BOONE

A NOVEL

Brooks Hansen
&
Nick Davis

SUMMIT BOOKS
New York London Toronto Sydney
Tokyo Singapore

SUMMIT BOOKS
SIMON & SCHUSTER BUILDING
ROCKEFELLER CENTER
1230 AVENUE OF THE AMERICAS
NEW YORK, NEW YORK 10020

SUMMIT BOOKS and colophon are trademarks
of Simon & Schuster Inc.

Designed by Carla Weise/Levavi & Levavi
Manufactured in the United States of America

1   3   5   7   9   10   8   6   4   2

Library of Congress Cataloging in Publication Data
Hansen, Brooks,
Boone : a novel / Brooks Hansen & Nick Davis.
p. cm.
I. Davis, Nick.   II. Title
PS3558.A5126B66   1990
813'.54—dc20   90-9624
CIP

ISBN 0-671-68108-7

TO OUR PARENTS

Contents

GOSPEL SINGERS SHOULD SING GOSPEL.

—a show-biz maxim

PROLOGUE

The Stage

Hugh Gardiner

We do with history as we please. That's what's so distressing. I had a letter from a student of mine some years ago, from England where she was living. She said that she'd seen a painting of Boone's in one of the prop rooms at the BBC and that it made her think of me. She was recalling the evenings we all used to spend driving into the city to see Boone's performances and then returning the same night for tea at my home. That was in late 1967, and she wanted to know what had happened to Boone since then. She was aware of his movie and the play, and the book, of course, but she said she'd heard he'd gone mad, and she wanted to know when.

Her question caught me quite off guard, I can say, but there

11

was something I recognized in the way she asked it, or perhaps it was the idea itself, of Boone having lost his mind—it's strange, but there's a need for reassurance there, I think. It reminded me of the things my students would say whenever we'd come back from seeing him. They'd sit in my living room afterwards with their tea and call him things like relentless and cruel. They'd shake their heads and wonder what the purpose was of being so ruthless. And I always tried to tell them, don't think of him as fierce. When you see Boone perform, think of it as something like finding a diary. I said, Imagine yourself in a stranger's bedroom, looking at the books on their shelves, at the keepsakes and pictures on their bureaus and end tables. Imagine even sitting on their bed, lying there and resting your head on the pillow. But then finding underneath the pillow a diary. Would you open it? Perhaps no—perhaps—but the temptation is there, and I asked the students to imagine the temptation always there, of reading and understanding the most private and intimate feelings of every person they saw, because for Boone it was. In his letters to me, he would describe certain people's faces as "perfectly legible," or their movements and manners as "graphic." The question for him was always whether or not to look, and I think he did at first—and I said this to the students—Boone reads our faces and gestures avidly, not because he's ruthless, but because he simply can't imagine that such expressive things could really want to keep their secrets. And my students would say, yes, but if that's so, if his intentions are so innocent, then tell us why everything he finds is so ugly? Why doesn't he ever look at people's faces and find something beautiful there, because surely there must be something to comfort us?

I never answered them. I didn't think it was my place, but I've discovered there's a funny thing that happens to that question over time. If it just lingers there, and we never quite get the answers or comfort that we're asking for, then I suppose we end up having to comfort ourselves. Years pass, and it's no longer a question, why doesn't Boone ever reassure us? The question becomes, "When did Boone go mad?" I was very reluctant to write my old student back and tell her—he didn't ever, that's just it.

Kelso Chaplin

It was 1967. I was finishing up at NYU Film Grad, but I spent a lot of time that winter shuttling back and forth between the city and Poughkeepsie to see Linda. Linda was a junior at Vassar, and she'd just started working with Hugh, who I'd met a couple years before at Fishkill when I'd been messing around with playwriting and screenwriting.

But one weekend that December I'd stayed in the city for some reason. I'd gotten together on Friday night with an acting friend of mine, Sy Page, who was also at NYU, and we'd decided to go down to this club on Grand Street. We'd seen an ad in the *Voice,* something like "Buddy D'Angelo presents Eton Boone." Sy wanted to go because he thought Eton Boone was this dancer who could manipulate things like glass balls and wands and all these minimalist props. He thought Boone was this guy named Arno Ponge, so we'd kind of gone down by mistake. We'd smoked some hash, and Sy had brought along his Arriflex because there was a film teacher at NYU, Billy "The Kid" Singer, who always told us to shoot anything that moved. That was his big line, and Sy took it to heart.

Of course, by the time we got all the way down there, it occurred to us that Jes' For Laffs didn't sound like the kind of place that was going to have avant-garde dancers. But we were there, we were stoned, we had the camera. We had to ask the manager if he minded us taking it in—this was Buddy D'Angelo. He was incredibly decent about it. We told him we were there to film Eton Boone, and he got us a table in the back, unobstructed.

There were only about two or three acts before Boone came on, but Sy didn't shoot them because he was actually running out of film. He'd shot the whole subway ride downtown from Eighty-sixth Street, these two women with their kids in strollers, so it's actually a pretty intense cut if you're looking at the original copy, from this fluorescent subway scene—which was way overexposed—to the pitch black of the club. The lighting there always sucked, but the sound's okay. We were sitting right beneath one of the speakers.

The first thing you see is this head bobbing up and down from the right. It's like a ghost. He's just wearing a white shirt that kind of blends into his face, and his hair isn't registering. You can't see his pants either, against the background. It's just this floating torso and all this applause. Not like a stadium, but it's a lot of people in a tight space, and there's a lot of hooting and hollering and loud applause.

Sy pulls in for a closeup. Just as this torso is trying to quiet the crowd, Sy gets him in focus, and he spots us. Sy's gone right in on his face, and Boone points a finger out at us. He says, "Hey. Back there. You two. Thanks for caring, but I don't show up on film."

Linda Chaplin

Oh, yes, he was hot. I mean, by comedians' standards. He wasn't Julie Andrews, right, but he had his little love affair with the media. Everyone had their blurb, and some of the lines were pretty entertaining. You'd pick up the *Voice* and they've of course decided that Boone is the future of stand-up comedy. They said his was "a voice a century in the making that it's going to take another century to repress." Well, okay. The radio critic on WNEW called him "Dr. Freud's Monster and a press agent's nightmare." "Man of a thousand fucked-up faces"—that was *Rolling Stone*. *The Downtowner* had a good one too—they called him "a fisherman in our national stream of consciousness," which again, you want to say, nice line, guys, but what does it mean? Why am I hearing about this man?

Well, the reason for that was simple—this man was making people extremely angry. Apparently, they tell us, he's doing celebrity impersonations, but from the response alone you know this isn't "You dirty rat," right, or "Judy, Judy, Judy." The celebrities aren't laughing this off the way they usually do. When Boone does Jerry Lewis, Jerry Lewis does not invite him on the telethon and throw his arm around Boone's shoulder. Jerry Lewis, from all accounts, considers legal action. When Boone does Diana Ross, Motown has to issue a statement. And by the time he gets to Richard Nixon, you've got reporters asking Nixon about it at the primary victory party in New Hampshire.

But the great thing is, for all this bluster and hoo-ha, none of these people has ever seen Boone. It's all just hearsay—they don't really know what Boone said about them because the man never did anyone twice. He was actually doing a different celebrity every single night. One of the papers even used to print an occasional what they called Boone watch, just to keep tabs on him. They'd give you his hit list for the week—Monday was Timothy Leary, Tuesday, Roger Vadim, Wednesday, Elvis Presley—he was all over the place, so you could just forget about trying to catch this guy, he was too slippery.

In fact the first I heard about him, it was this terrific little sidebar in *The Village Idiot,* just a little two-inch thing. Apparently some civil-rights group had caught wind of a routine Boone had done as one of those celebrity tag alongs on the Martin Luther King marches, a sort of lesser Tony Bennett-type. According to the story, Boone hadn't exactly emphasized the political correctness of what this lounge singer was doing. He'd just played it—exposed it—as Vegas grandstanding, very ugly, very show biz, all sung to the tune of "We Shall Overcome." So this civil-rights group decides to go down and see him, but the night they go, Boone is doing Shirley Booth and they've never laughed so hard in their lives. The whole routine was about wigs and orthopedic shoes, and the *Idiot* said Hazel had saved the day again. They'd even titled it something awful like, "Maid to Order."

Anyway, that was Boone's set up. That's the way he came to our attention, right, and it was terrific actually, just getting to watch from the sidelines, because you could see, this man is clearly irritating enough to be getting people's attention—all the agencies around town just keep huffing and puffing and stomping their feet—but you knew it was never going to amount to anything. Nothing was ever going to come of it, because apparently this man is so talented that he doesn't ever have to repeat his material. All that's really going to happen, right, is that the Boone myth, of this little rebel flinging lethal stones at all these Goliaths, just keeps growing and growing.

Kelso Chaplin

Sy's finally satisfied he's got him in okay focus. You can see that
he's young. He couldn't have been much more than twenty, but
he looks very comfortable up there. He's just kind of fumbling
around, scratching his head, throwing out ideas, and he's letting
these incredible silences pass—the hiss of the speakers is deafen-
ing—but he just keeps looking out over our heads as if there's
something in the smoke, he's thinking, and then he springs it. No
big segue. He just says, "I've been thinking about Richard Burton
lately," and it's actually pretty funny, it's not something you
notice watching it for the first time, but you can hear on the film
some people in front of us going, "Oh, Richard Burton" when he
says it, as if it's "Oh, he's going to do Richard Burton, I have to
gear myself for Richard Burton." These were people who knew
what they were coming to see.

Anyway, Boone doesn't waste a lot of time. He starts creating
this scene for us, he imagines it—Burton in his dressing room
before a show—probably *Camelot,* he doesn't say—and he imagines a kid there in the room with him, a theatre hand named
Julian who's been hired to keep an eye on Burton's drinking.
Boone even gets one of the club waitresses to bring him a bottle
of Irish whiskey from the bar, and a glass. So he sits himself down
in front of this imaginary dressing room mirror—we're looking at
him right through it—he pours himself a couple shots of whiskey, and then starts applying his makeup for the show. And as
he's doing it, he begins describing himself to this kid Julian,
feature for feature. It was actually one of Boone's favorite things
to do, if he could work it in—he liked to get the celebrity talking
about his own looks for a while, especially if it was a film star,
just as a way of finding the character. So he starts talking about
Burton's eyes, he's letting Burton describe them, and then his
forehead, his nose, his skin. He touches on everything he can, and
it's almost like hypnosis. When Boone's done describing a feature
for you, it just kind of clicks in. He says his mouth is straight and

thin, slightly pinched, and all of a sudden you can see it, Boone
gets Burton's mouth just perfect. So he finishes with the face, and
then he does the body, the way he holds his shoulders, the way
he moves his hands, his walk, everything he can think of until
finally when he's finished, pacing around this dressing room with
his glass of Irish whiskey in his hand, he is Richard Burton. It was
an absolute metamorphosis. The audience, some of them start
pounding on their tables they're so into it.

But he turns back to this kid Julian again, once he's set, and
he asks if he'd like his autograph. He takes the kid's autograph
book and starts flipping through it. He's being kind of glib, making little comments about all the names he recognizes, but then
all of a sudden he stops cold, and at first you don't know what
it is. He starts nodding his head. He sits back down in the chair
and he pours himself some more whiskey, but his eyes never
leave the book. He swallows the shot, then he looks up at Julian
and the word comes out of his mouth like a vapor—"Olivier."

Eton Arthur Boone, transcribed, December 8, 1967—
RICHARD BURTON

[Looks at book again.] Strange. *[Considers.]* I wonder what Larry was
wearing when he signed this. Do you remember? Was there a
crown on his head when he wrote this, Julian, or was there a great
big putty nose on his face? Who was he pretending to be? Because
I'll let you in on a secret, my young friend, and it doesn't leave this
room, but it's true—and pour me another drink, would you?
[Waits.] I'll pour it myself then. *[Pours himself a drink. Returns to the
mirror.]* Laurence Olivier is the shallowest man you will ever meet.
Sometimes I think there is no Laurence Olivier. There are only
clothes. There are costumes, crowns, elaborate makeup and then
that purposeless face of his to put it on, but it's just a prop like
everything else. He's all tricks, Julian, disguises and acrobatics, but
he gives you nothing of himself ever, don't you see, because
there's nothing there to give. How else do you think he's been able
to do it, go from part to part like that without leaving a trace? It's
that he's no character of his own for us to remember. He's like a
tire pump—inexhaustible, but completely hollow. *[Swallows his
drink in one gulp.]* Now pour me another, would you? *[Snaps twice.]*

Kelso Chaplin

We had no idea how ambitious and persistent he was going to be. You know comedians, they never want to stick with any idea too long, because they're afraid of losing you. But Boone, you could tell just by looking at him, he was there to explore. He was moving around the stage, and it was still clearly Burton, but something kind of animal was taking over. He was stalking. It was like watching a jackal go after his prey, except that Boone was hunting this man down from the inside. It was incredible. And you could feel it in the club too. This air had set in. Everybody was getting a little uncomfortable, they're not sure they really want to look at this thing, except they can't take their eyes off him. They had to know, Where's he headed? Where's he going? Because always, in every performance, there was this intense momentum, in every performance, a kind of steady crescendo that just kept building and building, until you knew that something had to give. Something was going to jam or bust or blow, and if you didn't look out, it could be dangerous. You could have Richard Burton's shot glass flying over your head.

Eton Arthur Boone, transcribed—*RICHARD BURTON*

[Standing, glaring out towards the audience, his focus fixed on a figure in the imaginary mirror before him.]

. . . I'll be there in everything I do, Julian, won't I, shining through every role I play, every jacket I wear, or crown—no King Arthur, no Alexander, only that—*[points into mirror]* Richard Burton. But don't blame me for it, Julian. Pity me, I did that for you. It's both our doing that I should shine so bloody bright. You've never been so tempting to seduce. The rewards have never been so grand, to be known from Rome to Hollywood, in London and Singapore, to have money and yachts, and the world's most beautiful woman at my beck and call for all the world to see, the whole world watching. Who could resist? Who but a cipher like Olivier? He knows nothing of desire, he hasn't the balls between his legs to feel it, but I have let it guide me, for longer than I can remember, in every gesture I have made, and I have been exposed for it. Look. *[Gestures easily towards mirror, indicating his reflection to Julian.]* I am unmistakable. Look how irrepressible is Richard Burton. Look in his eyes, Julian, and it's the same thing always—resignation. Look at his mouth—disgust and arrogance. Smell his breath—misery. And ask yourself why. "Why such contempt, Richard Burton? You've gotten what you wanted. Why such disdain?" *[Leans over, fingers on cheeks, stares at self in imaginary mirror.]* Because I'd no idea you were so easy. I'd no idea you'd cling like this. You should leave me now, Julian. Do. Get out of my dressing room if you know what's good for you. Leave me alone and tell the rest of them too. Out now, boy! *[Picks up glass.]* Leave me, dammit! Go! *[Hurls glass at the imaginary mirror, glass shatters on the back wall of the club. Blackout.]*

Linda Chaplin

Basically on any given night, you had two types of people in the club. The ones who left afterwards, never to return, and the ones who were going to keep coming back no matter what. And given the nature of what Boone was doing, that's certainly understandable. It's understandable that some people aren't always going to go for this sort of thing—maybe the imitation didn't click with them that night, or maybe they found the whole thing just too presumptuous and offensive. I mean, there's no doubt that Boone could be offensive. I remember taking some friends of mine one night, they were in from Madison, and Boone had done Diana Ross making love to the palms of her hands, and it was very awkward afterwards having to explain to them, you know, "He's not always like this."

But I actually think that in order to understand what Boone was doing, you really did have to see him more than once, because so much of it had to do with his sheer variety. I mean, here was a performer who one night you could see doing the Richard Burton, right, this very stagy sort of tongue-lashing, but if you went back two days later, which Kelso and I actually did, you'd see him doing just this beautiful piece on Sonny Liston, the professional boxer, which was absolutely heartbreaking. And if you went again the next night, who knows what you might get? Grace Kelly on the toilet? Kerouac mourning the death of Neal Cassady? Maybe J. Edgar Hoover getting ready to sodomize his page boy. It could be anything. The man was all over the board.

But what I think was so interesting, right, was that even as diverse as these routines may have seemed from certain perspectives, there was also something about them that was very much the same, and the more you went, the more you could see it— Eton Boone had his own antenna. He had his own hook, right, and if you were watching him with that in mind, you could see—Liston, Burton, Hoover, whoever it was—Boone was doing the same thing to each of them, and the best phrase I ever heard for it came from a teaching assistant I had at Emerson, Clayton Stern. It was very simple. Clayton used to say that Eton Boone really knew how to put someone in his place. I love that, because it's not just that Boone could knock someone down a few pegs— which he could, obviously—it's that he was able to take these well-known, public personalities and place them in very specific settings and circumstances that just completely illuminated them, where everything around them either seemed to reflect their identity or provoke it, or threaten it, so that in essence what you were watching was someone being made to confront himself. You were watching someone having to choose himself all over again, and what was always so disturbing, I think, was seeing how often these people didn't want to do it. I mean, it makes sense, I guess— people do hate being put in their place—but that's what Boone was doing, right. That's sort of the service he was offering, and I actually think that what started to be so thrilling about watching Boone wasn't really the celebrities so much or the imitations. It was the idea that Eton Boone could do this to anyone he wanted. You know, so look out, keep the house lights dim, right, because it really got to the point where you felt like nothing was stopping Boone, except for Boone, from coming out and doing you.

Kelso Chaplin

The whiskey glass broke about a foot and a half above Sy's head, so there's chaos on the film. The lights black out, you can hear Sy going, "Oh, man," like he's been shot, and the audience, after a second or two of complete silence, literally explodes. But it's not a happy sound. Most of them are applauding, but a lot of them, even the ones who are clapping, are yelling, just hollering, so you hear this mass wail on the film. Sy finally regains his composure and gets the picture in focus. The camera goes back to the stage, but the whole thing's dark. You can just barely see this dark figure, this outline of Boone feeling his way off stage, bumping into things. Some of the people in front of us have stood up, so you can't see him coming up the aisle, and by the time the lights come up, he's gone. The crowd's still going wild, but it's just the bricks now.

I

San Diego

1947—1966

From RUTH, by Eton Arthur Boone*

When I was twelve, my mother and I ran away from home. We never shared our reasons why, but I think that most of them had to do with my father. I once pictured our house surrounded and cluttered by loose rope, wound slack around all the furniture and sitting in heaps on the rugs and stairs. Mom and I would try and clean it up. We'd tie as many ends as we could find to the back fender of the car and drive off. We wouldn't see, but the lines would fly and untangle behind us. The braids would untwine. The

---

*Ruth was first published in 1975 by Hardcastle, Inc., New York. Portions of *Ruth* are reprinted here by permission of the Estate of Eton Arthur Boone.

coils would whistle away like tiny cyclones, and all the knots would slip. And when the ropes were finally pulled tight and separate, Mom and I would follow them back on foot to see where they'd come from. They'd lead us to Dad, they'd all converge in one enormous snarl wrapped impossibly around his crotch.

I don't imagine anymore that all the ropes would lead to him. I'm sure that some were fastened elsewhere, some that Mom would follow, but there's very little I could ever know about where or what to. She was dying. Cancer had been creeping through her body for years, and I think that when she escaped with me that June, she may just have wanted one more chance to get away, far away, and make peace with life before it began to fade.

We would visit the Southwest, down into Sonora then up through Arizona, and we'd follow the Zuni River into New Mexico. She wanted to take her time, take close looks, and she wanted her paint boxes and canvases with her. She was going to do what she liked best, and it seems I should have felt blessed to be asked along, but I was too frightened. I thought she'd want to know things about Dad, things I knew very well but would never tell, for reasons I hadn't yet admitted, except for one—a sense I suffered quietly that when she understood what had happened, she would die. Our trip was a kind of tempting fate, and even before we left I could feel it spread out before me savagely, as the last moments I could spend alone with my favorite person on earth, and as an awful and gradual means for her to discover what I had done.

Claire Sullivan

Eton had the very same color eyes when he was a little boy as his mother, the very lightest blue, almost bleached, but they turned more gray and green when he got older. Blue's stayed the same as when she was a little girl, which was very lucky, I suppose. She wouldn't have made a very good Hazel. Her given name was Ruth, but Blue was Blue, from the very moment she was born.

I remember being upstairs once at the Lemon House in San

Diego and Eton was so young—well, he must have been five, because I think Blue was six or seven months pregnant with Toddy. She was wrestling with Eton, trying to get a sweater over his head, and he was singing a song while she was doing it. He was teasing her with a song about eating booger peas, and when he was singing it, I was almost certain I'd heard it before but I couldn't remember where exactly. But then it came to me. It was a song that the CCC boys used to sing when they were working on the projects near Sullivan South, but of course it wasn't about booger peas. It was about goober peas, and I think originally the Yankee troops used to sing it during their marches in the Civil War. But I told Eton that I'd first heard his little song when I used to visit his mother down at Sullivan South, and she was just a little girl, not much older than he was.

Sullivan South was the loveliest fieldstone house on a small branch of the Delaware with just acres and acres of smooth green land surrounding it, and up the road a bit when we were all very young there was a bridge being built by the CCC boys, and I told Eton how horrified his grandfather had been at the thought of these hooligans so near the property. He used to curse President Roosevelt and warn us never to go near these dangerous fellows, which was very silly. I remember Eleanor, Blue's older sister, she was a teenager at the time and very rambunctious. She used to trot by on her horse, and the men would take off their caps and bow as she passed.

But when Blue was very young, she would go down to the river banks and paint. She would sit all day with a pad on her knees and her little brushes—my mother used to say Blue was like a Beatrix Potter let outdoors. And when these boys came singing their songs and building their bridges, she painted them as well. You know, Eleanor and I saw these young boys as people to flirt with, and Uncle Edwin saw them as people to fend off for the sake of his little women. But Blue only saw more things to paint—that's all—like trees and the sky, and now these great big men in shirtsleeves and coveralls, singing about goober peas.

There was a painting of hers we still have somewhere, that I was always trying to find for Eton, of the river with just half a bridge going across, and the men on it, working. When I was little I'd always thought it was so funny that Blue hadn't minded the bridge just going halfway like that. It would've bothered me.

Uncle Edwin just loved the painting, though—pretended not to know what it was of. He put it in his bathroom, so he could look at it while he shaved. He put the most extraordinary frame on it too, carved wood and gilded, that he'd bought in Baltimore.

Joe Boone

Blue and I met in Philadelphia. It was late summer of 1945—I'd missed going to the Pacific by two weeks. A friend of mine from the Navy named Buzzy Kaulgren and I had three days' leave from our base in South Carolina, and we had to drive up to Philadelphia to drop off some old DeSoto for Buzzy's aunt. I drove the DeSoto.

It was at a dance, Saturday night. Buzz and I were in our uniforms. His family got us the invites—he was from back East— very posh affair with a big band and all the women in those dresses that keep going straight ahead even when the woman turns in another direction, these chicken coops the women had to wear back then. I remember Buzz and I walking around feeling like security guards. We felt like we should have been checking people's passes or something, but we were just two soldiers trying to kill an evening in Philadelphia.

But Buzz, he was a terrific dancer, hell of a dancer, so he was busy for most of the evening. He ditched me midway through for a girl he ended up getting engaged to named Mamie Bosomworth. Anyway, I didn't know how to dance—somehow my father had never gotten around to teaching me the fox-trot. We were too busy shooting snake tails, which doesn't mean you shoot the tail. It means you beat a snake against a rock, stretch it out flat and then stick the gun down its throat, see how close you can come to shooting the bullet right out the tip of the tail. That's what my father and I used to do, and that wasn't going to help me on the Main Line. So I had to assert myself socially. That's it. That's why we met. Not a single shot was fired.

Sounds corny, but it was at the punch bowl. She'd been there with some fella named Ned Barnes. Poor bastard, killed in Korea, but that night he'd gone on to some other party. So there we were, talking by the punch bowl, stiff as boards and I never felt so comfortable in my goddamn life. I told her right off about my family, Texas, my dad. This was the first time we met, you have to remember, and I'm telling her about my dad and how he made my mother sit in the back of the truck when we moved out to Los Angeles.

Blue didn't say anything. I did all the talking, but not just to fill the air. She was so lovely. She didn't carry herself the way the other women did. She could have been in a cotton dress out at Mount Tamalpais, out in one of the meadows where we ate an entire watermelon once—that was maybe a year after we first got out to California. But if she'd been in a cotton dress you couldn't have seen Blue's shoulders, which I almost told her right then and there were perfect. It was that kind of thing, that just meeting her right there I could have told her what perfect shoulders she had, or how I couldn't believe her eyes, how beautiful they were, and it wouldn't have been some kind of line. You don't meet people like that very often, and when you do, you fall in love. I fall in love.

I asked her to marry me thirteen days after we met. She wasn't quick to answer, but she wasn't slow either. I asked her, we'd gone to Chadds Ford together, by the Brandywine, and I asked her there to marry me.

Claire Sullivan

The Sullivans always had trouble understanding. They never quite got Joe. He has such a hard humor about him. I remember a number of us all having dinner together in New York just after they'd been engaged. None of the parents, but Blue and Joe, and Eleanor and her husband Tom, Alice, who was the old-est sister, and myself. Just us. Joe told a story and he used the word "dago." I'm not sure Eleanor ever really forgave him for that. She just thought, and Alice did too, I'm sure, that Joe was just another one of Blue's ways of defying the family. You could see Alice wince whenever Joe used Blue's name, and I remember at the wedding, which was a great big affair out on the east lawn—Joe's father was there, drunk as a skunk, pulling on the tent ropes—and all Eleanor did was complain about how beautiful the gown was. It *was* a lovely gown, peau de soie, and just an off-white—an Eskimo could tell you—trimmed with lace that Uncle Edwin bought in Brussels. But all Eleanor could talk about the whole day was what a shame it was for such a lovely gown to go to waste.

They never really gave Joe a chance, you know. I lived not so far from them after they moved out to San Diego. They were in a little apartment near the ocean that Joe used to call "Sullivan West," and they were so happy. He was just out of the service, working at one of the radio stations, and Blue was teaching at the university. Her painting had become so important to her, and I think Joe was just the perfect balance. There's something about Joe, and I know it's going to sound odd in retrospect, but I've always thought of him as an honest man. For all his rough and tumble swagger, Joe is actually very simple with his feelings, he's close to his own surface, and I think that's what Blue needed. She couldn't really be bothered with people who didn't make themselves clear, and Joe, the way he'd take her hand in the front seat or bring picnic baskets to the studio she used to work in at the university, Joe made himself very clear.

Blue's father used to have an expression, which I'm going to have trouble remembering. He'd say if people were trees, most of them wouldn't even be honest enough to lean towards the sun. And it's true there aren't many, I think, but Blue found a man who would. She always said Joe leans towards the sun, and I think for her that may have been the most important thing.

Joe Boone

Right after we moved to the house, my father came down from L.A. and set up around ten minutes away. He was getting real old by that time, and he never liked California. He always missed Texas and the things he had down there. He'd been a sheriff for a while in Gilpin. That's where I was born, and Dad kept the peace. Nothing ever made him happier. He was a real charmer. When I was a kid, he used to sit me down on his knee and put his bourbon between my legs and tell me stories, prairie-shit romantic Western stories about horses instead of people, and all I can remember is looking at the hair growing out of his ears. To this day I think about the hair growing out of Dad's ears, and sure enough, you look in the mirror when you hit fifty, and there it is, you got the same damn thing.

Anyway, by the time he came down to San Diego, he was headed downhill. He went through about fifteen different nurses in two years—Blue really had to take over. Every week he'd call up, we'd ask how's your new nurse, and he'd say, I fired her. Blue would just go on up. She'd clean the house, do his sheets, make him roast beef and cucumber sandwiches the way he liked them. There wasn't a Mexican woman alive who could make a sandwich my dad could eat, but Blue's sandwiches were okay.

There were times he'd pretend to forget where he was—I don't know if he was pretending or not—he'd start calling you names like Poonjab or Silver. But you should have seen her, the way Blue handled him. She would take Eton, and he was just a baby still, and she'd give him to Dad and say, "Here, this is your grandson." And when Dad was holding Eton, it didn't seem to matter if he knew who the rest of us were. He'd get it all back. He'd say, "All right, all right. You're Joe."

But Dad knew more than he let on. I think he just liked having Blue around, and any time she did anything, he'd just look at me and shake his head. He even said it to me once. We'd come over for a visit and we were dropping off a portrait Blue had done of him. She'd brought her easel over one afternoon and they'd gone out into the mountains and she'd painted him sitting there in his spurs with his hat. No one else in the world could have made him sit still for it. But anyway, she and I had come over one morning to drop it off. We had to stay and listen to him complain about how all the nurses were stealing things, and right before we left—Blue had gone out already—Dad grabbed me by the arm and was looking at the painting she'd done, but he meant her. He looked at me and he said, "How the hell did you land that?" I wanted to say, "Dad, I don't know. I have no idea." I felt like the luckiest man in the world.

Claire Sullivan

Blue started bringing Eton into the studio with her in the mornings when he was still very young. The smell of turpentine and oils and paint thinner must have been second nature for him. I know he had a playpen in there for a while, and by the time he was too big for that, he was already painting. She bought him his own brushes and his pads, and from what I could see, he was a natural little artist, with a tiny blue smock and all his mother's painting mannerisms. Blue used to have a black-and-white photograph of Turner in her studio, studying his canvas with his elbow jutting and his hand on his hip with all the brushes sticking out. And sometimes when I'd come in, there'd be Blue intent on her canvas, with her hand under her chin, and then Eton with his hands on his hips and brushes in each. It looked like the three stages of the artist or some such thing.

But I never saw Joe in there, not in the studio at the Lemon House. I think he understood it wasn't his place. I remember asking Blue about a painting once, of sailboats. She'd gone to Monterey on a commission and done a whole series of paintings of sailboats and dinghies, and I knew that Joe hadn't gone with her, but I asked her if he'd seen them yet. She just said, "No, Joe doesn't really look at what I do," and it wasn't out of spite or anger or anything at all bitter. It sounded more like a comfortable agreement they'd had—that her work was separate and something he wouldn't necessarily be able to share in. I think that was one of the wonderful things about Joe, how well he was able to accept the fact that with Blue, there was this other very private realm, and if you weren't invited, then you just had to accept that.

Levi Mottl

I got my first glimpse of San Diego at about three o'clock in the morning, right off the bus. I spent the whole night roaming the streets, and I couldn't get over the quiet, coming from New York. The streets had a swabbed feel. The whole place just looked deserted to me, and it's not an impression I ever really got over, that something was missing. San Diego's always sort of struck me as the town out of a dull person's imagination. I didn't really feel much spirit there until I met Blue.

She was teaching one of the courses in the graduate art program at UCSD, a class in oil painting and color theory. I'd taken some courses at the League in New York, but I still wasn't comfortable with color, and I was looking to Blue's class to help me there. I was anxious to try my hand at the landscape around San Diego. That whole Southern Californian palette sort of swept me off my feet, the clay and purple in the mountains and that cornflower blue—I spent most of my time out in the hills with a canteen and a sketch pad, when I wasn't in class.

It was a while before Blue let us anywhere near landscapes, though. We opened with a lot of still lifes. We were drawing dappled pears one of the first days, a bosc, a red bartlett, and a seckel, probably—Blue was always sort of partial to the seckel. She was making rounds. The first thing she ever said to me was, "Do you see pears?" I nodded. She said, "I don't see pears. I see that," and she sort of waved her hand toward the plate. Her hair was auburn and there was a strand hanging down from a black velvet clip she used to wear for class. She was squinting out, and I remember wanting to see what she was seeing. I just stared at her and I don't know how long, but Blue you could watch sometimes and not even worry, because she'd get a sort of spellbound look in her eye. She could get it cutting a loaf of bread, watching the sky change—the simplest things—but as long as there was a shape and color to it, she'd be drawn in. She'd look, and it's not the way you or I would ever see things. It's not the way things are used to being looked at. I always sort of thought Blue made the world blush, and that's why it looked to her the way it did.

Joe Boone

There were very good years. They're always good years when you're building a family, aren't they? Everything worked. The kids were healthy, Blue was happy at the university. I felt like every day I was coming home to a house that was just sitting on air. A problem? A problem is some fat girl named Zabriskie hits Toddy on the pinky with a rock, or Eton's teachers are complaining that my kid is picking his nose for the other kids. You know, nothing you can't fix with a little ammonia.

And we used to have things we always did, little rituals. Wednesdays we'd take Eton down to the wharf to watch the fishing boats come in, see what they'd caught and pick out a fish, a swordfish, for dinner. We took him to see the battleships. You know, I can show you—we've got pictures of a very good time, of Eton up on my shoulders, all of us out at the opening week at Disneyland, Toddy in his stroller, laughing, the three of us with the mouse ears and Blue shading her eyes.

Levi Mottl

We would go after class to campus coffee shops—under turquoise canopies is where I picture it, with our portfolios leaning up against the third chair. I'd gotten to know her better when some work of mine was selected for a student exhibit up at The Art Center School, and Blue and I and some other students had taken the train up to Los Angeles together. The second semester, Blue had had to stay home for a month when Toddy got the measles, and that's when I started working as a teaching assistant for her classes.

I used to come over to the house, and Blue would take me out to the back yard. She'd stand out there and it was like watching her bloom. There was a lemon tree and the yard wasn't very big. It faced the ocean, just a half mile down the hill, so there was always a light salt in the air. At dusk the clouds would get a sort of salmon color, and shafts of light would spill through the leaves of the lemon tree and shift in the breeze. The house was stucco and Blue would point at the shadows on the white face and say how azure they were, to match the sky. We'd look at how the light would catch the hanging plants, or the shadows of the smoked-glass bottles she used to set out on the ledge. And when the lemons were out in the summer, they'd glint in the twilight. The yellow could just stain your eyes.

Claire Sullivan

I've never known Levi as well as I thought I should have. I think I always agreed with Joe, though. He's such an odd duck I don't think you find yourself wondering whether or not he's a threat. You'd come in and find him occasionally, out in the back yard, feeling the leaves of the tree, or crouching down, kneeling over something in the garden, pulling a worm out of the ground and holding it in his hands for Toddy to look at. He's so thoughtful with everything he does and says—he's so damn slow and steady, like the tortoise—but with those long limbs and wonderful long elegant fingers. And his poor face, that face, you can't help look- ing at it and thinking about the shape of his marvelous skull underneath, or his Adam's apple. It looked so vulnerable gulping there, like some trapped diamond that Eton used to talk about plucking from Levi's neck with his melon spoon. He'd make Toddy touch it with his finger. Levi would swallow and Toddy would go screaming off down the hall laughing.

Levi Mottl

I was sitting in a sort of semi-dining room that was just off the living room, and there was a piano. Eton had been playing when I came in, tinkering. He was around eight. He stopped and asked if I wanted to play. I'm not much with a piano, but I sat down and began "Clair de lune," which is one of the few things I can play with any kind of touch. Eton put his hands over his ears like so. He closed his eyes and pressed his forehead up against the piano. I wasn't sure what he was doing. Sometimes I don't really have much of a feel for children, and I think they know, like horses. He very slowly pulled the lid down on my fingers to stop me, and he asked me to play something louder. I consented. One of the few things I know in forte style is "The Battle Hymn of the Republic," so I began to play it as a march for Eton. He pressed himself up against the side of the piano again. I didn't want to burst his eardrums. I played lightly, but he got up and he was sort of impatient. He told me to do what he'd been doing, and *he'd* play. So I got down on my hands and knees and pressed my ear up against the side of the piano. Eton got up on the bench and began pounding the bass notes and stretching so he could floor the sustain pedal. I thought it was a strange sort of attack at first, but if you got your cheekbone flush and pressed your head up against the case just right, you could feel the vibrations trilling through your head. They'd sort of rattle your skull and you could feel your tongue start to tickle. Eton was just banging away, pounding the bass and I was down on the floor with my eyes closed, trying to feel the tickle slipping down my throat. It stopped suddenly. I looked up at Eton and he'd cocked his head like a rabbit as if he'd heard something, and very faintly from the kitchen you could hear Blue, "Shhhhhhhhhhh."

Toddy Boone

I remember pissing contests in the backyard, I remember him running around the house with a towel stuffed in the back of his shirt like a cape, I remember him coming up to me in the hallways at school and pinching my butt. We were brothers. We played. We had this giant pair of pants that had belonged to Grampa— they were even too big for Dad—and Eton and I used to get inside them together and walk around and Dad would pretend that he didn't know where I was. He'd say, "Eton, have you seen Toddy, I've got five hundred dollars for him." And Eton would say, "No, no, Dad, I'll take it." And then I'd stick my hand out of the zipper. Stuff like that, I guess. I remember afternoons at home, in the backyard. We'd just roll around out there for hours, and he'd pin me down and he'd have just drunk a Nehi, and he'd let this gob of spit drip out of his mouth, this long strand, and then suck it back up right before it hit me in the nose.

Joe Boone

Blue and I had a thing we called the Mazatlán lesson. We'd gone down to Mazatlán the spring before Eton was born. Blue must have been five, six months pregnant. She was more than showing, though. Eton was in there kicking away, and as beautiful a thing as all that was to us, you know how women can be. She was a little grouchy. But it's a beautiful place, and I was very happy at the time. We'd taken one of the paddleboats they had. We were out there in the middle of the bay and the sun was coming down, and Blue was looking beautiful the way a healthy mother can. That glow, that full glow. And I guess you could say I was pouring my affection on her, and sure it was hot, but I didn't care. I loved her and I was kissing her to death. But she was all grumpy and hunching up her shoulders. She said it wasn't what she needed right then. Not now.

And I told her something. I let her in on a secret, something I've always known. It's probably one of the things I'm proudest of having shared with Blue. And that was that love, or affection, or whatever you want to call it, well, some people act like it's an arrow, like it's this thing where the timing has to be right and you're doing it for the other person. If they're ready and they're willing, then it turns into a beautiful thing. And that's true—I'm not saying that isn't true—it can be that way.

But there's something else about it too. You know, sometimes love is something you just want to show. You have to let go of it. Maybe she's feeling hot and sticky, maybe this isn't the right time. For her. But it doesn't have to work that way. It's not this arrow that hits or misses. It's this arrow that says, "Hey, I love you whether you want to hear it or not." And you've just got to get it out. Half the time I'd have been happy to just kiss a brick wall and show it to Blue. It feels good to love someone, so do it and show it whenever you want. You don't do it just to make them feel good. You do it for yourself. That's the Mazatlán lesson.

Well, I jump ahead now to a time when Eton must have been eight or nine, somewhere in there. It was a Saturday afternoon, and he was in a terrible mood. He'd gone out on a friend's fishing boat, and he thought he was going to have a nice day fishing, but the kid's father, a real martinet I'd been in the service with, he'd made the boys buff the boat the whole day. I don't even think they got out of the dock. So Eton was storming around, banging around in the kitchen looking for something to drink, and I was trying to calm him down. I told him an embarrassing story about the man, back in the service together—he got beat up by a couple of hookers once in Honolulu. But Eton wasn't even listening he was still so mad.

Blue came in from the studio, and she had turpentine all over her hands, and she hadn't seen Eton all day, because he'd had to get up early for Christ's sake—the son of a bitch had been honking his horn in the driveway at five-thirty in the morning. Anyway, Blue hadn't seen him and went over to him where he was making a chocolate milk or one of his drinks, and he pulled away, you know, "Ma, your hands are all wet." You know, grumpy little boy looking for a shotgun. But she put her hands back on his cheeks. You know, she just wanted to put her hands on his cheeks, and she whispered something in his ear before she went upstairs. And when she'd gone and he'd finished making his milk, Eton looked up at me and said, "Dad, what's the Mazel tov lesson?"

Claire Sullivan

You'll want glimpses. We always look for glimpses, and the one I like to tell is of being upstairs with Blue, reading to Toddy, while Eton had been downstairs drawing. He was ten or so. It was late afternoon and we heard the door slam downstairs and the keys in the dish, all the noises of someone arriving home—the noises of Joe coming home after a rotten, rotten day. The door slams, he trudges into the kitchen, the refrigerator door opens and you could hear the bottles rattling around, and then one placed on the counter, a beer bottle. The pop and hiss of the beer being opened. The rustle of the newspaper. He may have kicked something across the floor, but then the unmistakable sound of Joe Boone's feet coming upstairs, and the change jangling in his pockets.

Now, I really wasn't there a great deal, but you know how you come to know the sound of someone's footsteps, the sound of them banging around a place. And Joe's feet came trudging up the hallway to Toddy's room—thump, thump, thump—and the door swings open, and there stands Eton in one of his father's jackets, with a bottle of beer in his hand and an enormous grin on his face, a very happy grin, almost as if he'd just heard a naughty joke rather than played one. Toddy was just howling with delight, which should tell you something about how accurate it must have been—and that he'd seen these sorts of things before. I don't know how Eton did it. I was just bowled over, all of us were, but Eton sauntered up to me, still smiling, this little ten-year-old boy with the devil in his eye, and he offered me the beer.

He was so delightful, just a delightful little boy, and he could do it on demand, that sort of thing. It was a very strange ability. You'd just catch him doing these sound imitations. He'd do them for Toddy mostly. I can remember them sitting at the dining room table, and Toddy would just start to giggle, because Eton would be doing one of his little tricks. He'd be twirling his fingers in his glass the way Levi used to. He'd have gotten out one of Levi's tall glasses, and he'd put the exact right number of ice cubes in, and just the right amount of iced tea. He fixed it so that it made the very same sound. Toddy and he would both hush up and listen, and Eton would twirl the cubes just so. Then he'd sniffle like Levi and they'd both burst out laughing hysterically again. He liked to do Joe chewing his food too, or reading the paper, folding it just right, smacking it in the middle, digging his finger in his ear and jiggling it the way Joe does. It was all very silly, I know, but I've never known a boy who could be so much fun to be around.

Levi Mottl

I was there four years initially. The last year or so I'd begun to incline towards a lifestyle that wasn't quite as easy to anchor. I went up to Big Sur a number of times in 1958 and spent several weekends that winter in San Francisco, and although I wouldn't say I felt any real desire to become a part of the culture that was taking shape up there, I'd liked the idea of getting out and exploring a little more, casting my line again. The world was starting to seem like something worth going out and seeing a little more of, and I think once I felt that tension in my limbs, the pull of the more nomadic existence, I had to admit to myself that the only thing stapling me put was Blue, and I never wanted to resent her. I just left at the end of the school year. I never spoke to her about any of it. I wrote her five or six drafts of a letter I never sent. I suppose somewhere I felt I'd be returning.

Claire Sullivan

Blue first became sick the winter of 1959. I doubt that there had been a lump there long before she found it. I don't think it shocked her. She had always considered herself almost too lucky a person. She had so many fortunes, and I don't think she really fought misfortune when it came. In an odd way, to her I think it might have seemed ungrateful.

Joe Boone

I came home with abalone one afternoon in December. I found her sitting in the backyard with a straw hat on her head. I remember sneaking up behind her with the abalone in my hand and she turned to me, and she was very pale. Before I could do anything she said she had a lump. For the first time in her whole life she looked scared. I took her right to a doctor, a friend of mine at the base hospital.

And you know, there are certain words in the English language, a word like cancer. It's a mean word. You know, some things it seems like you're waiting your whole life to respond to. There'll be some moment more horrible than anything else, and what'll you do when that moment comes? I wanted to strangle the son of a bitch. Okay, it's cancer, but don't tell me it's malignant. And he calls you in again and says, yes, it's malignant. And you just want to say, for Christ's sake, then cut her breast off. Get it off her. Cut my arm off. Anything.

But there were so many delays, so many tests. It looked like it was going away, but it didn't. It wasn't until the winter that she had her mastectomy, the first one. I don't think we were ever convinced it was all gone.

From RUTH, by Eton Arthur Boone

Dad had passed me an envelope in the kitchen, but I hadn't had much time to ask what it was. I was in seventh grade, and I'd started biking to school in the morning. Sixth graders rode the bus. Seventh graders rode bikes. Those with any social standing tended to ride in packs, and ours was a fairly well-oiled, synchronized operation, able on occasional mornings to get to Juan Cabrillo perfectly intact without braking. It was enough of a thrill when it worked that I used to eat breakfast with my backpack on so I could leave straightaway to hook up with the phalanx at Francis Avenue. Dad's request had been a small hitch. He'd handed me the envelope just as I was stuffing my pants into my socks. He said it was for my substitute teacher, Mrs. Cutter, and he held it out to me with his head turned, as if he'd been asking me to pick a card. I took it and left him at the refrigerator door, sniffing the milk.

He'd seemed out of sorts that morning, right from the start. He'd been different. He'd dressed. Every day since Mom had been at the hospital, he'd come down in his bathrobe, fixed us breakfast, and he didn't get ready for his day until both my brother and I were gone. But that morning when I got downstairs, he'd already showered, shaved, and combed his hair. He'd met me at the break-fast table in a tie and his coat was draped over the kitchen stool. He hadn't said a word until he gave me the note for Mrs. Cutter, and I'd left too soon for him to say anything after.

When I got out to the front lawn with my bike, I looked back in the kitchen window to see if my brother had come down yet. Dad was at the table, sitting with his hands in his lap. He looked like a wax figure in a museum. *The Union* sat at my brother's place, with the rubber band still wound around its waist, and the room was motionless but for the even sweep of the second hand on the wall clock.

I decided not to rap on the window or wave, and that morning I biked past Francis Avenue and took La Cienega into Juan Cabrillo alone.

Claire Sullivan

Blue was an angel about the mastectomy. She was so brave, but she did not fight. I remember seeing her in the hospital after the operation. She'd taken it all so calmly. She'd assured me that it wasn't life-threatening, that they could make a fairly clean cut of it and that she was actually very fortunate. But a few days after the operation I visited her and she was lying there, very uncomfortable having to be attended to, lying there so helpless, which was so un-Blue, and I remember her looking down at herself and she was in one of those awful smocks that they make you wear. She had the tag around her wrist and she spoke about her breasts. "I had a very pretty breast. They were very pretty breasts, don't you think?"

It wasn't vain, and it didn't sound like her—it sounded like the voice of a child, so sweet and scared. She lifted her arm very weakly and touched herself, and I'd never thought about it. All I could say was the truth, what came into my head, I said, "Yes, absolutely beautiful," because they were—she was. I said, "You are absolutely beautiful." And I walked over to her and held her and I remember I've just never wanted to love someone so much. She was like a little child there.

Levi Mottl

I'd worked for a number of months in a cannery in Vancouver, and then I'd gone up to Alaska in March. I'd taken a fishing boat up from Seattle to Juneau, and then sat in the back of a dump truck for eleven hours all the way to Anchorage. When I got there, it was the first time I called San Diego since I'd been away.

It's funny. I'd been so exhilarated, placing my call from the back room of a truck stop just inside the city limit, a place run by an authentic Aleutian named Dolly, and with a sunset so early in the afternoon. Everything had struck me as so extraordinary and wide, but when Joe told me, it was a bitter feeling in my stomach, a feeling that sort of had teeth. I felt deprived. That night I spent outdoors, watching the stars move more slowly than I'd ever been accustomed to seeing them, and thinking about her. Not about Blue in the hospital, but the Blue I'd first known.

It was an afternoon. I'd come in a little early and I'd just been waiting in the living room. There was a bathroom down that way, down a tiled hallway—of hacienda tiles. I could hear Blue in there giving Toddy a bath. He couldn't have been more than three and the wallpaper downstairs had wheels on it. I'd waited, made myself at home. I'd begun watering some of the plants, some fuchsia that used to hang by the sliding doors, and a baby palm. I was watering them when Toddy came running down the hallway laughing, and she followed him with towels. Both of them were soaking wet and neither of them had anything on. He ran right up to me. I caught him at my thigh, and she was three feet away, dripping on the tiles. I just stood there, with a tin watering pail in my hand, and with Toddy drying himself on my pant leg. It didn't last long. She covered herself, but there was an expression on her face I think I might have misunderstood, as if it had been casual, as if seeing her hadn't mattered. I didn't think it had.

And I suppose what I was feeling that night in Anchorage, passing a pipe with the man who'd driven the dump truck from Juneau, a man named Harvey or Charley whose brother was in jail, I was wondering to myself if this is what it took to see it did matter, that Blue's body had to be cut open. I know they tell you that you can't go home again, and I suppose I'd always thought that was because you change, but no one had ever told me that sometimes the reason you can't go home is because it's been ransacked.

From RUTH, by Eton Arthur Boone

I didn't see Mrs. Cutter again until the following week, after the second operation. I used to play in the upstairs hallway with an oversized yellow marble, wood blocks, and magazines. My brother and I would create whole courses with the blocks and pillows and weeklies, and the marble could follow only if it was rolled correctly, with just the right speed and spin. Most of the time it was distracted by the pitch of the hallway, which leaned south, down toward the living room. The whole house slumped in toward its center, so that if you lifted all its dividing walls and placed marbles at all its corners, they'd converge under the living room table, which was a big bronze platter on legs. They'd all roll and pat Homer softly on her belly as she slept, as if she'd swallowed a magnet for marbles.

Life and *The Saturday Evening Post* had the best surfaces for marbles, but they were kept on a rack in my father's den, and I didn't like to go in there in the afternoons, because when my father wasn't home and the shutters were closed, the den always seemed asleep to me, faint and airless. It was only 2:30. I was home early because Hector's birthday party had been called off. His mother's appendix had burst that afternoon, and I couldn't imagine that anyone would be home, because my brother would still be at Vega's All Stars, and my father had been taking his lunches at the hospital.

I crept toward the door of his den regardless and found it ajar. When I peered through the crack I saw my father kneeling between Mrs. Cutter's knees. Her skirt was hiked up. Her thighs were spread to welcome his chest, and her shirt was open, breasts bared for my father's frantic suckling. Mrs. Cutter's head was thrown back in an embarrassed ecstasy and her fingers rummaged awkwardly through my father's hair as he poured over her. I didn't stay long in the door frame, only long enough to see a single grind of Mrs. Cutter's full hips buck my father's head and upset his feast like a ground swell. Long enough to hear the slavish moans of two people who'd been beaten and to see her thighs close in on him more gracefully and her ankles hook and rub themselves, the way you'd imagine horses or swans necking. I slowly stepped back and out of sight. I didn't pull the door with me. I could feel my face flush and gave in to the pull of the house's center under the living room table, where Homer must have swallowed a magnet for shame.

Joe Boone

I don't know why. Something turns off inside. You stop thinking. You start just doing things because they're there. I just felt so damn alone, I think I'd have done anything to feel like it wasn't happening. When Blue got sick—I mean, I don't want to say this, because I loved Blue and I don't need to explain that to anyone, but Christ, how do you take care of a woman like that? She just pulled back. She acted like it was no one's business. I'd wake up and find her in the bathroom downstairs, sick and her whole body shaking, and I'd say, Blue, wake me up, but she never would. It was like she just took it in, you know. She accepted it, she moved on. And I couldn't do that. I panicked. I made a horrible, horrible mistake. But there's some things where you've just got to say, it happened. I can't do anything about it.

It's the part with Eton, I still don't know. I think I just wanted to have something with him. Because he'd just taken it in like Blue. He was like this little engine that just keeps going. He never cried. I'd go in his room at night to tuck him in. I'd ask how he was doing and he'd ask me medical questions. I just wanted us to have each other, see what we were going through—you know, not exactly, there's such a thing as fathers and sons—but I just wanted to grab him sometimes and say, "Okay, we should adjust. You're right. If there's a flood, you look for something that floats, I know, but it's still okay to stop for a second. It's okay to say, 'This stinks,' Eton. It's okay to know that people need help, that they can't do everything alone." And if he can see that—that we're not going to be heroes in front of this thing, this thing just beats us—well, then maybe it isn't the worst thing in the world.

I'm not saying it was the right thing to do. I'm not saying that at all. It was horrible and I'm going to have to live with it for the rest of my life. But I remember the second time, and this is not in the book. He was leaving to go, and I'd caught him on the stairs. I'd wrestled with it, but I saw him going. You go ahead and do something when it's wrecking you like that. I just gave him the note, Eton, could you do this for me? And he just looked at me. He reached out and took it on the stairs and put it in his bag. And I couldn't let him go just like that. I mean, I was trying to get through to him. I put my hand on his shoulder to say, you know, whatever, son, we're here together, aren't we? Thank him for that, and show him there was something strong about it. I wasn't looking for comfort. I wasn't looking for someone to tell me it was okay. Don't let people tell you that. Don't let people tell you that's what I needed. Eton knew what I needed, and he just looked at me to say, yes, he knew, I swear he did, and then he left.

Toddy Boone

Dad took me on a fishing trip, just four days up near Mount Palomar while Mom and Eton were in the Southwest. I know I was thinking that somewhere down the road we'd switch up. Mom would take me to the Southwest, and Dad would take Eton fishing.

I don't really remember what kind of fish it was that we were up there trying to catch, but I remember we'd gotten the wrong bait. We'd stopped off at a tackle and bait shop on the way up, and Dad said we'd been given a bum steer by the man up there. That was the first time I heard the expression "bum steer." And the night after our first day fishing, I said to Dad as he was tucking me in—we used to have a little ritual where I would have to tell him every night one thing that I'd learned that day—and I told him I'd learned that we'd gotten a bum steer and he should remember for when Eton came up not to go to that tackle and bait shop. But Dad said, "Eton's not coming up here. This place is yours and mine." And I knew he was trying to make me feel good, but I also knew it meant that New Mexico and Arizona belonged to Mom and Eton. That's probably when I realized things weren't exactly even Steven.

From RUTH, by Eton Arthur Boone

Santa Fe came as a relief to us both. I think the Southwestern landscape had worn our patience for shades of muddy pink and copper. I'd enjoyed our roughing days most during twilight and early morning, when lights and colors aren't reflections so much as the seeping of every surface, when each rock or strip of sky is a lamp shaded blue or orange. I think I learned most from these times of day because they convinced me that light doesn't play favorites.

I also learned that from my mother's palette. We were painting a landscape just outside of Magdalena, New Mexico. She was on a stool and I was sitting on the back door of the station wagon. It was twilight. I remember painting the landscape as it would appear in the brilliance of day and then shading my picture with what I thought was the grey of twilight. It's funny how a little boy can think shadows are grey when they so rarely are. When I was very young, I once asked my mother about the color of shadows and she told me that a shadow can be just about any color, but I said no. I said they were grey, grey cast on the color of a surface.

Outside Magdalena my mother won the argument with hardly a word, because she was able to find the colors of twilight with no strategy for shading. She saw the glowing copper on the face of a cliff and painted it. She saw the Dodger blue of the sky high above the horizon and found it on her palette. I saw a day washed grey and brown by twilight and I painted mud.

When it became too dark she walked back to the car and saw my painting and said, "There's really not so much grey as you think." She might as well have said there are no such things as shadows at all, just different slabs of color.

Claire Sullivan

Blue was very happy when they returned from New Mexico. I had lunch with her downtown not so long after, in a diner near the radio station. She looked well—I really thought the trip had done wonders for her—and she spoke about Eton. She was so proud of him. She said that Eton was painting better than she was, but she also mentioned she thought he was beginning to drift away from her, naturally, she said. I remember her telling me that it was something all mothers have to come to terms with. But you could just see, if she hadn't had to be at the hospital so much, if she'd seen him when she wasn't there, she might have wondered if it wasn't something more than just a boy growing up. It's so difficult to say after *Ruth.* I don't really know if I'm letting that book color what I remember. But I just hate to think that maybe Eton wasn't drifting at all. Maybe it was a different

kind of silence she was hearing, the silence that protects, that
hides. It absolutely crushes me to think about how painful it must
have been for such a young boy to go off on that trip having to
hide such secrets from his mother. That was Joe Boone's real sin.
My God, intruding on that wonderful, loving silence between
those two—the comfortable silence of painting the same landscape with someone you love—destroying that, that was Joe's
real sin.

From RUTH, by Eton Arthur Boone

We were staying at the Terminal Motel, which we thought was a
funny name. The Terminal was owned by a woman who looked
either Indian or Mexican to me. The sun had baked her race away
and she was just old. She sat at the front desk of the motel with
an infant in her lap the whole while we were there, and I remember
our second evening, when my mother and I were headed out for
dinner at a place across the road called The Taco Pit. My mother
stopped at the desk to drop off the key and asked, "Es su nieto?"

"No, no," the woman said, smiling and rocking slowly. "Dis my
little boy Garcia, my son." She leaned over the boy and rubbed her
nose against his. "Si, mi hijo." The baby reached out stiffly and
turned its head toward her belly.

"Su hijo?" my mother said. "That's incredible."

The woman looked up and smiled a toothless smile. "Mi sisteen
children." She lifted the boy up to my mother.

"That's amazing." My mother took the child in her arms. "Que
mujer." She looked down at the boy with a mother's longing.
"Your mother is quite a woman. Si, yes." The baby began to
squirm and was turning in my mother's cradle, stretching his
whole body toward her. She offered me the baby but he was
tugging at the silver chain around her neck. She stuck her finger
in his tiny palm and began rocking him. "Look at his ears. They
look like little shells, don't they?" I stood on my toes and looked
over at him as he continued to wriggle in her arms and reach
between the buttons of her shirt.

"No, Garcia." The old woman stood up from the desk.

"It's all right," my mother said weakly. The child strained his neck to reach for her, opening its mouth like a baby bird in its nest. And while the little boy groped for my mother I felt as never before that she was mine and would never be anyone else's again.

Toddy Boone

Dad calls it "that bad time." He just sort of lumps all those years together. When I was about twelve, I started wanting to know what the exact order had been, you know, when she'd first gotten sick, when the operations were, when Anne had started coming around, but Dad would just wave it off, he didn't want to talk about it. Eton knew. I was watching TV with him once up in my room—Dad had gotten us this TV that we used to roll into my room on Tuesday nights so I could watch "The Fugitive" and then go right to sleep. Eton and I were up there and I'd asked him if he remembered how it had worked exactly. He turned down the volume and just reeled off the facts.

It was almost exactly two years, according to him. She'd first gotten sick in late '59, the first operations were the following spring. Their trip was June of '60. She did okay from then until the winter and then she had uterine lumps—that's early, early '61. She was in and out of the hospital the whole last year, and that was the summer—again, this is according to Eton, but I think he was the only one really keeping track—but that was the summer Anne started helping out. Eton called her "Blanne." I probably first saw her right at the end of third grade. She brought me coloring books of "Bonanza."

Anne Richman Boone

I met Joe at a children's birthday party which both Toddy and Hilary went to. It was the summer. Hilary didn't get to be in San Diego very much, so he didn't have very many friends here, but my boss's nephew was having a party at the zoo, and I was able to get Hilary to go. It wasn't easy finding friends for Hilary, because of prejudice. I think Hilary had to face a lot of that. It's one thing to confront prejudice on your own as I did with Hilary's father Damon, but it's another thing to be the child of a mixed marriage. That's part of the reason I kept Hilary in boarding school after the divorce—at least they accepted him there as part of the community.

But little boys need friends, and in San Diego, Toddy was one of the first boys to play with Hilary. They'd first met at this birthday party at the zoo, and Joe and I had come to pick them up. The boys were in the same station wagon coming back, and Joe and I talked while we were waiting. Joe was so nice. I thought, what a wonderful sweet man, and what a horrible burden for him to have to shoulder. And he was there before any of the other parents, with a sweater for Toddy. And when the boys arrived, we saw they were in the back seat together, and Hilary looked like he'd been crying, and I think Toddy was the only little boy who would talk to him at all. Toddy was a very sweet little boy. They came up to us, and Hilary had cotton candy all over his clothes, and Joe said, well, let's have everyone over for dinner tonight and get everyone scrubbed up. I don't even think he thought twice about it.

Claire Sullivan

I visited Blue as often as I could, at least two or three times a week, but she actually told me that I might do better to set her mind at ease if I could stop by the house and see that things were running smoothly there, maybe fix the boys a real meal. Well, I did. I stopped by occasionally to see what I could do, maybe make a meatloaf or a casserole, things that keep.

But one afternoon I dropped by with some groceries and found a woman in the kitchen making a pie. She was very nice, really about as pleasant a thing as you can find in a kitchen. But it was a rather awkward conversation because I didn't know if she was there on a paying basis. She didn't look like someone you'd pay for. She was a very attractive package, with good, simple looks.

She struck me as looking like a blond Jackie Kennedy. Slim. She had on a pearl necklace. The only thing that was curious about her was how comfortable she seemed to be in that kitchen. Maybe that's why she seemed a little professional to me. But she said no, she said that she was just there to help Joe and the boys. She said, you know, we all have to pull together in times like these, and she'd sort of cocked her head when she said it, sitting at the kitchen table with her hands in her lap, and I remember thinking to myself that either here was the most gracious and kind woman on God's earth, or a madwoman had found her way into Blue's kitchen.

So the next time I was at the hospital, I had this very delicate piece of news for Blue, that there was a kindly apparition baking pies in her oven. I don't think that Blue had met Anne yet—in fact I'm certain she hadn't—but she gestured to calm me. She said, "Yes, that must be Anne Richman. Joe tells me he's found an angel to help out when she can."

Joe Boone

Lumps on her throat, in her neck. Back and forth for the tests and those damn vitamins. It's all just a blur. The truth is, the doctors, they didn't know what the hell was going on. And we didn't know how much to tell the kids—Do you tell Eton? How much can Toddy know? It seemed like it was all Blue and I got to talk about anymore. I hated all that damn strategy. I hated that every time I talked to Eton, it was just to tell him that she was getting worse, that it was probably just a matter of time.

Toddy Boone

I saw Mom and Eton dancing once. I wasn't in the room. I was looking in, into the living room where the record player was, and Mom was teaching him to ballroom dance. It was in the middle of the day. We had giant glass doors that opened out to the backyard, and the sun used to come in in the afternoon. Eton and Mom were just like silhouettes against the sliding doors, and they were laughing. It actually kind of scared me to see her up like that because I'd thought she was too sick, but she was laughing. They were stepping on each other's toes, and he was holding her, just rocking back and forth. I wish I could remember what they were dancing to. Someone like Nat "King" Cole. I don't remember. I just watched them, holding my breath. I'd remember it if I heard it.

Levi Mottl

I didn't think I should go back to San Diego. I was living in Saskatchewan, assisting at a school for the deaf there, and it hadn't been easy. I'd wake up at around six every morning and walk four miles to school, watching the sun rise. I'd watch the pink and ochre wash out the windsor blue, and think about Blue back in the hospital. I'd spoken to her a couple of times, but mostly to Joe. It didn't seem like she'd broken free of the hospital, but I couldn't imagine her being sick. I'd think about sending her some bottles of dusk in a box, to shine on her wall when the nurses weren't looking.

But Joe called after the hysterectomy. He said the doctors didn't think Blue was going to be getting any better, and he thought someone should be there for Eton. Joe said he felt like he'd lost him, and he asked if I'd come back.

I guess at the time I assumed Joe was just being a champ, giving me an excuse to return. I think to an extent that's probably true, but it was also true that Eton was in a shell. It wasn't hard to see why, the change in Blue was so dramatic. She looked completely different, sort of gutted. I don't think I could have imagined it, Blue shuffling across the floor, her hair so thin, her arms spotted and all the color gone from her face. The drugs she was on, it seemed like she'd retired from life, and I suppose I found it a little more stunning than I could take with any kind of grace or strength. I couldn't blame Eton for closing off.

We would go to the hospital together. I remember at the end of one of our visits, Blue's face. She'd tried to hold his hand while he was by the bed and all he'd said was it felt waxy. As he left the room she'd looked over at the wall and her eyes filled. I think it was for Eton she feared death most. She didn't want it because of him, and she looked at the wall and waited to be left alone. Before I left, she said, "Please tell him it's fine."

I drove back with Eton next to me in the front, silent and staring straight ahead. We drove out to the coast, but before we reached the highway he asked me to stop the car and he got out, and he got in the back, and we drove off again. I didn't take him home. We drove up along the coast, and he laid down in the back seat crying.

Anne Richman Boone

Once a week I would go do a shopping for them all, and this was one of the first times I had done it. I had all the bags out on the kitchen counter, and I remember I was putting the things away in the cupboards when I saw Eton ride up on his bicycle. And, you know, I felt awkward about being in the kitchen, alone in the house with no one else. So I got myself ready for him. I straightened my skirt and dried my hands. I got ready to welcome him and offer a sandwich or something to drink. I remember I'd even taken down a glass from the cupboard, and I'd poured an apple juice for him. And I just waited for him. I listened for the sound of the door. And I waited, and I listened, and I waited. And I waited some more until I started to ask myself had I really seen him. I was sure it was him, though. I'd seen him through the window, and he'd seen me. But he didn't come.

So I sat there, and I couldn't just leave all the bags out, so I put the rest of the things away as quickly as I could. I'd bought some things for lunch. I made him a baloney sandwich and put it on a dish in the ice box for him, next to the glass of apple juice. I just felt so awful. I went out the back door.

Levi Mottl

Blue reached out and took my hand one day in the hospital room very near the end. It was just the two of us, and she didn't say a word for a while, for a long time. Then she asked me to open the shades. The sun was streaming in, and there were roses on the windowsill from Joe, red roses, and her voice was very faint, hardly anything at all, and she said, "Look at them," and began to trace the roses with her finger. I put my head very near hers to see them from her angle. Our faces were very close. I could feel the warmth, and you could smell her sickness. She was having a great deal of trouble describing what she saw. She hadn't the breath for complete thoughts, and there was a thick, pale film across her eyes. Finally she managed to ask me what color I thought the flowers were, and the sun was flooding them. They looked red. I said, "Red. Rose red." And she said, she whispered in my ear, like the saddest joke, "Looks aubergine to me."

Claire Sullivan

She died on a gray, hazy day in late December, December 21, 1961. There's something very forgiving about the way someone finally dies after such a long, slow trial. The person leaves the body before the life does. We didn't lose Blue the instant she died—we lost her before.

I was there. I came in every morning, and the last few days she was somewhere in between. I read poems to her, poems that she'd liked best—Blake and Auden—but she was less and less Blue. Her face and her hair and her body, all settling for death. Her cheeks and mouth just lay there on her bones. Blue was gone and death had settled in, but it wasn't so horrifying. It seems right somehow, it happens so gradually but so distinctly. Death really does lay claim to you, and it's the same expression for everyone I've seen. Peace, and not at all the peace of the particular person. The person, your friend, your cousin is gone.

The last day, the last morning I came in, the smell in the room was entirely different. I knew that it was her last. I called Joe, who was still at home making breakfast for the boys, and told him to come down, that she was dying today. He asked me if he should bring the boys, and I've always been sorry for my answer, which I think was too abrupt. I said, "Not to see Blue. Blue is gone." But I'd been touched by Joe there. When he asked, I could see the side of him that makes him a wonderful man, such a really kind man. Because he was helpless. He wanted so much to do the right thing, but he didn't know what that was, and he wasn't at all ashamed to admit it.

He did something odd, though. He brought Eton. He left Toddy with Anne and brought Eton to see her, which mustn't have been easy. I think he must have thought that was the right thing to do. It may have been. I don't know. I was glad Eton was there. He walked right up to her, next to the bed, and he leaned over her. I think he wanted to kiss her goodbye, but he didn't. I think he knew he was too late. He didn't say anything. None of us did, until Joe. He said, "She loved you, you know, Eton. And that's something." Eton didn't respond, didn't even move. But I think that was the right thing.

From RUTH, by Eton Arthur Boone

The Terminal's only soda machine was in the registration office, which was a walk. Our room and the office were at opposite ends of the Terminal's L, but it was a clear evening. The air was cooling, and as I walked along the motel porch the ridge of the Black Range mountains looked like paper cutouts against the lavender sky. They looked flat, and I stared at them to see if the mountains would slide in front of each other like playing cards.

The desk was kept at night by an older man named Jimmy who

was bent and skeletal and whose teeth dangled off his gums like kernels of rotten corn. Jimmy was friendly to me. He broke my dollar and showed me where they kept the ice chest, in a room behind the office. I went in and began chopping myself some ice when I heard the jangle of the door and a couple walk in. They were drunk, and they needed a place. "Do you have rates for half-nights?" the man asked, and I heard the woman laugh. I wanted to see them, but most of the ice in the chest had melted into a single chunk, and I was having trouble chopping it. I had about a quarter-inch of what looked like a shattered windshield in the bucket when I went back in the office.

The man had on a white straw hat and a cream linen suit. His skin was burnt pink, and his eyes looked like olive pits covered in spit. They were dastardly eyes and they nudged both me and Jimmy in the ribs at the prospect of the woman tugging at his jacket. She was more native, with long black hair and smoother skin, skin pulled tight around her bones, except for her breasts, which swayed like water balloons filled to the nipple with liquor. Her nails dug in his jacket fiercely. She had their room key in her free hand, and as the man signed the registration, she traced a white spiral on his cheek with the tip of the key. Just as she was reaching its center, she looked at me out of the corner of her eye, flicked out her tongue and licked a three-inch trail up his neck and into his ear. She dropped the key in his pocket.

The man shucked her aside and she stumbled backwards, pulling up the straps of her dress like the cords of a grocery bag, to keep the fruit from tumbling out. She weaved over to the Coke machine, rummaged around in her purse, inserted a couple of dimes, and without looking at me, said, "Is that ice for your girl, little boy?" I said, "No, it's for the drink." She smiled and opened the glass door, pulled the last Coke from its slot, and turned toward me. For the first time I saw her completely, every drunken lap and swell. She said, "Well, I hope you didn't want a Coke." The man in the white hat snapped his fingers twice and dangled the key out in front of her. She turned back around and her body swished out of the office after him.

Jimmy gave a soft tongue whistle as the door clanged shut. He turned to me and said he was sorry. He called me fella and asked if I'd gotten all the ice I wanted. I said, yeah, and looked over at the soda machine with what must have been visible longing, because he told me there was a store about half a mile down the road, if I had my heart set on a Coke. I thought I did, and my mother was resting in our room. I didn't like being in the room when she was resting because it made me worry. So I had Jimmy point me in the right direction and started toward the road with the bucket of ice still in my hand.

By the time I'd made my way out to the edge of the road, the number 17 had me in its grip. I'd seen it in Jimmy's ledger, the room he'd given them. In room 17, that woman's dress would be slipping to the floor. She'd step out of it and open her mouth on his, slice off his buttons with her nails. The image pulsed in my brain like a slow strobe, a throb of blood, a blinking conscience that would rather see the deep blush of shame on its inside lid than that man and woman together.

She tugged at me, though. She kept leading me, to more and more doors, more sheets, more veils, more dresses slipping from her body, but only just slipping. I could not in my mind have had that woman completely for even a moment, but it made the image no less clear, of her stepping out of that dress and moving towards him. My blood rushed, and it raged with envy for the man, the one who got to go behind the doors with the woman, the one who folded down the sheets and accepted the body as it slipped out of the white dress. If I could somehow be a man, and have her carve spirals in my cheek. If I could have her come to me without questions, without suspicion, with nothing but desire, I would have done anything. I knew the lure of desire almost completely, and I felt in my knees and throat an ache to give in, to let it have me. And just as frightening and vivid to me was the longing with which desire wants a voice, wants to announce and proclaim itself like conviction, or like guilt.

It said, "If you want it, it means something. You need something, and there's no shame in that."

I turned around from the road and walked back toward the wooden stairs of the hotel porch. My steps were slow and tentative, but quiet like Indians as I walked along the planking, and the voice was very clear.

"All you've really got is what you want, and you can walk through your life pretending it isn't there, or that it'll go away, but you'll just drive yourself crazy. You're just a human being. Don't forget that. Wanting is what it's all about."

I stopped outside room 17 and stood profile in front of the window. The curtains were drawn and I could only see the figures in the room very faintly. I could hear their voices. The woman floated into the bathroom and the man was down on the bed waiting. He sensed me outside. He sat up and threw change at the window. I walked on as if I hadn't stopped.

"It's not going to leave you alone. Long as you want something, it's going to be there waiting. You try to push it away like you know better, like you don't need anything, but what you don't know is that's who you are. What you need, that's who you are, and somewhere you've just got to say, 'Okay, then, let's see it.' "

I keyed the door to our room as quietly as I could and pushed it open. I could see my mother's stomach rising and falling slowly with sleep. Her hands were over her belly and her shoes were on. I pulled the door closed and put the bucket down. I looked at my mother. I looked at her chin and her shoulders, her whole body lying there. I crept on flat heels into the bathroom.

The woman was returning to him now from the bathroom, with nothing on, with nothing. Her breasts floated and they were large and white. She smiled and slid onto the bed.

I locked the door and sat on the toilet. My mother didn't stir.

"It doesn't mean that all the other things don't matter. All it means is you're human. All it means is there's a difference between now and everything else, and right now there's something you want."

I was hard. I stretched my legs out and put my foot up against the bathroom door. My pants were straining, taut down around my ankles.

The woman knelt over him, straddled him, with her thighs spread muscularly, and unbuttoned him slowly. Her breasts hovered. They were heavy.

My mother lay still and I held myself in the bathroom, hard up past my belly button.

"And when it gets up close, right there in front of you, that's when you know you're alive. With everything else you'd never know. But having something right there waiting, saying, 'Come on. Come on, give in,' you don't give in, you go. You make that decision and that's the one moment in your life you know you're there. It's just, 'I'm getting that. I'm going.' "

I pulled once, and then twice.

The woman pulled him out of his zipper and held it in her hand like a bottle.

My mother's stomach rose and then fell. Her feet crossed.

I came, for the first time. It smacked my face and plupped against the wall behind me.

I hated him. I hated him. I hated him.

Levi Mottl

The funeral reception was at the Lemon House. It wasn't a big affair. The family. Some from back East. Some students from the school. Anne had prepared the place very competently. She'd made deviled eggs and placed them in a very neat circle around a dip for cauliflower and broccoli. It was a pretty attractive plate, and up until then, I'd liked deviled eggs a great deal.

But I remember I'd gone upstairs to help Toddy with a train set that someone had brought over for him. He was sitting on his bed in a jacket and tie reading the instructions, and I was down on the floor forcing the tracks together, when I heard a voice from the landing, a voice I couldn't quite place. I could just hear it calling out softly, with that knotted, thick throat that's like cloth, calling out, "Mom, Mom." It sounded like Eton, sounding lost, and I'd wanted to let it pass. I just kept on wrestling with the tracks and Toddy was still reading, but I heard the feet coming up the stairs further, and then he called out again, closer to the door, "Mom?" I put down the tracks. I stood up and went to the door. I opened it and there was a little boy standing there in gray flannel shorts and a white button-down. It was one of Alice's children, Blue's sister, and he couldn't have been more than seven, and he said, "Have you seen my mother?" I remember feeling I was going to vomit on the top of his head.

Joe Boone

I wasn't even seeing straight. You know, it seems like there'd been time, she'd been sick for so long, but you just can't prepare for something like that. It's still overnight. We turned from being this family—just because she'd been there—into this man and two boys, and how was that supposed to work? I tried. Jesus, I tried, but the three of us would go out together, just go see a movie, and Toddy said it right. We were driving back from seeing *The Music Man* and he just started crying. He said with the three of us together all it made him think was, "Where's Mom? Why isn't she here?" And I wanted to say, "Toddy, boy, this is it, from now on. This is what we got. We got to get used to it," but I just couldn't. I agreed with him. And we never got used to it. Driving in the car sometimes, right afterwards, I'd look at Eton in the rearview mirror—I feel like it's the only time we looked at each other back then—he's got his arms crossed and I can see it in his eyes. I don't blame him for it, it's natural and I don't blame him, but sitting there in the back seat, I know Eton's thinking, "I wish it had been you, Dad. You should have been the one."

Claire Sullivan

Four years. Four long years. I was just ducking my head in, but it seems to me that Joe spent the first year after she died simply working his fingers to the bone. I actually don't know if it was work that he was doing to pass the time—he may have been driving up and down the coast, for all any of us knew—but he certainly wasn't keeping up with the friends he'd had with Blue. Just holed himself up, didn't even return phone calls. He'd hired a housekeeper named Mrs. Milligan who I don't think any of them had particularly warm feelings towards. A great big Irish woman, she kept the place running, saw to Toddy, which is what it seems to me Anne should have been doing if things had been allowed to run their natural course. But Anne was a little frightened off by Eton, I think. It was very clearly Eton. He hadn't been gone for two months before Joe and Anne were officially engaged. Four years of them all moping about, dipping their toes in the bathwater to see if it's getting any warmer, and then the moment Eton left for Europe, everyone hopped right in. He must have been quite a little black cloud.

Levi Mottl

I stayed six months or so after Blue died, working at the University and checking on Eton. We'd take trips up the coast when we could, day trips, overnights on weekends up Highway 1. We explored, sort of painted the cordial white line between ourselves and everything else that was going on out there. We'd head out to the hills by San Bervasa where they have the red snakes, or go out on the fishing boats off Port Norma, and we had a good time together. Eton and I were a good match. It isn't that you need the same politics or sense of humor as your traveling partner. It doesn't even matter if he's half your age as long as he goes at your pace, and Eton did. That may have been an adjustment he was just naturally able to make, to find your gear, but the time we spent together back then, we gave each other the kind of company you get from a car radio. There. Soothing just for being there, ready to light, ready to tune into.

I'm not sure it was the best thing for Eton, though. I think coming and going like that, using the house as a sort of pit stop, probably just made Eton even more reluctant to be there in the first place. The way he'd get to his room when I'd bring him home—I'd drop him off, but he wouldn't use the front door if Joe's car was in the driveway. If he saw Joe's car, he'd go up to it, get up on the hood, and swing himself up on to the roof by the basketball rim. Then he'd walk across the garage roof to his window. I'd get out of the car to go say hi to Joe, and usually by the time he answered the bell, you could hear Eton's window slam shut.

I left in the middle of the summer, 1962, but before I did I made an offer. I told Joe I could take Eton on a trip after he graduated from high school, to Europe. It was a way of making sure that Eton and I would stay in touch, which I think we wanted to. I guess I also always felt a debt, learning from Blue and knowing her as I did, I had to keep a promise to be sure Eton always knew there was this special take on the world that had belonged to his mother. Joe knew it too. I think I always had his blessing there. So we sort of set this date, Eton and I, to go to Europe together after he graduated, and pick up there.

Toddy Boone

Eton used to take me out to dinner at this place just called Lunch-Annette, maybe once a week, just me and him. He'd take the car. He was too young for his license, but Dad never said anything. I have no idea if Dad remembers this, but he came into Eton's room with a ten dollar bill one time, and he said he'd pay if Eton would take me and Hilary out to Lunch-Annette, because it was Hilary's birthday and he was in from school. Eton just looked at Dad and I remember him saying, "Who the hell is Hilary?" He knew, I think he just wanted to hear Dad say it, Anne's son. Could he please just take Anne's son out for a birthday dinner? We didn't. Eton said no. He didn't even look at him.

Dad ended up taking us, just Hilary and me and Anne. We went to the restaurant in the Coronado, special treat. We'd gone in all dressed up, Hilary was in his uniform. People were staring at him the second he came in. It's like we'd brought in a freak. Halfway through dinner he said he was feeling sick. He just sat there with his chin on his plate. I remember the three of us singing happy birthday to him while the waiter brought out the cake, and no one else joined in. They all just sat there at their tables, clearing their throats.

Hilary Richman

I was born in Bethesda, which is an awful place. I went to grade school, I went to public school there till I was in the middle of second grade. Then this unfortunate incident happened and my parents moved me to a military school, which is where I was until my parents divorced, after we'd moved to California.

Actually it was funny. It's a racial incident, which I recount with glee. I was in second grade and it was at a Christmas party. First of all, we lived on the base, so the school had a lot of military children, and there was this grotesque little boy who was fat and his father was a general or something. He was just horrid. At the Christmas party we had hot chocolate and he was drinking a little mug. He said, "This chocolate is just the color of your skin, you cocoa face" or something like that. I looked over at his hot chocolate and took it and I threw it at him. He was hospitalized. It wasn't boiling—apparently it was very hot, I don't know. So they asked my parents to move me to a different school, which they did. The worst part of it was I had to write a letter to the little shit, apologizing. I'm sure he's in the service now.

Claire Sullivan

Hilary was an adorable child truly, an adorable little brat. I never saw him that much, and when I did, I doubt I was in the best of moods. This was when Blue was really quite ill. He'd come down from his school on vacations, and occasionally he'd come over with Anne to help make something. A very delicate little tawny boy with the most beautiful face, I can see him in Blue's kitchen peering about and watching us all chop up vegetables and such things. And occasionally you'd glance over at him. He was a boy but he still stared like a baby, so unafraid, and like some very dear babies, when you caught him staring he'd give you his wonderful little smile. He must have been very uncomfortable in those situations, and I imagine anywhere he went, because he was so extraordinary. This lovely little boy tiptoeing about the kitchen with his roll of apricot candy.

Oh, but he had the foulest habit with it too. He used to have those rolls, those fruit rolls that are just sheets of dried apricots or some such thing that Anne used to make, and he had one in the kitchen one morning. I was in there starting a ratatouille, and he'd come in the way anyone's bound to when they hear someone fumbling about in the kitchen. He'd taken one of these new rolls, and he was standing right next to me, and he opened it and unrolled it like so and laid it out flat on the counter. And then he brought it up to his face and licked it, he licked it all over. And he was peering out of the corner of his eye as he did so, gleefully. He proceeded to roll it back up. Well, I looked over at him and I said, "Hilary, what on earth are you doing?" And he said, "I'm licking it." He said, "I'm licking it so that if anyone else wants one, this is the one that I've licked. Would you tell the others?" Would I? I felt rather obliged to.

Joe Boone

There was a weekend, a Friday night, and the kids weren't around. Claire had taken them up to Los Angeles, and I'd called Anne. They were having a carnival down by the wharf, and I asked Anne if she'd like to come with me. We'd gone places together before, just the two of us. We'd go on walks down by Imperial and talk. She told me about Damon and all that, how rough it had been. But there was something different about this night, I think Anne felt it too. She looked terrific. Had her hair up. We'd gone down in the early evening and just walked through. They'd set up some fish stands. We danced. They had a mariachi band set up in the square, and we danced. Her hair looked like gold, and we walked up and down the wharf, up and down, dancing to all the different bands they had.

But I'd had to go back to the car. It got dark and it was getting cold, so I'd gone back to get us sweaters. I sat in the car for about ten minutes, just sitting there. And then I went back to the wharf. It looked beautiful at night. All the people, and the lights hanging, streamers, piñatas. It was like being a kid again, and I saw Anne sitting on one of the tables, with just the red checker tablecloth. She had her elbows on her knees and a paper cup in her hand, and she was nodding to people when they came by. She looked sleepy. She looked beautiful. And I guess it's just a matter of enough time passing for you to see it. You've had to just wait for all the pain to go away. You've had to get through that period where no one could really help you, and then one day you just see her sitting there, same lady who's been there all along, and all of a sudden you know you're looking at your future. You're looking at the rest of your life.

Hilary Richman

Look, can I just say, I hated that part of my life. That part of my life just sucked. I mean, the idea. No one knew what to do with me. My mother was an army brat like me, but I don't think she ever really wanted me to be in the military. God, I hope not. My father did. He wanted me to be in the Navy, and he'd give me little planes which I always broke and had to hide from him. But my mother, I don't know. After my father left for Manilla, she took me out of Hammond and enrolled me at Hoyt, which was precisely the same thing, only in California. I just think it had been so ingrained in her from her own childhood that this was the way you dealt with a child growing up, which was to give them military structure, that that's what she did with me.

But I hated that place. I deplored it. I wrote this poem when I first got there. I was eleven years old and I wrote this poem for some English assignment. It stemmed from a dream I'd had. It was just this very vivid dream about people singing and it being a very painful experience, something like they couldn't stop singing even though their ears were bleeding. So I wrote this poem which I thought was excellent for an eleven-year-old about the military, and I gave it to my teacher. And I don't even think he read it. He just smiled and took it away from me. I ended up being called into the Colonel's office, the headmaster—the members of the faculty had to be called by military titles, even though most of them weren't even officers. So I go into the Colonel's office, with these fucking World War II maps on the wall, and he stands there and reprimands me for writing this what he called obscene piece of literature. This man is just marching around this office in these boots and yelling at this poor little eleven-year-old kid for writing a fucking poem. I couldn't believe it. I was eleven years old and I was surrounded by these completely ignorant fascist idiots.

And I would write these long teary letters to my mom telling her how miserable I was and begging her to get me the hell out of there. I used to literally sit at this public phone in this hallway in this dingy dorm, with these lobotomies running around rat-tailing each other. I would literally sit there every night having to read this disgusting graffiti all over the booth, just waiting for her to call. It was pathetic. She would come see me occasionally. She would come up from San Diego because she was so lonely too, but she never really talked about taking me out. They are such awful places. They're awful awfully horrible places. They step on your mind and fuck with you and ruin people. I have terrible memories of them. I guess I'm obviously bitter.

Toddy Boone

Eton and I went to see Grandpa Edwin in Philadelphia when I was about eleven. Dad said if we played our cards right, it would be the only business trip either of us would ever have to make. We stayed about three weeks. They were getting ready to sell Sullivan South, so the upstairs had all been cleaned out. Eton and I had the whole floor to ourselves. We slept in sleeping bags in this room that used to sleep about six nannies. It was a fun trip. It was different. We were treated like little princes and we had this whole big house to run around. We'd play moonball over the house and at night we'd watch TV with Grandpa, and Eton would make up songs on the piano for him.

But the last night there, we were up in our room in the sleeping bags just talking, and Eton said he bet that Dad and Anne had been spending nights together while we were gone. I was pretty shocked. I said, "What are you talking about? They wouldn't do something like that." And Eton just said, okay, let's bet. He said it was probably the only reason we were there in the first place, just to give Dad and Anne a chance to spend the night, but I told him he didn't know what he was talking about. He was just being a jerk. So we bet. We hooked pinkies up there in our sleeping bags.

We didn't really resolve how we were going to figure out who was right, but Eton just said we'd know, and we did. The first night back we knew. Anne made dinner for us. She brought over a meatloaf, but when she came in Dad didn't even get up and go to the door. He just stayed in the living room, but it wasn't just that. It was the whole dinner, the way it felt. I remember looking at Eton during dessert. He was tonguing his spoon at me.

Joe Boone

I tried to talk to him about it. I tried to tell him that Anne and I were taking it easy. We weren't rushing into anything. I wanted to be honest with him. I wanted him to know, and he'd nod and say fine, but the whole thing still felt rotten. There were stretches there it seemed like he was never home, but we still felt like we had to sneak around. She'd have to tiptoe in, because we didn't know, he might have been up there. We didn't want to make a noise. If she was over visiting, we'd just sit in the living room sipping our drinks. Even when we went out to dinner, we'd find ourselves whispering. And he said to me once—I'd been trying to sit down and explain it to him—he said, "Don't tell me it isn't romantic, Dad." And I wanted to say, "Dammit, Eton, it isn't romantic. It's not romantic with you up there with your door closed, like we're just trying to hurt you. Anne cries." Jesus, she wanted to get to know him so much, I'd tell her what a great kid he was, but we're still having to sneak into the kitchen to touch each other. Two years of that, and that's what still stinks. Anne and I look back at these years, and we should be seeing how happy we were and how grateful we were for each other, and all we can remember is feeling like criminals in our own home.

Hilary Richman

Joe Boone was an asshole. He really was. I'm sorry. I hate for my mother's sake to say that I don't like him, but we all know I don't like him. He was just so full of shit. I couldn't deal with his father act, and Mom knew. But she would practically confide in me, just because I guess she had no one else. That was probably a mistake. You know, you've got your mother calling you on the phone saying, he's invited me ballroom dancing, and what was I going to say? Great, Mom, wear your taffeta blouse? I mean, the most I could say was, Mom, do what makes you happy. And what makes my mom happy actually, what she told me, is being allowed to tell someone, "Why don't you wear that shirt?" Well, Jesus, here I am, I'm a twelve-year-old fuck-up at the other end of the phone and my mom's telling me, you know, it's the little things, and I just go, Mom, if it makes you happy, go ahead. I just pretended I didn't care. It was fine. It's what she wanted. But I really objected to Joe Boone. Maybe I was too young to know it in so many words, and I certainly had no objections to Toddy or E.B., who I hardly even saw, but I never trusted Joe. Not that he ever trusted me.

God, I remember this Christmas vacation. I brought a friend home to San Diego. I guess I was the equivalent of a freshman, thirteen, and I had basically one friend. His name was Frisbee. He was a complete freak. All he did was play Frisbee and do drugs, and his mind was just completely gone. I thought he was fascinating. I don't know what the fuck he was doing at Hoyt in the first place, but he was just the best to hang out with. I think he was like an Eisenhower or something. Frisbee Eisenhower. But he'd been completely tripping at some school function so they put him on probation and his parents had basically told him to fuck off, so I said well, come to San Diego with me, and he did.

He came down with me for the Christmas holidays, and Christmas day we all drove to Joe Boone's house so we could pretend to have Christmas. It was something to just laugh at. E.B. was hardly even there. Joe Boone had gotten my mom this scarf, and Frisbee and I escaped out to the back lawn with this flask he took from Joe Boone's liquor cabinet. We got completely smashed, and I think Frisbee actually pissed on these flowers they had.

But Joe Boone came out and started yelling at this kid, who was obviously fucked up in the first place. Joe Boone was just incredibly mean to him. He was yelling and yelling and telling him that he'd ruined Christmas, he was intruding on a family Christmas, and he certainly made me feel that way too.

We went back inside finally, and my mom was there, and Joe put his arm around me. He gave me this transistor radio. What an asshole. I'm sorry, but he was.

II

Europe

Summer 1966 — Spring 1967

Peter Finney

My father told me once, Beware the man from nowhere. Beware of him as a character in a play and beware of him in real life, because in either case, he's capable of anything. No family. No home. No mark on him. He's a knock on the door. You rush to it and through the peephole you see him, someone unfamiliar, twiddling his thumbs, whistling at the sky, innocent. Beware.

What a wonderful, horrible, humbling moment, to have spent your life as I had, having to resort to effects when I was at a loss, as I so often was, a scowl to effect my disdain for it all, and then to have a mere boy enter your life, stage right, and demonstrate an ability, such an ability. You could feel it in your throat each time he would do something new, My God, he's touched with two such precious things—instinct and independence.

So prepare to be humbled, my father should have told me. Let the stranger in, by all means, but pray that he's courteous, pray that he's younger and that he aspires to younger roles, because having to compete with him stroke for stroke—and this elaborate warning we conjure from my father, mind you, the great Franklynne—don't compete with him stroke for stroke, Peter, because this boy from nowhere, with no home and no legacy, has no limitations either. He can sound like anything, look like anything, act anything. So beware. Be wise. Take him under your wing.

Levi Mottl

We were in Europe together about six months. We made a sort of circuit, starting in Amsterdam and then swinging around the continent clockwise until we hit Paris in the winter. Joe and Anne announced their engagement sometime in the fall, when we were in Italy. I'd called Joe from a post office in Florence. He said he wanted to talk to Eton about it, but Eton wasn't with me. He'd taken the day in Siena, and I told Joe I couldn't promise Eton would return his call. They hadn't spoken the whole trip. Joe said fine, he didn't insist.

I told Eton that same night, in our pensione. We were lying in twin beds separated by a table lamp down on the floor, and I didn't really understand his response, except that after he was finished and we'd turned off the light, I suppose it was the first I realized he wouldn't be going home. He told me about Blue's Christmas presents.

Blue had died just before Christmas, and she'd had presents for them all. Eton said there'd been a painting for each of them and a present too. She'd had Claire do her shopping, and Christmas day they all opened their paintings together, just the family. Eton's was one of the ones she'd done in New Mexico, a gas station with a range of violet mountains behind, which Eton ended up putting over his desk. But after they'd all opened their paintings, which Eton said hadn't been a lot of fun, only he and Toddy had opened their presents, shirts that Claire had bought in Santa Barbara. Joe didn't open his. Eton said Joe just left it under the tree, and later he'd put it up in his closet. He never opened it, and Eton said he'd asked Claire once what was in the box, and she'd told him there were wine glasses, two of them, that Blue had asked her to get. Eton said every time he saw Joe drinking wine, he always thought about the two glasses Blue had bought for him, sitting up in his closet. He said he thought about the wine glasses they had downstairs in the cupboards breaking, and Joe would go out and buy more, and he'd never know that there were two up in his closet, waiting for him, from Mom.

Harry Hampton

Okay, I first met him at Harry's Bar, of course, in Paris. This is pretty near the end of the continental portion of his trip, when he's just hitting his stride as a traveler, by which I mean he's realizing people aren't sticking to him. I don't remember who I was with—whom—some nose job whose dad knew Art Buchwald probably, but I was in Harry's when they come in, tail end of the Frommer trip, Boone and Levi—hard to believe it was Levi because he didn't make much of an impression on me, but later, years later when we're in New York, Boone said it was. Anyway, they practically still have their backpacks on when I first see them, and Boone's young. He's younger than me. What the first note says is, "He acts like he's just grown into his skin and he's taking it for a spin, ninety miles an hour."

Okay, now I don't know how much that does for you. Probably not a lot, but what's more interesting than what the note says is that there's a note there in the first place. Back in Paris, see, I used to carry two notebooks with me. I was working at the *Herald-Tribune,* two years out of college, had a place on the Rive gauche, a pretty nifty setup, and I carried two notebooks with me wherever I went—one for reporting, which means checking quotes with Reuters, and one for fiction, which means shit. I was still writing fiction, and I used to take notes—images, ideas, comments, anything I thought I might be able to use in my writing. You know, "ideas are like birds," I'm saying to myself, "and if a pretty one flies by, you've got to have a pen around to shoot it down." That, needless to say, is a note, dated January of 1965, so I'm twenty, twenty-one years old.

But also and most important is, I'm taking notes on people. As far as I'm concerned, anyone I meet is fair game. If I have lunch with some Yugoslavian chef I'm interviewing for the paper, I take my reporter notes, but when we're finished, there's a good chance I streak home, pull out my fiction notebook and write down some really ballsy description of his nose. "His nose," say, "looked like a baked potato," ha-cha-chaa. So if you look in these notebooks, Hampton's Parisian period—and there's a good half dozen of them—that's what you're going to find for the most part, just little one-two punches on anyone I happened to meet. Say, "Pierre"—or no, "Girard," who was a real weasel, "Girard will push his mind only as far as it can easily go, but no further. Not where sweat's involved." You know, all as if someday I'll walk underneath a trolley car, some cop will find the notebook in my pocket, read it, rush it over to Methuen, and before you know it, they're giving guided tours of my mother's icebox.

Anyway, the point is, I took notes on Boone too—I couldn't help myself—but I'll tell you something, no one ever made me feel like a cheaper whore doing it. That first night in Harry's, Levi'd gone back to their hotel, and the two of us went out for a walk, out around the Latin Quarter, and even right there I'm feeling it. I've known the guy three hours, and I've already got this crotch-ache ambivalence going. Part of me wants to get back to my room right now and get something down, like "he's grown into his skin" or another one I'll share with you. Say, "B. sweeps in like a jet airplane, with all the noise and from the same height, content to watch his shadow flicker across the land," tra la.

Okay, but the question is, do I want to be doing that, or do I just want to walk down the goddamn street with the guy? This is my problem. This is my condition. I'm chronic, and basically I'm always trying to do both, within and without. "Does that not explain," I wonder, "the distant aspect of all the greats?"—a note. But am I great? Is this how it's done? Well, you tell me. You hear the notes. No. The notes are an embarrassment, and they do real violence to most of the people they're trying to describe. Because

Boone, for instance, was not, he never was, and I'm frightened to death there are people out there who are going to tell you he was, but he was not walking around in some cape like he's the second coming of Lord Byron. He did not have rocks in his pockets, and he did not howl at the moon. But the problem is, if you take a look at my notes, if someday there's a lucky trolley car and the notebooks do get published, you could end up thinking that, and I just want to get it said now that that's not Boone. That's a kid who wanted to write too damn much. That's me.

I mean, that first night, we went over to the Île de la Cité really late, and we were talking about Europeans or something. We're behind Notre Dame on one of the small streets. We see a party spilling out maybe twenty yards in front of us. People are leaving a party, and there's light on them, street light, and all of a sudden on our right, we both look up and there's a woman leaning out her window, second story. She was probably only four feet above us, but she had the window open, and the lights were off in her house. She was wearing a white slip and carrying a little dachshund in her arms, and she was crying. Beautiful, but she was crying, and then she pulled back inside. We didn't stop. We just kept walking, and I could hear her rattling the window. She was having trouble with the lock, but Boone was moving us along, past this thing, this vision. I didn't know what was up. Finally I had to say to him, "Could you hold on a minute?" And I stop and I take a note, which I happen to have here—"The dog's ears flapped like angel's wings"—and Boone just stood there waiting for me while I was writing, standing right there in the middle of all these people adjusting their collars. That's not a note. That's a memory.

Levi Mottl

The only time Eton and I ever really got the chance to paint together was in Europe, and I always thought that was too bad. Eton said something in his book about painting the same landscape with someone you care for—when you've finished painting together, there's a sort of silent pact that's formed between the two of you and whatever you've both been looking at, the buttress of a cathedral or a drift of blue lupin. It's not something that really hits with everyone, but it did with Blue, and it did with Eton.

The best work I have with me is from Bakken, which is an amusement park for the people of Copenhagen. It's very torn and tattered, much more picturesque than Tivoli, and if you get there the right time of year, the walk there is shaded by a canopy of intensely green trees, and that's where Eton and I stopped to draw the passersby. It must have been May or so, June.

Eton was always more interested in passersby, in human figures, than either Blue or I. Art was more of a speed sport for him. He never really had the patience for less fluid structures like architecture or even nature, and that really did set him apart from Blue. Blue was so concerned with the blocks of color that make up a vision. For Blue, it was all sensual—a still life, a landscape, a human face, they were all just things that light hit on. But you have to have tremendous natural skills to see that. A teacher of Blue's—Oscar Greenough—he once put it that you have to have the open mind of a chess master.

At Bakken, I'd sketched a group of children standing on line at a snack stand. Eton came over and when he saw what I'd done, he said I seemed to have a pretty firm idea in my head of what a group of children looked like. It was sort of brash, but true. He said all my figures looked like they'd been stamped from the same cookie cutter. So I offered him my charcoal. I asked him to draw the figures and see if there wasn't a sort of family resemblance there too. I gave him my tree stump and wandered off to get myself a Danish cruller, one of those garlic-and-butter–drenched crepes, which actually gave me pretty rancid breath all the way through Denmark. When I returned to Eton, he'd already done five or six sketches. He ended up filling the whole sheet, and I actually brought them with me today.

You know, I was looking through these and deciding which ones to bring, and I really am glad I kept them. I don't think I'd want to look at any of them more than once a year. They're just sketches, but there's always something a little more personal about sketches—less space between the paper and the hand. If all paintings were as personal as Eton's sketches—as these right here

I'm having such trouble finding—I don't think we'd hang them on our walls.

But here they are. These are the Bakken sketches. The children had all kept circulating, but you could still match them up with Eton's drawings—maybe one was standing on line now, tugging on her mother's skirt here, or this little gentleman hiding behind the poplar. Eton had just been sort of skeet-shooting. And I remember watching his pencil dash all over the paper and him making a sort of show of it, like the men who twist balloons into poodles and giraffes for children. They say your hand can have a kind of intelligence, a memory for what it likes to do, its favorite steps, but Eton's hand was more like a marionette. It never looked like it had any ideas of its own, and it never would have confused one child's forehead for another. It was what Blue called having an honest eye. You can even see, right below where I've dated it here. June, '66. "The honest eye—children at Bakken."

I wish we'd been able to do more drawing like that, but Eton's interest flagged. He started playing games. In Hamburg, I remember we'd pitched camp in one of the squares and were painting a cathedral there. Eton was settled out in front of a hotel, right by some tables with flamingo pink umbrellas. He was about fifty yards away from me, catercorner across the square. I was painting an old man sleeping with a long pipe in his teeth and a covey of sparrows at his feet.

I took a break at some point. I went over to get chocolate from Eton's box. One of Blue's teachers when she first came to the coast told her to always bring bars of chocolate with her on painting excursions for a quick shot of energy. It's a habit she passed along to Eton and me. We'd always have chocolate around, and at some point midway through a session we'd take a breather and share a Tobler, just sit with each other until we were ready again. So I went over for a chocolate break and took a look at what he'd been doing.

I've painted and sketched out in public with a good number of artists, all with their own particular customs and manners—a Ukrainian, Louie Beklov from the League, who used to beat people away from his canvases with his brushes and flick his paint thinner at you for just glancing over his shoulder. I don't think Louie would've taken too kindly to what Eton had done. He'd painted the same man I had, but he'd tried to do it from my angle.

the grave of Gertrude Stein. All of a sudden he's got a bee in his bonnet about Gertrude Stein. Off he goes. I pick up my dick, say good-bye to my Hungarian friends, and go over to join him. So there we are, we stand there in front of this friggin' tombstone, I'm serious now, for forty-five minutes while Boone's asking me every goddamn question you can think of about Gertrude Stein, who is she, why have I heard of her, where'd she get her brownie recipe, and on and on until finally I tell him, "Hey, Curious George, if you're so interested, go to the goddamn library." I mean, maybe he was interested—I don't really know, he probably was—but I just thought he was messing with me. The afternoon I'd planned for us was going over like a lead balloon, the bums are a washout, so Boone decides to make the best of it by standing there and yanking me around with some pop quiz on the rose-is-a-rose lady.

So anyway, that's where that note's from—the one about his mind wandering—and I've got a million others. And I could try to remember what they're all talking about, but you'd get the message pretty quickly—Boswell here is out of his league. "Was he such a buccaneer before the eye patch?" There's a pearl—he had an eye patch for a while because he'd hurt his eye. "Conversations like jazz," I don't even want to go into—"Jamming." Or here, actually. This is Harry the merciful, always allowing that maybe it's just me. On Boone's performances—"As they grow in number, they grow in strength as well, don't they? Until you start to," quote, "wonder whether he's turned the tables on you. Maybe you are the one detached and whirring"—especially since you're so goddamned busy looking at him—"and maybe he, and only he, is really engaged." Close quote.

Levi Mottl

The day we left each other, Eton gave me his last present. We were in Paris. It's funny. We'd been spending more and more time separately as the trip had gone on, just afternoons at first, in Vienna, or days, but then longer stretches in Italy. We'd go to separate towns, and at the beginning, whenever we'd hook back

up, meet at appointed places at appointed times, Il Papiro in
Florence or the Trevi Fountain, Eton would have things for me,
gifts he'd bought from windows, and stories to tell. And most of
the things he got—swizzle sticks and casino brochures, different
kinds of chocolate—most of the gifts were fun, but they all reminded me of a clay ashtray that Blue used to have in her studio.
Eton had made it for her in a kindergarten class. It had been
glazed a sort of teal blue, with the imprint of his hand stamped
in the middle and his name carved in with toothpicks. Just a gift
you make and show, but I'd always noticed it had a kind of life.
It was always somewhere new, by the easel or on top of her file
cabinet or on the bench where Blue stacked her frames. And it
wasn't that any one of Eton's gifts in Europe ever kept turning
up like that, it's that they all seemed to be part of the same
gesture.

But as the trip had gone along and Eton's side trips became
more extensive, I noticed I began to hear less about what he'd
seen, and I was getting fewer of these gift items from him. I think
he was just sort of easing his way towards the day we'd be
splitting up. But the last night we spent in Paris together, he did
have something.

We'd found our only two ties and had gone to a restaurant
right opposite the stock market. We had tartare, both of us, and
just before dessert, he gave me some drawings he'd done while
I'd been off in Bordeaux. When he handed them to me, it was
another one of Eton's ways of sort of packing a tender moment
in yesterday's paper. He said, "Take good care of these, Levi. We
don't know when I'll be getting another chance to give someone
a present." Then he just handed it over.

They were two drawings actually, on the same page. He'd
drawn them in the style of some da Vincis we'd seen in the Uffizi
together, these sinister caricatures da Vinci had done of the Flo-
rentine man in the street, but Eton's drawings were of me. He
called one "Levi the European" and the other "Levi the American." It was funny, the difference. The European one he'd cap-
tioned "alone with his opinions," and the expression was very
severe. The eyebrows were knitted together and the lips curled
into a snarl. I actually think Eton may have been saying more
about Europe than me—it looks like all my concerns are either
political or philosophical. But the American face he'd drawn he

just called "Alone." He must have been thinking back to when I'd first been in San Diego working with Blue. There was a quiet panic he'd caught in the expression, the way the Adam's apple was risen, or the pull at the corners of the eyes. They wondered if anyone was going to call or whether bringing flowers was ever appropriate. Eton might have titled it, "The Man Who Brings Potted Plants." We sort of had a laugh about it, and I remember showing the drawings to a little boy at the next table who'd kept asking us if we knew what we were eating. I remember being afraid he was going to stain them.

Harry Hampton

All right, so this is what it's all for. This is why, in the end, I loved the guy and I'm glad as hell he came to Paris. He'd left right around Christmastime. We'd said good-bye, I'll be in touch, we'll talk. A couple days later, I find an envelope taped to the wall in my apartment. It's from Boone, and what was inside I still have. This is the note that kicks the shit out of anything I ever wrote down about him, and the great thing is, it knows it. It says just this, and I'm quoting directly—"What he found inside the envelope, he read once and then taped on the inside back cover of his fiction cahier, ashamed slightly that it had taken someone else to give it the postscript it so richly deserved, ten nails: 'That Harry, he really always was an asshole, wasn't he?' "

Amalie Hindemuth

I spent New Year's Eve with my friend Bebe and her boyfriend, Jack or John, some generic name like that, in some pub near the British Museum. I'd written Peter that I would continue the tour but that I wouldn't be with him anymore. It was very depressing.

That was New Year's Eve, ringing in 1967 with an absolute whimper.

The following day, New Year's Day, I was very depressed. I wasn't even drinking the night before. Bebe and her boyfriend, Jack or John, they were wonderful but they were obviously very much into whatever they were doing, and I had no place there. So at about eleven A.M., while they were still snoring loudly, I got up and went out. And I remember it was a fairly chilly day, and it wasn't a very sunny day, but I was wearing sunglasses because my eye was black and blue and I didn't want to go down the street like that. Actually I probably looked much odder wearing sunglasses so early in the morning. But I was very depressed and I went and bought about three éclairs for myself, and I went into South Kensington to Holland Park. It's a beautiful little park, you know. It's where they have the peacocks.

I sat on a bench and was very morose and was thinking about what I would do after I ate my éclairs. And I watched the peacocks. Very few people were in the park since it was New Year's Day. And this boy, this young man, comes walking by very slowly and he starts to watch the peacocks. He sits down on the bench next to mine, and he looks at me sitting there with my half-eaten éclair, and I'm still wearing sunglasses. He's wearing sunglasses as well. Nobody else is wearing sunglasses. There was no need to. It was very queer. This was Eton.

He looked very young. Definitely younger than I was. I was twenty-one, but I had been living with Peter for a while by then, so of course I was much older than anyone else my age. Eton was looking at me and smiling, but I was just so very curious as to why he was wearing sunglasses. I thought, "Why is this boy sitting on this bench on New Year's Day wearing sunglasses?" Of course, here am I sitting alone on this bench on New Year's Day with my own sunglasses, but I had a black and blue eye and I was eating my éclair and minding my own business. But he kept sort of looking at me and it's hard for me to believe we were strangers, but I didn't know quite what to do, so I offered him some of my éclairs. I said, "Would you like some?" which was very brave of me because I never did things like that. And he said, "Yes, I would love a bite."

He was very happy and very jovial almost, and he smiled. And I remember thinking to myself, "My, this boy seems to be

lonely." I was right. He came over and said, "Would you mind
if I sat on your bench?" It was obvious he was an American, and
I said, "No, not at all." And he did. There were only two éclairs
left, and I gave him one. They were wonderful éclairs. He took
it and he ate it and he said finally, "Okay. I'll ask. Why are *you*
wearing sunglasses?" And I said, "Well, I'm wearing sunglasses
because I had an accident and I'm covering up. I have a black
eye." And he said, "Small world." I said, "Oh, really? You got
into an accident and have a black eye too?" And he said, yes, he
did.

We started talking. He introduced himself and said he was
Eton Boone, which I thought was a very handsome name, and I
even told him so. And I said, "Well, I'm Amalie." And we chat-
ted. I told him I was an actress. He was very easy to talk to, really.
Physically, my initial impression was that he was smallish—he
never struck me as particularly large except when we would go
to the beach. For some reason he looked bigger on the beach. He
was rather thin. Light brown or dirty blondish hair, and rather
unkempt. Attractive. He was smoking a cigarette and he gave me
one. Later on, I saw his eyes, these stark eyes, sort of gray-green,
which were beautiful. Very attractive man, but not at all the kind
of large attractiveness, the Peter-type large, tie-you-up, beat-
you-up large, which I alternately am afraid I found very attractive.

But soon enough, we began to talk about the peacocks and the
peahens. Occasionally, people would go by and, as you know,
peacocks have their feathers, right? They have these lovely blue
and green and yellow feathers. But the peahens, the female peacocks, have nothing. I mean zip. They have nothing. So the men
have this lustrous plumage, and the women have these little
stumps, and it's remarkably unfair.

But occasionally people would come by and what was so interesting to notice was that people, even children, would only
feed the peacocks, because they wanted them to come by and
spread their wings and show off their beautiful feathers. The
peahens could have starved to death for all the people cared.
And I mentioned this to Eton, and he said, "You're right. The
peacocks have the feathers, and the peacocks get the éclairs.
Maybe if we give the peahens some éclair, they'll grow feathers,
too." And he took my napkin from me and he took off his dark

glasses and I could see there was a red splotch on his eye and a thin black crescent underneath, and he said, "You feed the pea-hens." And then he sort of lowered his voice like this, "and I'll distract the peacocks."

So I went over to the peahens with the éclair, and Eton went over to a group of the peacocks and sort of began ripping up the napkin and tossing it down at them like food. He was doing it very deliberately, almost like one of those mimes or whatever, you know, as if it would fool the birds more the better he did it, and I was watching him, because he had become very animated, very much alive. His body was really very exciting when he let it be, and he kept telling me to hurry, "Hurry, Amalie, they're starting to catch on." He used my name, and I remember—I was laughing and watching him sort of stuff a napkin down the throat of this peacock—I remember thinking that he had used my name and that we were going to be friends.

Peter Finney

St. Alban's, early January. We're six weeks into the *Lady Winder-mere* tour. A colossal headache. C.L. has taken over producing the show in lieu of Shawn, which was like putting a blind man in the crow's nest for all C.L. knows about the business half. Amalie tells me she's met a young American, an Oscar Wilde fanatic who will be in the audience that night, and she says that I'll like him.

He came backstage after the show. He was wearing a wrinkled seersucker jacket and black slacks with a torn pocket which he'd attached with a safety pin. His hair wasn't long, it didn't hang, but it was overgrown, and he had sunglasses.

I asked him where he was from and he said America. I asked him where in America and he said the coast. I asked if he was on vacation from college and he said no, not particularly. He said he supposed he was very, very close to being a "hobo." He said he was a safety-pin away, and I asked him if he'd enjoyed the show and he said yes, it looked like fun to wear all those clothes.

Amalie Hindemuth

We came back to the bench after feeding the peahens and we were sitting there, and it was a bit uncomfortable. You know, you've just met this person, you've played this game with the peacocks but really you don't have very much to say to each other, but he said, "I lied. I'm wearing sunglasses because I jabbed a paintbrush into my eye." He was sort of laughing about it, but of course I thought, how horrible. I tried to make a joke, though, you know, "What a very clumsy thing to do," or whatever. But I couldn't leave it at that. I said, "I lied also." I don't really know what possessed me to say this to this person except I liked him a great deal and after all, he'd told me the truth. I said, "Somebody hit me. My boyfriend hit me." Eton said, "Did you hit him back?" and I said, "No." But then he leaned in and he was sorry and he said, "Can I see?" And I took off my glasses and he took off his glasses, and he smiled and said, "It may not be right for faces, but that's a hell of a color, Amalie." And he kept on looking, and his expression changed—and his expressions could change very dramatically, you know, and it made me very uncomfortable—but he put my sunglasses back on my face, and I told him, I said, "He's not that bad."

C.L. Hull

Oh, it was Pete, there's no shred of an argument there. Pete was the one saw it right off, because Boone wasn't even a member of the company to begin with. Fuck no. He was just there as a lackey, fixing up sets and toting makeup trays about. But what it was is we lost our Dumby, the company fat man, which is a fairly accepted turn of events with a traveling company like

Ratliffe. Along the way your flotsam and jetsam will be falling by the wayside, once they realize they haven't really that innate understanding of what it means to actually *be* an actor. So you really have to catch as catch can from time to time, if your company zeppelin decides mid-tour that he's got to go run the family cutlery business and no longer has time for Mr. Ibsen. You know, *I'll* wear a pillow for a night or two, double up in a pinch, but you have to be a man of true vision to look around at what's at your disposal and say, "Well, fuck, we have a little bit of a problem here, don't we, but can anyone here tell me why our young Mr. Boone couldn't step in and give it a go?" 'Cause, you know, all Boone's done up to that point is place a few prank phone calls on behalf of Pom Whitley, our road manager, who went absolutely bonkers for them. Boone would ring old ladies in Derby and tell them things like he was bringing over their new horse or they'd won some bucket of Borneo oranges. But, Christ now, being able to take the occasional piss at Mrs. Figgililly doesn't necessarily clarify the idea that the man's going to make a trustworthy understudy or actual full-fledged company member. Not by a long shot, and in a role like Dumby, which is really screaming out for the likes of a Robert Morley, who in the hell in their right mind would hand it over to a skinny American punk?

Well, Peter fucking Finney would, that's who. And let me tell you, my friends, if he hadn't, if he hadn't looked at your Mr. Boone and spotted something of substance in there, and if he hadn't the consummate respect due a man of his stature in a traveling theatre company of his own making—and mine, I'll allow—well, if all that doesn't happen, then you can all just go home to your can of beans and put away your tape recorders because there's no book here. There's no Boone, right. There's no fact of the matter that when a young man was young and was very much adrift in the sea of life, he had the good and great fortune of stumbling into the very generous heart of one of the thespian art's finest minds, Pete, who you'd all be more aware of, I assure you, if it weren't for fucking Franklynne, whose Hamlet I did see and thought paled by comparison to his brilliant son's, and of course Albert, who completely fucked up Pete's career. Real shame.

Peter Finney

He could actually be quite brazen at times, in his own secret way, and it was always something of a pleasant surprise to see it. Eton was normally so respectful and quiet. I remember just after he'd taken the Dumby role, something he'd done for me. He'd had a habit then which wasn't much appreciated by some of the more methodical company members, of playing jacks before performances. In fact, the noise had been so distracting that a few of them had petitioned me to please stop the American boy. So I'd gone in search of him before a performance in Camberwell to catch him red-handed. He wasn't difficult to locate. I had only to follow my ears—that ba-thump ba-thump and rattle of the jacks, and his "Onesies, twosies, threesies" echoing down the corridor—and there he was, sitting cross-legged on the floor of one of the back dressing rooms. I stood above him with my arms folded, my demeanor wholly dark, and in as commanding and lordly a voice as I could summon, I told him that as of some recently issued grievances from his fellow actors, his career as a jacks champion had come to an end.

He looked up at me and said, "You mean C.L., don't you?" Yes, I nodded. "C.L. doesn't like my jacks," he said, "C.L.'s not very good at jacks." Well, yes, I explained, that may have been so, but regardless, and despite what some of us may have felt about him, the man, as producer and veteran member of the company, did have certain attendant rights, and out of deference to those, or at the very least to his persistence, one in Eton's position ought to show a measure of respect for his methods. "Oh," said Eton, "the methods." And there was in his voice a hint, the slightest challenge, or even solicitation, so I pursued, and the end of it was Eton's asking me to do something rather playful.

The makeup table that Eton had found for himself was standing up against a partition, and he asked me to go to the other side and listen. I did. It was a game. I stood behind the partition and told him I was ready, and it began. From the other side, I heard the scrape of his chair being pulled across the floor, out away from the dressing mirror, and then a tremendous weight dumped into it like a sack of drunken potatoes. I could hear him beginning to fiddle with the makeup tray, plucking at the brushes and pads, and if it hadn't been for the monstrous, simian breathing that slowly began to wheeze and cluck from behind the partition, I might have thought that Eton was simply making up his face for me, that any moment he would appear in front of me as Pierrot. But I knew very well from all that congestion that Eton was making fun of C.L. Hull.

Now, C.L. had always been something of a frustrated circus clown, it's quite true, but everyone in the company had learned to turn a blind eye to it and the layers of powder and paint he'd occasionally appear on stage with. But apparently Eton hadn't been so polite. In fact, not only had Eton taken note of C.L.'s makeup, he'd memorized the whole ritual of its application, which I could hear very distinctly from the other side of the partition—the initial scan of the makeup tray, so careful and slow, as if it were an artist's palette, then the frantic search for the proper base or rouge, his hand sweeping across and scattering the bottles. The sound of him patting his rough cheeks with a sponge, or balling up a whole packet of tissue and jabbing at his face with it. The way C.L. would grunt with each little punch, it was precisely right, or the painful croak as he smeared the eyebrow pencil across. And then his lips smacking, pop—it was a symphony of C.L.'s mannerisms, and it was uncanny. I hadn't known myself how familiar I was with C.L.'s routine, but I found the more I let my imagination go with Eton's performance, the more convinced I was that he'd slipped through a trap door in the floor and that C.L. himself had taken his place at the mirror.

I was desperate to see how he was doing this, of course, so I cheated. I've no pride about things like that. I peeked around the corner, and I'm very glad I did, the sight was so remarkable, of Eton with powder and rouge caked on his cheeks and forehead, leaning over the table with his head in his hands, staring at himself in the mirror with such bleak and sallow eyes. This young man—he could hardly have been twenty years old—but capable of making his eyes droop in such a beastly way. It was breathtaking, and I wondered to myself, what would have been the harm in letting me see this?

But I withdrew. I didn't know if he was finished or not with his play—he'd begun sobbing and gasping and letting with some

other unmentionable nether things—but I said from the other
side of the partition, "Very well, Eton, right-o, I'll be going now."
I made my way to the door with a wave over my head, but as I
reached it, he called out. He said, "Pete!"—a frightening imitation
of C.L.'s cockney patois. "Pete, bloody hell, make the boy stop.
Those blasted tin stars are piercing my brain!"

Amalie Hindemuth

Eton would always go to the workshops Peter held in the afternoons, but he didn't ever volunteer. He'd just sit off in the corner
with his orange next to him, pretending to read the *International
Herald-Tribune.* Peter would always ask him, "Eton, would you like
to play?" and Eton would always say no, so Peter—and I'm actually fairly certain he did this intentionally—we often had the
workshops right after lunch, and Peter literally started getting
Eton drunk during the lunches. He'd just continually fill his mug
until certain days, Eton would be staggering over to wherever we
were holding the workshop. He'd have to lie down for the first
parts, and even nap sometimes. You'd hear him snoring.

But there was one time at an old church in Birmingham. Peter
had positively drowned Eton in warm ale, and it was the first time
we ever got him to play Mister Freeze, which is this very tradi-
tional sort of acting game where a person gets up on stage and
begins just by doing anything he wants, you know, pretending
to sweep something up with a big broom if that's what he wants.
But then Peter would say "Freeze," and the actor had to freeze
there for a moment and then begin something completely different based on his position, again and again like that.

It's a very fun game, but it still hadn't been easy getting Eton
to play. When Peter asked him, he kept saying no and trying to
lie down in his pew until finally Peter and C.L. went over and
literally picked him up. They actually carried him up and sort of
deposited Eton there in front of the altar, and it was even a bit
tense, you know, with Eton and Peter sort of squaring off like
that. Eton was trying to drag himself off, but Peter just said
"Freeze," and it began that way, with Peter just by force of will

freezing Eton before he could get off. It was like this dance between the two of them, until Eton finally had to sort of give in
and go with it, you know, but once he did, it was just extraordinary. I've really never seen so many characters just spring out of
someone, really from nowhere. There was a jet pilot and a street
urchin, and a lady trying to find a slip under her bed, and an old
man applying for some sort of worker's dispensation, standing in
a queue at the veteran's office. They were all so thorough, you
know. There was one of a dancer who didn't speak at all, but I
can still see it so clearly, the way he would sweep his toe across
the floor. Eton was so precise for someone who had no training,
and his switches from one to the next were so fast. I remember
when he was doing the man with the broom, when Peter yelled
"freeze," the broom became a shovel, and Eton was a grave digger
burying his brother, which was just stunning. He did one with
his hands up in the air, fixing the time on a street clock in Glas-
gow, which turned into a guillotine that Eton was sharpening in
the middle of the night during the French Revolution. It was very
frightening.

And of course Peter was positively glowing. He just kept pacing back and forth on the sidelines, shouting "freeze," sort of
challenging Eton to continue. He must have kept Eton up there
for three-quarters of an hour. There was one scene of a Chinese
Ping-Pong-paddler that Peter must have let go on for nearly five
minutes, as this sort of dare to see if Eton would become flustered
or just stop. But he didn't. He was very self-assured. He just kept
hitting this invisible ball back and forth and sort of grunting to
himself in Chinese, keeping score. He played whole rallies, and
it went on for so long that Peter finally threw some coins up at
the altar to see what Eton would do, but he didn't do anything.
He just kept playing, this very long rally in the middle of a sort
of shower of coins that Peter was tossing up at him. When he
finally won the point, he'd given this mean sort of quick look over
at the referee. You could just see it. And then he'd served the ball
again. He had such dignity.

But in any case, after forty-five minutes or so of this Mister
Freeze—and I really don't think I'm exaggerating about the
time—Peter finally let him stop. He'd called out, "Enough," and
Eton had sort of collapsed on the stage with everyone applauding
like mad, which you're not supposed to do. C.L. and Theo, who
played Lord Darlington, had gone and picked him up and carried

him down the center aisle—he sort of did this Queen Elizabeth
wave at us all as he went by in their arms, and Peter had lifted
his fist to him— they'd carried him out into the graveyard next
to the church and I actually think he got very sick out there.

Peter Finney

Eton and I used to go to the parks in London when the company
wasn't out in the provinces. We'd take plays with us, not just
plays, stories as well, whatever the human voice could speak.
We'd take them to Hyde Park or Kensington Gardens, sit on a
bench and read to each other, listen to the pace of a speech, the
cadence of a stanza or thought.

Once, though, I remember we'd been sitting by the Peter Pan
statue in Kensington Gardens—it was one of our venues—and
Eton would read from these plays and poems and stories we'd
bring, apparently so well that it began to capture the attention of
the people around, who were mothers and nannies with their
prams mostly, the people who shared our schedule at this time.
I'm not certain if Eton was aware, but gradually, subtly, day after
day, we, or he, had begun to attract a little crowd. No one came
specifically to sit at his feet certainly, but it became a spot that
certain mothers and grandmothers would return to, to listen.

And I don't think that Eton had really noticed until one afternoon two grandmothers who'd been given a day with their
grandchildren approached Eton after he'd finished a passage of
Kipling, and asked if Eton wouldn't mind reading some stories by
Hans Christian Andersen that they had with them. Eton took the
book, and it actually surprised me. He very nearly declined. I
know that that's what he'd wanted to do, just from embarrassment, a shyness, and in fact we didn't go back the next day. He'd
been very embarrassed by it, which I think you can understand,
for that's the difference, you see. There is first the ability to take
what's in here and express it, and he had that from the very start,
an intelligence, a talent, but a talent like long legs are a talent to
the runner, or wings are a talent to a bird. He possessed it. But
beyond this there must be a willingness to exercise it. We are all

great actors in our minds, but there must be something of the showman too, or something generous.

And I told Eton something, after he'd read the women their story, read it to their children, and not really so well, not when he'd understood that there were people listening, people looking to him for something more than fun. He'd shrunk. But as we walked back along the Serpentine, alongside all the ducks and swans, I told Eton something which I heard first from my father, who claimed to have heard it from an artist friend of his, but something I've actually heard elsewhere, attributed to several others, but still so much worth saying.

It was the last my father saw of his friend. This man was on his deathbed with a tumor in his skull, an enormous tumor that had deformed its shape and grown beneath his right eye in a giant hideous lump so large he could no longer see, and he said to my father, "I know, Franklynne, I know what my tumor is made of. I know what it is. It's made of every painting I did not paint. It's made of every song I did not sing, and it's made of every child I did not touch. This tumor is made of every moment I could have expressed myself and chose not to."

And I asked Eton not to do that. Don't keep. Don't do it all in your wonderful head, please. There's no virtue in keeping it there. It's deadly. It only becomes regret.

C.L. Hull

You can throw a fiddle at your fucking Isaac Stern and I've always said he'll entertain you for a half hour at the outside. Give us any longer than that, and I don't care if he's playing in his jockstrap with a fishbowl on his head, there's only so much you can take. But as Christ Almighty is my witness in heaven, give Eton Arthur Boone one of those rubber fart bags and he'll have you rolling on the pub's sawdust floor till your socks are damp. Christ, what a riot he was. You know, he just proved it, something which I believe is the acknowledged truth among the blessed people of this earth who didn't somewhere along the line get society's nasty whipping switch shoved up their bum, that well-crafted flatulence is pretty well the most basic form of human entertainment there is, from the fucking Neanderthals right up to your bloody Oxford dons, everybody loves a nice cut.

I think he'd picked one up in some novelty shop somewhere along the road, and he'd play with it in the van on the way to a show in Nottingham. Start complaining to the driver, "Christ, Nigel, please pull over, I'm really having some pains here," and then he'd crack one with the fart bag. Nigel would practically drive us smack into a fucking tree. He'd really take our lives in his bloody hands. Or when we were at the pubs after shows, Boonie'd point out some poor sod up on a stool, just an innocent little bystander having a pint to himself, and the game was coming up with what his gas might sound like. Boone would just look over at the fellow, or the barmaid for Christ's sake, just pass a glance her way and "Fffffffffffff!"

'Course the very idea, right, of Boone harnessing any of that energy and unleashing it on stage in the full support of a company production—which is what Pete and I, may I say, worked so bloody hard trying to get him to do—Christ, you'd have had another Newley on your hands. But see, for all his brilliancy as a sort of party entertainer, he didn't really show the respect, you know, that is so essential to the performing endeavor. I mean, this is art, you have to keep in mind, and you can't just fuck it up because it happens to tickle your funny bone to come out on stage with tissue paper up your nostril or a bit of parsley stuck in your teeth. I mean, I enjoyed working with the man—he was a true naturally innovative mind—but I was always rather convinced in looking at him on stage, you know, with Nigel's merkin pasted on his chin, that his one true artistic intention was to get me to blow my fucking lines.

Hugh Gardiner

Once every few years up until quite recently, I had been in the habit of visiting England, usually in the summers, but in the spring of 1967, I was on sabbatical and had been there for six months already. My purpose, in addition to keeping up with old acquaintances, seeing my friend John Kinsey, of course, was to look at the theatre. I've always had an interest in regional theatre, and I was at work on a study of Bertrand Sand at the time. John and I would normally head up to the Edinburgh festival in the summers and spend a fortnight or so at Stratford. But on this occasion, we happened to be in a charming village in Surrey called Reigate, and it was there that we attended Oscar Wilde's *Lady Windermere's Fan*. John had seen its director, Mr. Peter Finney, in a production of *Man and Superman* in London, and been very impressed.

I'm afraid to say, though, that the production of the Wilde play wasn't very memorable, except of course for the performance of the young American who'd been so terrifically miscast in the role of Dumby. John, I remember, had suspected that it was only the way that the young man had combed his hair which had captured our interest. He'd brushed it all straight up in the air and greased it. It was quite an effect, but I prefer to think that there was another explanation—and I believe that time has vindicated me on this score—for the fact that midway through the first act both of us found that our attention had been focused almost exclusively on this relatively insignificant role. When he was on stage, I ceased to follow the plot, my attention was so rapt with him, and when he was offstage, I found myself wondering when he would return. At the intermission, I can remember racking my brain, trying to recall the plot of a play I hadn't seen in some dozen or so years, hoping that it might take a turn to allow us to see more of this young actor. Oh, no, I can tell you, if it were only that he was different, that he was miscast or makeshift, I wouldn't remember it as I do. It was talent, rough, unschooled, but manifest. Our word is "charisma."

For one of his scenes—and this was the second night I'd gone, without John—Boone's hair was a bit more normal, but he came on stage with a yo-yo in his palm and spun it throughout the action, even as he spoke, and it wasn't so much the aptness of the gesture—that, I would have to allow, is open to debate—it was the simplicity with which he was able to perform it. Everything he did was played with so much ease and naturalness that its effect on stage, in the midst of this otherwise mediocre production, was riveting.

After that second night, I decided to write him a note. It had long been a practice of mine to write performers whom I admired.

I wrote to Paul Scofield after seeing Peter Brook's *King Lear* in 1964. There was Bert Lahr's work in the original *Godot,* of course, in 1955. But with Boone in Reigate, my intentions were different, I think. I can say that something about his manner had delighted me so personally and unmistakably that I wanted to do more than offer encouragement. I wanted to extend my hand. He was obviously quite, quite young, so I told him that if and when he returned to the States and felt he needed any help with anything, he could look me up. I could see what I could do.

When I returned to London the next week, there was a reply waiting. He said I was the first person ever to call him Mr. Boone. He thanked me, and he seemed to appreciate that my praise had come so unexpectedly. He said he found the kudos of a stranger very exciting, much more so than the encouragement of a friend.

Amalie Hindemuth

I took Eton to my parents' house when we were in Bath. I'd actually planned on bringing Peter, and my mother had been very excited, but at the last moment he hadn't been able to go. Really, I think he'd just been bored by the idea, but I'd promised my mother a guest, so I brought Eton with me. Eton had said that he would come and act like Peter if I liked, but I told him no, he could come as himself, and he did, and it was very nice. I remember he played my mother and sister something he'd made up on the piano that sounded like carnival music, and at dinner every time he would ask my mother for the Yorkshire pudding, he'd say, "Could I please have some more bread, Mrs. Hindemuth?" which she thought was very funny.

After dinner, I took Eton on a tour of the house and the back garden. It was early spring so there wasn't much to show yet. Eton asked me questions about how we'd played in the garden when we were younger and what our favorite hiding places were. It was very cold, and we sat down on this swing that my father had hung from the chestnut tree, and it was very foggy. We just sat there and you could only see the lighted windows of the house. And it actually wasn't ever fair when you sat in this seat, because only one of you was ever able to see the other. I was just looking at Eton against the fog, and he was sort of staring out into the dark with his feet swinging back and forth, and it made me so sad, because I felt like I was as close to him as anyone, and I asked him if he had any plans for when the tour finished, and he said, "Amalie, I don't have plans for tomorrow." And then we kissed. I kissed him. We kissed and then we stopped. I don't really know why we'd started. I don't think it was quite passion, but we stopped. He said it just made him feel like Peter, which was very strange, because he really wasn't like Peter at all. Peter was so Peter. Peter was so there, and solid, and so being Peter at all times, but Eton it was more a matter of trying to find. And for us I suppose that kissing wasn't really ever the way to do it.

Peter Finney

Towards the end of the tour, we were able to spend more time in London than we had previously because our final dates were in the nearer counties, and so Eton and I had been spending more of our afternoons together working with plays and scenes in the parks, and I think it was there, on benches under the rare English sun, that we finished with that part of his education that I could help him with at all. Not so much really, or a very great deal—I'm not prepared to say what good I might have done Eton—except that it was in my presence at least that he'd come to understand why a true actor acts, if he has the courage, and that is simply to live more than one life.

We would often stop in bookstores on our way. We'd pick up one of the Samuel Frenches or diaries to take with us and read from. And sometimes if we'd found something we liked, a speech or a passage, we'd return to it several days in a row. There was one I remember, from very near the end of the time we were together, that he'd taken from a lovely book we'd found. I don't remember the name. It was about a parish priest in Strasbourg, and towards the end of this little book the priest says a prayer. He's been secretly in love with a young girl from the parish, who comes to him once a week in the confessional and confesses her dreadful ambivalence about whether to join the convent or marry. Her family had wanted her to wed a colleague of her father's, whom she did not love, of course. And it's a wonderful prayer which the priest makes. He makes it the night before her wedding, which he is to perform, hating himself, loathing himself for letting it happen, loathing himself for the love he feels for this young bride, and loathing the life she might have had as an alternative. Tremendous prayer, and it had such a range.

I can remember the first time Eton read it. We were in Warwick Square, because I had a friend who was living there and loaned us his key, and Eton I can still see thumbing through the book and finding this invocation near the end of it, this wonderful soliloquy was practically the first thing he read from the book, and he read it aloud to me. "Dear Lord," and so on. He controlled it rather well for someone who hadn't seen it before and who didn't know the characters. And when he was finished, he'd liked it so much, we both had, that he gave it another try. Even better. And the next day, he read it to me again, and it was still better, much better because I think he'd taken the book overnight.

And so, for a number of days in a row, which I can remember well because they were all in Warwick Square, Eton performed this prayer for me. But he did more than perform. He breathed life into it, and it was astounding, watching the prayer change from day to day, the slight adjustments he would make as the words grew more real to him. It was like watching blood find its way from line to line. He'd begun with certain moments of it, single sentences that had been so true to him at the start, but as the days passed, one phrase would reach out to the next, and the one before it, until the whole prayer was drenched. It was remarkable, and as he performed it again and again, I began to wonder who there around our bench, who could push their child in a pram or tend to a bed of roses with a trowel and say that it was any more real than this Alsatian priest in Warwick Square?

But the fifth day. It had become already a character that Eton carried around with him, an idea or a voice that was always there, and I remember as the sun was setting, I'd said, "It's time for the prayer, isn't it, Eton?" He wilted in front of me. It had been a lovely day and when the sun fell it grew even lovelier. I can remember him leaning back and looking up into the trees, and he said, "I don't want to." I was surprised. I asked him if he'd grown tired of the prayer, and he shook his head. I said, "Has it become too easy for you?" And he said, "No, it's become much, much too hard." I said, "Bravo." Now do it.

Amalie Hindemuth

The tour ended before June. Peter had an arrangement with the National Theatre where he would go during the summers, and that was the summer that Olivier had nearly worked himself to death. They needed help, so Peter had invited Eton to stay with him in London. I know that Peter was very interested in introducing Eton to all his friends there, but Eton had begun to feel a bit restless and I really think what he'd liked most about Ratliffe was that it moved, you know, it never stayed anywhere.

I had decided to go to New York. Things with Peter hadn't been very good for the most of the spring, and I'd never been to New York, and I think as an actress, there comes a point when you really have to go, don't you, I mean to find out. So I was going there. And not really in any way to compete with Peter, although I know that's the way that most of the company saw it—most of them I think were under the impression that some sort of menage had been taking place amongst the three of us, which is perfectly ridiculous, because I tended to stay away from Peter for the most part when he was drinking, which he was, incessantly—but anyway, I invited Eton. He'd never been to New York either, and I suppose I'd sort of known he would accept.

But before we left, Peter had taken me aside. He'd taken me out to dinner at the Connaught, and I'd thought it was to say good-bye, you know, to say whatever our problems have been, I still love you and I'll see you, or things like that. But he took me out to dinner, and all he'd wanted was to make me promise him that I would see to it that Eton continued acting. He said he would be writing people he knew in New York, Broadway people—he didn't mention a thing about me—and he said that if Eton wasn't acting within three months, Peter himself would fly to New York and kidnap him.

Levi Mottl

I didn't have much contact with Joe after Eton and I split up. I'd told him that he and Anne should probably go ahead with their plans and not to wait for Eton. Joe knew. He wrote me a card, which found me months later in Ibiza where I was staying with my friend Lance. Joe had written it just after I'd left Paris. He said he didn't blame me for anything I might have had to do with Eton's leaving. He said he didn't blame me at all, and I never knew if that meant he did or he didn't. But it wasn't long after that, after Joe's little card had finally caught up with me in Ibiza, that I got their announcement. They'd been married in early July, 1967, the summer of love.

III

New York

Lionel Thubb

I cannot rightly say that I have any vivid memory of Eton Arthur until an evening when he had come and seen a performance of mine at the Village Vanguard. A number of us, comics and musicians alike, had gathered after the show at a coffee shop in Sheridan Square, and I recall Eton Arthur had secluded himself at the farthest and cornermost seat of our table, as was his habit, so it was a while before I was even aware that he was present. And in fact when I first saw him, his head peeking out from behind a dessert menu with a malted already in front of him, I needed reminding from a dear friend of mine, Ms. Kristl—"Who is the gentleman at the other end of the table who seems to be taking the ice cream floats so seriously?" She told me that was Mr. Finney's boy, Eton Arthur, wasn't I aware? That was Amalie's friend, who Ms. Kristl herself hadn't taken the opportunity to meet until this very evening, when apparently they'd all shared a dinner together before the show. And I asked her, well, what did she find? Was he as thoroughly captivating during the first course as he was during dessert? Ms. Kristl leaned in close and said with the inimitable sass that propelled her career far beyond the point her best material had abandoned her, "Lionel," she said, "I don't know what it is, because he was a perfect gentleman, but that boy there"—who was by this time vacuuming the bottom of his drink—"he'd scare the milk out of Mary."

Amalie Hindemuth

We were living together up on Twenty-first Street in a building called the Shangri-La, and he was working as a security man in a clothes store. I was studying with Lee Strasberg. Peter had written a letter for Eton which he was supposed to take to Lee, but he never did. We went together the first time to watch one of the classes, but Eton never introduced himself and he didn't seem very interested. I think he felt that classes like that are filled with actors, and I don't think Eton ever considered himself an actor. Really, I don't think Eton particularly liked actors. He said he never saw one that he couldn't read.

What he liked was the stage, which was very clear. We were going to lots of clubs when we first got to New York just because I don't think we had much else to do, jazz clubs and folk clubs and what comedy clubs there were back then, but I never really felt that Eton was as interested in the performers as he was in just the stages themselves. You know, if we went somewhere and saw a comedian or a jazz musician that we didn't like, he'd say they were wasting the space. That's the way he would say he didn't like someone. Lionel didn't waste the space—Eton just used to love the stories Lionel would tell, about his family from down South and all those sorts of things, and there was a black singer named Vargo who used to wear an enormous pink dress with rhinestones and stamp her feet. But other than those two, Eton used to say that the people we saw never really took advantage, you know, because, when Eton looked at the stage, I think he just saw this sort of endless possibility—especially a stage like the one they had at Jes' For Laffs. It was so simple, just this small black square and with the lights so dim you could only see the microphone and this very stark brick wall in the spotlight. I remember walking along West Fourth, coming back from Jes' For Laffs, and Eton saying, you know, "That's anywhere—that's what they don't understand. That's anywhere you want it to be."

Lionel Thubb

Jes' For Laffs was at this time perhaps not yet as renowned a club as some of the places in midtown such as the Improvisation or the Blue Angel, or even those in the Village such as the Vanguard or Cafe Wha?—it was, in fact, a stutter-step up from a strip joint. What Jes' For Laffs had that these other clubs did not, however, was Buddy D'Angelo, and I am by no means alone in feeling the loyalty I do to Buddy and to Grand Street. It may not have been the most impressive establishment to those further along in their careers, but Buddy was never overly concerned with comics who'd made the big top, as he liked to put it. He took far more pride in discovering and developing talent. Surely it's not every club owner who would have looked past the danger in putting a down-home Southerner on stage, wet behind the ears and green as Granny's pea soup. Didn't bother Buddy. Buddy saw what you had, not what you didn't have.

Now, all it was that Eton Arthur really and truly had on the night he first took the stage at Jes' For Laffs was a little too much to drink. I had invited Amalie and Eton Arthur to the club one evening in late summer, secure in the knowledge that on a lonely Wednesday night they would have no trouble finding themselves a table, where I could join them after my act. Jes' For Laffs was really much more of a bar on such nights, and I can tell you that Eton Arthur was making ample use of all the facilities. In fact, it was upon one of his many returns from the club loo that Eton Arthur retook his seat, slapped his hands together, and said, "So tell me, my country bumpkin South Carolinian, most likely to secede, when do I go on?'' Well, the attendance was so sparse that evening, and I admit that I was rather compelled by the idea of seeing the shoe on a Yankee foot that I decided to take my friend up on his drunken offer. I told him to keep his seat for just a moment, so as I could ask the club owner if a talented friend of mine might take his stage.

Fortunately Buddy and I both suffer the same vice, the vice of gluttony, a weakness for butter and brown sugar, and we were both particularly vulnerable to my grandmother's recipe for sweet potato pie. So in exchange for the promise of two Macel Thubb mouth-watering delectables, Buddy yielded the stage to a newcomer. It was, if you will allow, that easy.

Amalie Hindemuth

The lore, which I can't really personally verify, of how Eton got on stage the first time—it's sort of one of those stories that everyone understands differently—but the one I remember best is that Rich Bahssin, who was this very hostile comedian with hair on his neck who I didn't like at all, he had apparently dropped some acid the night before and was still sort of tripping at the time that he was supposed to go on the next night. He'd been an absolute disaster during the first show, so when the time came for his late set, they'd decided to get a replacement, and Pietro Goldberg, who was another comedian, a nicer man, he had suggested it should be Eton because he knew that Eton was interested. And Buddy had asked who Eton was and Pietro said that he'd worked with Albert Finney, meaning Peter. So then Buddy was supposed to have asked Lionel or someone like that who Albert Finney was, and Lionel had said Albert Finney was Tom Jones. So the story goes that Buddy let Eton go on that first time because he'd thought Eton had worked with Tom Jones. It's really very silly.

Buddy D'Angelo

How you gonna forget a guy like Boone? Before I even had a chance to meet the guy, you know, he's just gonna do a couple songs, that's what L.T. told me, but he just gets up on stage. Looks out at the audience with a big grin on his face. Waits. Doesn't say a word. Just stands there, smiles, walks over to the piano, sits down on the bench. He's doing it all very slow, very in control, you know, and I notice that. He's a pro, pros don't care how long it takes 'em. So he's sitting there at the piano, slumping over a little, and then he looks out, just starts shooting these quick grins at the crowd. Boom boom boom. His eyes are jumping all over the place. But they don't know what the hell to make of this kid yet. I don't know what to make of him. How'd he get up there? Hey, Buddy, since when?

But he starts playing. He starts playing the piano with his left hand. Left hand only. He's messing around, trying to figure something out, and he's having a little trouble at first. He can't get it, hits a few clinkers. Takes him a while, but then he starts to find it. He gets a few notes together, and he builds it, over and over. And finally he gets what he wants, this boogie-woogie–type jazz thing. Dum-dum-dum-dum-dum-dum-dum-dum. You know, accompaniment. He sits there and he plays this thing, very happy, he's got the shit-eating grin, full steam ahead. A few people start to clap along with him. L.T. turns around and gives me the thumb's up. And the kid's playing it. That's all. We're all waiting for the right hand, and I'm thinking it's just gonna turn out to be some bullshit college song. You know, I'm gonna get Tom Lehrer, Jr., up here singing about trichinosis.

But he just keeps playing. He keeps playing with his left hand and he's got his right hand on his leg. It's sitting there like a dead fish, and he's looking at it like it doesn't belong to him, like, who put this hand here? But finally he brings it up. Up comes the right hand, but he doesn't start playing. He starts digging in his ear with it, cleaning his ear. You know, he pulls his finger out and looks at it, what he's dug out from his ear. Keeps playing. What the hell is this? Who is this kid?

He gets these Kleenexes. There are these Kleenexes up on the piano and he starts pulling one out. He pulls one out and just lays it on his leg like he's some kind of Mandrake the Magician. But what he does is, he wipes his finger on it, with the earwax. He's playing the piano and cleaning his ear. That's it. That's an act? And he starts doing it with the other Kleenexes. He starts pulling out these other ones and doing the same thing, and stuffing them in his pockets. I don't know how many, but he's reaching around in back of his head and cleaning his other ear, there's one he blows his nose on, there's one he wipes his face with, he wipes his pits, and I'm back at the bar thinking to myself, Mother of God, please don't let him start wiping his ass or I'll have the cops in here like flies on horseshit. But he's putting all these Kleenexes in his pockets, and he just keeps playing. Nothing else, just playing and then every now and then he opens his mouth like he's gonna start singing, but boom, he goes right back to the Kleenexes. This was his first performance, you gotta remember, first time ever up on stage.

Okay, so he finishes—you know, big crescendo ending, ba dum baaah. He gets up to take a bow. He starts looking very serious. He's got his arm up like he's in Carnegie Hall, but you can see he's got about three boxes stuffed in his pockets. So he's standing there and now he's acting like a matador or something— keep in mind, he hasn't said a goddamn word since he got up there. And he gets one of his Kleenexes, you know, one of the dirty ones with the crap from his ear, and he tosses it out at the audience, just flinging it like some kind of matador doing whatever the hell it is, you know, flinging his beret to some Spanish lady or something. And he does this with maybe, I don't know, a lot of Kleenexes, from his pockets. He's pulling them out of his sleeves, he's bending over and pulling one out of his sock, and he's tossing them and blowing kisses too. One for here and one for over there and back by the bar for Claudia. And then, real slow, he mouths, "God bless you all." He takes his bow and backs off, his arms are up in the air, and the place is going crazy. I never saw anything like it. I invited him back as soon as I could get to him.

Toddy Boone

Right after the wedding, in July, we got this postcard from him with a picture of Babar on the front, and it was addressed to "Dear famille." He said everything was fine and that he'd started performing at a club called J.F.L. None of us knew what J.F.L. was. Anne thought it was a jazz club. I remember Dad saying, "What does that mean, he's playing bongos?"

C.L. Hull

He was trouble, was what he was. You could smell it from the word get-go. I'd come over a bit after Amalie and Boonie pulled their little coup, their little American tryst. Pete had asked me to give Boonie a look, have a gander at what he's up to because, you know, fucking Pete, he just thought the sky was the limit. So when I came to New York—I had some work in a small picture by Carol Ludlow—I went and saw him, and I had no fucking idea what he was up to. But I called up some very important people, not that I was trying to impress anyone by any means. I'm not taking Dickie Attenborough down to Soho to shine his bloody boots, but they're people for whom I have a great deal of respect, and I would tell them, "Relax, now. Take your shoes and socks off, here's an old pal o' mine, very entertaining young man, has a way with a fart pillow and Oscar Wilde, so let's see what he's up to," and fucking shit, what happens?

Completely wacko. It's like he's thought up these jokes in the fifth dimension or wherever the fuck it is. Like he's come out there with a kettle in his hand—this is the first thing I saw him do—he's come out with a tea kettle, and he takes some water from someone's table, puts it in his kettle and slaps it on a hot-plate he's got there on his piano. He's complaining about being a little under the weather—it looks like he's swallowed a clove of fucking garlic—and he says he needs a cup of tea. So he starts in on the—what is it?—banter, right, he's telling a perfectly nice story, which I could not remember if you promised me Julie Christie in return, but he's got this kettle going behind him and, Christ, I mean everyone knows where he's headed. He's in the middle of this nice little story when the kettle starts up. It starts hissing and hissing until all our fucking ears are bleeding, and Boone was standing right there next to it, stiff as King Tut's prick, shrieking his fucking head off along with it. The whole audience—and my guests, I don't mind telling you— are crawling under the table and positively gob-smacked, and Boone's standing there just wanking around with the burner like it's some fucking aria. His Teapot Aria, is what I like to call it.

I mean, he pulled it off. He was quite adept at working a crowd and sensing the mood of a room and all—he really had mastered the give and take that is so essential to any performing endeavor—but I wouldn't advise taking your father-in-law —or a fucking dog, for that matter. Really wacko. I wouldn't have trusted him with a ten-foot pole. I mean, another time— because I did enjoy myself and went back on a number of occasions—I'll never forget, because it's something I'm quite sure he lifted from working with Ratliffe. One of our little exercises was trying to create a scene without the use of any fellow actors. Pete was a fucking master. Pete could make you think you're at fucking Ascot if that's what he wants. But Boone, I must say, was no slacker in that department himself. I mean, out he comes, tiny little stage, and he does a scene about this young pug who's being dragged along on some street-gang jaunt. They're all harassing some poor beggar, standing around with their knives drawn—including Boonie's boy, of course, only he's the only one we're seeing. Brilliantly played, if I may say. You could just see them all prancing around Boonie, all diving into some miserable victim. And Boonie's boy was absolutely pissing scared. He's got his knife drawn, but he's just watching, when all of a fucking sudden—you're looking at his face, right in his eyes to see what's going on when all of a sudden blood, bloody fucking blood, spurts right up onto his face.

Christ! What a brilliant move that was, the victim's blood all over his face and his shirt—really something—and then you look down at the poor bastard, this little kid, and he's digging the knife into his bleeding thigh. Blood just drenching his trousers. Really revolting. Christ, they must have been pissed with him, Boonie's out there trying his little novelty tricks on the audience. Just a great scene, made everyone want to fucking barf up. I mean, there's a performer for you.

And the other comedians, they must have wanted to string him up scrotally. I mean, here they are, coming in and telling the same jokes night after night, why'd the chicken cross the road and blah blah blah to get on my fucking nerves, every single night, and then all of a sudden in walks this kid, balls high, and the only theatrical training he has, and I'm not trying to take credit, my friends, but all he has is Ratliffe under his belt, where it was cardinal that you mix it up night to night, where maybe one show Pete hits this word, and the next night I decide to play the garden scene as a sheepdog—not literally, mind you, but thinking about a sheepdog. That's where Boone was coming from, so it was quite natural that when he comes in he absolutely blows these little shits away, I mean, right out of the water, like sitting ducks.

I'll tell you what it was actually, seeing Boone after all these music-hall plebes had done their little song and dance. I'll tell you, my friends, it was like going to a steam bath, the finest steam bath in all of Kyoto, and getting yourself a fine full-body massage with all them oils from a lovely young genji girl, and then having her shove a Nazi-spiked billy club right up your bum. That's what it was like, my friends.

Buddy D'Angelo

Hell, no, I didn't love everything the guy did. But he drew. He drew right off. People never knew what they were going to get from this guy, so they'd come in just to find out. See, that was the thing—kid didn't have an act, he was changing it every night. He didn't even tell jokes, and who ever heard of that in '67? You know, there's comedians today living off jokes they wrote ten years ago. But in the sixties, forget about it. They could do it in their sleep. You gotta understand, they weren't going on TV all the time, so they could keep the same shtick and no one would notice, or if they did notice, that's what they wanted. That's where you get the people, "Hey, Jackie, tell the one about the Jew at the Waldorf."

But Boone, he's not doing jokes. One act I remember, all he does is three things—four things. He comes out with his hands up like this, like he's got the goddamn Shakespeare skull up in front of him. He goes right up to the edge of the stage, and he says, "I see England," and I'm thinking to myself, oh Christ, I'm getting some John Barrymore for the late set. He's playing it like "Friends, Romans, Countrymen." He says, "I see England . . . I see France . . . I see Buddy's underpants." He bows, very gallant, turns to the other side of the crowd, same goddamn attitude. He does, "Chinese . . . Japanese . . . dirty knees . . . look at these," flashes his tits at all of us, bows again, and I'm telling you, they loved it. They're going crazy for it, but he's not even finished yet. He goes and stands right in the center of the stage and he opens his arms and then grabs himself. Says, "Milk . . . milk . . . lemonade . . . 'round the corner, fudge is made." The place, I thought one lady was gonna die, she was screaming so loud. And as he's going off, he's through, he can't take it anymore, he's staggering right out to the street and he's got tears practically streaming down his face, he's going, "Beans! . . . Beans!" Just wailing. "The musical fruit! . . ."

Amalie Hindemuth

I was waitressing downtown at a place called Francesca's, so I wouldn't get to see him on stage very much, but often Eton would walk me down Greenwich to the restaurant in the afternoons. And sometimes at the end of the walk we'd stand outside the restaurant and he'd say, you know, okay, Amalie, what would you like? And I'd just say the first thing that came into my head, you know, an astronaut, or a koala bear or really whatever, and whatever character I'd said he would try to do that night. You know, because it was always characters that he liked best. So I would give him my suggestion, and once I remember he said, you know, your wish is my command, and really the whole night, I would be taking people's orders, bringing people their food and arguing with Francesca, but I would just be thinking about Eton and about contributing my small part, you know. And then when he'd come home, I'd have waited up for him, but we wouldn't talk about how they went. We would just go downstairs to this little deli on Eighth Avenue. We'd get pastrami sandwiches and eat them together at the kitchen table, and he would wash them down with enormous gulps of ginger ale.

Buddy D'Angelo

Okay, you can't do that forever. You've got people coming in, and they're not there for bullshit. They're there for one thing. These people, the school people I'm talking about here, I talked to them, they were there for one thing, and that was his—what are we gonna call it? What are you gonna call it? His impressions? Acting? *Esquire* magazine comes in one night and calls them his "poisonalities." The students called them "expo-zhays," "expo-zhures," exposures—I don't know what the hell, I don't know French.

We called them his "Sammies," because that's the first one where I didn't know what the hell he was thinking. He's just standing there pretending he's Sammy Davis, Jr., for some reason. He's talking about his jewelry and his singing and dancing, and all of a sudden he leans into the crowd and says, "But, you know, I'm still just Frankie's little nigger." My life flashes before my eyes. That's it. The roof is gonna cave in on me. My license goes out the window, and I'm gonna be spending the next six months in jail. What the hell was he thinking about, I have no idea. I have no idea where any of it came from. You know, the guy's been coming out doing these knife tricks, or these pooh-pooh pee-pee jokes, and all of a sudden, this. I practically chewed his head off afterwards, he's saying, "Buddy, it just happened." Yeah, well just make sure it doesn't happen again.

But, next day, Alex Bahssin comes in and asks me if Boone was gonna do another Sammy tonight, because Alex missed it and that's all anybody was talking about, and that's why we called them his Sammies. His Sammies. That's where everything changed, but I don't want to talk about it. I don't know where it came from. I'm through talking about it.

Lionel Thubb

Eton Arthur had been on its trail for some time, and when he finally found it, his particular invention, it truly was like watching temptation in action. The first I can recall seeing was of Lyndon Baines Johnson, though it was not the imitation so much that captured one's attention, or what he said, it was watching him give in to the idea of doing it.

If I recall, he'd just been having a little fun with our president, showing off his scars. He had even gone as far as placing himself before a mirror in the White House, finding every little nick on him, leaning over, checking between his legs, over on his shoulder blades. It had not lasted long, though. Eton Arthur had tried to move on with his routine, but he'd liked the idea of the mirror, you could see that. It was as if he'd caught the scent right there, because in another moment he was right back in front of it again, this imaginary mirror in the president's dressing room, and dressing himself, from the socks up. He couldn't make up his mind if he wanted to keep dressing the president or come upstage and start entertaining these kind folks again. He tried to do both. Put on a sock, mumble to himself, and then come out and tell a joke or two, then back to the White House. Whenever there was a lull, back to the White House he would go, back to the White House mirror, finding an undershirt, finding another scar and muttering to himself. And every time he'd go back, he'd stay a little longer and mumble to himself a little bit more, till soon enough, there was more of our president in more of our president's clothing than there was of Eton Arthur.

I can remember him putting his hands on his cheeks and saying, "God damn that face." And I would bet my final dime that

that is where the imitation turned, looking in an imaginary mirror and seeing an imaginary face and thinking to himself, "God damn that face." It just flowed from there on. If he could damn the face, he could damn the nose and he could damn the jowls, but if he could damn those jowls, he could admire his height and his sturdy Texan hands. No telling where it would stop, but one thing was for dead certain—if the president stayed for too long in front of that mirror, it was just a matter of time before Eton Arthur would catch his eye, and who knew what would happen then? He'd begin to string together the ideas that he found inside. "Well, well," he'd think, "if Mr. Johnson thinks this of his face, then he must also think that. And if he thinks that, he surely thinks this other thing." Swinging from vine to vine in another's mind, once he'd found his way in, was very much the impression. Or like watching an alley cat tip over a garbage can when he smells a fish dinner at the bottom, and rooting through till he's licked the bones clean. Oh, the mighty gumption of his burlesque. When he'd finished dressing, he took the president to Arlington, he took him to the cemetery, how perfectly merciless, and stood him before the flame.

Amalie Hindemuth

I remember right when they started, you know, he probably hadn't even been doing them for two weeks, but the club owner was nervous and wanted him to go back to some of his older things, little bits that had worked well, but Eton would come home and be so excited, you just knew that these impersonations were the only thing that interested him anymore. He would eat so fast. He would stand at the kitchen counter drinking a whole carton of milk, and he would walk around the apartment making fun, you know, pumping his fists like a boxer and jumping on the couch and things like that. He would stand on the kitchen table with his head up in the kitchen lamp. Or in the shower, he would sing things from *West Side Story,* and I'm sure the whole building could hear him. I remember him coming right in the door sometimes, pretending he'd kicked it in with his feet, and saying, "Yabadabadoo, Amalie! I am home."

Eton Arthur Boone, transcribed, * *February 4, 1968—*
JACK KEROUAC†

Anyone see the paper today? Here, see this? "Neal Cassady,** beat hero, forty-three." Beet hero sounds pretty appetizing. Sounds like it would stain your teeth. But Neal Cassady's dead. Dean bit it. How do you think Jack babe's taking it? Is he still up in Lowell, you think—Kerouac? *[Inaudible voice.]* He lives with his mom, right? *[Inaudible voice.]* Okay, thanks. No, I don't know where the hell I'm going tonight. My dog ate it. But thanks, ma'am, seriously, thanks for helping out. Okay, it's her fault if I fuck up.
[Sets stool in front of him. About to begin, interrupts himself, waves hand up and down. To audience.] Imagine bars. *[Sits on stool, puts head in hands.]*
Neal died. Neal died. Man. *[Looks up, responsive.]* Neal Cassady. Dean? You know—Dean? *[Listens.]* No, not James. Dean. Dean Moriarity. What's with you, you never read *On the Road? [Looks,*

---

*Unless otherwise indicated, all the transcripts of Eton Boone's stage performances which appear in this book have been provided by Kelso and Linda Chaplin. Over the period of eighteen months from December, 1967, to May, 1969, Mr. and Mrs. Chaplin filmed nearly every late Thursday night performance of Eton Boone at J.F.L., Grand Street in New York City. It is through their diligence and generosity that we are able to present these documents of Boone's stage work, but Mr. and Mrs. Chaplin have offered their material only on the condition that the following be understood, in Ms. Chaplin's words: "That the transcripts are just that—transcripts. They lie flat on the page and cannot possibly convey the profound emotion of Boone's stage work. The pacing, the accuracy of his vocal impersonation, and most of all the manipulation of the space, his gestures, his movement, his posture—all of that is lost in the transcript. Still, given the importance of the exposures both in the context of the popular culture of the period, and in the brief history of Boone's career, it seems essential that the reader be provided at least the opportunity to imagine what Boone was able to do."
†Jack Kerouac (1922–1969) was a prominent member of the Beat Generation. His best-known work is *On the Road*, published in 1957.
**Cassady was the real-life Dean Moriarity, hero of *On the Road.*

smiles.] Well, there's a cop for you. He can smell a man's breath from fifty paces, but all Deans are named Jimmy. *[Pulls cigarette out of shirt pocket, puts it in mouth, unlit.]*

[Snorts.] Yeah, and we'd talked about doing ourselves in. Late-night sessions plotting out our perfect good-byes, but we agreed—suicide never really made the right spiritual sense. Plus, "Death's here now, babe," we knew that. "It's here. It's been hanging around waiting ever since Pink Thing saw itself in Mama's mirror, the moment Infant You first said, 'Hey. Hey there, look at that, there's me.'—it's all dying from there on." We agreed. And if you shoved a mirror in Neal's face, sure, he'd die a little for you too, he could be so full of shit. But that's only if you slowed him down, 'cause most of the time, you put Neal at the wheel of a Cadillac, and he's the only person I ever saw live. He's the only person ever forgot himself. 'Cause life best lived, my deputy friend, goes one-ten on the straightaways, hate to say, it goes one-ten wherever the hell it wants—that's what Neal showed. The decisions you make then, man, you should have seen him, he was beautiful. Got to make a decision in an instant or it's your neck. *[Snaps.]* You've just got to flow.

Like writing. Neal was the best teacher I ever had, but he didn't have to say anything. It was in his hands, the way he'd hold a steering wheel. One-ten on a two-lane bridge, he's trying to pass a string of cars right in the teeth of an oncoming semi, Neal still holds the wheel like it's a baby bird, says, "Stop mulling it over, babe, just go." Same as writing. You've got to do it like you're telling dreams,* just do it. Then what you set down, if the cliff falls to your right or your left, or if the theatre had a red velvet ceiling, that's important, that's what you need, is what you remember from a dream right when you wake up. That's writing, babe. Hold that pencil in your hand like it's a baby bird, same thing, and Neal made it so easy.

A three-week dream that trip was,† I just had trouble seeing it for a while. Eight years of getting my ass kicked by words and

---

*In 1961 Jack Kerouac published *Book of Dreams,* an account of his dreams written directly upon waking.

†The main action of *On the Road* is a three-week cross-country trip taken by Dean Moriarity and Sal Paradise, the fictional Jack Kerouac.

ideas, till finally I just said, the hell with it, I'm not gonna think about it anymore, I'm just going to do it, like I just rolled out of bed, like it happened. No novelly gothic architecture, just life out there, courtesy of Neal, and get it down fast as you can, Jack. And all the choices you've got to make sitting there at your typewriter, they come bearing down on you, headlights blinding, they say, "What's it going to be, writer boy? Just the fact she blew you at the Greyhound station or what it felt like too?"— those choices, you just blow them right off the road, don't play chicken with me, boy—Neal's life goes too fast to fuck with what it felt like. "And besides, there'll be other women down the road," I can hear him, "don't you worry, Jack." Aw dammit, Neal, there's so many choices. You're the only one who ever made them easy.

[Takes deep breath, looks up at jailer. Snorts. Takes cigarette out of mouth.] I should probably light this. *[Snorts again. Puts cigarette back in mouth, takes matchbox out of breast pocket, lights match, holds flame a few inches in front of cigarette, watches as flame burns itself out. Cigarette still unlit, dangling from lips.]*

Choices, choices, and the writer can't make a damn one without his subject matter. Can't even decide if he wants a light. Kerouac, shit. Carraway.* Yeah, there was a beaut, a mistake a fella made at a party introduction way back—"Like you to meet Mr. Carraway."—aw, but I wouldn't correct him because he hit it. That's it—Carraway watches, stays outside, just keeps trying to throw pegs at everything, but he hasn't had anything real good to aim at in years, goddamn decades. He's nothing without his subject matter, and now his greatest victim is dead official. West Egg blew, buddy—look in the news. *[Points to paper at his feet.]* Pulled over to the side of the road and perished. Jesus Christ. So what are you going to do now, Jack? Chapter ninety-nine? Epilogue. Isn't that what you do? Yeah, write it, writer boy, write it down good as you can. *[Pulls a pen out of his breast pocket, sets paper on knee.]* Like a dream then—I sleep. *[Tilts head, resting on pressed hands, then awakes.]* I wake up, notebook's waiting and what've I got? *[Writes.]* "Neal's dead . . . Died . . . Isn't anymore . . . Had a drink . . . Got drunk."

---

*Nick Carraway was the narrator of F. Scott Fitzgerald's novel, *The Great Gatsby*.

[Looks up at jailer.] See, but that's yesterday's news, dep. That's a thirteen-year-old story now—statutory limit's passed, so I'll fess up, I'll fess up, I can't take this shit anymore. *[Raises hand.]* I did it, I killed him. There's foul play, officer, and me and my writing are the guilty party—we're the sinners worst of all because we try and deny it, but we are, we are, me and my pen and pencil–friends and ribbons and typewriter keys, we took the beauty's life, the whole steering strong, feeling fine, fucking fast to a blissful beat, beauty of a beautiful beautiful man's life. Took it, shot at its wheels, and he didn't even know it. He'd be saying to me, "I'm thinking of ending it, Jack. I'm thinking of calling it quits," and I'd just want to say, Neal, babe, you're dead already, can't you see? Look at you, Neal, you and your self-conscious self, moaning and groaning. Shit, man, I am sorry. I didn't mean to do you in, I didn't mean it, because Neal never had seen a mirror, even a rearview mirror, with the white lines lick lick licking beneath his wheels. He was free, but that book comes out eight years later, big stuff, big hit, and never again is Neal the same. Never is. He's dead, dead, dead, and he's dead for real this day of February 3, 1968, and I've got nothing to write, I got no dream no more, I've got blues I could listen to, but I've already thought about those too much. Just shut me up. Get me a cup so I can rattle this cage, drown out the rattle in my I-am-bullshit, I-am-bullshit brain.

[Puts hands over ears, rocks back and forth quickly, grunting. Brings matchbox up to the side of his head, strikes match trying to make as much noise as possible, drops flame to ground. Quicker and quicker, he strikes seven more matches next to his ear, grunting louder with each one. Throws matchbox down, puts head between hands, sobs.]
Neal died. Nothing.

Kelso Chaplin

Sy developed the Burton as quickly as he could, and probably no more than a week later Sy and I and Linda spent an evening looking it over in a cutting room at NYU. Linda was in love with him. I liked him, and I actually liked the film a lot too. And if

Linda liked it, and I liked it, it was just a matter of time before it got to Hugh.

We took it up to him for one of his little student get-togethers, "Teas for Tuesday." Hugh used to have students over to his place once a week, basically just to hang out and talk, and this Tuesday night in the middle of December, 1967, Linda and I brought up a copy of the Burton which we'd blown up to 16 mm for him. Hugh actually had his own projector and a bunch of films. He had these 2,000-foot canisters of *Citizen Kane* and *A Man for All Seasons* and actually *The World, the Flesh, and the Devil*—they were the three I knew about. Now he's got a VCR and a Betamax—he was the first to get them all—and a video library that takes up a whole wall of his closet. Anyway, Linda and I got there, and we pulled out this film. We asked if it was okay. We got out his projector and took down the painting above his mantel. There were probably about six or seven other people there, and we all sat down on the floor with our legs crossed to look at the thing.

We'd decided not to tell Hugh what it was. We just told him we had something to show him. We wanted this figure to emerge totally out of context. So the film just flickered on Hugh's wall, and he was doing his thing, sitting back in his big armchair. He had his cane over the arms, and the glass of sherry—it was all Hugh, he was smiling like a Buddha. And it's not that long a show—you should check, I think the Burton's 5:45—but when it was finished, we all just sat there in the dark for a moment. Someone got up to hit the lights, but Hugh stopped him. He's got that gentle voice, but it's so soft it's almost like you have to listen to it. He said, "Don't touch the lights. Kelso, put it on again."

So we all watched it again. This time Hugh was sort of leaning forward, really studying it. You could hear him mumbling to himself as he was watching, these little notes in the margin, like "Mmmm, indeed. Yes. Marvelous." When it ended, Hugh got up and left the room. We all just sat there, and when he came back, he was carrying a folder. He opened it up, took out this piece of paper, and placed it down on the coffee table. He just kind of left it there and went back to his chair, sat down and waited. Linda bit. She sort of scrambled for this paper, and when she got the nod from Hugh, she read it out loud. It was a letter from Boone that he'd written from England. Hugh had a letter from Boone—pretty far out. The only part I remember is Boone saying, "Do be a stranger." So Hugh'd pulled this awesome rabbit out of his hat, and when we were all finished shaking our heads, he said, "Kelso, I'd like you to go back to New York and film him some more. He was just beaming. He said, "And if you could, would you mind leaving us the address of that club you found him in?"

Hugh Gardiner

Of course it was a captivating thing. I was agog. No one had ever done this before, and yet it was so simple. Isn't it always simple? There is tragedy in all our heads, and he was not afraid to expose it, nor was he afraid to use any of the means at his disposal—the shared cultural terrain. Finally here was someone to admit that these cultural figures are our gods. We can read their stories in the tabloids as though they are myths, of their marriages and divorces, of their fights and petty jealousies, their battles with alcohol and pills, and it is worthwhile, I think, to read them and see our own vulnerabilities revealed or reflected in their lives. But isn't it inevitable that there should eventually come a person who will scrutinize these people, heedlessly and scrupulously, someone without reverence or discretion? Boone. I marveled at the self-evidence of it that popular culture had progressed so far without there being some figure there to examine it from such immediate range, to see the language that is in body and gesture and give it voice. To ask, what is it that we see, and what would it sound like if it had the courage to speak? This is what all the *exposures* were about. They were satire stripped of satire. They were not ironic. They were not timid or indirect. They were what all art wants to be desperately. They were themselves.

Linda Chaplin

Hugh graduated from Princeton in 1944. He got his Ph.D. in English Literature at the University of Chicago, and the dissertation he wrote there on Keats's letters was published around the time he first got to Vassar in 1951. He did a little campus hopping for a while in the fifties, especially at larger universities—Yale, I know, Cornell, Hopkins—but I don't think that's ever been the kind of teaching that really interested Hugh. He's been in Poughkeepsie pretty steadily from 1959 or '60, spending the academic year at Vassar, and his summers just down the road in Fishkill, where he heads the writing colony. He's been published a number of times, mostly essays and articles on the Romantic poets, but his real passion, and he'd be happy to admit this, is teaching. Quite simply, Hugh is the best teacher I've ever encountered, just the gentlest, most encouraging man. He's one of those people who has the ability to make people express themselves, and what could be more important than that?

Now, his personal life I can't tell you much about. We've never really known, right. As gentle and generous as he is with his ideas, he's also an extremely private man. What we do know is that he's from this very large, wealthy Delaware family of athletic shipping-magnate types who weren't all that crazy about turning out an academic, I'm sure. I think he has very little contact with them. And we also know that one of his sisters, Emily, was born with cerebral palsy and that Hugh took full responsibility for her. She lived upstairs at his place with a nurse, and I don't think anyone ever met her face to face, but sometimes you'd see glimpses of her. You'd see Hugh taking her out for walks or driving her places in the fall when the leaves were changing.

I saw them once actually. It was a beautiful spring morning. I'd come by to drop off a paper, and I heard Hugh from out back. He was out on his little patio, so I wandered back there and I saw the two of them through the bushes. They were sitting there with breakfast tables set up, and a pot of tea between them. Emily had her napkin tucked into her collar, and Hugh was reading to her from a book of Shelley. It just about broke my heart.

Hugh Gardiner

I wrote him the moment Kelso and the others left. I reintroduced myself and told him of Kelso's film. I wanted to let him know how much I admired what he was doing, and congratulate him on his remarkable courage, because unless he'd been inspired by some divine touch, these performances of his must have involved him very deeply in a kind of thinking from which most of us shy.

I invited him to write me, as I suspected he might wish to let go with his feelings. We are all bound to wonder at what we do, and certainly Boone was no exception. From that very first film, I felt safe in assuming that he wondered a very great deal. Here was a man intending to practice the self-consciousness of others on a nightly basis. A record of his own reflections would surely be of great use to him, a journal of sorts, that I would gladly keep. My motive was to hear him, to let him vent whenever he needed. I would listen, and that is all I tried to convey to him in that first letter. That is all I ever tried to convey to him.

I was very pleased that he did write. He wrote me very quickly, and we began the correspondence.

Kelso Chaplin

He'd cued up the music, the theme song, "I Love Lucy and She Loves Me," so this scratchy recording plays the first few bars in the dark. When the lights come up, she's just standing there— he's got on this hideous plaid pantsuit, and gobs of bright red lipstick, topped off by the wig, this bright orange beehive, and he's waving at us and smiling. He's looking a little wistful, and he gets up to the microphone and says, in this croaky menopausal voice, "I'm so honored." That's all he needs to say. It's Lucille Ball and she's accepting an award, some lifetime achievement award someplace. She puts her hand to her chest, she says, "As a woman," and her wig topples down over her eyes. She tries to fix it, and she knocks the microphone stand over. She leans over to pick up the stand and kicks it across the stage. It's just shtick, it's kitsch, but it was right out of one of her shows—wacky situation, Lucy embarrassed, Lucy trying to smile, and he milked it just like her, you know, with those wide ostrich eyes. It's a great imitation, just visually. I mean, you don't see Boone at all.

Anyway, Lucy fixes herself, straightens herself up and looks out at us, and she says, "I need a cigarette." Someone tosses one out, and she drops it. She leans over to pick it up and smacks her head into the mike stand. Finally she gets the cigarette. She puts it into this holder she's got and winks at the guy who's given it to her. He gets up and lights it for her, and the thing is, for a second there she's very smooth, very sexy. And you go, shit, yeah, Lucille Ball *is* a woman. She's not just a clown who gets trophies stuck on her head and tries to get into the Tropicana. She's a woman. She says, "As a woman in this business," and she takes this drag off her cigarette, this incredible, sexy drag. We can't even believe it's Lucy, but then she breaks into this coughing fit. She just starts hacking—clown again. She sort of steadies herself, she looks out at us sort of wide-eyed and says, "Has anyone got a drink?" Same guy stands up and hands her a glass. She says, is this water? Guy says, no, vodka, and she looks at us, shrugs, and just tosses it down in one gulp. Smacks her lips, gives us that big Lucy smile and wipes her mouth. Smears the lipstick all over her face. It's great.

But she goes to give the guy his glass back, and she stops. She sees these lipstick stains on the glass, and she's just gazing at them. It's dawning on her too now—she's not just a clown. She even spots the lipstick on the holder and takes another drag. She keeps kissing the holder and looking at the mark—just this great loving gaze—but then she has another coughing fit. She doubles over wheezing. The wig slides down again. Finally, she turns herself around, and crouches over with her back to us trying to make herself presentable. She's poking at the wig. She takes out a compact and looks at her face, and you can hear a little bark

when she sees the lipstick. She starts trying to fix her face, rubbing her cheeks, poofing the wig. When she's finished she stands
back up and spins around to face us, and it's great. She's a circus
clown. The wig looks like Bozo, and she's got the lipstick in a big
clown smile, and the diamond mascara. Everybody starts laughing at her, and she begins to lose it. She's looking right at our
camera now—I pull in for this coyote-ugly close-up—and she
says it, "I . . . hate . . . Lucy." The music starts up on cue, the
closing music with the canned applause, and she's looking right
at us and just begins wailing, the big Lucy "Waaaaaaaah!"

Amalie Hindemuth

I can still see him and the things he would do, the things he would
sort of have to do for the impersonations. He would watch television a great deal and read magazines. He'd just stare at the pictures in *Life* magazine, because that's how he worked mostly.
He'd find a photograph in a magazine that he sort of connected
with or read something from an interview. He didn't like to read
biographies so much or listen to things that other people had to
say about someone. He was more interested in just a single line
from an interview, and he would copy it down and look at it, or
he'd snip out a picture and keep it in his wallet. He'd have a dozen
of them at a time in his wallet, and sometimes you'd just find him
staring at this picture or this little slip of paper, because it's
almost as if it wasn't the big things he was ever looking for. It was
more I think just finding that one sentence and staring at it and
sort of letting it grow. Do you know what I mean? I mean, not
this expansive sort of thing, like this expansive plain of whoever
it is, more like just drilling a hole wherever the ground felt soft
to him. Does that make any sense?

It was even almost like watching an animal before the kill or
something like that. He'd pull the picture out to look at and then
put it back in his wallet, back and forth like that. It was as if he
just couldn't resist, you know, and when he got like that, you
knew he'd have to do it soon, even though I think nine times out

of ten he knew perfectly well it was going to end up being very hard on him. I mean, there wasn't ever any sense of, am I good enough? He wasn't thinking to himself, can I do this? Will they like me? It was more, should I do this? Can I take this? But the answer to that question was always yes. Yes, you know, for now, I have to. It's what I do. I can take it, and I will.

Lionel Thubb

The other comedians were none too pleased. Mr. Caporale would sit at the bar and complain to Claudia, "Is this a nightclub," he'd ask, "or Lincoln Center? These people are dead." He may have been the first to notice, without exactly putting his finger on it—the patrons weren't dead, they were the same. The same people were coming night after night, and they weren't coming to see little ol' us anymore, the comics. They were coming to see a repertory company of one, name of Eton Arthur Boone. A very difficult crowd to play to, I can assure you. I recall Mr. Schacter storming offstage one time, complaining that a lady at one of the front tables had actually corrected him in one of his routines. Or another time when a rather large group stood up and left in the middle of the evening. They were going for dinner, they explained, and wanted their table saved for Mr. Boone's set.

Fortunately for myself, I as an entertainer was possessed of the two virtues that we members of the undercard needed most at Jes' For Laffs—a repertoire the size of a lounge singer's and an intonation that was just as easy to ignore. So it was that I came to be almost as regular a fixture at the club as Eton Arthur himself. My act most often preceded his, and vividly do I recall spotting Eton Arthur's head at the bar as I neared the end of one of my tales. I'd see him standing at what Buddy called the blocks and then hear Kelso Chaplin's motion picture camera start up—vroom vroom—as the crowd began to murmur and shift. "I shall not be taking your time any longer" was my au revoir. "My tale for this evening is through, and I see the next performer is champing at the bit."

Eton Arthur Boone, transcribed, February 22, 1968—
J. EDGAR HOOVER *

What's that? Hoover, hunh. All right, okay. Vrrrrrrrrrr. I suck, I just suck. There's your Hoover. Oh, all right, all right, Hoover. Hoover, Hoover, Hoover. You know, it's funny, I saw him on Chet and Dave† the other night. J. Edgar, right? Yeah, I was thinking about him. That's a nice trick he's got. I mean, what the hell *do* we know about J. Edgar Hoover? What do I know about J. Edgar Hoover? . . . Yeah, yeah, exactly. What does Hoover know about me? There's his trick, sir. "Get me that file on Eton Boone!" Right, that's it. Can I have that chair? Thanks. Watch your head. Great . . . Hoover. You think Hoover crosses his legs?

[Sits as if at office desk. Leans over, presses imaginary intercom button.] Get me the file on Ethan Boone! How's that? I don't give a hoot in hell, Shannon, just get me the file, double time! Watch this. Ten, nine, eight, seven, six—*[Knocks.]* Ha! Enter. All right, just put it on the desk and leave . . . You waiting for a citation, Shannon? You'll get yours. Now amscray! Hunh? Yeah. Sure. Four o'clock.

Good little foot soldier. See the way he takes orders? Knows which side his butter's breaded on. "Yessir. Nossir. Right away, Mr. Director." Here bright and early, stays till midnight if I do and then some. Reports in triplicate. Clean. Bright. Efficient. Scared shitless of me. *[Laughs.]* Yeah, they all are, aren't they? The men's room here's wired, they all know that. Shannon knows I've got a tap on his place in Georgetown. Sure, sure. His mother calls him "Beasty." Beasty looks under his bed at night. Good for him.

Because there's gotta be fear. Can't have morality without fear, and the people aren't afraid anymore. Afraid of the darkies maybe—hell, yes, up in a Baltimore alley at three o'clock in the morning—but it looks like we got them licked now. Yeah, they're not going anywhere. But I mean the flag and having a little respect,

---

*J. Edgar Hoover was the director of the FBI from 1924 to 1972.

†Chet Huntley and David Brinkley were co-anchors of NBC's "Huntley-Brinkley Report."

that's what I'm talking about, and keeping the cities safe for good decent American citizens, cleaning the hippie scum off the streets, the commies and the pinkos. And if that takes putting a little fear into some of you people, even the good young people of this country—and they're out there, God bless 'em—well, fine. You should be scared of me.

And you are. I can feel it. In the back of your minds, you know J. Edgar's on the job. *[Falsetto.]* "Did you hear that, Madge? Was that on your end, or was it me?" *[Laughs.]* Or "Who let the plumber in, crumbcake? Our pipes were fine. And son of a gun if that bulb doesn't seem too strong." *[Laughs.]* Yeah, you've gotta be looking over your shoulder every now and then, fella, making sure everything's on the up and up, because you know if it isn't, if there's a little something stinking in your closet, The Man's going to know about it. *[Thumbs his chest.]* No telling what The Man knows. He's got that invisible network out there, and he's got those files. Want to see?

[Takes an imaginary binder out of top drawer of desk. Smiles.] Yes, yes, let's see here. Paper clip, anyone? Where's my coffee? . . . *[Sips.]* . . . All right, let's take a look, what do we got? Kempton, Harvey. Journalist, Chicago. No relation to that pansy-ass in New York. Led a student group in the fifties at Oberlin. On behalf of the cafeteria workers. I remember that. He was in on that? Little pantywaists. The leader of the union was a card-carrying member, for Pete's sake. Now he's working with Lowenstein? Well, that's easy as pie.

Knock off another before Shannon gets back. All right, all righty. Let's see, what do we have here? Glass, Roger. Lawyer for CBS out in L.A. Let's see. Hmm, hmm. Got a family, kids. Community chest, PTA—what the hell's PTS, Shannon? On the straight and narrow is Mr. Glass. Sure, sure. But what's he doing in Frisco every two weekends? Meeting with a fella named Ashish, that's what. Friend of his. Good and great friend. Tall guy. Hung like a horse. You want to see pictures? *[Laughs.]*

'Cause let me tell you something. It's all in here. *[Holds the binder in the air with both hands.]* I got everything I need. I got pictures. I got clippings. I got reports, and it's not just the journalists and the writers and the homo teachers. It's any one. Any size. The Kennedys. Sure, sure. Bobbsey Twins. They thought they had me. They had some Harvard scum tailing me in '62, but they were out of their league. Jesus, the shit I had on those two. Talk to me about the Carlyle corridor, Jack.* Salinger† was a pimp. What the hell'd they think they were gonna do to me, leaving trails of shit six miles long? They didn't even have the guts to try.

No one would. *[Points to man at first table. Stands up, menacing.]* You want to, sir? Come on, come on. Take your best shot. I dare you . . . Ha. Thought so. Just watch yourself, mister, 'cause I'm all over you. You think Junior'd like to know what Daddy did to his gerbils, Cheese Butt? Or you, ma'am. *[Points to lady at third table.]* I'll rip you apart from inside. Think I'm bluffing? Take a look in my eye, ma'am. You want me to check the file? Say the word. 'Cause I see some trips to the clinic, lady. I see some two-hour lunch-breaks that have me thinking. And you there, next to her, Mr. Charlie Cuckold, yeah, does she know about your Memphis wives? I don't think so. No, well okay, then, you're in the bag. Anyone else? Any takers?

What about this Ethan Boone character? Goddammit, where the hell'd he put it? Here. Let's see. Here's a growing file. Kid's been ruffling some feathers. We got Sammy, we got Judy. Harold Stassen?** And Jesus, he's doing *me* right now. This kid's doing me! He thinks I can't hear that? Listen to him. *[Listens.]* Come on, kid, come on. Do something, kid, call me a faggot . . . What's the matter, scared? Scared? . . . Say something . . . Ah, he's not going to do it. He knows—he can't pull that shit with me what he pulls with the others, because I could blow his life to hell like that. *[Snaps.]* Nail him on possession if that's what it takes. Yeah, I got a bug in every beer bottle he ever bought, and if you don't think Ethan Boone knows that, you're crazy. We're in the intrusion industry, him and me. Got each other's secrets, got each other by the balls, and we're not letting go. *I'm* not letting go—of his or anyone else's. *[Extends his hand, cupping.]* Got the whole world's balls right here in the palm of my hand, and I'm starting to put the squeeze on, feel it? So nobody moves until I say. I say move, move.

---

*It was reputed that President Kennedy used a secret underground corridor of the Carlyle Hotel in New York City to usher women in and out of his suite there without notice.

†Pierre Salinger was President Kennedy's press secretary.

**Boone performed routines on Sammy Davis, Jr., in late September, 1967; Judy Garland in November, 1967; and politician Harold Stassen on January 21, 1968.

I say stay, stay. I say turn over, you turn over and drop 'em. And if I want your eyes shut, you shut 'em now. Don't you look and don't you listen or I swear to God I'll blow you wide open too. *[Rips belt from belt loops.]* Shut your eyes!

Shannon! In here, double time! I've got a mood, and hit the lights when you come in, I don't want to see your friggin' face! You got five minutes, mister, let's move!

Linda Chaplin

Comedy's very young. Well, obviously, you have your court jesters and Aristophanes, right, but I mean comedy as a business, as a full-blown American industry. It's still in diapers in the '60s. No one has really done imitations alone, as the entire perform-ance, really until Vaughn Meader and the *First Family* Kennedy albums in the early '60s. You need the media ball to get rolling for impersonations to really catch on, right. Without film and television, there's nothing we can all recognize like that, and throw money at.

So that's what you've got to remember, that in 1967 or '68, comedians are still trying to figure out what they can and cannot do. A code of ethics is being formed and not because there are these edicts coming from Uncle Miltie saying this joke is kosher, this one isn't. The code is having to constantly adjust to television and this new incredible media machine, this juggernaut, right, what we're now calling "infotainment." Specifically around the question of impersonations, too. Lenny Bruce broke rules, he tested limits, but Lenny Bruce was talking about concepts, about laws, about language. And that helped. That paved the way for a lot of the things Boone was allowed to do, but Boone wasn't talking about laws or about concepts. He was talking about spe-cific people. He was, generally speaking, an impersonator, liter-ally, the first in-personator.

Because it almost comes down to these schools, right. On the one hand, you have these people like David Frye and today, Fred Travalena and Rich Little and Marilyn Michaels, who are doing these very soft, but also very funny, imitations. They're just sort of poking fun at these figures, and they're successful at it—that's a perpetual industry, right, it's going to be there as long as pop culture is, people imitating other people and making fun of them, playfully.

But then you've got Eton Boone, right, and even though you can't exactly trace comic lineages, there are performers today who are a part of that legacy. Robin Williams, right—he'll sort of pop inside these heads, Jerry Falwell, and it's outrageous, but he's only there for a millisecond—that's Robin Williams, electron comic—he doesn't develop anything, and he never really stops being Robin Williams. And then you've also got the more feminine performers who do take the time to build characters—Lily Tomlin and Jane Wagner, or Whoopi. When they do a character, they really want you to understand her, or him. They let their characters talk about themselves, and talk to you, at length, just like Boone. But they've changed it too, right. Their soliloquies are so well-crafted, they're so obviously organic that they've really taken it away from the pure spontaneity of Eton Boone. And they've also taken it away from actual people, celebrities, people in the audience. Lily and Whoopi are doing types.

So it's a trade-off. It seems like either you're going to get the spontaneous, outrageous brilliance of Robin Williams, or the crafted depth of a Whoopi, but not both—only Eton Boone ever did both, and who can really blame these other people for backing off a little? That's what a legacy does, it teaches, it learns, it develops, and what we learned from Eton Boone, the forefather, right, is that just turning your lasers on real people—whether they're stars or just these regular folks who happen to wander into a comedy club one night—that's much, much too dangerous.

Amalie Hindemuth

If I could hear the television from outside the door when I was coming in, if he'd turned up the volume like that, I knew it hadn't been easy. It didn't mean it hadn't gone well, it just meant it hadn't been fun. Or if I walked in and he was reading a sports magazine or a letter from Professor Gardiner, or writing one—these sheets and sheets and whole yellow pads he used to go through. You could just see that he was trying to flush all these things away from him, just be rid of them. He wouldn't even answer the phone. I would have to answer it, because most of the time it would be someone wanting to talk to Eton about what they'd seen at the club. They wanted to get angry at him or thank him or things like that. They'd ask me if I was his girlfriend, or they'd want to send food—just the strangest things. They'd send books, or they'd call to make requests, you know, "Please ask him to do so-and-so. My friend and I would love to see that." And I would leave their suggestions for Eton. I'd write them down and leave them on the mail table, and I don't really know how often he'd take them. It was sort of like leaving food for a cat—one second, you look over and it's gone.

But really what I remember most is just coming home from a show I was in in Brooklyn, and he'd be sitting there in front of the television with these jelly beans and candies in front of him, these big bowls, and he'd pour them out onto the table and arrange them in patterns. It was all sort of "give my senses something else to deal with," in a way. I mean, take me and beat me with a broom, just as long as it's something new. But please, Amalie, don't ask me how it went.

Buddy D'Angelo

Yeah, you bet we were unprepared. People calling up—"Hey, are you the guy that got Boone?" At first, you're a little pissed—"We got Boone, yeah. We got Holly Kristl and Lionel Thubb and Alex Bahssin and we got Maury Schacter and a million other guys." But maybe you stop yourself after the tenth guy calls. Finally you just give in, you tell 'em, yeah, we got Boone, four nights a week, we're the ones. And you keep getting calls, and people are stopping you on the street about the guy, so you take out an ad. You're cooking. You got lines halfway to Chinatown. I mean, you tell me in 1966 that you're ever gonna have to make a reservation two weeks ahead for the late show on a Tuesday night at Buddy D'Angelo's J.F.L. I tell you you got rocks in your head. I mean, Jesus, fella, let me get some earplugs, I hear my ship coming in. No bullshit. My ship comes in, and it stays there right at J.F.L., my SS *Boone* stays with me for nearly two years. He starts the Sammies in September of '67, and he stays right through to the end, right through to May of '69. One stop. J.F.L. Guy never went anywhere else. We went through the fucking roof.

Excerpted from BAY WINDOW, San Francisco, April 29, 1968

THE VIEW FROM GOTHAM: ETON BOONE'S VANISHING ACT?
by Carey Hogan

The stage at the comedy club Jes' For Laffs in New York's Greenwich Village is momentarily bare late on Saturday night. After six or seven opening acts and two or three drinks for the paying customers, it seems like nothing but good cheer has come from the microphone stand that everyone now stares at with such palpable anticipation. For a little while longer, it remains bare—that extra beat, as if to tell you, Down That Drink. Get Ready. The Party's Over. Here Comes Eton Boone.

And here he does come, a polite and well-groomed young man wending his way through the crowd to the stage, dropping muttered excuse me's along the way. As he hops up and starts lowering the microphone to his height, you are caught off-guard by his appearance. It's not just the silk pajamas he's wearing. It's his manner, so mild. Can this really be him? He seems like too nice a guy.

He won't keep you waiting. His eyes begin to sparkle with delight as he reaches into the breast pocket of his silk top and pulls out a Sasieni pipe. As he glances leisurely around the club and begins filling the pipe with tobacco, his legs stiffen and his shoulders rise. You realize it along with everyone else; the sparkle in his eyes doesn't belong to that kid who came up on stage just a few moments ago. Eton Boone is gone. Someone else, someone you know, someone whose name is on the tip of your tongue, has replaced him, and he's lighting his pipe up there on stage.

"Good evening and welcome. I'm glad you could join us." That tight and easy smile clenching the pipe between his teeth. You've seen that smile before. You've almost got it now. But who? A table of six to your right has begun to squeal with laughter, and you want to kick yourself. Finally, the bald man in the denim jacket up front can't help himself. "Hef!" he screams, and the whole club erupts. The tension's broken. Now let's wait and see.

. . . I'd like to show you around the place. Barbi—you've met Barbi haven't you?—She's a very special lady. Barbi, say hello to our guests. Hmm. Yeah. Now why don't you go fix them a drink . . . Very special lady. Oh, there's Joe Williams. I think he'll be kind enough to sing for us a little later on. I first met Joe back in 1961 when he—oh, here's Dick Shawn. Hello, Dick . . . Yeah, yeah, hn. Good one. Always on your toes. Yeah, yeah, sure, I'll see you later . . . Very funny man. Funny man, Dick Shawn. I enjoy his work a great deal. Oh, I think I see our drinks coming. And look at the lovely young lady who's carrying them. Her name is Linda. Linda, why don't you say hello to our guests. Yeah . . . She's a very special lady. One of my favorite people in the world. She's going to be appearing in our May issue. Plans to be an actress. Did you get what you wanted? Oh, good.

So Hef leads us on a tour. We meet a few more celebrities: Peter Lawford, Red Buttons, Jim Brown. We travel through different rooms at the mansion, and as he takes you along, you're thinking, Well, this is good. This is very good. Eton Boone has transformed himself into *Playboy* publisher Hugh Hefner for sure, but you still don't know what all the fuss is about. In fact, you think you'll have another drink. You always did want to rub elbows with Hef. And Eton Boone is so good, you almost stop wondering how he got so good so quick.

"Oh, I don't really think it's that tough." He's granted you a few minutes for questions after the show. You almost expect him to have a towel around his neck, but all he's got is a bottle of Schaefer in his paw. He's doing his best to recline on the tiny folding chairs the club provides its customers. He looks about as tired as anyone is bound to at 2:00 A.M., but at least he's the same kid who came out on stage an hour and a half ago.

"I think wanting to do it is half the battle," he says between swigs. But how? "You get a mental image. Look at their eyes, listen to the voice for a second. As long as you've got the voice in your head, it'll come. Just keep in mind no one's really an adult." He sure makes it sound easy, but you aren't buying.

Born and raised in San Diego, Eton Boone seems an unlikely candidate for pop stardom. The son of a radio executive and an artist, Boone reels off the facts of his life as if they were statistics off a baby-boomer's collector's card. He's 5′ 9½″, 145 lbs., 21 years old, throws right, hits right, has one brother, five years his junior. His mother, the artist, died of cancer when he was fourteen. He left San Diego four years later and hasn't looked back. No college. No degree. No resume. Nothin' but talent.

Boone admits that there isn't much about his early bio that would put him on a collision course with the New York comedy stage. And he didn't spend his formative years peeking over Hef's hedges either. If that was the way it worked, Eton Boone would have had to peer over a hundred different hedges. Well, not exactly. By his own count, Boone has toured club audiences through the minds of just about seventy-five celebrities since he began his unique impersonations last September. Figures ranging from Elvis Presley to Dean Rusk, from Sonny Liston to Sonny Bono, from Julius Rosenberg to Louis Armstrong—no star is too big or too small for Eton Boone's galaxy, which, you started thinking about an hour and a half ago, seemed like a pretty pleasant one.

And yet Eton Boone's star treks haven't been entirely free of controversy. That's why you came, isn't it? To see the guy who's got Sammy Davis, Jr.'s press agent talking lawsuit. "He'll cool down," Boone says with a peculiar air of resignation, and he's right. There's a shoe box in the Jes' For Laffs manager's office downstairs that has Eton Boone's name on it. Stuffed inside are the latest complaints, threats and kudos that Boone has earned, but something about sitting with him, something about watching him light a cigarette, tells you this shoe box is nothing but a holding pen for the circular file. "No, I read them," he says. "But they go away. People forget, or they decide to let it be, I guess."

Does that mean Eton Boone doesn't take his mail seriously? That same peculiar air crosses his handsome, would-be carefree features. "Well, that's tough. I think people eventually realize that the deal with what I do is, these routines come out of here, and they just evaporate." It's late, and his mind is tired, but he drains the last of the beer and keeps on. He knows you don't have much longer. "I never do anything twice. I try not to press anything. There's still a threat, I guess, but it never lasts long, and that seems to make everything okay."

Sure, maybe. That and the fact that Eton Boone's not playing stadiums, and that, to his knowledge at least, none of his victims has ever attended a performance. Because it's not a pretty sight. It seemed easy enough for a while, seemed like maybe it would drift away harmlessly the way Boone says, but that's not how it turned out, remember.

Hef kept touring you around. Didn't he show you some back issues? Sure, and then that gallery of Playmates on the wall of his billiards room. And hadn't it been one of us who first pointed it out, who asked him whose picture that was in the corner over there, next to one of Jayne Mansfield?

. . . Hmm? Oh, that's Marilyn, of course. She was our first. Called a sweetheart of the month back then. That was 1953. We were going to call the magazine *Stag Party*. Glad we didn't. Has a sort of seamy feel, don't you agree? You'd have to sneak that one under your raincoat. *Playboy* isn't about the stripper girl, it's about the girl next door. Look at her there, waving at us still—hello.

[Hefner takes photograph from wall.] Marilyn had already been out to Hollywood by the time she came to us, but there was still that quality about her, of Norma Jean, the gal who wants to please. Look at her smile there, see her eyes. That's the perfect look. Every move Marilyn made, there was a question, Is this right? See it? "Is this right?" Lets you say, "Yes. Yes, Marilyn, that's right." Marilyn was perfect. *[Hefner lights pipe.]* Tragedy. *[Hefner inhales, blows smoke.]* The photograph, though, it doesn't know what happened. I keep it right here on my wall where nothing can get at it. *[Hefner gestures around him.]*

You can feel it here in the pool room, can't you? Look at all these eyes, covers going back some fifteen years, staring out of the frames— brown, hazel, blue. Or the hair, brunette, blonde, redhead, look at that—doesn't matter. There's something the same in each, isn't there? What is it? I ask all my guests—what makes them all so seductive? Dick said breasts. Funny man. But you know what I think it is? They're photographs, that's all. They're eternal. That's the sexiest look of all, the one that doesn't change. Same look, same pose, every time. Look at the skin there. Always that smooth, that perfect, and the flesh, you feel you can reach out and touch it, don't you?

Hef wipes the photograph of Marilyn with his sleeve and puts it back on the wall. He relights his pipe and surveys the whole wall, smiling proudly. Then he turns back to his guests and closes his eyes. You can almost hear Joe Williams crooning as Hef starts snapping. His timing is off. He smiles at us and the look on his face is warm, but eerie.

That's Sam Ellis on bass. Regis says the only thing that keeps time
at the mansion is Sam on bass. I like that. Have you seen any—clocks?
No. Didn't want that here, like a casino. I told them that when they
were building it. I said I wanted people happy, enjoying themselves
without the face of Father Time looking over their shoulder. He's not
invited. I want a pool, and land and games and entertaining friends.
I want a place where whatever you want, you can have—more ice in
your drink, fresh can of tennis balls. I want the same beautiful women.
Just look around you. Smell that, can you? *[Hefner takes a deep breath.]*
. . . That's the mansion. You can smell the leather, women's perfume,
and the alcohol. Listen . . . the ice melting in people's drinks, the
chinkle-chankle of the gameroom, Joe at the piano, and all the conversations. *[Hefner listens.]* . . . That's Dick, did you hear that? Dick's laugh.
[Hefner, eyes shut, starts nodding.] This is right. This is what I wanted.

Hef keeps his ear cocked to the hum of the mansion, but something's made him stop for a moment, slowed him up. His shoulders
are hunching a little more, and the smile has begun to look like a
frozen twitch. He moves to his billiards table, and as he speaks,
he's leaning over the felt and sliding the cue ball at us, bouncing
it off an invisible bumper and letting it roll slowly back to his
hand. His eyes are in a trance.

I actually went out to a roast for Joey a few weeks ago. Dean asked
me. Black tie. It's nice to get out there every so often, but I can't stay
as long as I used to. Start to feel that ticking again, and I see the women.
Gabe's wife, Monica DeLisio, used to be so beautiful, such a lovely
young lady—May, I think, '61, pictorial up in a Vermont cabin, Hur-
rell—she was wandering around the party afterwards in the dress she
was wearing when I first met her. Still a very special lady, talked with
her a while. Seems happy, had some television spots, but I couldn't
help seeing all the changes. Hair used to be longer, lighter. Breasts were
falling, and I looked at the skin below her neck, rougher. Just the tiniest
flaws, like cracks in the paint. Time just pulls at everything, doesn't
it? Should have kept her here a little longer. She'd still have that youth,
the quality, the skin would still be so soft, perfect. You can see around
you, all the young ladies walking around here, so special and lovely,
don't they all have it? Never change. And they know, they're safe here
from what's out there, tick tick tick. The women always have a place
here and they know it.
[Hefner looks back at frame of Marilyn, takes it off wall.] So does Marilyn.
Marilyn will always be here with me, just like Linda and Barbra, Kelly.
This is right, Marilyn. This is the right thing you're doing. I'm glad

you're here. . . . Oh, Marilyn, why don't you see if anyone needs anything? Marilyn?

His face is inches from the frame, and even if it seemed like he was joking when he first called her, the way he waits there for an answer has you wondering, has he been indoors too long? He glances back at you quickly, but there's no reassurance in his smile.

She doesn't seem to be in the mood for it just now, but I see Linda coming our way. You met Linda, didn't you? Linda's a very special lady—I'm sure she'll be glad to refresh any of your drinks, if you like. Just ask her if there's anything else you need. I'm going to go hunt down Barbi . . . Enjoy.

Sure, sort of. But while Hef may have been saved by the belle, no one else was. No one stayed to refresh their drinks. They got out of Hef's never-never land as quick as they could. But you had to stay and listen to Eton Boone tell you that it was all okay. It was all just supposed to evaporate.

But it didn't evaporate. Eton Boone knew that. It went out and got in cabs and buses and subway cars, or maybe it decided it needed to walk home. But it didn't vanish. And you think to yourself, Eton Boone knows that too.

Hugh Gardiner

I had gone in and seen him with my students several times that winter. We would sit in the back and watch from there, but by late February, Boone and I had exchanged enough letters, and I had watched his talent develop to such a degree, that I resolved to go into the city alone and introduce myself in person. I thought that it would be the next logical step, and I must tell you, the prospect of actually meeting and talking with him I found quite thrilling.

For you must understand the captivation. As much of my life as I've spent in theatres and clubs and cabarets, it's still rare that I see a performance actually fulfill the promise of the stage.

Those moments of waiting are so electrifying, aren't they? What is it Garrett writes? That however old we are, when we see a stage unoccupied, we are all children again, climbing into the red velvet seats of our first *Nutcracker.* Dazzle me, we say. I am innocent. I am here to look. But so often we are disappointed, I find. All of the excitement we bring to the moment of the performance begins to drift almost the moment the play or the show begins. It's even more true of the spectacular productions. The energy which came so effortlessly from the simple elevation, the lights, the focus of a stage, all slowly dissipates behind useless pageantry.

And I think for those of us who know that feeling of being anesthetized by spectacle, we spend our lives waiting for a performer like Boone, a man who would not disappoint the lights, and the reason for that was simple. He did not act. That night I went to see him in the late winter of 1968, he did a piece on the reluctance of Eugene McCarthy, so noble but still uncertain, of politics and himself. It was a magnificent performance. One could feel the energy coming from the stage, of a man engaged in the pursuit of another man, seeking him out, seeking out just an instant of pure understanding, and giving out to us something we'd have thought was impossible to give—a moment of empathy for another human being.

As I say, I'd come with the intention of introducing myself, but as I sat and watched his performance, I saw verified on stage all of the concerns that Boone had been suggesting in his letters to me. There were such an extraordinary number of forces at play within him, keeping this talent in balance. He'd written vows to me that he should never treat the ability he'd cultivated as something he could leash and unleash on the people in his life. I'd read them over and over, but only that evening did I understand the importance to him of secluding his insight.

When the performance was through, he came down the center aisle of the club, and as he passed my table, I could see that he was still in the grip of the mind he'd found on stage. His eyes were set elsewhere, and even as I considered standing and introducing myself, I was pushed back down in my seat by what I think was a finer impulse. For I could see then that introducing myself and telling him in person the regard in which I held his work, none of that would have been a help to him in the least. That would have been for me. For him, it seemed that finding some way of managing and preserving the separate arenas of his life was the most important thing, and it occurred to me then the relevance of the relationship we'd already begun. As I watched him take a beer from the bartender and leave the club by himself, I resolved to provide him, through the letters, with a companion who would always listen to him, without judgment or self-interest, someone who would remain unknown to him as we generally know people. I would be his silent confidante. And I can tell you, at the risk of sounding perhaps a bit proud, that it was a very lucky decision on my part, for both of us, and there is ample testimony to that fact.

Linda Chaplin

Oh, don't even think about it. You'd have a better chance of getting into Fort Knox than seeing any of Boone's letters. I know. I've tried to get Hugh to release them, and I do think the idea tempts him. I mean, it's definitely something he thinks about, just because he'd like to be able to share them. Gosh, when I was at Vassar, I can remember how much he would go on about them and talk about the sorts of things they'd been writing each other. But I think that as far as letting the actual documents out of his hands, he's always felt, and still does to this day, that those letters are basically a world unto themselves, and if we all just ducked our heads in, we could only misunderstand, we'd violate it somehow. He's probably right. There was that awful mix-up with *Harper's Magazine* in 1975. They got hold of one, and Hugh nearly left Vassar he was so upset. And I know that he was approached by the people at Hardcastle maybe about ten years ago, but they were asking for some kind of exclusive rights, and they couldn't promise how many they'd use. They basically just wanted to purchase them, so Hugh had to say no. I'm sure no one's even seen a word of them in years.

Amalie Hindemuth

Eton moved out in the spring. He'd just said he was going to and, you know, it was very difficult, because I wanted to help him, but I think I just finally had to admit that maybe the most I could do was let him go. Because by then, of course, it had spread well beyond just these photographs in magazines and things. You'd be with him on the subway—he really loved and hated the subway, I think, because it was all there, you know, all these faces and lives just parading on for you to look at, and Eton simply couldn't help himself. People would come and sit opposite him and you could see him sort of fall into it. He'd cross his arms and put the palm of his hand on his face, and just look, and he'd wear dark sunglasses so people wouldn't know.

I actually remember more specifically once a taxicab ride we'd taken home very very late one night, and the driver was one of those very beautiful, very proud big Caribbean women with a lovely wrap around her head, and she had her little boy sitting up in the front seat with her. There wasn't a license, so we couldn't tell where she was from exactly, but for the whole ride we watched this little boy turning around in his seat and looking out the window, and the mother every so often trying to settle him with her hand. He was absolutely adorable, and I'd given him some brownies that we had with us for some reason, but I knew that Eton had just been mesmerized. He didn't say a word the whole ride and it was very dark, but he had his hand up over his mouth as he watched. You could tell that they'd both just over-whelmed him. At the end of the ride, we'd gotten out and Eton had to stand there on the street corner and wait for it to pass. He said that I should go on, and I just sort of left him there bending over with his hands on his knees, and spitting into the gutter. But that was very near the time he'd moved out. It had just been getting so awful like that, but there didn't seem to be anything else to do.

Eton Boone, transcribed, March 7, 1968—
*JANIS JOPLIN**

Janis, man. I was watching a clip of Janis at Monterey. Couple
nights ago. Yeah, friend of mine working on a TV show about it.†
Did you see that? *[Inaudible voice.]* You were there? You were actually there, in Monterey? Geez. I'd have gone but I'm not allowed
in that state. Got a look at Janis, though, in this documentary.
Some nice footage of Ravi Shankar too. About a half hour of it.
Thanks, Rav. *[Hits mike with forehead. Snoring sound.]*
    Yeah. But she, she was outrageous, man. Janis. She's so fucking
jacked, man. Yeeow! Look, she gets you talking like her. But
it's a sad, sad story somewhere, right. Somewhere, shit. It's right
there. Blues, blues, blues, blues. Right. Hold on, hold on. Dig this.
*[Leaves stage, returns with flask of Southern Comfort. ** Glances around, looking for something that's not there. Shrugs.]* All right. Here we go then.
[Begins stamping her foot, trying to get a rock/blues beat started.] Yow! Cha-
cha-boom-quack-quack. *[Nothing. She stops. Tries again.]* C'mon
baby. Cha-cha-boom-quack-quack, cha-cha-boom-quack. Stomp.
Stomp. *[Nothing. Stops. Looks back behind her.]*
    Hey, hey, man, what is this shit? Where are my boys? *[Looks out
at audience.]* What is this, man? Look out there. Look at you all.
Man, I can't see you all, except for this chick here with this look
like, this look like, look at you, man. Yeah, you. Keep your legs
crossed, sister. Yeah, but there's a whole bunch of people out
there, man. I can feel 'em. I can feel you, but, where the fuck did
they take my band? . . . Hey, who's the boss here? I've got some
blues to work off, baby, and someone stole my band. How'm I
s'posed to do this alone? How'm I s'posed to make it without my

---

*Janis Joplin was the preeminent white female blues singer of the late
sixties. She died in 1970.

†*Monterey Pop*, the Leacock/Pennebaker documentary about the 1967
rock festival in Monterey, California, was originally slated for television.
It was eventually released in late 1968 as a feature-length film.

**Southern Comfort, a blend of whiskey and molasses, was Janis Jo-
plin's liquor of choice.

Big Brother?* I gotta, gotta have that umph. My chug-a-chug-a-quack-quack. My thump, thump. Hunh? Thump, thump. Hunh? Chug, chug. Right? You like that? *[Addressing young woman at first table, left.]* That's it, right there, right? You never thought you'd see that. *[Shimmies for her.]* Stomp, stomp. Yeeeeeow! Yeah, 'cause I'll tell you something, sister. If my boys were here, you'd see—it's better here, baby, better up here with my boys, my Big Brother, than it's ever been with any man, that's the kick in the ass. Much better here, right, for Janis, and I know—I get myself fixed the same way. I get all dolled up with a little Southern Comfort.

Un-hunh. There's nothing a little Southern Comfort won't fix. Give me a little of that, baby. Yeah, you give me enough of that juice and it'll half kill me. See? But that's the deal, baby. That's the deal. Get that chick out here half-dead and we'll try to keep her alive with a little stomp-stomp, a little chug-a-chug-a-chug. Right. That'll keep her on her feet. That'll keep her heart pumping, baby, that's what makes it beat. A little chug-a-chug-a-chug. And that's entertainment, baby. That's a show, but where is the band? Where the fuck is it, man? Are you back there, baby? *[Looks behind stage, returns.]*

'Cause I kinda feel like I'm starting to slip, man. Got some blues to work off here, baby, gotta have my fix, my little Davie-Davie-whack!† Whack! Oooww! Chug-a-chug-a-quack-quack. C'mon, c'mon, man, a- c-c′ c′ c′ c′ c'mon, man, I can't do this alone, man, and you know it, people! You, you know it out there. Stage says get half-dead and come out here and we'll see what we can do, but now you go changing the rules. Well, fuck this shit, man, help me out. Someone get up here and boogie with Janis. Man, we don't need the drums. Just get up here, baby. Get up here. Break down this fucked-up barrier, man. You and me. Yes, you chick, you chick, you chick. Get up here, baby, and do me a favor. I've got some blues to work off. I've got some—

Hey? Hey! Shut the fuck up, man . . . You shut up. I'm up here. I'm ready baby. Janis is up here and she's pouring her heart out. She's spilling her guts out all over the stage, man, and she don't need your talking, man. I don't need that . . . What's that, what's

---

*Big Brother and the Holding Company was the name of Janis Joplin's backup band in 1968.

†Boone could here be referring to drummer David Getz.

that you're saying, man? I know, I know. Janis knows. What is it, "Woman needs a man, ball and chain." "Bitch on stage needs a man." Well, let me tell you something. Let me tell you something. Janis needs more than a man right now. Always needed something more than a man . . . That's right, feel it, fuck it, shoot it, lick it, suck it, man, whatever, give me something. Right now, man. Janis is slipping. *[Laughs, falls down.]* It worked, man. It worked. You took this chick's blood away. Took her blood, took her band, man. You did it.

[Lies flat on her back.] And man, and you just wanna know what it's like. That's the shit. That's all you want. Wanna hear it from the other side, what a ghost sounds like. Huh. Well, I got some bad news for you, baby. Sounds just the same. Sounds like *[starts to wail refrain from "Ball and Chain."]* Way-ooh-whaaah-oooh-whaah-oah-ooooh-waaaaaahn! Sounds like, help me, baby! Somebody help me. Get me where I'm s'posed to be, because, baby, baby baby baby, I just don't know where it is! *[Laughs.]* Hear it? Sounds just the same, just the goddamn same—'cause this ain't life, baby, this ain't life. This is something different. Because Janis didn't leave nothing for Janis. All of it's stomp, stomp, that's the kick in the ass, that's better than any man ever, my little Davie whack-whack, and he ain't even here. Ain't none of them here. Don't be doing that, man. Don't be leaving Janis up here alone. She's trying to break down that barrier, man. Don't be leaving her up back there alone.

Hilary Richman

It was just incredible how people didn't see it, acting like he was cruel, like *he* was too mean. *E.B.* was mean. Please. People are so stupid, they couldn't even see it was them. He wasn't the mean one. He wasn't the petty one. He wasn't selfish and egotistical and grotesque. It's just what he saw, and let's face it, they all wouldn't have come to see him if they didn't agree. You know that. If people weren't such ghouls, if they didn't all like coming and watching him do his little fuck routines, then they wouldn't have, you know, flocked the way they did.

I mean, it didn't have to be like that, but just look at who he's dealing with. I mean, how far do you have to go? The bar down the block. Just go outside. Anywhere. Just walk down the street, and you'll see it. They're all just complete petty liars, they lie to themselves all day long, and I don't know what they expected E.B. to do about it. Sit there and say, oh, you're all so beautiful? Well, maybe if they hadn't all been so busy lying to themselves, they might have seen that that's what he *was* doing a lot of the time. I mean, people just don't know the difference. He wanted to, E.B. wanted it to be better and more beautiful, of course he did. No one wanted more for it to be like the good ones than E.B. Why the fuck do you think he was doing it?

Linda Chaplin

We actually have Hilary Richman on film. It's great. It was at Jes' For Laffs. It was an evening during the spring of '68, and Kelso and I were there in our usual place, setting up. We had this wagon full of equipment from the Vassar Audio/Visual, so we used to have to get there at 7:30. And this gorgeous young black man started hovering around us like this woodland fairy, right. We'd seen him sitting at his table when we came in, just perfect and compact with such fair smooth skin, but he'd come over when we were setting up. He had a drink in his hand, and finally he just asked us, "What are you filming?" He was very timid in a way, but when he finally sort of popped the question, he was almost confrontational. He said, "Who are you here to film?" We said Boone and he sort of huffed. He said, "Why?" and we said there were people interested in what Boone was doing. Again he said, "Why?" I said that a lot of people were very excited by Boone. And then he said, to me, "Are you excited by Boone?"—this very forward remark. Finally Kelso sort of turned on him and asked him what he wanted. You know, "What *do* you want?" And he just smiled.

I have to say, there was something very charming about him. He was very snooty and all, but he had this wonderful, beautiful face, and when he smiled and looked at you—I'll get crucified for this, but it was like Garbo—when she looks into a man's eyes it just kills you, right. He would bat his eyelashes at you and give that little coquettish grin. It was amazing. I mean, this is someone I'm sure people would just go up to on the street, right, and tell him, "Excuse me, you are very attractive, you just are"—I mean, I'm sure he got that.

But it was also the way he acted. God, it was such a performance. He wanted the camera to make love to him, right—he'd just been drawn to it. He said to Kelso, "Is the film in?" and Kelso said yes, and I remember Hilary leaning over and looking in the lens and saying, "but it isn't on." And he stood up and took out a pack of cigarettes and picked one out with these lovely fingers and he waited. He waited for a light. I couldn't get over it. Finally Kelso flipped him a matchbook but he just took it, looked at it—this was wonderful—then he looked at me and said, "Would you do this? I don't like matches." He said, "I always think they're going to flare up in my hands," and he gave this sort of parasol smile. So I lit his cigarette, and he had this fabulous expression as I was lighting it—he was looking at me and his eyes were glittering, and once the cigarette was lit, he just stood there and waited. Finally he said, "Do you wait for Boone to turn it on?" And we said yes, and he walked away. He walked up towards the stage with his cigarette. The lights were better there, and he stood there just smoking. It was irresistible. Finally I said to Kelso, "Oh, go ahead, just film him. He wants it so much." So Kelso turned it on and it's a fabulous shot, he's just standing there by the stage and he doesn't react at all. Kelso zooms in on him and he takes a deep drag, he turns perfectly profile and does this slow, beautiful French inhale. Oh, "Get me that boy!" right. "Get me that face!" Hilary was great. I loved Hilary.

Hilary Richman

There was a spring vacation. Toddy and I went and stayed with E.B. in New York. E.B. and Toddy hadn't seen each other in two years, and I went along because I had nothing to do. I mean, San Diego. Please. San Diego sucked. I was coming from this ridiculous military prison and I just had nothing in that house. I slept on this couch in E.B.'s room, with fishing pictures of E.B., and I had to go out to dinner with Joe and Anne and listen to Joe's jokes. It was ridiculous, I hated it, so my mother said I should go to New York with Toddy.

I don't think Joe wanted me to. Of course not. He should have been happy I was out of his hair, but he didn't want me to get in the way of this big family reunion he'd set up. He just didn't like me in the least, and he was completely petrified of E.B. E.B. was like this danger man, so I think the idea of me going too—I mean, what was going to happen to his little golden boy in Hilary and E.B.'s clutches? But I went and we had a wonderful time. I finally felt I was somewhere I could breathe. I was sixteen. We went and stayed for two weeks. I had a wonderful time. Toddy and I went back the next summer. We might even have gone two or three times, I don't really remember. Amalie would know.

I remember one thing from the first trip, though, because it was the first time Toddy and I saw him. We'd gone to see E.B.'s show. He'd gotten us this table on the side, and I'm sure we were both just sitting there with our drinks like, "Aren't we just the hottest shit in Manhattan?" And after about a zillion hours of these morons telling knock-knock jokes, E.B. had come out and done his thing. He did Jerry Lewis talking about how comedy is supposed to work and this weekend he'd had with Charlie Chaplin, and I remember just looking at it and thinking, "Jesus Christ, you know, look at fucking E.B." I couldn't believe it. I was just sitting there like, finally. You know, finally someone has the guts to get up and say, "Look, I don't care who the fuck you are, you're full of shit." I mean, this guy, I've hardly ever seen him in my life but he's my fucking stepbrother, and he turns out to be this genius. I was just completely blown away.

But afterwards, we had to go to this party someplace to find Amalie. For some reason E.B. felt compelled to go, so we had to take these three subways uptown and walk through this incredibly dirty New York rain to find Amalie. When we finally got there it was like this opium den. It was incredibly dark and smoky, and you could just hear Amalie and all these English morons crawling around on the floor. They were under this plastic Twister mat and laughing, we're so funny, we're so groovy, hardy-hardy-har.

I wanted to leave immediately. I didn't know what we were doing there in the first place, and I don't know how the hell E.B. could even stand it, but he just disappeared. He'd gone into the kitchen for light. I could see him through the opening, in this bright white kitchen with this completely black frame from the party. E.B. was just standing there opening and closing the icebox door with this little pickle in his hand, and then he sat down at this grungy kitchen table. He was just sitting on this orange metal chair, and this woman came into the kitchen. She got a beer from the icebox and then stood in front of him, and she put her hand through his hair. She looked like this Joe Namath stewardess with all her eye makeup and her hair and this beauty mark, and she leaned over and kissed him. Then she took him by the hand and sort of pulled him off the chair and into the dark room where everybody was, and it just made me feel so ill. I felt so bad for him.

And I don't know. I didn't want to feel bad for E.B. I just wanted to get away. I went off and I hid in the bathroom. I had to go down this incredibly long hallway, this ridiculous hallway. It was like a railroader and they'd fixed it up like it was supposed to be some psychedelic jungle or something, with all this toilet paper hanging down from the ceiling, these streamers taped up and these big red light bulbs. I went into this bathroom and just sat on the toilet, but then these two people came in and wanted to use it together. I think they wanted to shoot up or something or fuck, so I had to go in to the bedroom. I just stayed there with the lights out.

I remember just sitting on this radiator and leaning up against this giant window, and I could see the entire hallway from in there, and then I saw E.B. He was coming down the hallway through all these streams of toilet paper, and he didn't see me. He was just walking straight ahead like a car wash. All these toilet paper things were blowing on his face, and he stopped. He stopped there for like a minute just to feel it, and you could see him breathing. He was just letting these things brush his cheeks and face, and I know it sounds ridiculous, but I'm just back there looking at him, like, shit, there he is. The guy who was up on stage turning all those people on, there he is, and it's E.B.

But then he came into the room, and he saw me. He said, "Are you waiting for the bathroom?" And I said, "No." And he said, "Are Boopy and Doopy in there?"—I don't remember their names. I said, "I don't know, it's two people." And he just sort of nodded, and we waited there. It was just so dark, and the window was freezing. It felt like the back of my head was wet, and I could see his eyes. The whites of his eyes were just sky blue, they were this incredible color, and I just felt like my head was fucking glued to this window. I was just frozen. I don't know.

Kelso Chaplin

Hugh was pretty obsessed with him. He was incredibly into the films. We'd gotten this schedule going. I'd film one of Boone's Thursday performances and then develop it over the weekend at NYU so we'd have it in time for Hugh's teas on Tuesdays.

This one time, though. I was working part-time as a projectionist at the RKO downtown, and we were showing an old Buster Keaton—*The General.* I was up there setting up the third reel one afternoon when Hugh walked in. He looked like he'd just come from the reading of a will. He was in a three-piece suit and he seemed really fragile. He pulled up a stool and just put his hands on his knees. He didn't say anything at first. We both just sat there and watched the movie together for about ten minutes, and then he said, completely out of the blue, "Kelso, I'm worried about him." I didn't really know what he meant, but then he started talking about the letters. He said Boone's letters had been getting pretty desperate, and Hugh was worried that Boone was in trouble. He talked about the precariousness of what Boone was doing, the importance of what Boone was doing, the importance of our doing whatever we could to help. I don't know how long it lasted, but it was this intense little speech, and when he was finished, I don't think I said anything. He asked if he could stay and watch the rest of *The General,* so we sat there next to each other and watched it. It was a very weird little visit. He left right after the movie was finished, but he asked me if I'd come up early the next Tuesday, because he said he had an idea.

So the next Tuesday, I took the early train. I had the Syd

Barrett with me, where Barrett basically waits for his acid to kick in. When I got to Hugh's, we put it on and watched it together, just Hugh and me in his living room with the shutters closed. Hugh groaned through the whole thing—the Barrett actually was an incredible performance. No one could vouch for the imitation, it's true, but Boone absolutely turned the club inside out, just shattered the fourth wall, and it looked like the whole thing was making Hugh sweat. I'd gotten up to rewind it for a second look, but he stopped me. He went over to his bureau and took out this leather-bound check book. He offered to start paying me for the work I was doing. He said he wanted me to "monitor" Boone for him, stay close, make sure Boone wasn't killing himself basically. He actually wrote out a check for a hundred dollars right there, and he made me promise I wouldn't tell Boone that we'd even had this discussion. He said, "You mustn't let on what you're doing, Kelso. He mustn't know." It was incredible, and that was it. I was probably still sitting there with this check in my lap when people started coming in for tea. Linda came in, and I've got this check in my wallet from Hugh to babysit Boone basically. We rolled the Barrett again for all the students, and then we analyzed it for two or three hours. Hugh never even looked at me.

Eton Arthur Boone, transcribed, March 14, 1968—
SYD BARRETT*

> *[Takes tab of paper out of jacket pocket. Puts it to mouth, licks once. Twice. Tastes. Licks a third time, and then puts the whole tab in his mouth. Chews it. Takes sip from glass of orange juice and swallows. Stands. Looks out as if over the edge of a building.]*

---

*Syd Barrett was one of the founding members of the British psyche-delic rock group Pink Floyd and was its lead vocalist, composer and lyricist from 1966–68. Allegedly, Barrett's heavy experimentation with hallucinogenic drugs, primarily LSD, strained his relationship with the band and may have led to his departure from the group in early 1968. It has been suggested by Amalie Hindemuth that Boone may have seen one of the group's free Hyde Park shows in the early summer of 1967.

Waiting, waiting, waiting. Feels like waiting's all I do here these days. What's it, lag time, eh? Me as lag time, waiting up on me mum's Cambridge rooftop. *[Peers out over edge of stage.]* S'like in Victoria Station, eh, waiting for the train to come in. Or King's Cross, with the great big King's Cross clock—*[half-sings]* "and the lad he sat all day but never did it tock." Had to kill a little time till his vision did arrive, till Piper* came and took him.

We could kill the time together—shall we? Let's do. I have brought the knife, swallowed it like a carnival junkie, d'you see? Would you like? I have some more. *[Extends his hand.]* Vision's on a black market, friend. That's our age. Like some? *[Waits.]* No? *[Shrugs. Comes up to the edge of the stage again, leans over and looks, as if down at train tracks. Stares at the palm of his hand. Moves his fingers individually, slowly, then quickly.]*

. . . No, not here just yet, not quite, but you can feel a change, you can, just the taste in your mouth, the way it sits in your stomach, its breath. Same as what you do there. I can see you. There in the station pub, shall I imagine you? *[Leans over with hands on knees, peering out.]* There, there, swirl your glass below your nose. Smell it. Very evil stench, liquor—not very nice at all, but once it's inside the old tum tum, once it's flowing in your veins, well, there's your best friend back. And that sip's all you need sometimes, isn't it, the reminder. That's why you do it. So you can feel it again in your mouth, all through you, hear it say, "There is something else, my friend. You haven't forgotten me now, have you?"

No, I haven't. I won't forget ever, because it's true there's something else. I have seen it. I have seen the world go all angel-filled. I have held colors in my hands, and I have tasted songs. I have seen the breeze, watched it push sounds and light, felt cobblestones melt beneath my feet. I have felt the steam of London grates rise up through me hot, and my bones have frozen like icicles. I have breathed in the air from an angel's lungs and felt her all through me, telling me it's so.

And when my mates come too, I have tried with all my might to share, I have. When they're along, and we stand side by side

---

*"The Piper at the Gates of Dawn," Pink Floyd's first LP, was released in 1967.

and watch a kitchen window go stained glass right before our noses, I have said, "Remember this, please, let's remember this. This is what's been kept from us all along," and they say yes, they do, they see it as I say. "There's sense to be made of this yet, Syd, senses we never dreamed of." And I have dreamed, dreamed for us all.

But then I've felt the dream go too. The angels flee, I know the sound of it, their wings flapping away say, "Baaaaack now, Sydney, back from whence you came. No, no. 'S'not yours, little Syd, little Cambridge pup." Isn't fair, though. Isn't fair! Vision so warm goes so nasty cold and leaves you alone in the dark. Where's warmth, then? Where's light? In friends? Mates? Well, go to them then, once it's done, once you're back in sanity and ask them, "Do you remember, how wise the roses in the garden are? 'Member?" I've looked deep in their eye and asked them, but all I see are angels fleeing, narrowing down into pinpoints till they're gone, and then they smile their vegetable smiles for me, say, "No, Syd, I can't be sure anymore." "But you were there! You saw it, you did. You said you did."

But no, it's back to stodgy sense for them, it's back to the tool-kit world for building boxes, and all you're left with then is yourself, and you look at the sky, and it's just barely breathing, on the point of expiration when moments before it was so beaming, and you say to yourself, "This isn't quite so right. This isn't as real as what the kitchen window showed me, as what the Piper let me see. I have to get back!"

[Stops. Cocks head, puts hand to ear, listening.] He is coming, though. Can you hear? But no, vision approaches not by air, not by sea, but by feel. *[Looks at hands.]* Show me, you. I've done mine, now you. *[Presses left palm with right hand, expression transforms. Amazement. Delight. Undulates his hands in front of him, giggling.]* It's here. Prayers are answered, gifts are opened, the Piper has come just like he said he would. Glory day! *[Extends his hand to audience, flat-palmed.]* See? *[Wiggles his fingers.]*

[Takes out a book of matches, lights one, holds it. Takes a cookie wrapper out of his pocket, rolled in the shape of a cylinder. Lights the wrapper, which then flies up toward ceiling and then floats down gently. He tries to catch it on his nose, laughing hysterically. Blows it out toward audience.] "Step up! Step up! He fast becomes the madman, right before your very eyes! He sees it's amazing, this one, yes. *[Leaps from stage, prowls through crowd.]*

Ripper's on the loose, beastly beastie, feeding on meat, the animal, the fangy beast who sees, the toothpasted soothsayer, and what does he see? Soothsayer sees . . . *[surveys club with hands on hips, looking up at ceiling]* . . . sees *dark*. Dark, so bloody pitchy black, but bright lights too, like stars. *[Looking at lighting fixtures.]* Soothsayer sees stars, sees ethereal sky right here and don't deny it. Soothsayer sees end of universe, its very edge—brick wall. *[Points at stage.]* Brick wall's where it ends, right? But look at the bricks close. Can you see the bricks? They're dancing! They're dancing, Sydney boy, can you see?" "Yes, I do, they do." "Promise, then." "Promise, yes. *[Puts hand over heart]* 'I do solemnly swear these bricks dance. I do solemnly swear ethereal sky hangs here, pitchy black and brightly lit with expanding dancing wall of bricks at very edge.' " "Edge of what, Sydney boy?" "Imagination!" "Yes . . . but?" ". . . Imagination dances!" Yes! Who else sees it?

[Sweeps through audience looking at people.] Who sees it, who sees it? *[Addresses third table, two men.]* Here, you fellows from King's Cross, from the King's Cross pub, with your noses stuck in the *Sun*. Can I have your attention for a moment? You, sir, do you—close the paper for a second, would you please? *[Jumps up onto table. Crouching.]* Now, look. *[Points at wall, addresses man on left.]* Do you see? Come on, King's Cross newspaper junkie, put your smudgy *Sun* away, and look for me at the bricks, edge of ethereal sky. Can you see they dance? Look at them! *[Man shakes his head.]* But they are, look at them! *[Waits.]* No? *[Man relents finally, nods.]* You're lying! *[Syd delighted, hops off table, pointing.]* You're lying, cheater! Liar, liar, pants on fire—you don't see. I can see it in your face, the Piper lets me see. No hiding here, friend. Everything shows, every smile, every tear still shows, and how you cry, I can see, and how you laugh, and which comes easier, I can see, and I can see, sir, sir newspaper junkie of King's Cross row, I can see that no bricks ever danced for you.

[Looks up, searching.] Who else, then? Who else? *[Moves on to other tables, prowling.]* Beastly beastie finds . . . *[choosing]* you! You. Warm you. Sweet, beautiful you. *[Crouches by woman, mid-forties, delicate, hair swept up into a beehive.]* D'you see? Shake your head if no. *[She shakes her head.]* No, and I can't tell you, can I? No. I wish I could. May I sit with you? *[She nods. He places himself in her lap very gently, takes her hand in his, looks into her eyes.]* Do you not see what's inside, dear Mum? Do you not see what I am? Do you not see that the whole world's here, begging to be set free? *[She shrugs, uncomfortably.]* But

Mum, you must. *[Traces her face with his fingertips.]* You should try for me, because I will not be here much longer. I need you to see for me, I need you to believe, that I know. I know it's happening, Mum, I'm going, but I choose it, I have to, and if you could see it, you'd be coming too . . . *[He places his hands on both sides of her head, pulls her face inches from his.]* Look, Mum, look! Can't you see? Look in my eyes. Look at me. I'm leaving. Don't you—won't you please see?

[She says nothing, frightened. He kisses her on the forehead and gets off her lap, pushes himself away, starts walking backwards through the club, looking at her.] Then I'm going. I'm going, Mum, but when you think of me, remember I said good-bye. I said good-bye best I could. If you'd looked, you'd have seen—all what I did and all what I said, all that I sang and all that I breathed, all was my invitation to you and all was my farewell. You should have seen. *[Looks at club, opens arms.]* Anyone? *[No one moves. He lowers arms, turns, leaves club. Barely audible, from Grand Street.]* There you are, Piper! I'm here! Show me all! *[Shouts and screams trail out as he races down Grand Street.]**

Hilary Richman

Joe and my mom had laden Toddy and me with all these gifts we were supposed to give each other, from them. I have no idea what they were thinking, but I had these packages for E.B., and Toddy had these presents for me. It was completely absurd. But finally we just decided to get it over with, so we had this little party. We were down at E.B.'s place on Perry Street, on the second floor. Amalie was there, and some Spanish guy who lived way uptown and grew pot on his terrace. We all just sat there and mocked the whole thing. Toddy got this shirt that was like ten sizes too small, and I got these hanging silver balls from Joe, these ridiculous click-clack things that are supposed to show conservation of energy or something. Gee, thanks.

---

*Boone did not return to the club that evening, despite a stomping ninety-second ovation from the crowd—K.C.

But I'd given E.B. this sketch pad that was supposed to be from my mother. It actually wasn't even a sketch pad—I think you just call it a painting block or watercolor block, which Joe Boone had gone out and bought for my mother to give to E.B., but they were trying to pass it off as my mother's present. It was ridiculous. I even remember Amalie making E.B. read the card out loud, which was very my mom, you know, "Heard you were *drawing* well at the club. Thought this might help you with your comedy *sketches.* Hope you're having fun at your new *pad."* You know, "Love, Anne." It was just ludicrous and I was thinking, who do they think they're dealing with? Like E.B. isn't going to know this was Joe's idea. The whole thing was absurd.

Anyway, at some point E.B. and I had to go out and get some ice. This Spanish man had some drink he wanted to make that needed cucumbers and something like eighty-five pounds of ice so we could take them up on the roof. So E.B. and I went out to this place called The Food Box, and we were walking there and I just told him—I couldn't help myself—I said, "You know the watercolor block is from Joe Boone, don't you?" And he just smiled. He said, "You think?" like, no shit, Hilary. And I asked him if I could write the thank-you note. You know, "Dear Anne, thank you so much for your present. Gee, I guess you really know me now. Love, E.B." I mean, that's what they wanted, right? It would have made their fucking year.

But E.B. was still trying to act like it was perfectly normal, even though I could tell deep down he thought it was comical. And I don't know why, but I just wanted him to admit it. I wanted him to keep playing. I was talking about Joe and my mom, and telling him about Joe trying to have these conversations with me about shit like military strategy and taking me to this golf range. And E.B. started imitating him. He started doing these imitations of Joe Boone, of things like Joe clearing his throat, and Joe's golf swing and blowing his nose. I couldn't believe it. I was in heaven. I was practically jumping up and down on the sidewalk.

And then, I don't know, it just evolved into this imitation of Joe buying the sketch pad. It was like this performance. E.B. said Joe Boone had gone to this store that was all the way on the other side of town from the radio station. He said he'd gone right after work, and E.B. was acting it, how Joe Boone would walk into this Schiavoni's Art Store with his slacks and his keys, and how he insisted on hunting around for this pad without asking anyone. E.B. said he probably spent twenty minutes just wandering up and down the aisles trying to recognize it, and I was like, "An hour, please. He probably had to sit down five times." But it was incredible how much it was like Joe, just with his hands in his pocket, his fucking vibrato whistle. E.B. was on the street doing this, pretending to go up and down these aisles, and looking at all these pads and shit and paintbrushes and not being able to make up his mind. But then he finally had these two pads and he couldn't tell which one was right, so he goes up to this man, Mr. Schiavoni, and he's holding these two pads in his hands, and he says, you know, "Which is the one Blue used?"

I just shut my mouth. I mean, I'd been so turned on, I guess I hadn't even been thinking about it. But when he said this thing about which one was his mom's pad, I don't know, it was so fucking sad, the whole thing just stopped. We just kept walking. We bought the ice at this place from this cretin who was in there behind the counter, and on the way back, it was total silence. We were walking along like some dirge until finally E.B. said he was sorry for saying the thing about his mom. He said it wasn't nice of him to ruin the fun.

And I don't know. All I can really remember is being pissed off that he'd said that. You know, I was just thinking, "E.B., Jesus. You don't have to protect me." I mean, maybe with everyone else, maybe it was true, he had to apologize for seeing how fucked up they all were. He practically had to wear these fucking horse blinders all day long just so people wouldn't freak in his presence, just so they could sleep at night. But I just thought, you know, fuck them if they can't deal with who E.B. is. Then they should just leave, I mean, if they're going to be so selfish and hold it against E.B. just because he sees who they really are. I mean, wasn't. I just wish I'd had the guts to say it to him, you know, "Don't you ever fucking do that to me, E.B. Don't you ever apologize," because he had nothing to be ashamed of. Fuck, I mean, what E.B. did, it was the most amazing thing, it should have been such a beautiful thing, the way he could look at you and just see, you know, just know, and I wanted to tell him. I would have grabbed him and said, "Come on, don't stop, E.B." but I didn't. I didn't want to freak him out.

Kelso Chaplin

April 4th, Martin Luther King was killed, and Buddy closed the club. It was a Thursday, and actually Boone didn't show up till about ten. I was at the club with Buddy, the two of us were sitting and drinking, talking about anything, you know, The Bowery Boys—anything to keep our minds off it. Buddy'd already called everyone who was supposed to perform that night, but nobody was ever able to get hold of Boone. We figured we'd sit and wait for him to show, then we could all go home.

When he finally got there, he was looking very nervous, just pacing and jittery. The place was empty. We asked him if he'd heard about King. Yeah, yeah, of course he'd heard. Everybody'd heard, but Boone came in and he said, "Yeah, I'm going to do his assassin." Buddy and I just looked at each other. Boone said he'd been out walking in Riverside Park all evening, thinking about it, but Buddy told him to forget about it, the place was closed. Boone looked at him, then he kind of slapped his hands together and kicked the ground. It looked like someone had stolen his cab. You know, and I was thinking, what's the deal here, Boone? Martin Luther King.

But you only had to look twice to see what was going on. He wasn't saying, "Dammit, I had a routine." He was saying, "Dammit, I blew it. I went ahead and thought about the assassin, and I'm not going to be able to get rid of him." And he looked at us and said, "You know, it's not like I ate a bad piece of fish," meaning he couldn't just go take a shit and flush it all down the toilet.

Well, I don't know. Boone was pretty weird. I don't think Buddy really understood what Boone meant, but he left. He'd had enough. He left Boone the keys, and we said we'd lock up. So it was just Boone and me there. We were sitting at the bar, and he'd really been hit by the assassination. He was saying, "Man, I just couldn't believe it when it happened." He said, "I couldn't believe someone would do that," but then he looked at me and said, "But now I can." And he said, "Want to see?"

Well, all right, when everyone was in the club, I guess it felt kind of safe. And behind the lens it was even safer, but sitting there alone at the bar and Boone asking me if he could get up on stage and do his James Earl Ray for me before any of us know who James Earl Ray is—no way, man. I really didn't want any part of it. Not fun. Not safe. I mean, I would've been doing him a favor, I know, but when he asked, I just wanted to finish my beer and get the hell out of the club. Linda hated me for this—you know, the command performance of a lifetime—but you just couldn't want to see it. No one could.

So I went back to Hugh. Next time I saw Hugh, I gave him back his check. I said, the other night he came in and wanted to do King's assassin. Hugh just shook his head. He said, "I know, I know. He wrote me about it." He looked helpless.

Erin Hirt

We met, it was a friend of a friend–type thing. I had a girlfriend Janice who worked with me on a lot of shoots, and she knew this musician Pietro Goldberg. Boone had seen my picture in a Sealy's ad she and I did, and he said something to Pietro. I guess Pietro sort of took it from there. There was a show at the Armory for this Italian guy who did giant prints, and Janice said to me, he's here, Boone came, he wants to meet you. She kept asking me if I was scared, but the problem was, I didn't really know who he was. Everyone was acting like, he's here, he's here, but I didn't know who they were talking about. I'd just go out on the runway thinking, which one is he, but I couldn't even find Pietro. Boone told me later they'd been in the back drinking Orange Juliuses.

We saw them afterwards. There's this big room with animal rugs where they waited for us. Janice and I came out and the two of them were on this bear rug and Boone had sneakers. Pietro had flowers for Janice and Boone had one foot up on this bear's head. He just looked so young. I guess I'd been expecting someone older, but he was my age, and we started talking. He was asking a lot of questions about modeling, and we showed them how you're supposed to walk, and what you're supposed to do with your eyes, and he was listening. He looked amazed by the whole thing. Janice was telling stories about it, she was talking and talking, and he was staring at her and smiling, but I just didn't know who he was. So finally I said, "So I don't even know what you do." And I remember Janice kind of covering her mouth and laughing. She said, "Boone is the hottest comic in New York." And I said, "You tell jokes?" because he didn't really look like a guy who would tell jokes, and he just said, "I do what I want. Arthur *is* my middle name." It was very funny, it was very funny when he said it, but Janice had no idea.

But then we had to leave, we had to get downtown, so they walked us out and got us a cab. Pietro gave Janice these flowers, and Boone said, "Hold on," and he reached into his pocket and gave me half a Hershey bar. Janice and I were in the cab and she was saying, you shouldn't even think about eating it.

Amalie Hindemuth

I suppose she was very attractive. Very. She had long red hair and was very thin. Very fine features. She had a face like a doll in a way, like a Barbie doll, or one of those cutout women from the paper cutout books that you can put the different dresses on. You know, she was one of those women who could get away with wearing something chartreuse. But it always surprised me, and this is not to say anything against Erin—I don't really know her very well—but I suppose with Eton I was always very wary of estimating how important something was to him.

Erin Hirt

He would take me out to Sheep's Meadow. We would go to the boat pond in Central Park, in the summer. We'd get a rowboat, and he wouldn't be high or anything like that. He'd row out to the middle of the pond and say, "Sorry, out of gas," and we'd just sit out there. He'd talk. He said once when two people had the same thought at the same time, that's what angels waited for. He talked about how angels always knew, and that's what they liked to watch, when two people were thinking the same thing on opposite sides of the street. And he would talk about how he used to think it was such a funky sight to sit there in the boat right in the middle of nature, with these enormous buildings shooting up all around and with us right in the middle of it, and it's hard to say the way he said it, but I know I was wearing just a simple white cotton dress that he liked. It had this beautiful stitched collar, embroidered, and he said, "The people up there in the buildings are looking down from their windows and they're thinking, 'Red hair, white dress, and that guy keeps waving his hands around.' "

Hugh Gardiner

You must understand. Though I never once questioned devoting myself as I did to his career and to his life, there were drawbacks to our arrangement, certainly—I'm thinking in particular of the beginning. It took some time to know the limits of my province. He wrote me quite often at this time, you see, perhaps twice a week, to express the concerns he'd been having with his work, and as many of those concerns as I tried to address in my responses, I was wary of overstepping my bounds and offering advice when it hadn't been solicited. The Piedmont show is a prime example that comes to mind. If I'd occupied a less discreet position in his life, I might have advised him against participating in such frivolous pursuits. But I withheld my opinion. Unfortunately, at the time I didn't think it was my place.

Buddy D'Angelo

Sure, sure. Hey, look. Man does not live by stand-up alone. I don't care who you are. Okay, today, sure, but what a life. Boone, he never would have wanted to travel like that. He liked J.F.L., J.F.L. liked him, but you need a little something, just for the future, you know, and I told him I'd see what I could do. Boone said, sure, so I call Hank. I figure, why not? Hank's a friend, it's a New York show, and God knows they needed writers. I think Solly and Bert were the only two there for the summer. ABC had given Hank a summer slot to see if he could get a jump on the competition. It was his last chance, and he was going crazy.

Jesus, first thing Boone does, though, I get a call from Hank. He says they were having their first meeting together, the four of them, throwing around ideas. Boone says he's got one, first time he opens his mouth. Bert and Solly are sitting there, let's see what the kid's got. Boone says, okay, we've got some comedian out there on stage telling rotten jokes, you know, "and boy are my arms tired," the vaudeville crap—Hank's telling me, can you believe this? with Solly and Bert there? Solly and Bert *wrote* those goddamn jokes. But Boone wanted these two canes to come on from opposite sides of the stage, you know, to drag the guy off. Tomatoes are flying up at him. The canes, they're fishing for his neck, they both wrap around and pull from opposite sides, and plop, the comedian's head falls off. It goes rolling around the stage telling the same rotten jokes, "so I bit him."

Hank says, "Buddy, what the hell are you giving me? This is 'The Hank Piedmont Show.' " I say, "Hank, wake up and smell the coffee."

Bert Niemann

I met Hank in the early '60s. I was in Vegas doing some spots, hanging around. You know, *there* was a time. *There* were people. It was fabulous. You had Sammy, you had Dino, you had Peter Lawford, you had people who were fun to be around. Hank was putting together this little show with Nabisco, and he was scared. He's a nice guy, but deep down, I'm telling you, he's a scared little kid. You know, there's people in this business that kind of loaf around with the big boys—ah, but he shouldn't hear this from me. Hank knew that I wrote for George Burns and Fred Allen so I knew what it was all about. I was there at the beginning. He asked me to come East and write for him, and I said, "What the hell."

We wanted solid, good, old-fashioned comedy. You can tell me about your Eddie Pryors and all this business, this garbage that you see today. But the comedy that works, that gets to people, is the old stuff. I don't care what they're doing now today with the dirty words and God knows what, but if you do a good old-fashioned sketch with a doctor and a nurse, or a fish down a man's pants, people laugh and no one's gonna change that, am I right? Nowadays, I could go around, I could go to a college, I could do old jokes, and the kids love it. Look at Bob Hope. You know, they never heard these things before.

These days, it's a whole different thing. No one knows how to write a good four- or five-minute sketch, you know? And the variety shows are full of these disco numbers. Music like that doesn't fit into a variety-type show. You can't go from a comedy number to a big sexy dance with a lot of tits flying around on the screen. Because you need a wholesome kind of atmosphere. The whole world is screwed up. You can't do a show that you could do thirty years ago, where the whole family could sit and watch and laugh and sing and have a good time, because we're doing everything for eleven-year-old kids. All the movies coming out, everything on TV, it's all for eleven-year-old kids. What the fuck do they know?

Erin Hirt

He used to buy me clothes. I would get home and there would be this dress waiting for me on the bed, this box and maybe some flowers. I'd open the box and it was like being in a play because I would put it on and it still smelled new, and I would sit in the kitchen with the radio and wait for him. He would come over from the club really late, and I'd be wearing the dress he'd gotten me, and the buzzer would ring. It was really a loud buzzer from downstairs that he would hit three times just to let me know he was coming, because he liked for me to answer it wearing the thing he'd gotten me that day. When I would open the door, he would smile and say, "Miss Hirt," and I would turn around for him.

Linda Chaplin

Boone started to have problems with our filming in around the fall of '68. Somewhere along the line, he'd sensed a change in his career. He felt it before we could, right, and he didn't want the cameras there recording it.

I'm trying to think now. We have thirty-one exposures on film, and I think we missed about four or five weeks, so that's thirty-six weeks, call it nine months from about the middle of January, '68. So it must have been, what, early September. He came up to us one night after a show—it's the Rose Kennedy, which Kelso isn't that crazy about but I actually think is fabulous because he does so little talking. He just comes out on stage, and she's just heard about Bobby. She just starts weeping, this horrible, croaking weeping, and anger and rage. Kelso's right—it doesn't really go anywhere, but it was horrifying and wonderful to be there.

Kelso probably would've liked it better if he hadn't been doing the camera.

Well, anyway, Boone came up to us after the show as we were packing up to leave—and this is something that he'd never really done before—but he asked if Kelso and I would consider not filming him the next Thursday. He said he thought there could be more stuff like the Rose Kennedy, and we might not want to waste our film on it. We didn't really say if we would or we wouldn't—Kelso and I just thought he was trying to be polite. But we actually did bring the cameras the next Thursday, and that was the last exposure—or I guess the second to last exposure—that we ever got on film.

Kelso Chaplin

He'd been trying to stretch himself all summer. He'd been getting away from the formal exposures—meaning you take a celebrity and work from the outside in—but that's still what the crowds were coming to see. And this night he was a little edgy. He was resisting. There were a ton of suggestions about who to do. Peggy Fleming, Joe Pine, Jackie, Ringo Starr, on and on. He was just shaking his head. I have this on film. You can see him thinking over Ken Kesey, but for the most part, he's really trying to stay away. He handles it okay, but different for him. He says, "Look, maybe we'll get to them, but I had something else in mind, and if we screw around now, we may never get to the sexy parts." And right then a voice shouts out from the crowd, "Do Larry Storch!"

Boone puts his head against the microphone and thinks about it for a second and just laughs. And he looks out at the audience and smiles. There was something really strange going on that night between him and the crowd. That's a real strange smile. He looks out and says, "Well, I'm not sure enough of us know who Larry Storch is, sir. Maybe we should do someone we all know a little better." He starts looking for the guy who said Larry Storch, and he says, "Sir, could you please stand up?" I had to move the camera over, so you lose Boone for a second, but you can hear him saying, "Can we turn the lights on this gentleman?" Someone tells him they can't, so he calls out to a guy named Rudy Hack who used a flashlight in his act. He says, "Rudy, could you toss out your flashlight? There's a guy here I want to get a look at." There's this gap, it's just black because I can't find anyone. The whole club just sat and waited for Rudy to work his way up to the stage.

Finally, Boone gets the flashlight and shines it on the guy. He says, "Is that you there, sir? Are you the one who suggested Mr. Storch?" And the guy nods and laughs. Everyone's a little nervous at this point, especially the guy. He's medium height, a little tubby, bald, and he's got sideburns coming down, no mustache, just the beard, but he's nervous as hell. Boone catches him in the face with his flashlight and says, "Holy shit, it's Ahab's little brother." But as Boone's asking the guy for his name, he's looking at the guy, but he puts up his right hand and he's sort of waving it at us like this. I didn't really know what he meant at the time, but apparently he wanted us to turn the camera off.

Eton Arthur Boone, transcribed, September 19, 1968—

[Inaudible.]
——What's that?
[Inaudible.]
——Sorry, sir, you're going to have to speak up. There are about seventy
   people here trying to hear you.
——Glenn.
——Lem?
——Glenn.
——Glenn? Just Glenn? You go up to a cop on the street and tell him your
   name is Glenn and expect to get home?
——Glenn Hupert.
——Thank you, Glenn Hubert.
——pert.
——What?
——pert! Hu*pert!* My last name is Hupert.
——Good for you, Glenn Hu*pert!* How many n's in "Glenn?"
——Two n's.
——Two. Unh-hunh. And how old are you, Glen-n-n-n?
——Forty-three.

——Forty-three. I am half your age, Glenn Hupert. Where do you live?

——I was born in St. Louis.

——Un-hunh. And where were you born? Wait a minute, you just told me. Where the fuck do you live, Glenn Hupert?

——New Rochelle, New York.

——Glenn Hupert, forty-three. New Rochelle, New York. By way of St. Louis . . . is that St. Louis, Missouri? . . . Glenn.

——I'm still here.

——I know you're still there. You're not an easy fellow to miss. Now, is that St. Louis, Missouri?

——As in the World Champion Cardinals.

——Oh. "As in the World Champion Cardinals." Glenn, you dork . . . Answer me this, Glenn Hubert. Pert! Pert! Answer me this. How'd you get here tonight?

——Took the parkway.

——Well, put it back, Glenn, Jesus Christ. Just kidding. I'm kidding, Glenn. It's been that kind of day.

——I know the feeling.

——Bet you do. Hey, Glenn, who's that there next to you? Is that your squeeze box? Glenn. Is that your wife? Did you drive in with your wife?

——No, sir. This is—

——That's not your wife? Who the hell is it? Glenn Hupert, did you just come in here and sit down at someone's table?

——No, sir. This is a friend.

——Ever been married?

——No, sir.

——Lotta broken hearts in St. Louis, I'll bet . . . All right, Glenn, you can sit down.

——What?

——I said, sit down. Wait. Just a second, Glenn, let me get another look at you . . . okay, thank you. Thank you, Glenn Hupert.

Glenn Hupert. Glen-n-n-n Hupert. Born—nineteen . . . 1925. Birthplace—St. Louis, Missouri, home of the World Champion St. Louis Cardinals . . . Grew up watching the Cardinals. Now, New Rochelle. No baseball team in New Rochelle . . . Take the parkway in to see the Yankees. I have some friends I go to see the Yankees with. I don't know them very well. Tried to follow the Yanks for a while. But I'm still a Cardinal fan. Who'm I trying to kid? I even rooted for them when they played the Yankees a few years back.

Everybody at work knew I was for the Cardinals. It gave 'em something to say to me. And that, well, that was okay. That's something . . . They could say, "Hey, Glenn, how 'bout those Cardinals?" "Like that Brock." They could say, "Lookin' pretty good." And I could say, "Sure are. Sure are, Phil." Like, "thanks." And they knew if they were watching the game with me, and some of them did, some did, they were watching with a Cardinals fan . . . Glenn Hupert, Cardinals fan.

I have a Cardinals cap. You bet. I've had quite a few Cardinals caps in my life. I don't know where mine is now, I was looking for it just the other day. You ever lose something and you think you know where it is but you can't find it? Yeah, you too? I know the feeling.

Know what else I know? I know the feeling of being in Yankee Stadium going up to the souvenir stand to buy myself a Cardinals cap . . . And I know the feeling of standing in line to buy beer with a Cardinals cap on my head, with a little Negro kid looking up at me, and me looking down at him and thinking, "You bet. Darn right, I'm a Cardinals fan. And I don't have any hair on my head." You know the feeling? . . .

Mmm-hmm, and the feeling of sitting in Yankee Stadium with these people who aren't really my friends, and watching the scoreboard the whole game, because the Cardinals are playing the Phillies, and when the Cardinals start to pull ahead in St. Louis, these people turn to me and say, "Hey, Glenn, you see the Cards got three in the seventh?" And I say, "Oh, yeah," as if that wasn't practically the only reason I came to the Stadium in the first place.

Yeah, I know that feeling, and I also know the feeling of going home after the game, driving these people back up the parkway with my Cardinals cap on, and thinking about what's in the refrigerator, and do I need to stop and buy food, or can I wait till tomorrow? And when are the Cardinals coming in to play the Mets? And what order do I need to drop these people off in? And what am I going to do tonight? And how long before I get to go to sleep?

Maybe I do need to get something. I need some milk for the morning, goddammit, so I stop at that store off the exit I always stop at, where they had the holdup, and I get some milk and maybe a TV dinner—they usually still have the salisbury steak on Wednesdays—and I see a girl in the store, and she's got shorts on, and I can't help myself—I want to fuck her. Want to . . . I wanna . . . ah, shit, I can't even cook up a fantasy any more. I can't think of what might happen that I could get that sixteen-year-old girl home with me.

But I wouldn't really want her to see my home, anyway. It smells. It's depressing. For one thing, there's too much Cardinal shit around. And I've been using the same towel as a tablecloth for a couple months, and who knows when was the last time I cleaned the toilet bowl?

I'd pay for a room, that's what I'd do. But I just can't think of what would make it happen. She's attracted to guys like me? Would she be doing it on a dare? I've got to have fantasies where the girl is having sex with me on a dare. Shit. And I can't even think of interesting ways to do it with her. Just want to fuck her, maybe from behind. I don't know, I want to fuck her, and I know I'm not gonna.

So I get home, I open the goddamn door, and I have to pee because I had three beers. And while I'm peeing, I take off my Cardinals cap and look in the mirror. The cap's left a little red line around my head, and my head's itching a little. I look tired. I look tired and old and fat. I don't look a single thing like what I used to look. But it's still Glenn Hupert, and I'm thinking, "Glenn Hupert, what the heck are you doing in New Rochelle?

New Rochelle's for families, for Rob and Laura, not for tired old bachelors from St. Louis. Need a change, Glenn Hupert, need a change. Need to do something so you don't have to look at this same ugly mug every day, goddamn double chin.

"Two ways to skin a cat, Glenn Hupert. One—sweat it out and lose some weight, or two—don't shave." Well, I'm too fat to exercise. Besides, I like this. I like being a big man. I'll like being a big man with a beard.

Mustache didn't quite work. It made my mouth look tiny, and someone once told me that my upper lip looks like Marlon Brando's. Yeah. "We got a thing here in the state of Louisiana called the Napoleonic code, by which . . . by which what belongs . . ."—Aw, fuck it. Just fuck it . . . So I shave it off, and I just go with this look—

Ahab's cousin. Fuck him! One of the girls at work said it looked groovy. Groovy enough that I've got a date here. Groovy enough that I can wear my black turtleneck and take the parkway into New York, take my date to dinner and then—comedy club. Little place I know. Grand Street, just for kicks. Guy named Boone someone at work told me about. Bet no one's ever taken her to a comedy club before. I paid for dinner. I'll pay for this.

Maybe she will fuck me. She will, she will . . . Can't drink too much. I've already drunk too much. Drunk enough to say that stupid thing about her eyes. But they are, they are . . . Drunk enough to call out "Larry Storch" and show everyone how much fucking TV I watch. Drunk enough that when the guy makes me stand up I start stammering like a retard idiot and tell him where I'm from when he asks me where I live. Drunk enough to let that Cardinal thing slip. Jeez, you think he got enough mileage out of that? . . . Drunk enough so that all I can do now is smile and laugh along with the rest of these assholes, and keep turning to my date and laughing, "Pretty funny, hmmm? He's good. Yeah. Ha ha." Drunk enough that I'm sweating like a pig with a beard, so that I'm gonna stink like a monkey cage if I do get lucky and we do fuck.

Hey. Hey, now, asshole. That's about enough. All right? Fun's fun . . . Yeah, yeah, okay and I just have to keep smiling—you gonna keep this up? You gonna keep on with this shit? Yeah? Okay, just so I know . . . I cannot believe I opened my mouth. Goddammit. I am a dork. Okay, could we just go back? I was gonna tell them about it at work tomorrow. But now . . . This is turning into a nightmare. Turn back the clock, let's go. Back in time. Why in the hell did we come here? Why is this happening? What can I do? Did we get the check?

Maybe another drink. You want another drink, honey? Oh, goddammit, he caught me, "Uh, yeah, two more beers, or whatever she had." Stop it. Stop it. "Yeah, two more of the, whatever, the same things we had." Fuck. He's looking right at me. Goddammit. What does he want me to do? What does anybody want me to do? Folks, any suggestions? What can I do? Can I leave? No, it'd be too pathetic. But he could do this all night. He could do this all goddamn night, and there's nothing I can do. I could get up and go to the bathroom and hope he's gone when I come back. Dammit. I could, I could say, "Okay, okay, joke's over, ha ha. Very funny, Mr. Comedian. Now just stop." Show him I'm getting pissed.

But c'mon, how long do I have to put up with this? I'm getting pissed. *I* am. *I* fucking am. This is some kind of joke. Yes, yes, all right, very funny. Now cut it the hell out. No one else is finding this particularly entertaining, you know. No one's laughing. They've stopped laughing, and now he's the one on the spot. You're on the spot. You're on the spot now, buddy. What am I saying? No, he's not. He's just a mean son of a bitch. What does he care? He's just—well, I don't know what he's doing now. He's not doing anything. Is he? No, he isn't. He's not doing a goddamn thing. Hey, asshole, get the hell off the stage!

Any other requests?

Thank you. Good night.

Linda Chaplin

It didn't take long for the crowd to leave after that one. Really, not a lot of fun. I remember having to watch this poor guy, the original Hupert, watching him walk by Boone at the bar and everyone pretending not to look. Kelso and I wanted to leave too, but Boone had given us a real hairy eyeball when he walked by, so we'd stayed. He came back to us after about ten minutes, after everyone had gone, and he had a bottle of beer in his hand. It looked like he'd calmed down. He just walked up to us, and Kelso said, you know, okay, we won't bring the camera anymore. And I didn't even know if I wanted to come back at all. Really. Just too cruel.

But then, as Boone was standing there, this vision comes in the front door and walks up, very gently and timidly. This apparition, walking so slowly, you know, as if she was sort of stepping from one lily pad to the other. And she stood there and said, very quietly, "Boone?" He turned around and took her hand and introduced us to this beauty. This was Erin Hirt, this model, his girlfriend. She had a beautiful dark green dress on and black stockings and this full head of unbelievable, really gorgeous red hair. This red-haired American beauty. She was so stunning you almost forgot what had happened, what Boone, this man she was holding hands with, had just done to this perfectly innocent bystander. I ended up just looking at their hands. They were holding hands, and their fingers were so tightly hooked, you know. I guess they just sort of excused themselves and left. Kelso and I were breathtaken. Kelso said, "I guess I wouldn't have been too pleased to be here either if I had that waiting for me." Well, yeah, honey.

Erin Hirt

He had a lot of trouble sleeping. I would wake up and he would have the TV on with the volume way down, and he would be sitting on the edge of the bed. I sort of got used to waking up and seeing him at his desk writing a letter with the TV on, or down at the edge of the bed, and he'd rub my feet.

This one time I woke up and the set was on, but he wasn't there and he wasn't at his desk. He was in the bathroom. I could see him. The door was open, and I could see him in the mirror all huddled over the toilet and he was really sick. It wasn't drugs or anything. It was a fever or something, and his whole back was sweating, and I went in and sat on the tub and got a washcloth for his back to cool him down. He was just shivering and all sweaty. We ran him a bath, and I went and got him a bottle of ginger ale and this Crazy Straw that he'd given me as my stocking stuffer. So he got in the tub and it was this tiny little tub. It was too small. You'd always hit your head on the faucets, but I feel like we spent the whole night there with him in the tub, and me sponging his back.

We hardly said anything at all, but he did apologize. He'd say he was sorry that he was just treating me like this little rose. And I know every time we were supposed to talk, he just wanted to watch TV. He'd come in and he'd turn on the TV and I'd lie down on the couch with my head in his lap and he'd scratch my head. That's the way I'd fall asleep usually, in his lap. And Janice would say, "You've got to help him, really help. He's got to let you in," and I would have to explain to her that that's just not how it was with him. He was really hard.

Buddy D'Angelo

He did this one thing I used to love. I'm not a big fan of television, I've got to tell you, but you could always tell when he did something. This one he was actually in. He played this character called El Bijet. I don't know how they got it on the air. You know, he comes out as this nearsighted Mexican knife-thrower. El Bijet. There'd be some Mexican maiden tied to a post, and this evil bandolero or whatever they're called with the mustache is whipping her, and the maiden says something like, "If only El Bijet were here!" Then you'd hear the Mexican brass—ya ta daaaah!— and Boone comes out in this spangled yellow getup, long johns, and a giant black sombrero. He does the Superman pose, hands on his hips, and he says, "Iyam El Bijet!" And then he'd start throwing knives and hatchets all over the place. People start running for cover like crazy. A chicken goes flying across the screen. I don't know. I thought it was funny.

Bert Niemann

I remember the first time I went out on stage. I was a skinny little seventeen-year-old kid from the Bronx. It was a little vaudeville show in Newark, and I had a partner, Manny Seiglemann. Seiglemann and Niemann, it sounded like a law firm. We went out, and we did the jokes with the hats and the little dance and the yaka-yaka-yaka. We were all right. We made a few dollars. You know, it makes you feel good. People are laughing at what you've done. It makes you feel like you've brought happiness. It's a beautiful business to be in.

But he didn't get that. Boone never got that. Solly and I, we'd be walking around the room, throwing things out. Say, "Okay. A dumb guy in a lingerie shop wants to buy something for his wife, and the sales clerk thinks it's for him." Boom! We'd just throw something like that out and make something of it, you know, just the two of us, or Hank too, just have fun with it. But when Boone's there, we'd start the same thing. Say, "Okay. A guy walks into a lingerie shop and wants to buy something for his wife," and Boone would say something like, "and he only has one arm" or "and he's bleeding in his left ear" or "and he has pink eye" or something. You know? It was a family show, but he just didn't care. He didn't give a shit what anyone thought. It was, "What do I feel like doing or writing? And I'll do it." That's not what entertainment is about. It's about the people who are working at keeping this country going, and it's our job to make them feel happy, make them forget their troubles for a little while. We're not there every Thursday night to piss them off. We're there to make them laugh, for God's sake.

Erin Hirt

The winter, right around Christmas, was really tough. His brother and Hilary came in, and I was supposed to take care of them. I didn't really know what to do with them. I took Toddy up to the Cloisters. We had this great afternoon up there in the snow, but Hilary hadn't come. Hilary was tough to deal with. He sulked a lot, he stayed in the apartment. He went out on his own and he'd come back with dope. He and Boone smoked a lot of dope together, which left me and Toddy out, because he was really a clean kid. I really liked Toddy. I didn't know so much about Hilary, though.

He and Boone would go up on the roof. His mother called one time and I had to go up on the roof to find them. They were up there smoking. Boone was wearing a pea coat and it was getting dark. They were over by one of those round things on top of the chimney and they spin. They were just standing there, and Boone was spinning one of these things and blowing it like a pinwheel with his breath, and I had to go back inside and tell Mrs. Boone that I couldn't find them.

Toddy Boone

Hilary was ridiculous in New York. New Year's Eve, our second visit, we'd all gone bowling, me and him and Eton and Erin Hirt. It was this bowling alley about three blocks from where Eton lived. They actually had a picture of Eton up on the wall—his was between these glossies of Ernest Borgnine and Art Carney, which Dad would have loved.

But we'd run into a bunch of people who knew Eton, NYU people and comedians from his club. They had about four lanes and waved us over while we were still getting our shoes. We all had to play together, and I don't think Eton had really wanted to. I think he'd just wanted to have New Year's Eve with the family, but Hilary—it's the first time I'd ever really seen him like this. All these new people, champagne, party hats, he put on a real show.

First of all, he refused to use the same ball twice. He kept going up to other people asking if he could use their ball, and he'd shine it up with a towel and say, "Why, hello, big ball." He tried holding three in his arms at once, and he'd dropped them all—he almost broke the floor but everyone loved it. And whenever he'd take his turns, he'd go running halfway up the alley to count his pins. If it was a gutter ball, he'd turn around and pout for everyone, but if it was a strike, of course the whole place had to know—he'd shimmy back to the seats saying, "Melikelikiama."

After a while, though, I guess he got a little bored with the game, because what he ended up doing, what really stole the show, is he started playing with all the women's hair. It's like he'd opened up this beauty parlor back by the shoes. It started with this woman from NYU who had blond hair. Hilary had gone up to her and told her it looked just like his mother's—which it didn't at all, it was just blond—but he started touching her hair and petting it and telling her how he used to braid Anne's hair when he was home sick from school, so of course this lady asked if he wanted to do hers. Pretty soon, everybody was crowding around and before you knew it, every woman in our group was going up to take her shot with one of Hilary's braids on the back of her head.

Except Erin, of course. She'd been up front at the scoring table with Eton the whole time, and what you have to know is, Erin Hirt had the nicest hair of anyone I've ever seen. Her hair was just beautiful, full and smooth, and it had all these beautiful colors, so while all this baloney was going on with the other women, what everyone was really waiting to see was if Hilary had the guts to do Erin's hair too. Problem was, Eton's hand was in it. He was rubbing her neck. It's like his hand was back there saying, "Stay the hell away."

So Hilary goes ahead and does it, of course. He kneels down on these coats behind her chair and moves Eton's hand. He actually picks Eton's hand off the back of her neck and starts braiding Erin's hair. I couldn't believe he was doing it. Everyone's standing around oohing and ahhing, and Hilary is out of his mind with all the attention. He's humming to himself and separating her hair into different strands, but he's really tugging it too. He's yanking her hair. It really made me uncomfortable. She was having to jerk her head back every time he pulled it, but she didn't say anything. She and Eton both just sat there with their beers looking straight ahead, and I couldn't figure out, why were they indulging him? I wanted to lean over to Eton and say, "Come on, man, smack him. I'll pin him down, you drop a ball on his chest," but he didn't do anything. He just pretended nothing was happening.

Hilary Richman

We'd all just been hanging around watching television. We were at E.B.'s place and we started watching *The Blob,* which was on the late show or something, this movie which I've always hated because of the first time I saw it. I saw it at a drive-in with my mother and my father. We were taking a trip down to Georgia to see my father's family and I'd begged them to go to this drive-in movie, and we did. I don't even think I gave a shit what was playing. I was like seven years old, or six, and it was in Richmond. I was so fucking happy about it. We just went into this drive-in and it was the three of us in our own car and all these other families in their own cars, and my father got us hot dogs and I sat up in the front seat with them, in between them, and it's like one of the few happy times I can remember.

Probably the only reason I can remember it at all is that my mother started crying. She started crying in the middle of the fucking *Blob,* and I couldn't believe it. I couldn't believe she was ruining this beautiful thing with the three of us in the drive-in. We left early. We had to drive out of the parking lot past all of these other cars, and the whole trip ended up sucking. My grandparents were complete assholes to me. They wouldn't even deal with me, and I can remember my father yelling at my mom, yelling at her in the kitchen, showing her how you're supposed to fold up the milk carton before you throw it away. The whole trip sucked, and I blamed it on my mother for crying at this drive-in.

Anyway, this movie was on when we were in New York and everyone was insisting on watching it. Everyone was being really loud because we'd been drinking. Even Toddy had. So I just went into the bathroom, and I ended up taking a shower. The movie just depressed me so much I went and took a shower and I stayed in there because you never could at Hoyt, just stay in the fucking bathroom.

So I must have been in there a while, I don't know. I was standing over the sink just in this towel and washing my face, and I looked up and E.B. was in the door. It wasn't all the way open. He was sort of behind the door, but he was standing there with this beer in his hand and I don't know how long he'd been there. I saw him in the mirror and he was looking at me with all this soap all over my face. And I could tell he was doing it. He was looking at me and I could only barely see him, but I could see his eyes and it just absolutely froze me, it was so intense. I mean, I don't know what I was expecting, but this was practically physical. It was like, "Whoosh!" His eyes just bored right in, they were like these drills or something, and I wanted to say, "Stop. Jesus." Because most of the time, let's face it, you don't know what the hell you're feeling. You have no idea how unhappy you are because you're too busy fucking around making yourself unhappy, but now E.B.'s standing in this doorway, and it's like he's decided to look and see for you. You know, all this shit that's mine, these feelings that I don't even want to deal with, they're right there on E.B.'s face. I actually had to look at them, and I mean, it scared the living hell out of me—Jesus Christ, I was completely freaked out—but it was amazing too, you know, just E.B.'s face, E.B.'s eyes. It's like he's the one person who's figured out that if you just look, it isn't so hard to know what it's like for someone else, if you just look. I'd never felt anything like it in my whole life, just so fucking *known.*

I don't know. It probably only lasted two seconds and then it stopped. He was standing there looking at me like, "I'm sorry. It just happened," but then he closed the door. He said the light was reflecting in the television set, but he was just as fucked up by it as I was. I know he was.

Hugh Gardiner

I went to see him in late February of 1969. I was no longer receiving the filmed exposures at this point, so to keep track of him, I'd begun venturing to the club in person again, alone, normally equipped with a small tape recorder and a commonplace book. I was aware that his work had grown more troubled, and I don't believe that the television program had been much of a help in that regard. One could sense that his creative juices had become rather acid. That evening in particular, in February, his energies were diffuse, directed at the audience, thrashing about rather than focusing. The crowd was wary of him too—perhaps they'd heard of the incident with the Hupert fellow or perhaps it was simply his manner, but no one wanted to risk provoking him. One gentleman, though, made the mistake of requesting that he do El Bijet, the rather tame satire of President Johnson that Boone would do on the television, and Boone's fury was evident.

Transcribed from the tapes of Hugh Gardiner, February 1969

——Who said that? Who said El Bijet? You? What's your name, sir?
——*[Inaudible.]*
——What?
——I said I'm not gonna play that game.
——Don't be a dork. "Oh, no, I'm not going to play that game. You shan't swallow me in your trap, Mr. Boone." C'mon, pal, lighten up, what's your name? Hey, miss, what's his name? What's his name? Are you with this man?
——No. *[Inaudible.]*
——Who is with this man? You, ma'am? Did you come in here with this gentleman?
——Yes.
——You're with this man, you're his wife.
——*[Inaudible male voice.]*
——Haven't we established that you're not playing my game, sir? Ma'am, pay no attention to that man. Now what's his name?
——Jerry.
——Jerry. That's a lie, ma'am! This man's name is not Jerry!
——*[A second male voice]* Just lay off. Do somebody else.
——Oh, you're all chickenshit, you know that? Yes, you are. Look, someone give me that man's real name. Not you, ma'am, you lied to me. "I'll lie to him, get him off track, get him off this thing, get him talking about something else." Well, it won't work, Missy!
      You, there! You, laughing. "Oh, that's funny, I like what he did to her." What's your name?
——Jerry.
——Oh, fuck you, sir. Just fuck you, okay? This is no joke. How the hell do you want me to perform if you won't give me at least your fucking names? Cheap shit, chickenshit, bunch of fucking inconsiderate idiots . . . "Jesus, this guy's really hostile. What an asshole. I'm ready not to forgive him for this. Bring back the Southern guy." Fucking idiot. "Well, okay, maybe we had better leave. I'm not kidding. Maybe we'd better just go. Honey, get your coat." Yeah, maybe you'd better. Fuck you. "Well, fine, fuck you too, Mr. Boone."

Hugh Gardiner

It was another punchline of sorts, a very clever bit from a critical point of view, and the logical step in the progression. That's part of the reason I've kept it all these years. He'd succeeded in performing one of his imitations, reading and manipulating the thoughts of an entire audience despite their steadfast resistance. Clever, entertaining in retrospect, very clever, but none of this overturns the fact that it was ugly, the act of someone screaming to be let out. So it's with a great deal of sadness that I review that scene in my mind, because of course I knew it meant that something was going to have to change. He wasn't going to be able to go on much longer with the exposures, so that period in his life—really in all of our lives, of there being a young man willing and capable of exposing conscience in this extraordinary way—those days were numbered.

But of course I didn't want that to change what Boone and I had been able to establish in our letters. Our relationship had taken on a life independent of his stage work, and I feel safe in saying that neither of us wanted the evolution of his career to place our arrangement in jeopardy. Rather, I felt that his career and our correspondence should evolve as one, so I began for the first time to think in terms of the future. If this is what's come of his exposures, then one in my position had to recognize that maybe it was time for his ambition to transform itself, perhaps no longer to be this piercing psychological needle, as it were. Give the boy bigger brushes, and let him work in thicker brushstrokes.

Lionel Thubb

In May of 1969, Buddy D'Angelo was inspired to throw a fifth anniversary party for the club. It was closed to the public. Only the Chaplin couple were to be allowed in from the outside, to film it for posterity. And a few members of the local media, of course. Buddy invited as many comedians as he could to perform and pay their respects, remember when, reminisce. The evening's final performer had been slated for some time—if Jes' For Laffs was indeed "The House that Boone Built," as Buddy was fond of calling it, then it seemed only fitting that Eton Arthur should close the show.

Buddy D'Angelo

The Night the Shit Hit the Fan. I swear to God, I'll never live this down. This is the last time I talk about it. Okay. The night the shit hit the fan. Fifth anniversary show. The place is packed. I'm in a tux. I'm emceeing, and everything's going great. We're making a bundle, everything's doubled, passing around a hat. Dick Gregory drops by. Marty Allen does a set, kills 'em. Bahssin, Holly, L.T., everyone's cooking, and I'm saving Boone. He says before the show he's got a special tribute ready for me, which we never get to see. But he's sitting with the Piedmont people. They've got a table right in front, Hank and Niemann and Solly. Jimmy Garner's there too, he'd hosted their show that night and brought me down a bottle of champagne. So it's midnight. I introduce Niemann, and I go sit next to Boone and Jimmy.

Niemann gets up on stage, and I'm thinking, hey, why not? Crowd's in a good mood. Old guy's got something to prove, wants to see if he's still got the old magic, let him. Piedmont had gone too. He'd done a quick little thing on Canada. He still had it. But Niemann. I was never crazy about him. I'd seen him up on the belt in '62. He was something, that guy, a real piece of work, and he gets up and does his shtick.

He bombs. Dies. In the frigging toilet. He just doesn't have it. But then he starts doing the shtick, "Hello, hello, is the mike on? Can I get a little feedback?" You know, the panic-button stuff, and it's going right down the tubes. I look over at Boone and he and Jimmy are clenching their teeth, trying to smile. Everyone is. No one's laughing. The place is a goddamn tomb.

But Niemann won't give it up. He tells some old clunker, I don't know, "I told you to say DiMaggio," and there's nothing. Sounds like we're at a golf tournament. And Niemann—I swear to God, I'm not making this up—he leans out and he says, "I know you're out there, I can hear you breathing." I'm not making this up, he actually said it, and Boone just buried his head on Jimmy's shoulder.

Kelso Chaplin

This is probably the most valuable piece of film we own. Linda and I were at our usual place in back, and Buddy'd gotten some extra lights, so there's no lighting problem at all on this one. The third reel begins with this old-school guy, Niemann, doing material that I swear to God was thirty years old. Maybe it was funny at the old vaudeville places, Linda would know. So it's interesting footage from a documentary point of view, kind of a comedy warmed over. But where it starts getting really priceless is when Niemann catches on—with the rest of us—that he's flopping. He starts gesturing to Boone at his table near the stage, sending rescue signals. He goes, "Eton, get up here and talk to these kids. I can't do anything with them." He starts to turn it into an introduction. "Yes, that's right," he says. "Eton Boone, my fellow writer on 'The Hank Piedmont Show.' He's your man, isn't he?" Nice. "He's sitting right down here by the stage, and he's getting ready to entertain you, so why don't we just get him out here. Eton?" Eton, help! I'm drowning! Somebody, send me a line!

Boone's very lazy about it. He pulls himself up on stage, he's wiping these mock tears from his eyes, and I know Buddy's pissed, because he had this big introduction he'd read for us earlier. But Niemann opens his arms to Boone—Linda thinks he says, "my boy"—and the crowd starts to applaud. They're being polite. But the two of them are up there hugging and Niemann tries to make his way offstage, but Boone holds on to him—he doesn't let him go—and he says, "Bert, this feels so good. Don't leave. I don't want to say good-bye. Let's stay like this forever." Niemann starts playing along—he has to—he's patting Boone on the back, but you can see he's dying to get off. He starts saying, "No, they're all yours."

And that's when it really turns ugly. Boone says, "Who?" Niemann says, "Them. Out there. Your people." Boone says, "What people? I can't hear them breathing." And Boone turns back, looks back at Niemann right in the face, very close, and it's that weird smile—he says, "I can hear *you* breathing, Bert." He places his head against his chest. "I can hear something. I know you're in there. I can hear you breathing. I can hear a little elf in there. He's screaming. 'Get me off! Let me go! Let me go!' " This tiny, tiny, fly voice. Niemann's trying to laugh, and you can see that look on Boone's face, you can even hear Linda saying, oh no.

Boone starts doing him. They're still locked in this embrace, and Boone is looking right into his face. He does Niemann right in his face. Boone says, "I can take a joke as well as the next guy, Eton. You know, I worked with Manny Siegleman before you were born." He just starts mocking him. "I worked with Manny Siegleman before you were born, and if you could work with Manny, you could work with anyone. Siegleman and Niemann, sounds like a law firm." And then comes a terrific moment. Niemann looks at him with a big, sweaty smile, totally panicked, and then plants a big Bugs Bunny kiss right on his cheek. Boone looks right back, exact same smile, and kisses Niemann. They're both staring right at each other, and then Boone, this terrific rapid-fire Jewish voice, he says—you should get this from the film so you can get it word for word, but I'll do it for you—Boone says—

Eton Arthur Boone, transcribed from J.F.L. Anniversary film, May 9, 1969, BERT NIEMANN

Well, this is ridiculous. He's copying me. This is copy cats. Hey, Boone, I was doing this when I was eight years old, for God's sake. Very funny stuff. Oh, this is comedy, Mr. Boone. Next you'll be, uh, dipping the girls, the girls' pigtails in the ink or whatever. Who the hell can't do this? I can do you, you know. You wouldn't be so tough, Mr. Young Genius.

Kelso Chaplin

And the amazing thing, the amazing thing, is that Niemann actually goes for it. He answers him. Niemann pushes Boone off and says, "Sure," but you can't hear him that well because he doesn't have the mike anymore. "Sure, I could do you." That's Niemann, and then Boone says, "Yeah, that's what I'll do. I'll do the son of a bitch." Niemann reaches back to the piano where they've set up everyone's props, even Boone's from way back, I guess, and he grabs one of Boone's fake knives, what he thinks is one of Boone's fake knives. You know, he still wants to play along—these guys never want to admit they can't keep up. He says, "Yeah, I'm Eton Boone. Mr. . . . Mr. Revolutionary," and Boone is sticking the mike out so we can hear Niemann better. "Mr. Revolutionary with the knives and whatever. I can do whatever I want." Niemann lifts the knife up into the air. "Ha ha ha," and then plunges it into his stomach.

I've looked at this more times than the Zapruder film. His eyes pop out. His mouth drops open. He's just stabbed himself with a real knife, a fishing knife that Maury Schacter used to use in his act, and there's this moment where no one knows what the hell to do—except Boone.

Eton Arthur Boone, transcribed—BERT NIEMANN

Oh, God. Oh, God, I've stabbed myself. That little shit. That little shit. This was a real knife. I'm bleeding. Someone get up here and help me. Why is he talking? What is he, a maniac? I think I'm bleeding to death. I'm dying. I think I'm dying. Bert Niemann, dying on stage. I'm dying on stage and this little schmuck is still doing me. Hey! Hey, would someone get the hell up here? Hank, where the hell is Hank? What, are people turning on me? Are people afraid of this little schmuck? He's not going to hurt them.

I stabbed *myself*. Hello, everybody, I've stabbed myself. I'm dying. I've done the stupidest thing maybe anyone's ever done on stage. I can't believe I did this, and he's enjoying it. Look at the little bastard! Jesus Christ, where the fuck is everyone? Where's my wife? Honey, Jesus, you're a nurse, get your ass up here. Solly! I'm bleeding here. Turn on the lights, for God's sake. Buddy! Somebody! I know you're out there, I can hear you breathing.

Kelso Chaplin

This has all been very fast, no more than forty-five seconds, and then Boone stops. He looks out at us all and he's himself now, and he says, "Is no one going to help this man? What are you, beasts? He really is bleeding." And then mayhem breaks out. People start rushing the stage. The lights come up. Some music starts playing, somebody's thrown on Benny Goodman. Boone turns off the mike, puts it back on its stand, and walks off. Piedmont's up there. They bring up the lights. Niemann's wife gets up there, and she is a nurse, and here I am the worst of all, because I'm still filming. The last thing you can hear is Linda saying, "Kelso, turn it off."

Bert Niemann

Why should he change? Everyone was telling him he didn't need to. He had all these people around him all his life saying, "Oh, Boone, whatever you do, it's new, it's wonderful, it's brilliant, you're a genius, you're a sensation." Why did he have to grow up? He could just go on stabbing people and offending people and pissing people off, because everyone loved it.

He must have been on the drugs, or drinking. I don't know. And of course, I look like a fool. Everyone thinks, "Oh, Bert, what a fool, and the guy doesn't even go to jail." I mean . . . I don't want to talk about it. I could show you the scar. Can you imagine? Can you imagine if I'd died? People would still think, "Oh, Bert, what a fool." No one ever thought, "Eton Boone, what an ass-hole."

Hugh Gardiner

Kelso called me late that evening and told me, and of course I knew that this was the end. I wanted desperately to see the footage, but I thought, no, charity is often best when it's blind. I wrote him immediately, but not a letter of condolence or of reassurance. I didn't want to join rank with those who were sure to make a tar pit of this unfortunate scene. Rather, I wrote him a letter I'd been ready with for some time, to be perfectly honest. I wrote of the future, about where he might go next, and what possibilities I felt were still open to him.

England was the possibility that he seized on. I know that many people had suggested he go to Los Angeles, but we both felt that he'd have some difficulty there because his exploits would surely precede him. He'd made no friends in the past eighteen months certainly, and I imagine that the Hollywood powers that be may already have considered him something of an *enfant terrible.*

In England, on the other hand, it was my feeling that he'd have a better chance of sneaking in unnoticed. He could grow there and learn things that he wouldn't have been able to in New York anymore or Hollywood. We could broaden his scope, open his eyes to history. It's one thing to be able to understand the celebrity mind or probe the momentary consciousness of the people in his audience, but it would be quite another for him to turn his focus to the really great minds of history—to Shakespeare, Keats, Yeats, Tolstoi. The possibilities were endless, and though I understood I'd be unable to oversee his education alone, from my seat in Poughkeepsie, I thought I might introduce him to John— John Kinsey again. I thought John might be able to take Boone in hand, be a sort of cultural guide. It was the correct next step. Boone had come to a crossroads, to be certain—we both saw that—but I wanted him to grow, not flee. I made that very clear to him in my letter.

Of course, what I could never express to him was my nearly insurmountable regret at the simple fact that we most likely wouldn't be seeing the exposures again. I'd known that this time would come, and I certainly never doubted that Boone would find new, equally fascinating paths to follow, but I was still terribly saddened at the inevitability with which it had all passed, and the fact that as hard as Boone and I had tried to maintain the balance necessary for his work on stage to continue, we finally had to concede that not all of the forces at play were ours to tend. Boone had changed, to be sure, and grown more disenchanted as time had passed, but the people who came to see him had changed as well. Towards the end there'd been an increasing number who were coming to see him as though he were a monkey in a cage, rather than a man who had something so vital to tell them. I suppose it was their way of doing away with him. No one likes the gentleman who says, these are shadows on our walls. Not now, nor ever, I should think. So, England.

Erin Hirt

He took me to the Plaza. He'd gotten some severance pay from the TV show, and we just went out to spend it. We'd gone and seen *Rosemary's Baby* and some people had recognized me instead of him. They'd come up to me because of this ad I'd been in, for shaving cream, and Boone had introduced himself as chopped liver. Then after the movie we went to the Plaza and had champagne cocktails in the Oak Bar because they were so expensive. We were sitting at the window and he asked me if I wanted to come to England with him. He said he had no idea what he was going to do. He said he had no idea how long it was going to be. He just said, if we don't like it, we'll leave.

IV

England

John Kinsey

It had just begun to rain when he arrived at my doorstep, and he hadn't an umbrella. There was a box of Maria Mancini cigars tucked under his slicker, though, so I knew it was he. Hugh and I make it a habit of exchanging Scotch whiskey for Havana cigars at the least provocation, and I think Hugh was hoping to endear his young friend to me by having him deliver such an extravagant gift. His hair and shoulders were very wet and he asked if he could use the loo. He went off. I opened the box to examine the cigars and found a note waiting for me, from Hugh, in an envelope. I didn't open it. Eton returned with his hair combed and parted. His face looked very fresh, braced by the weather, and I found myself very warmed to him, much more so than I'd anticipated. I suppose I hadn't been expecting someone so sanguine, and it comforted me.

I asked if he wanted a cardigan of mine, because he looked cold, and we went upstairs to my dressing room to find him one, a navy blue one that my wife had given me. It was much too big for him. The sleeves fell down past his fingers but he rolled them.

The rain had begun to fall torrentially, and there is a window in my bedroom, nine feet high and roughly four feet wide, that looks out over Lamb's Conduit. Eton walked right up to it and looked out at the rain. He asked if that was where I took my breakfast, looking out over the street in the mornings, and I said yes, sometimes, but more so when my wife had been alive. We would sit by the window together, with the Queen Anne candlestick table between us, and have our toast and marmalade. I asked Eton if he wanted a cup of tea, but he turned and pointed at the cigars, which were on my bed. He said he'd never had a cigar. I was delighted—surprised at my delight, but very willing. I went downstairs to make sure all the windows were closed and took two snifters for us from the drinks cabinet and some calvados. By the time I returned to him, my room had darkened, but he'd taken the oil lamp from my mantel and set it on the table in front of the window, lit. We sat in the chairs beside it and I poured us both snifters. We toasted to his arrival and then lit our cigars by the oil lamp. His face was radiant as he lifted the flame up close to him. His cheeks and forehead were beaming amber.

We both looked out at the rain. People were coming home from work, and so from the depths of the downpour, which held more light than a clear evening might have, small black figures would slowly emerge, the umbrellas of people on the street, bobbing up towards us one by one, or in twos and threes. They would come right towards us and pass under the archway just next to my house—they marched underneath us as if the building had opened its skirts to them for shelter. It was a very memorable, very dear sight, and with our golden reflections faintly there also, the ends of our cigars hovering like fireflies.

To the left was a bakery, and above it a cooking school that was run by a friend of my wife. Two of the umbrellas snuck inside the door and moments later, a pale yellow light turned on in a window above where they'd entered, but the rain was too heavy to see what was inside. We watched some more of the people straggle home until the rain lifted a bit, night fell very quickly, and we were able to see inside the first window across the way women with large, white, beefy arms, rolling out dough with pins. Eton asked, and they were the only words he spoke as we sat there, "What do they make?" I replied with my only two words, "Pastry dough." That was all we said to each other, from the moment of our toast to the moment night had fallen completely and we'd finished our cigars. We simply sat there and let the brandy settle and the tobacco smoke curl up alongside the draperies.

When he had finished, Eton put the end of his cigar in the dish and stood up. He said, "Thank you," and smiled gently. I said, "Tomorrow?" He said that he had to look for a place with Erin. "After tomorrow," he said. The rain seemed to have cooled the evening, and he asked if he could borrow my jersey for the walk back to his bed-and-breakfast. I said certainly. I led us downstairs by the oil lamp, lent him an umbrella, just in case, and he left.

The whole house was very dark afterwards. I was a bit lonely, my company for the past hour had been so flawless, so I went to every room turning on the lights, and remembered Hugh's envelope in my pocket. I read it in the living room, with the wireless playing. It was a note of thanks for accepting Eton's company— very, very clever, Hugh was—and then a list of books I might have for Eton for when we next saw each other. I was very disturbed by it, even then. The flame was there. My mischief had been kindled. I burnt the letter.

Erin Hirt

We found a flat in Bayswater. It was on the third floor and it had these nice bay windows but we never really decorated it. He wouldn't let me put up curtains. There was a couch that was rotten underneath, so we got a cover for it we bought on the street, an Indian print that was always pulling out. We'd sit on this couch and read at night and eat Dutch pretzels, and every time we moved the blanket would untuck. We'd have to get up and shake the salt off and tuck it back in. Also our first bed there was old and the mattress slumped in the middle. Boone said it was like waking up in a burial pit because our arms and legs would be asleep. He'd have to crawl into the kitchen in the mornings, and he'd kneel at the stove with his hair all messed up making the tea and waiting for the feeling to come back into his legs.

We didn't even get a TV until he started working for "Color by Numbers," which was the only show we ever really watched. It was about this detective who was also an artist, and Boone's first job was just to do the detective's paintings. Frank Smythe was playing the detective, and his brother-in-law had been doing the paintings but he got fired for drinking, and so Boone just stepped right in—I guess they all knew Peter Finney or something. But every week we would wait to see if they used the painting Boone had done of me. They'd always begin the show with a pan of this detective's art studio. They'd go across all his paintings and there was one of me, but the TV was black and white so you couldn't really tell. He'd painted it right when we first moved in, one morning when it was about five o'clock. We'd get the sun reflected off the windows across the street, and he said the colors on my skin were mandarin and blue, but my hair he just couldn't get. He said he probably just didn't believe what color my hair was, so he couldn't get it.

C.L. Hull

Frank told me. We were at the Beefsteak Club, little party for Tony Newley that Frank and Bertram Lilliquist had put together, and Frank tells me they've got Pete's boy painting sets for them on their little detective series. Christ, I nearly spit up. I mean, all due respect to Frank because it is work, after all, and I think he did a wonderful job with it under the circumstances, but "Killer by Numbers"? Fuck me.

I mean, Eton Boone, I knew, he can't be doing that kind of plebe work now. He was an artist, and I think you'll all agree, he'd really been doing something there in New York. I didn't know what the fuck it was, but ingenious sorts of things, I'm sure, and I even at the time, I don't mind saying, did think to myself, well, Boonie, you know, he should be quite pleased. It's not everyone who gets a chance to really express himself like that. It's a miracle he got away with it as long as he did. But then you turn your back for one fucking minute—I go over to Norway to make a lovely little picture with my friend Maurice Mickelwhite, *The Gazelle Boy*—I get back to London and they've got him painting these fucking prop paintings.

I mean, it just shows, doesn't it? The big cheeses catch a whiff of your genius and that's that—boom, down you go. And just think of the man's spirit—riding so high, Boonie'd been drinking champers out of Pat Nixon's B-cups for the last two years, and now this. Must have fucking crushed him. I mean, when Frank told me, it made me want to put down my knife right there, go straight over to the BBC, walk in their big brass doors, find my way into the fucking director-general's office, turn around, pull down my trousers and take a giant black shit right on top of his bleeding desk calendar. There's your fucking prop painting. Poltroon.

Christ, and I'll tell you, I wanted to get through to him too. I mean, you have to stick together on these things, you have to show some solidarity. So if I'd seen him, I swear, bumped into him wandering on down the halls there with his little shit sketches for these buggers under his arm, I'd have told him, "Boonie, my friend, buck up. We have all been there, we've all had to wear the banana suit, but the point is keeping in mind that nothing is an accident. If you've done it once, if you've sashayed on down that red carpet with the world's tongue up your bum, then by God there's no reason it can't be lodged up there again someday. Never lose faith, man. Courage."

John Kinsey

At the very start, I was getting letters from Hugh at a nearly delirious pace. I was taking Eton out at least once per week, but Hugh would write as if I'd had no contact with Eton, as if he and I spoke in different tongues. He'd say, "Boone quite enjoyed the Altman Library. Why don't you take him there again?" Oh, thank you, Hugh, may I? Or, "The LSO he rather liked. Why don't you check its schedule for the winter season? Perhaps Mahler." Oh, perhaps, Hugh, yes. And he would send reimbursements.

I think he simply wanted to know what I thought of Eton. He wanted a second opinion, which I'm afraid to say I withheld, not because I wanted Hugh to suffer, but because he'd have found so unsatisfying the things I had to say. Truthfully, I didn't want to say anything. I didn't like us comparing notes that way, cataloguing Eton's development as if he were a laboratory rat. And I don't think that Eton was particularly comfortable with it either. He was wonderful, and I confess my fondness for him grew in leaps and bounds wherever I sensed his resistance, or better, his apathy towards Hugh's Baedeker. His nonchalance in the art galleries, the interest he took in security men as opposed to the paintings, I've come to think it all may have been for my benefit, a friendly bit that he knew I relished, but I did. At the Gridiron Club, listening to Percy Shropingham-Dowe's epic free verse, I savored every delicious snore that brayed through his nasal passages. They sounded to me like the most elegant rebuffs imaginable of Hugh's whole queer plot.

Because the pleasure *I* took from these outings with Eton had nothing whatever to do with cultural insight. What I enjoyed most was the walking, the strolls to and from wherever we'd been dispatched for the evening. We walked distances I wouldn't have dreamed of on my own, all the way from Ozymandias, the bookshop I keep in Whitechapel, to the Tower of London, across the river and then back again and along the embankment all the way to Charing Cross and then back to Lamb's Conduit. I even bought us a pair of handsome walking canes with mallard heads, mahogany with ivory bills. We walked everywhere, to neighborhoods I hadn't visited since before the war. And never taxis if it rained—the bus on occasion, because there's more to see—but anything to stretch our time together.

And the conversations came and went so comfortably. We spoke of the things in front of us. We talked of the people on the street, the buildings, windows. But we never felt compelled by long silences to speak. Silence was a comfort. Silence was a friend, it led us its own way, sometimes so far astray that we'd completely forget where we'd intended to go, or decide at the back of a queue for tickets, oh, hang it, there'll be other nights for this, let's go for tea at Endicott's. We'd stroll along Regent Street. We'd look in all the shop windows, at antique clothing for Erin—hats and wraps and shawls. And he never made me feel that there was any place he'd rather be than by my side. No, it became very clear to me, the more time we spent together, the less inclined I was to let anything, anything other than his desire to return to Erin, guide us on our way. It was perfect companionship, beyond compare, and yet even while I enjoyed it, I fear I understood that I enjoyed it, like a book you can barely finish you want so badly to go back and read it through again.

Hugh Gardiner

Our letters were never more alive and electric than when Boone was in England. I was at work then on a study of Rupert Brooke, and I would use my office hours for that. Of course I was still giving at least two lectures per day, and teaching a course in creative writing, so I kept a fairly busy schedule. But there were at least one or two evenings per week when I could set everything else aside, when by ten o'clock my desk top was clear and all I had to consider was Boone's last letter, and my response.

It would be there waiting at the top of my desk. I'd have a cup of tea there beside me and let it cool as I read. I would take the letter out of the envelope, lay it flat, and at first just look at the handwriting for a moment, to try to see the mood he'd been in, if it was the same as last. There could be no telling. He was so eager to explore new ideas. You could even feel it in some of the things he'd send, that he hadn't quite given something the time it might have needed to simmer—a letter on Thomas Hardy, I remember, he wasn't very kind. But then most of the time he'd go back and reexamine his thinking. He'd work through it, and of course it was very exciting for me being able to read the words of an artist who was still so young, whose theory wasn't quite in step with his practice. It was thrilling to watch his mind develop, really right there before my eyes.

And of course, his letters weren't about intellectual matters only. Just as often, they were quick impressions, descriptions. I remember one, a lovely portrait of Miss Hirt sleeping. That was an extraordinary piece, and what was so moving about it, to me, wasn't just the blazon of his sleeping beauty, but that with no problem or concept demanding of our attention that evening, he did not put his pen aside and join his companion so soon. He chose instead to look at her and think to himself, "I'll send Hugh this."

Because the point of these letters wasn't ever to reach conclusions or create works of art. The point was to include them comfortably but faithfully in our days. It was the practice itself, the ritual of writing. And it was just as much a ritual for me, and one that I held dear, responding to him, even if sometimes my reactions had to be tempered by discretion. I never wanted to distract him, you see, the intensity of his writing could be so stunning. The immediacy with which it reflected his states of mind and changing ideas indicated an engagement with his own thinking that was quite solitary, and I didn't want to jeopardize that by calling too much attention to myself.

Soon enough, though, I think I came to understand the measure of my province, and the things I could say without apprehension. And once I had, the letters became very easy for me, and very soothing. I would make notes to myself throughout the day about what I wanted to mention to him, even as I edited my Brooke or lectured the students, and slowly the letter would begin to take form, so when time came for writing, it felt as though the words spilled out of my hands. They rushed through me, they flowed, from sentence to sentence, to paragraphs, to whole pages, but always tamed by the idea that we'd be writing again, that there would always be other opportunities to share.

And having that constant in my life, a place I could go that was so apart from everything else, and so perfectly honest, it was very cleansing. It's a true wonder, how in a six-page letter that concerns nothing but his first visit to the Tate Gallery, all the grub that you've carried with you is flushed away. It's a very natural process, and I fear that fewer and fewer people understand it anymore. I know that I miss it greatly. It is a lack in my life now.

Erin Hirt

I cooked him a really nice meal once in the kitchen, a giant fish soup with mussels, and I'd made bread. I don't cook that well, but neither of us liked English food. So I made this really nice meal, and I'd bought wine and put a rose in a vase, and he came home from the show, and we just sat there. He didn't drink any of the wine, and he tried to make a joke. He said, I feel like I should have a ring for you or something. Which didn't mean, next time warn me, Erin. It meant, cut it out.

C.L. Hull

But thank God for resilience, because there is a certain resilience to the true artistic spirit. It's just that sometimes you have to play the cards you're dealt, that's the key, and I have to say, for all the fucking genius people are liable to heap on Boone's back, it's really the fact that he was able to take advantage, you know, of what they were giving him, and what they were giving him, all those bucktooth sods at the detective program, was a very wide berth. They were petrified of him. Frank said so.

Artist, in the first place. That's enough right there for most people to call the dogcatchers, but you take that mainstream pea-brain attitude and put it in combination with the fact that Boone really was a complete loon—well, then you've got yourself a bit of leverage. And Boone sees that. He says fine, let 'em all think I munch on Hitler's balls for breakfast, because you know what? There's a measure of respect there, and he knew that, that every society has a certain admiration for the madman, they really do. So he lays low, kicks a dog every so often, roots through the waste cans, and in particular turns in a set of paintings for that show, I'll tell you—Christ, I went over to take a look at them with Frank one time and what I'd like to know is, where the hell did this bleeding detective get his hands on so much fucking mescaline, because these things were from the planet Mars. Wild stuff, really wacko, thrashing sorts of things, with bodily organs and animal heads and eyeballs flying all over the place and these white, nightmare masks. All right out of his head, I could tell. Frank loved them.

But, you know, Boonie, he was just taking a piss at them all. He was just fucking with them. 'Cause he knows now, now that he's established himself as every bit the wacko they thought he was, that when he finally pulls himself together enough to actually write something down—because I happen to know that he was interested from the start in maybe actually *creating* an episode—well, you tell me. Christ, it's yes sir, no sir, Mr. Boone, whatever you say. Appease Dr. Dementio here, Pablo Schizo, because who knows what the hell he's going to do—but listen to him too, that's what I'm saying. They're going to listen because in the first place he's got that madman authority about him, and secondly, let's agree now, the man could actually write one hell of a detective program when he put his mind to it. Frank was actually the one to see that it got made, the first episode he wrote.

Fine show. Excellent program, I mean, from a very sort of television perspective. Nominated for a BAFTA, and I myself actually appeared in it, the first one Boonie wrote, as a favor, you know. "Bloodlines" it was called. All about blood, the power of blood, brotherhood. Wonderful stuff. Two brothers, artists in the West End, and they hate each other's guts. Cain and Abel setup, and I unfortunately got killed right in the first scene, but I think we really did establish a palpable sibling feel, which anyone will tell you is just about the most difficult, you know, family dynamic to play. See, the other one, my brother, who was played by the gifted French actor Henri Charteaux, he stabbed me right there in the first scene, in the stomach. I think I only had six lines, but Henri, the other brother, he just leaves the body for dead. But it isn't, see, because I'm not. I'm gasping and moaning, and what I do is, as my dying gesture, I reach into my belly, right into my gut so my hand's covered with blood—because that's what an artist is doing, my friend, he's working in his own blood or else he is not a very good artist—and finally I reach up and smear my brother's name all across the canvas—a big red "Colin," if I remember. Smashing scene.

Anyway, by the time Henri—oh, Christ, it couldn't have been "Colin," then, could it? Something French. Anyway, Henri gets back and finds me dead, but when he sees what I've done—you know, the "J'accuse" right there on his canvas—he rings up Scotland Yard, gives them the old crocodile tears. But before they get there, see, he's outdone me again, bastard—he's painted over the canvas. He's done a sort of collage, and it turns out to be his masterpiece, which Boone actually did a very fine job with—very gifted man, for Christ's sake—and Henri tells everybody it's his final tribute to the greatest artist he's ever known, me, and right in the middle of it, there's his name, written there in his brother's blood. Fantastic stuff. I think Frank figured it out in the final scene, tossed Henri out the window.

There's a great deal to think about there, there really is, and I believe people would have a much higher opinion of television altogether if it were all like that. But, you know, Henri, Frank, myself if I don't mind saying, and Boonie behind the old typewriter, you're obviously not going to find that everyday. That was a very special program.

John Kinsey

I asked him about Erin every so often, where she was, how she was, but I'd have done just as well to ask him who she was, because she hadn't come with us anywhere, and Eton hardly said a word about her. And of course it's very difficult trying to get a picture of someone you've never met. Every new piece of information about her I found even more surprising than the last, they all required such drastic revisions of what I'd been piecing together in my head. That she was a professional model—I'd thought perhaps a writer with thick black glasses and elegant high cheekbones. That she was a redhead—I'd pictured black, jet raven black. Even that she was Irish—it was all very difficult to manage.

So finally I insisted. There was a fashion show on a pleasure boat that Erin was apparently modeling in, and I pressed Eton to get me an invitation. We went together, and it was quite an introduction, I must say, for her to be literally parading out in front of me for inspection, to see if in essence she was anything like what I'd imagined. I was very excited, and the setting itself, when we arrived, it was thrilling to be among such revolting society.

When the show began, all the models came out at once. I asked Eton which one was she, but he wouldn't even say. He said, "Guess." I did miserably. We were very far away and they were in hats. I think Erin may have passed three times before, by process of elimination and nothing else, I said, "She. She's the one, isn't she?" "Very good, John. Yes," Eton said. I was able to see her several more times, up and down the runway, and I did stare, I peered to get some understanding. She seemed very pretty, very attractive, but I couldn't get much more than that. She was fairly mannequin, which was only her job—she was quite professional, it seemed to me—I didn't count it against her.

After the show, the boat transformed into an enormous party, where my presence, I promise you, was quite exceptional. Erin found us finally. She was with someone else, another of the models, who was excessively tall and slim. Erin came up and she'd let her hair down, extraordinary. She'd taken off some of her makeup and was carrying her shoes in her hand. She hooked arms with Eton and said, "I know you hate makeup," but she kissed him on the cheek anyway. They turned to me. Eton said, "Erin, I'd like you to meet a friend of mine. This is John Kinsey," and I suppose I'd been expecting something normal—she might say that she'd heard so much about me, or "Yes, I've been looking forward to meeting you," but I was absolutely stunned as she turned to me, she extended her hand and said, "Oh, hello, are you one of Eton's friends from the television program?" I was flabbergasted. She had absolutely no idea who I was, none whatsoever. Eton and I had been seeing each other now, two or three times a week for the past three months, and she hadn't a clue of me. And I might have held it against her, in a very irrational but natural way—how could she be so oblivious, after all, not even to know of me, her lover's other axis—but for the effect of her presence, for as lovely as she was physically, even more lovely was something in her manner, something trusting, something at that moment very happy just to be with Eton. He reached into his pocket and told her that he had something for her, and he pulled out a handful of Rowntree Gums. He said, "The greens." She took them and she kissed him again, again on the cheek, but so openly and unsuspiciously that I found in an instant the mystery of this Erin Hirt was quite solved. She was a beautiful young woman, frighteningly pure of heart. My imagination had been far too complex, I hadn't needed to use so much of it. The new mystery, though, or the thickening one, stood there stiffly beside her, looking out through the crowd over my shoulder, with his jacket sleeve hooked anxiously by her tender arm.

Erin Hirt

The way I remember it, even when I'd gone up North, it was raining. He'd be on the bed and his hands smelled like soap, and he'd have just gotten home. I'd have gotten out of the shower, so my hair would be wet. We'd have goosepimples, and the pipes would be banging. This is the scene I would remember when I was up North. It was like when we could get up there, when we could get up to our room, everything would be okay. Just with the rain outside. He liked to have me stand there, he'd want me to stand there because he said it was his only chance to see all of me. And I'd just be out of the shower.

I don't know. I don't know if I can say this. I don't know what the rest of his life was like. I don't know how he acted the rest of his life, but with me, when the two of us would be alone and not have to deal with anything else, just being alone with him was really the best and, I don't know, you should know that. You should. Like his hands, you should know. They weren't big, but they were beautiful and very graceful and in control. He would just run his hands very smoothly all along me, very smoothly. He could do the whole thing without touching, and we'd end up laughing because of this energy that would be there. There really was. The pipes would just be banging and it would be raining, and maybe even you could see us from the outside, but I just didn't want to move.

Carlo Esteban

I first met Eton Boone in January of 1970. He showed me the Beethoven testament and told me his idea. We met for eight straight nights after that, in February, and prepared a twenty-six page treatment of the film. For two and a half months we let it sit while we completed our other projects. He was working with the detective series. I was reediting *An Ulster July* for theatrical release, but that is where he had first seen my name, on the television documentary—I had been in Ulster in the summer of '69 shooting a film on the Catholic civil-rights movement when the troops moved in. The summer of 1970 Boone and I worked again, nights, at his flat in Bayswater—on the screenplay. The fall we spent in casting and production, securing lots, sets, and supplementing our finances. We began shooting on January 23, 1971, and wrapped on September 11. It was slow. We had shot 83,000 feet of footage. Midway through the editing process, in December of 1971, Eton Boone left England. I finished editing the film myself. These are the facts of our association.

THE HEILIGENSTADT TESTAMENT*

O my fellow men, who consider me, or describe me as, hostile, stubborn, or misanthropic, how greatly you do wrong me. You do not know the secret reason why I appear to you to be so. Ever since childhood my heart and soul have been imbued with tender feelings of goodwill; and I have always been ready to perform even great actions. But just think, for the last six years I have been afflicted with an incurable complaint which has been made worse by incompetent doctors. From year to year my hopes of being cured have gradually been shattered and finally I have been forced to accept the prospect of a permanent infirmity. . . .

Though born with a passionate and lively temperament and even fond of the distractions offered by society, I was soon obliged to seclude myself and live in solitude. If at times I decided just to ignore my infirmity, alas! how cruelly was I then driven back by the intensified sad experience of my bad hearing. Yet I could not bring myself to say to people: Speak up, shout, for I am deaf! Alas! How could I possibly refer to the impairing of a sense which in me should be more perfectly developed than in other people, a sense which at one time I possessed in the greatest perfection, even to a degree of perfection such as assuredly few in my profession possess or have possessed—O, I cannot do it; so forgive me, if you ever see me withdrawing from your company which I used to enjoy. . . .

I must live quite alone and may creep into society only as

The Heiligenstadt Testament was written by Ludwig van Beethoven after his retirement from Vienna to the small village of Heiligenstadt in 1802. The Testament, which concerns the suffering and isolation brought on by Beethoven's loss of hearing, was addressed to the composer's two brothers. It has been suggested by Levi Mottl that Boone may have first become aware of the Testament during their trip through Europe in 1966.

often as sheer necessity demands; I must live like an outcast. If I appear in company I am overcome by a burning anxiety, a fear that I am running the risk of letting people notice my condition. . . . How humiliated I have felt if somebody standing next to me heard the sound of a flute in the distance and I heard nothing or if somebody heard a shepherd sing and again I heard nothing—such experiences almost made me despair, and I was on the point of putting an end to my life—art alone restrained my hand. For indeed it seemed to me impossible to leave this world before I had produced all the works that I felt the urge to compose; and thus have I dragged on this miserable existence— truly miserable, seeing that I have such a sensitive body that any fairly sudden change can plunge me from the best spirits into the worst humors—patience, I am told, I must now choose for my guide; and I now possess it—I hope that I shall persist in my resolve to endure to the end, unless it pleases the inexorable Fates to cut the thread; perhaps my condition will improve, perhaps not; at any rate I am now resigned. . . .

Urge your children to be virtuous, for virtue alone can make a man happy. Money cannot do this. I speak from experience. It was virtue that sustained me in my misery, and owing to it and also to my art I did not put an end to my life by committing suicide. . . . Well, that is all—joyfully, I go to meet Death— should it come before I have had an opportunity of developing all my artistic gifts, then in spite of my hard fate it would still come too soon, and no doubt I would like it to postpone its coming—yet even so I should be content, for would it not free me from a condition of continual suffering? Come, whenever you like, with courage I will go to meet you—farewell; and when I am dead, do not wholly forget me. I deserve to be remembered by you, since during my lifetime I have often thought of you and tried to make you happy. . . .

Thus I take leave of you—and rather sadly—yes, the cherished hope—I brought with me here of being cured to a certain extent at any rate—that hope I must now abandon completely. As the autumn leaves fall and wither, so has my own life become barren. I am leaving here almost in the same condition as I arrived. Even that high courage—which has so often inspired me on fine summer days—has vanished. O Providence—do but grant me one pure day of joy. For so long now the inner echo of real joy has been unknown to me—O when—O when, O Divine Power—shall I be able to feel it again in the temple of Nature and in contact with humanity—Never?—No!—O, that would be too hard.

Ludwig van Beethoven

Heiligenstadt
October 10, 1802

Carlo Esteban

The idea was very simple. To treat the life of an historical figure with the cinema verité technique. Boone had been inspired by two things—*The Heiligenstadt Testament,* and the Bob Dylan documentary, *Don't Look Back,* which Leacock-Pennebaker had made of Dylan's British tour in 1965. The challenge was to put these two things together—to try to understand this very romantic and passionate expression of suffering, Beethoven's, but to see it on our own terms, through a handheld camera. Boone said it would be like taking a tape recorder to the opera. You would miss some of the high notes, yes, the arias will be thin, but perhaps you will pick up the snoring of the lady next to you, or snickering in the chorus, and that is new. The opera we have seen, we know the opera, but now can we wander around inside it, hear the diva's backstage tantrums. This is what our technology lets us do. It allows us to be there as it happens. So Boone and I wanted to know, how did history look before we knew these were heroes, before we knew that any of this mattered, or would last? These are questions we want to answer, using the cameras on our shoulders and pointing them at Beethoven and the tragedy of his deafness.

John Kinsey

I had bought Eton a megaphone, the idea seemed so preposterous to me, a great big red one. We'd been out to dinner at an Indian restaurant in Knightsbridge, and Erin too. To that point, you must understand, it all seemed like some great joke to me. The very idea of Eton at the helm of a film set, directing all the lights and cameras and traipsing about with actors in wigs, I could see that it was quite intoxicating, but also very silly, and so I'd given him the megaphone, which I'd just happened to see on Portobello Road that day. He was very happy with it. He used it to get the waiter's attention and everyone else's in the restaurant. I felt as if I'd given a kazoo to a little boy. He was very pleased.

We spoke about the idea as we ate. I suppose I may have asked about it, just to tease him, but as he answered me and we continued to discuss it, I could tell that he'd developed the idea much more than I'd thought. He explained certain specific scenes he had in mind and the ways that they would work, angle for angle, and I must say, I'd never seen him quite this way, chewing his food so quickly and gulping it down. Eton had savored things so well normally, tastes, aromas, sounds—he was well beyond his years at telling the difference between blends of scotch—but I felt that night as though the three of us might just as well have been in a Pimlico pub having fish cakes. Worse than that, it didn't even seem that Erin's or my company was particularly necessary. Eton could have been explaining his ideas to any passing stranger, or posting them on church doors. He was talking about books he'd read, biographies and diaries, and when I asked finally about the possibility of its actually happening—I'd become very concerned—he said that he'd been discussing the idea with some of the people from his program, and that he'd actually found a filmmaker to work with. He told me that he'd been scouting certain locations around London, and that there were even certain props he'd already been pinching from the studio where he worked. He went on and on with these frightening details until finally I asked him, still somewhat skeptical, "Have you looked into how much such a thing would cost, Eton? Do you have an estimate?" "Oh," he picked up the megaphone and whispered through it, "maybe sixty-thousand pounds." I was momentarily relieved. "Sixty-thousand pounds? Well, where on earth would you get that kind of money?"—fool, John. Oh, but he was quick at his food again. He put down my gift, an embarrassed grin. He wouldn't even admit it. He kept mumbling. Erin told me finally. "Mr. Gardiner," she said. "Mr. Gardiner will match the funds that Boone and Carlo can come up with."

Hugh Gardiner

It was an extraordinary decision to commit himself to a project the size of *Heiligenstadt,* and I would perhaps have advised a challenge of smaller scale except that he'd been so frustrated by the work he'd been doing at the television program. "Color by Numbers" had been convenient, to be sure. It had given him the opportunity to learn about the more technical aspects of film and television production. It enabled him to experiment with scripting and plot, but I think that ultimately his ambitions were too great to be tamed by such light fare. He needed to move on, but he wasn't interested in the slow grooming it takes to become a filmmaker—that was very clear. He wasn't interested in being a filmmaker. He was interested in producing the effects he'd been imagining in his head, and when he described them to me, it was such a natural outcome of the thinking he'd been expressing in his letters, that I was quite convinced of his vision.

He'd seen a similarity between the Testament and the exposures, and yet Beethoven's piece he found to be slightly unsatisfying. He didn't really think that it conveyed so well, even at its most anguished, Beethoven's depths. It made reference to them. It announced them, but it did not convey them. So Boone had wanted to explore those depths for himself. To do so, however— and this was perhaps the most intriguing aspect of the project to me—he would have to reverse his normal creative process. With the exposures, you see, Boone had been observing the behavior of a man, and from that behavior he would distill a single soliloquy that could bring us closer to understanding the person. With Beethoven, and with *Heiligenstadt,* he would do the reverse. He was taking a soliloquy, the Testament itself, and from that he would evoke the life that preceded it. It was a wonderful idea, I felt, for Boone to challenge himself with this new strategy. It was surely worth attempting, because he could only grow from the experience, and what else was our purpose?

Carlo Esteban

Every idea, when you begin, seems impossible and also very simple. Even as I think of it now, I feel both the possibility and the impossibility of making this film. Impossible, because how could you ever hope to create the sense of authenticity that you will need for this? Authenticity is not so hard if you are following Monseignor Meegan up in Northern Ireland, or Bob Dylan on his tour of Britain, because these things were true, they were happening. But if it is a period of Beethoven's life that you want, this is impossible. Everything will have to be perfect. The sets will have to be perfect, the language will have to be perfect, the dialogue, the direction, the acting above all, will have to be perfect, because if anything is off, the label on Beethoven's inkwell or the style of candlestick, the illusion will be broken, and what is our film but an illusion? We will be reminded of the creators, we will lose the creation. So it is an impossible thing we were intending to do. This is one mood.

But here is another. Is it not also very, very easy, what we are setting out to do? If there is competence and understanding all around of what we are trying to do, the actors understand, I understand, the cameramen understand, then every frame is an instant success, because the idea is so good, the idea is so compelling. What is that good is always very simple. So in this light, in a good mood, it is a very possible thing we are doing. It is essential, revolutionary, the right idea at the right time, and this you should never pass up.

And what makes it even more possible to imagine, and more

exciting, is that this is a collaboration. I am not alone. There is someone else's desire there, someone else's energy. And this other person, do not forget, is Boone. Boone, he is a bottomless pit of energy—and no doubt. Doubt we do not need. Vision, we need. See the possibilities, and from the start, Boone did. Time after time, I can remember, we are at his flat in Bayswater, and we have been brainstorming. We have been pacing back and forth, Boone has been bouncing a ball, standing on furniture—his head is always up near the ceiling. He can go from the one end of the living room to the window in the kitchen without touching the floor, using nothing but chairs and desks, and tossing down pillows like hopscotch in his green wool socks. But now it is getting late, and we have come up against difficulties which seem impossible. Boone is down on his knees cleaning the rug with his hands, and I know that it is getting near the time for me to leave. Let us sleep on this, we say. Let's see how this looks in the morning. I would go home. I would go to my family, I would find my daughter Lucia is sick with pneumonia and I must take care of her, or the sink is clogged, there are bills, there are my mother's troubles back in Montepulciano, and I am hoping, Boone, will you know what to do with the film tomorrow, because I do not. I have lost the time. I have lost the hope.

And every tomorrow, I would get there and he would smile and say, "Carlo, everything is fine. Our trouble was this, and we will turn it to our favor." If it is a scene that wasn't quite working, when the sun comes up, he has made it work. The scene felt claustrophobic last night, this morning the scene is about claustrophobia. If the problem was money, he has found new money. He says, I have six thousand more pounds, don't ask me where. If it is tracking down the right coats, a spencer or Beethoven's Prince Albert, Boone has found the address of a shop in Bath. Every night, which I have begun frustrated, hopeless, and guilty that I have to tie my children's shoes, Boone has been understanding what we will have to do. His mind has not left the problem since we said good night. He has been listening to the music. He has been reading Von Breuning's diary and the biographies. He has found the solution to our problem, and when Boone finds a solution, he tells it to you as if it had been obvious, as if we have been lucky once again to discover that this is the way it should be. And when he is finished explaining this, he would look at me and clap his hands together, and hold them—this meant we were agreed, we could go on. And every time he would save the project from disintegrating in these early stages, I am thinking, well, I will make this up to him when the shooting begins. When the cameras are rolling, I will make this up to him.

Erin Hirt

He moved this giant desk into the flat after we'd moved in. We had to move a bureau out to make room for it, but that's where he'd sit at nights. That's where he'd do his writing, but sometimes he wouldn't even do anything. He'd think I was asleep. He'd come in and lie with me for about ten minutes, and then when he thought I was back asleep he'd go out to the desk and sit there. All I could see were his feet crossed below the desk and the joint burning in the ashtray. The only move he'd make was picking it up, and then I'd see him put it back down again, and he'd just sit there. When I woke up, he would be next to me.

John Kinsey

I redecorated my study at Ozymandias. We are so stupid about ourselves sometimes that we have no other way to notice our moods but in bending to our desire to move this chair here, this sofa against the back wall, perhaps move the lamp to the other side of the desk. That room had become so dank. It seemed to me to be growing must and cobwebs where just a year earlier it had been my citadel, the room to which I returned day after day to find peace in the books I pulled from my own shelves. Well, I could hardly stand the sight of it now, and the reason was resentment. I resented the place. Oh, it felt like a jail cell to which I'd been sentenced.

In the first six months or so when Eton was in England, you see, our lives together had created such a handsome braid. We'd seen each other three or four times a week over the spring or winter—because I can remember us all trudging through slush, a mad Christmas Eve hunt for a goose. I can remember Erin in her fur-lined leather coat and mink hat. I can even see the blotter above my desk, filled with appointments, dates, meeting times. "Meet Boone at five at Piccadilly Circus." "Buy groceries for Eton and Erin, at home." "Reserve two tickets, ballet on the twenty-fourth." But as time slipped away and the film began to supercede all else, mentions of his name perceptibly dwindled. And when they did appear, they were rather pitifully calligraphied in my stylograph. "Eton? Tea? Ludwig Van permitting."

By the following autumn our visits were so rare that they came to assume a significance that no evening should have to bear. I'm sure I flew to the door when I heard a knocking and rather shamelessly tried to keep them as long as I could. Five-course meals, with port and cheese, anything to keep them, and in my mind always thinking, worrying, "Don't go, I'll start a fire. Perhaps we can listen to the 'The Ring' or the complete Sonatas. Anything, yes, I'll talk about your silly soundtrack if that's what you'd like. I'd rather you just stayed, you two. Take the guest room and be here when I wake." But then I'd see a young man in the street the next day who might have Eton's step, it would level me, or a woman in the British Museum with Erin's cascading red hair.

She even surprised me once, at Ozymandias. She walked in, in those tall puss'n'boots, Anouk Aimee gracing the book shop with a visit. I showed her back to my office. We had some tea and biscuits and a lovely chat. Talked about nothing, really. Tried desperately not to talk about him and the fact that we both seemed to be waiting for something. She didn't stay long, she never stayed long, but even in the time that she was there, one couldn't help seeing the fullness of her feelings for him. Feelings not deep, but flawless. He was an almost complete mystery to her, the way an adult seems to a young child, such an astonishing lump of worry and intelligence that she had absolutely no means to fathom—only love or not love. And Erin found Eton wholly lovable, she did—that was her gift—to see him all at once like a stuffed Pooh bear and a white-bearded god who smiles down on us with puppet strings tied to his fingers. She loved him completely, and without a glimmer of understanding.

I remember her leaving, pointing her toward the autobus that would take her to her shoot at Trafalgar Square, and watching her cross the road as she looked through her handbag, a woman so artless, with all her love blown gently in the direction of a man whose brain was so clearly elsewhere. It made me want to see him even the more, but all I could do was turn round and head back to my lonely office. "Yes, perhaps the globe ought to be on the shelf. And if the desk were by the window, I could see the people's feet as they stroll by. Yes, move it over there." Either that, or go at it with an axe.

C.L. Hull

Ludwig van Beethoven. Fuck me, what a challenge. Really terrifying prospect in a way, a part like that, because you know, it can just eat you alive. Except that's the sort of thing you can wait your whole fucking life for, you know, so when the chance comes along, even if you can foresee the fact that it might really fuck with your insides, you have to dive at it. You have to take the risk. Because the rest of what you're asked to do in this life, even if you are lucky enough to be an artist—but especially if you're an artist, that's what I'm saying—is crap. It is absolute, verifiable shit. Because when you are an artist, what you are, and I'm sorry to say this, my friends, but what you are is a dog. You are essentially a dog who goes from one bone to the other. That's the only way. You eke your art out where you can. It's really a matter of individual—I don't know what you want to call it—individual circumstance, luck, kismet, karma. You just have to take your chances. That's what the true artistic life, I believe, is all about.

Beethoven knew that. I studied for the film, I read up on the man.

Carlo Esteban

Boone himself had had no intention of getting in front of the camera. He had hoped that Peter Finney would be able to do it, but even Peter Finney, I had my doubts, because this was not stage acting. This was a camera closer than any actor has yet experienced. I had thought perhaps not even an actor at all. Let us just get someone who is right. But this was not my area. Finney was unavailable. Hull was there. Boone said trust and we will see. I had never worked with actors before. I have not worked with them since.

Casting was set in September. We rehearsed for two months with the major roles before shooting. The sets were not ready, I had not yet assembled a complete crew. This gave Hull time. Boone would sit with him, listen to symphonies with him on a stereo that Hull had stolen from the National Theatre. They would read passages together from the diaries, and Bursy's letters. One afternoon, they went to Beckton to meet with deaf people who could give Hull insight. But still nothing was working.

One night we are at Boone's flat, Hull and I and Boone, and we have been discussing the role. How can we get Hull to understand Beethoven? Perhaps, I am thinking, if you imagine music is bullshit or rum-vomit. But I say nothing. They are the actors. 'An actor prepares,' and Hull has a plan. He says that he wants to listen to the music, *Eroica,* and when he feels his mind merging with Beethoven's, when he feels Ludwig's light, he will write out the entire *Heiligenstadt Testament* from memory. If he can do that, he says, he will have tapped Beethoven's genius. Very well.

Boone says that he has some of the wardrobe in his bedroom. He goes in and comes back with a cardboard box that he places in front of Hull. Hull digs through and finds a wig and a nineteenth-century smoking gown to wear. He admires himself in the mirror. Boone is sitting on the radiator now with a beer.

"The spitting image," he says—of Whistler's mother, I am thinking. This is absurdity. I should probably have left the room. My vibe, I am sure, was not positive. But Hull takes foolscap out of the bag that he's brought with him. He had aged it the night before by soaking it in white wine—theatre's gain, he says to us, was science's loss. Boone raises his beer to Hull, and Hull takes out cotton plugs and stuffs them in his ears. He gives us the thumb's up and shouts, "Let us begin!"

Boone jumps up to turn on the music. We sit and stare at Hull, who is crouching on the sofa. We listen to two measures. "Louder!" yells Hull. "Make the fucking music louder! I want to hear it in my soul." The man's ears are plugged. Boone is adjusting the volume, louder, still louder. Hull is raising his hand like a conductor. The windows are begining to rattle, the paintings are shaking. Cracks in the plaster are streaking across the wall. Suddenly, "Perfect," he says. "This is perfect. This is driving me fucking crazy." He listens. He is sitting there with his face in his hands, slobbering, his eyes are closed—"the madness, the madness," he says. Boone watches from the radiator, smoking a cigarette.

Finally inspiration strikes. Hull leaps to his feet. "It is time!" he shouts. "I am ready!" And at the top of his lungs, "I *am* Ludwig Van!" Boone looks at me from the radiator, a smoke ring for me. "I need a pen! A pen!" Hull shouts, and Boone points me to his desk. "Hurry! I will not be Beethoven forever!" I lift up the desktop, and I look inside. I give Hull his pen, but what I see in this desk is amazing. I see letters, hundreds of them, stacks and stacks of letters. Some are bound by rubber bands. Others are loose and stuffed in slots. They are just dumped in, but the desk is clogged, and they are all from the same person. Each one has the same stamp on it—Hugh Gardiner, New York. Our investor.

Hull is having spasms at the dining table, drooling, his eyes are rolled up in his head. I look past this. I motion to Boone, what are these, all these letters? Should I know about these? The man gives us thirty-four thousand pounds, are we in trouble? Boone looks at me. Nothing. But he gets up from the radiator, turns down the music, and he looks at Hull. "Ludwig," he says. Hull does not answer. Boone cups his hands. "Ludwig! Ludwig Van!" he shouts. Hull finally turns to him—he has his hand to his ear—"Alas, my good man, I cannot hear you," he says. "Speak up. Shout, for I am deaf." Boone goes over to him. He slaps him on the shoulder and points over to me with these envelopes in my hand. Hull looks at me, the wig crooked on his head. He is livid. "Fucking shit, whoever you are," he says. "Get the bloody hell away from my bleeding manuscripts!" He storms over to me, rips the letters from my hands, and throws them back in the desk. He turns to Boone. He is pointing at me now. "Get him the fuck out of here!" Boone looks at me and shrugs. "Herr Beethoven says you have to leave."

I left. I was glad to. Again I am going home confused and doubtful, again I am hoping that somewhere between midnight and sunrise, Boone will have fixed it, he will have turned Hull into someone I can stand working with, he will have turned Hull into Beethoven.

John Kinsey

It was at this time roughly that I received a letter from Hugh that I'm afraid I'll never forget, which is too bad, because it was an unfortunate moment in the history of our friendship—it was to me. It had been some time since Hugh had last written me—I think he'd sensed my reluctance to respond, or he may have been bored with what I'd had to say. In any case, this particular letter, which must have reached me sometime in the autumn of 1970, was very different from any I'd so far received. It was a letter of tremendous fret. It seemed as though it had been written with trembling hands, as I suppose many of them had, but this one was much more explicit with its worries.

It concerned Boone, needless to say, and me. Hugh said he'd sensed from Boone's letters that I had developed an attachment to our young friend that may not have been in all our best interests. In the first place, he said, Eton's talent was the most important thing, didn't we all agree, and the movie represented a very important juncture in his career, so now was not the time for me to be pouting about like a silly schoolgirl. Furthermore, he said that Boone had been behaving differently in his more recent letters, and I even think he was laying me to blame for it. He said that Eton had begun asking questions, questions about Hugh himself that were making him very uncomfortable, I know, because once he'd finished with these strange, vaporous descriptions of Boone's new-found curiosity, Hugh advised me, he very nearly warned me, not to discuss him with Eton. And of course I hadn't—from propriety alone—but to see it set down in such a subtle and nearly sinister explanation, that Hugh did not want Eton thinking about him in any way whatsoever, I began to understand for the first time that Hugh was frightened of Boone. He was petrified, and the whole thing might have amused me but for the way Hugh closed his letter. He ended by saying that if I persisted with my behavior, if I pursued my infatuation with Boone, I would be in trouble. He said, "You don't know him as I do, John. He has the power to hurt you."

It was such an offensive thing to say, and I didn't know what Hugh's design was, whether this was some kind of threat or intimidation tactic on his part, or whether he'd gone completely mad. But it positively infuriated me, and I suppose my final reaction was this—to wave my finger at Hugh from across the Atlantic, shake my head and advise him under my fiery breath not to be hoisting his own absurd fears onto my relationship with the boy. Obviously he is threatening you, old friend, and I don't exactly know why. I'd never claim to. But please don't advise me with your own torment. It isn't fair, Hugh. It isn't polite. It isn't very dignified.

Joe Boone

Hilary's grandfather died in 1970, October. Hilary was at Harvard—it was his freshman year, I think—and Anne had to get him back. It was Damon's father, but she had to tell Hilary. The funeral was in Georgia, and Damon was going to be there.

Hilary had been very hard. He hadn't been coming home the way Anne would have wanted him too. He wasn't using his home as a home. He wasn't using his Mom like a Mom, and he was very tough to control. We'd seen him a couple weeks over the summers, and when he went off to Harvard, he didn't ever come back for vacations. It was very hard on Anne. She'd wanted it to work, she'd wanted it to be some kind of family, we both did, but it just felt like we'd both lost a son. We'd lost two kids in the trade, and that hurt.

Anyway, she'd told Hilary to go do this thing for his father, and we'd sent him money for it. Anne and I had gone down there too, and Hilary never showed. We tried to call him up at Harvard the day before the funeral to see what was going on, see where he was, and one of Hilary's roommates said Hilary was in England with Eton. That's where Hilary had said he was going.

So there they were. These are the two boys we're losing, and now they're together over there. It was very hard. Damon looked like he was going to blow, and Anne, it really shook her up. And I know she didn't want it to seem like being with Eton was the worst thing in the world, but it's hard to control your reactions sometimes.

I had to call Toddy to get Eton's number. I didn't have it on me. We got his number, and we didn't even know who should call. But I called. Ten times, I called. We had to leave messages, but finally, Eton calls back. He got us the day after in the hotel room, and I asked him, is Hilary there?

Now, he laughed. I can understand why he laughed. I can understand that, but at the time, I just wanted an answer. I said, is he there, goddammit? And I don't know what it was with him, he says, "Hold on, I'll check." Pause, gets back on. "No. Sorry. Why don't you check his room?" And I say, "Look, now's not the time. He says he's with you. Is he there?" And Eton said no, he wasn't. He said he hadn't even heard from him since he left New York. And I don't know why it is sometimes. I don't know why you sometimes believe, sometimes you don't. Sometimes you don't believe a single goddamn word, it just feels like they're thumbing their noses at you. And Anne was there next to me and she was in tears. I got so angry. I just wanted an explanation. I said, "Goddamn it, Eton. You two ought to just think sometimes, you ought to just think about what it feels like back here, and why we have to feel like goddamn criminals for just wanting to have our own lives." We didn't want those two to go. We wanted the family as much as any two people ever did, but they just made you feel like a criminal, and I'll take it, but I could never stand seeing Anne have to feel that way. I just said, "Look, Hilary respects you. Now can you just get him to do something for Anne? If he isn't there," and I didn't know, "but if he isn't there, then would you just write him a letter or something." I wasn't asking for myself—I never did that with him—I was just asking for Anne. And Eton, goddamn him, he said something like, "Great idea, Dad. Help me write it." He says, "Dear Hilary," and I didn't know what he was doing, but he just goes into it. "Dear Hilary, you're needed at the house. You should know how needed you are," and I'm sitting on the bed next to Anne. I'm listening and I can't even believe he's doing it. He says, "Please come to the house. Wednesday night was very important to me. I need you. Blue is still drifting."

I just hung up.

Camille Walker

There's always the pull of Hilary. I met him in Cambridge. I was teaching at the writing program at Harvard, tutoring. It was at Sirocco over on Brattle Street, in the basement. Hilary was there drinking. We'd both gone to hear a student of mine, probably for different reasons. Actually, probably not. We both wanted to fuck him.

Hilary was a sight, a very beautiful little man. He was leaning over the bar, writing on the bartender's cast. The bartender was a friend of mine, and Hilary's apparently, named Malcolm. Malcolm had a broken arm and Hilary's knees were up on the bar stool displaying his ass to the club. I went up to get a drink. Hilary and Malcolm made me one together. Hilary put the straw in, and I told him that it was quite an act. Hilary said, "I'm his little monkey," and then he pointed at Malcolm. "And he's my organ grinder." I said, "Is that how he broke his arm?" and Hilary clapped his hands.

I had every intention of sleeping with him then. He seemed young, but he knew the ropes. *Un poisson dans l'eau,* as they say. He was wearing alligator boots and a Qiana shirt with a jungle on it and beige pants, not khaki, that grabbed his ass. I took him back to my table and we had a naughty little conversation. I asked him where he was hiding his tail, and he said, "It's wrapped around my leg, sister."

But I don't want you to get the wrong impression. Conversations with Hilary were risqué, but rarely were they word games. The game was "will you play?" It was *osé*. It was "you've got me now, can you keep me?" Hilary turned his attention to you. He stirred your drink and licked your fingers. He looked at you. He didn't look at you. Hilary played with your clothes while you were wearing them. He took my scarf, a silk scarf, and ran his fingers along it, and when Hilary's hands began to play with your clothes, you never knew quite where they were going to end up. He was like one of those pickpocket magicians who nab your wallet or your watch while they're talking to you. I always expected Hilary to look up at me and say, "By the way, Camille, aren't you forgetting your IUD?" Voilà.

That first night, we went to the Cantabrigian Inn. Hilary wanted to go to the Cantabrigian because they had full-length, three-panel mirrors in the bathrooms with side lamps. He said they make you feel like Gloria Swanson. So that's where we went the first time, and the first time with Hilary is a treat—I'm sure it was for everyone. There's no one like him. I've never been with anyone like him.

We were at the registration desk. I was signing in with one of my parents' credit cards and the marble counter came up to our chins. Hilary was standing next to me smiling at the man, and as I was signing in, he unzipped me. He unzipped my pants and fingered me right in the lobby.

Eton Arthur Boone to Hugh Gardiner, November 16, 1970. *

Dear Hugh,

Cézanne keeps nagging at me. When I belch, I taste his paintings. I haven't found the book you mentioned, though—I'm not

---

*This letter has been reprinted by permission of *Harper's Magazine*, where it was published in the May issue of 1975, under the heading "Indecent Exposures." The editors of *Harper's Magazine* have acknowledged that the names "Nina" and "James" are fictitious.

sure I want the book—but I went back to the gallery alone today, and I think that he was lucky—his weakness was for nature, not for human nature. I can imagine him returning to his easel and his view of Mont Sainte-Victoire. Throughout his home all the still lives pose in vain—the bowls of fruit, the sleeper, the eggs in the dish—every day he passes them by and makes his way back to his easel by the window which overlooks Mont Sainte-Victoire. He has settled on it, one image to paint, to see without concept or understanding, a single sacrifice to his art. When he sees a peach, he still wonders if it is ripe. When he sees an egg, he wonders if it is fresh, and the sleeper in his bed is warm and welcoming to him, nude. But when he looks at Mont Sainte-Victoire, he has painted it so often, there is nothing there but shape and color to speak to him, no other sense to make of it. Like a word he has repeated so many times it's lost its meaning, Mont Sainte-Victoire is no longer a mountain to Cézanne. It is not vegetable or mineral. It is no distance from his door, and as long as he sits at his window, it is as if he had never seen it before, every time.

Credit the painter, the stakes of his game are profound, but safe. The mountain is innocent, and what Cézanne does is gentle, we can see. He loves the mountain. With each new painting, he forgives the mountain everything we ever did to it. He reinvents it. Lucky Paul, for nature to be weakness.

But these aren't mountains out in front of me. There's a boy across the street who beats off at his window every night, hoping someone will stop and watch. Nina and I have discovered him. She averts her eyes. I am enraptured. A mountain blushes once a year and is blocked from my view by buildings, but this boy here sits right in front of us and blushes nightly, thrusts, jiggles, pants, grows, comes, wanes, and his eye is on the street the whole time, yearning for a witness. Tell me who is more irresistible than man, with all of our uncertainty pounding away in his chest, boom boom boom. Look at him, he has desire. He has need. He has intention. He is a ravenous identity, a liar, preserved in all the images I keep, they'll be with me until I die, of this lusty boy here, cleaning himself off, bittersweet, disappointed, spent. There are photographs I've studied too, from New York, just as etched in my memory, of Dylan playing chess, or Nixon's "v" for victory. Phrases. "Who the hell is Lana Turner?"—LBJ lies prostrate, begs for our mercy. Or the sight of Judy Garland on Paulo's television

set, up in Washington Heights. She turned around as if the angel
of death were there behind her, but the look on her face was
relief—she'd tipped her hand. ("Did you see? Did you see that?"
Paulo nods and hands me the pipe with his toes. *"Ceci n'est pas un
orteil."*) Their words, their faces and gestures draw me out like the
song of a Berber flute, and I listen, I gaze, I study, but I do not
forgive them—it's not my place, and it's not my place to reinvent
them either. I cannot. I submit to their desire, and they desire to
be understood, they desire for us who look to reaffirm their flailing
personalities. So is this love I feel when I return to them, or the
arousal of a much fiercer instinct, to see all the hate and pain in
someone? To eat the peach, to smash the eggs, to fuck the sleepers
from behind.

Nina deserves better, and so does James. I am sometimes
frightened to be with Nina, for fear I might be swept inside her
momentarily, or to think of James as he closes the door after
we've said good-bye. Right there, on the brink of giving in and
allowing their minds to roll into mine, I would want to reach out
to them both and say, "You know, if my love meant anything, I
would feel it for you, obviously." But then I would relent, I
know, allow myself the simplest games I used to play. There are
roses just inside James's gate that must stare at him every morning he leaves for Ozymandias, or books on the shelf in his office
that wait for him to arrive. He must see them every day, and
with that simple incidental fact, we are let in if we want. We
have picked the lock of his brain and we can go, we would, but
for the fact that I know it would only lead somewhere so ugly to
me, only show me something sad and imperfect, thrashing,
unexpressed, something naked and ashamed, pleading to be pun-
ished—I would oblige. Isn't that all we have to give each other,
the satisfaction of our desires—suck on arrogance, beat the
sheepish, rape the insecure—it's what they want—and then
watch the monsters grow. Watch them devour perfectly good
lives. That's all I see, if I look, and I have not yet learned to do
anything but thrash in the presence of that fact.

Or compensate, like Cézanne, with a sacrifice, but for me a
human sacrifice. Can I? Oh, please, oh please, oh please, I beg—it's
just this one. *Paul* got one, and this will be the last, I promise. Plus,
it's for my own good. Everything else will be safe and sound now,
won't it? All the other everyday things can go back to being. We

can see the peach blush and imagine its tang, Mrs. Garland can
have her makeup back, James can leave the door and go upstairs
to bed, and all the energy that went towards stripping the world
of its bland grey suits will settle savagely, for me, or nothingly, for
Paul, on a single victim of our fetish. Someone, or something we
could never resist—it isn't in our nature.

Look at him, sulking somewhere in a corner of a couch,
huffing, ripping through a magazine with his feet tucked underneath him. He is supreme. He has seduced the military man, a
major, from his bunk at check-in, just fifteen years old. He
watched the guy struggle face to face with his regulation-shiny
belt buckle, and from that moment on he's known that no one,
not even the major with his tattoos and decorations, can resist
the lure of such pure arrogance, even on a sophomore's beautiful
face, an arrogance that comes from being so hateful and knowing
it, that he is irrevocably un-alike, the most exotic mutt. A
"marabou," a *"zambo," "fustee," "griqua"*—he lists them on his
fingers, he tastes the words—*"sacatra," "cafuso,"* a "high yaller,"
and he can smile because he knows, he tilts his face moonward—
yellow nothing, he's warm gold, alchemical, and more beautiful
for his mongrel breeding than a Burmese cat. Regal. Imagine his
eyes, resting on the major's shiny bald top bobbing up and
down—there's the moment that changes a young man's life. He
said, "I wanted to look down on that fucker, I wanted to see his
mouth too small, and I did." And he saw one more thing, too,
that has been his secret, his ticket ever since—he saw that all the
rest of us who belong and make up the rules have one thing in
common: we are perverse. Perverse, perverse. We want what we
shouldn't, always, and that will include him—always. Legal exalts illegal, consent exalts taboo, and we exalt him, the perfect
anomaly, lovely and grotesque. He confounds every meaning we
ever concocted—no race, no gender, no father, no home—no rule
but his own desire to see us gape. I have watched it. He plays at
being extreme, deviant, absurd—because what else is there for
him? he has no stake in our approval—And he has *become* extreme finally, deviant, absurd. He has become a freak of his own
self, and there *is* heroism in that, I'm sure, to turn up the heat on
yourself until all the fat burns off. His moods are full throttle.
His voice pinches, scrapes, caresses, slugs, and his gestures are all
like a stage actor's, exaggerated, but he possesses us with them,

because there bare-ass naked on the surface of every flagrant mannerism is a perfect blend of loneliness affirmed and arrogance asserted, a confrontation of emotions so pure it turns our repulsion into awe and then burning desire, to indulge his game, to get down on my knees and unbuckle his pants too, just to see, to submit, and then become part of him for a moment. See how pure is that arrogance if I believe it for you, how pure is that sorrow if I feel it with you, how pure is that hate of yours, let me taste it. Let me hear the steady revving of your tirade, and where it always leads, if we should ever dare to question your motives—you say, "Look, shithead, let's get one thing straight—I didn't ask to happen. No one asked me, 'Do you want to come in this world and have nothing and be fucked up because they'll never know what to do with you?' Because if anybody had, if anybody'd had the brains to say, 'Do you want this'—this absurd, absurd situation—do you know what I would have said, E.B.? I'd have said, 'Fuck you, asshole. Fuck off. No.' But they went ahead and did it anyway, didn't they, these fuckers who only thought about themselves, they made me, and now I've made myself, and now you're going to have to live with me, and you're going to look, and you're going to want it, and you're going to worship it, you perverse, perverse imbeciles you . . ." on and on and on. Is there anything we'll ever hate more than him? Is there anything we'll be so helpless to resist? If we could love him, there'd be no limit to our perspective. There would be no perspective.

Good night.

Boone

Camille Walker

I'd come up to him with a long bottle of Mexican beer in my hand which the Cantabrigian used to have stocked in the refrigerators, lots of different bottles. Hilary was sitting on the bed looking up at me. He pressed the bottle in between my legs. I held it there and he started kissing its neck. I said, "Hilary, you are something special." And he looked up at me, with his tongue around the top, and he said, "Camilleon, I am sex. That's all."

He was—back then. Before. This is your introduction to the most sexually gluttonous man you'll ever meet, and that fall was vintage Hilary. He had someone different every day, every night, every afternoon. Sex, sex, sex, breakfast, lunch, and dinner. Libraries, bushes, bridges. Anywhere. And the ways you would hear about them. Just little hints. They became gifts. He would wear a new bracelet or a chain and you would have to ask him, Hilary, where from? Have I seen that before? "No," he'd say. "It's courtesy Mr. Edwards." He had a whole museum in his room, a cabinet full of love beads and other tributes, most of which came from the older men. He was a real hit with the older crowd. The man in city government, the one from the K-school who gave him a black opal scarab right in the middle of a Coles seminar. The attorney on Brattle Street who had offered him plane tickets to Montreal. He was the one with the two little boys that Hilary used to see on their bikes—"Oh, The Married Man." But the others, the younger ones, they were less emotionally draining. They didn't give as many presents, but they were quicker pops. Hilary could wedge more of them into a single day. I remember how he used to slide through the crowd at the Pudding, very smooth, very Ipanemac. "Slept with him. Slept with her." He'd touch them as he passed.

Now there is a reason he gets all this attention, very simple reason. Hilary was the sexiest man I have ever known—and I don't mean outside, in bars. That's a matter of taste and a lot of people, I'm sure, thought Hilary was a little ridiculous, but I'm talking about during the act. That's where a lot of Don Juans run into mechanical difficulties, but Hilary was perfect. Flawless. He loved flesh. When he pulled your clothes off, he said, "I'm a choir boy who's never seen flesh below the neck." And when he took off his clothes, he'd say, "I'm a choir boy who's never been naked." His body was like a boy's, like Donatello's *David,* but he moved like an animal. I used to just look at him. He'd be prowling around the furniture, or washing me in the shower, and his only concern was pleasure—his, yours, both of yours. And if you had objections to that—if you tried to get him to think, he'd turn you over on your stomach—and apologies if this doesn't sound very liberated, but I don't care, this is Hilary—he'd give you what you wanted. And that doesn't mean gnashing teeth and violence, necessarily. All it means is that Hilary knew what you wanted before you did. He didn't read minds, he guided them. His hand on your thigh meant that's where you wanted that hand, and that went for his mouth, his teeth, his ass, anything. He constantly let you know what you wanted.

We even used to lie there together afterwards. I'd tell him about a man I'd been seeing, and I'd just say, "Hilary, dear, give me a fantasy." And he would tell it to me. The meeting place. The touches. He would tell them like poems. He would lie there and imagine it, describe the body and what I'd do to it, what the body would do to me. His imagination was sexually perfect. The things he would see, there were no limits.

Toddy Boone

Hilary's birthday, Eton sent him something from England. It sort of surprised me, I guess, at the time. I was at RISD, but I'd gone up to Harvard to visit Hilary for his birthday, and he said Eton had sent him the funniest present he'd ever heard of. It was this shoe box filled with all these strange things Eton had collected for Hilary. I remember Hilary taking it down from his closet and putting it on the bed, and he started pulling out all these envelopes and plastic bags, which were marked. One envelope said, "Fingernails of the Cast and Crew" and another one was "Hair." There were also two little jars. One was labeled "A Jar of English Rainwater" and the other was "A Jar of English Mud." And Hilary spread everything out around the bed, and he said, look at what the best part was, and he spilled this whole envelope that was marked "Toenails." He said, "Look, there are like a hundred of them." There were a lot. They were all the actors' toenails, and he was swirling his finger in them. He opened up the envelope of hair, and they were in locks mostly. Eton had put in a key, with a sample of each person's hair next to their name and whatever they were doing for the movie, which hair was the other director's, which was Beethoven's and which was his own. There were about ten clumps, and Hilary was taking them all out showing me, showing me the blond and the gray and saying, wasn't it gross. He took them all out. He had the hair spread out all over the bed, and I asked him which one was Eton's, and he said Eton's wasn't there anymore. He'd taken Eton's out.

John Kinsey

But it is December. I have seen neither Eton nor Erin in a fortnight. I have been for some time down in Dover, attending the funeral of my cousin Henry and overseeing the reading of his will. Henry, who was an only child, had been left a pair of beautiful ivory combs by his mother, Harriet. Alas, Henry died a bachelor, and apparently never found anyone whom he felt deserved his mother's gift, and so left the combs in his will to dear dear cousin Victoria. Dear dear cousin Victoria, however, had passed on in 1967, and presumably Henry never got round to adjusting his will. I suppose I was remiss as the family solicitor.

Nonetheless, these combs remained, floating about with no one to claim them and no one really, other than myself, cognizant of their existence. I might have let the family know and chaired the ugly tug of war had not the combs, to my mind, so clearly been intended for a beautiful young lady whom I'd met not so long ago and who had shared with me in a discussion at Ozymandias her fondness for a particular volume of O. Henry. To see these combs, so refined, the purest ivory with a simple jade inlay, to see them stuck abruptly in the pitiful gray nest on Aunt Vanessa's head, well, it would have been a crime. But to see them resting in Erin's dazzling mane, oh, it would be like seeing the crown upon the Queen's head. Or a carnation in a white bowl of water. Sometimes, figures meet. I snuck the combs back to London.

I had not told my young friends in Bayswater that I had been away. I don't know that the thought of me had passed through their brains during that time, so it was with no sense of ceremony that I tried to contact them again. I knew Eton was keeping late hours, and was not surprised that my first few phone calls went unanswered. But one evening around eight, just before closing the shop, I rang up again. I had thought ahead. The combs were with me, wrapped in tissue and resting in my jacket pocket. Eton was home, thank goodness. "Hello." "You're there," I said. They're there. "I have a present. May I come over?" "Yes, John, but hurry, we were just going out." Going out? I flew. I grabbed the O. Henry volume and flew. With wings on my brittle urban heels I sped to Bayswater. And standing outside their door breathless, my hands were shaking uncontrollably, I remember feeling in my pocket for the gift. Is it here? Is it here? Yes, old fool, you remembered.

Finally, the knob turns, slowly, so slowly, the door is opened, and there, standing before me in all his diminutive, Mediterranean glory, is Carlo Esteban. "Carlo, where are they? Are they in the kitchen?" "They?" says he. "You mean Boone?" Boone was seated at the kitchen table, I could see, spooning porridge into his mouth. There was no sign of Erin. I stomped up to Eton, huffing and puffing. "Has Erin gone?" I asked. "Is she left already?" He looked up at me with an alarmingly dull expression. "Erin?" he said, "she left last week." Left? Where is she left for? "She's gone up North for a while, John. She'll be back, but it's no good with her here and the film." He said this to me. It was no good with her here and the film. Well, then dash the film, Eton—my goodness.

I was still breathing heavily from the cold, and with him there so nonchalant and Carlo putting golf balls in the living room, I began to feel a bit stupid. I'm sure my hair, what there was of it, was flown every which way, and I doubt that Eton was accustomed to seeing old men in such a frenzied state. I tried to excuse myself almost immediately. But he asked, was the gift for Erin? Yes. "Well, John, I'm very sorry. But I'll keep it for her if you like." No, I will keep it for her, Boone. I wasn't going to leave it with him, not with the one who had banished her for being too great a distraction. And as I made my way down the stairs, even closing the door to that odious flat, I was livid. "Damn them both. Damn them both." And of course it wasn't Eton and the exiled Miss Hirt whom I damned. It was Eton Boone and Hugh Dunleavy Gardiner. Oh, as I made my way home, and I walked the whole way, I could think of nothing but how those two deserved each other.

Carlo Esteban

There were 164 shooting days. That is an absurdly high total for the sort of film we were trying to make, for any film, but we had had to abandon our hopes of sticking to the original plans. Budget was not a problem as much as deadlines. We did not keep deadlines. You can see in the log book, days sixty-eight through eighty-seven—"Concert scene, concert scene, concert scene"— and from this we got only ninety-two seconds of film. Ninety-two excellent seconds, but nineteen days is too much for a minute and a half. The screenplay came to mean nothing. None of the narrative elements were working, Beethoven's relationship with the nephew specifically. So very early on Boone had started trying to convince me that the success of the film would be a matter of shooting everything that occurred to us and then putting it together later.

This was very frustrating to me. I had wanted to shine here, to be an influence on the set that could keep us pointed towards our plans—this is something I am able to do—but he is right, and that is even more frustrating. We could not do what we had planned. Hull was not up to it. Timmy Weld, the boy who played Karl, the nephew, was not up to it. Our screenplay was probably not up to it. But when I am working with Boone and he is making these changes, I would think, does this not disappoint you, Boone, or anger you a little? I did not want to see him throwing chairs or berating the actors, but I wanted to see, for my sake, some regret. Was he ever committed to Beethoven, or was I mistaken? Did I misunderstand?

Boone's answers to these questions were the logical ones, "What does it matter what we wanted if we cannot get it?" and he would point at Hull, dunking crumpets in his mug of scotch. He says this and he goes straight to work, because there is no time for regrets. There is always something to do, even if it is teaching Hull to write with his right hand. Boone is saying to me—but not in words—you may question my commitment to

Beethoven, Carlo, but to the project, to the filming and production, you have only to look. He was there when I left, reviewing the dailies and setting up for tomorrow, and he was there before I arrived in the mornings. Most of the nights, I do not think he ever went home. I would find him shaving at Beethoven's porcelain shaving bowl in the mornings, and then as the rest of us would arrive, he would go to each, help each, always active, driving the lorry, overseeing the embroidery of the wardrobe people, helping select the stencils for all the trompe l'oeil in the ballroom. For that scene, the banquet thrown by Madame Bernier for Karl, Boone built the set, the size of an indoor tennis court, in two and a half days. I would stop what I was doing sometimes and watch him, up on the ladder with his bucket of blue paint, robin's egg he makes us call it, spattering it with a roller, and then hopping down the ladder when the crew brings in a chandelier. He helps them attach it to the winches, and as they lift it, he pulls out a bulb or cracks off a few of the more ornate hangings. By the time the chandelier is in place, he is somewhere else. He has pulled the grip aside for a quick lesson on how to use the boom, or he is reviewing a dozen petticoats with Maureen. The crew would call him Doctor Sleep, because he seemed to need so little. He would sneak it in. There was a couch in one of the offices that he would use. He would say take ten, and he would go into this office and sleep. This had been the secret to Jesus' success, he said, fifteen-minute naps.

But then he would come back out. He would run his face under the tap and he would be ready again. Available to the actors. Available to the technicians. Available to our cooks, the Old-hams, helping them with their Cornish pastries and their pork pies. It seems to me we ate nothing but pork pies on this shoot. Boone would hand them out with bangers. He would eat standing up, even when we were outside, at Beethoven's cottage in Staines, what Boone called the beat sessions when we beat my friend Tony Denham's house into nineteenth-century condition. We pulled down bricks, splashed it with muddy water and charcoal, beat it and slashed it with shovels. You would hear Hull from inside—"It's a good thing I'm deaf, because I'd never be able to compose with that fucking din outside my window." I remember Boone passing out the pies in the late afternoon, tossing them like horseshoes, and then spinning around, spotting Sela Finch, who played the prostitute. Her scenes were not until later, but she had come by to help, and while the rest of us ate, he and Sela sat over by Tony's well and Boone smeared tar on her teeth.

Erin Hirt

Up in Scotland, whenever Gail asked about him, who was this guy back in London and what was going on with us, I had this ID picture of him in my purse. We'd gotten it at Victoria Station with his eyes closed and my hands in his hair. Gail and I would go to these little inns for dinner after walking around these fishing villages all day, and I would always take out this picture of Boone and put it down on the table. Gail was seeing this guy back in London who played bass, and she'd talk about him. She'd tell me about these songs he would write, and the way he would stand when he was playing. She'd ask me why I didn't talk about Boone, but I just didn't. I always just wanted to finish dinner and get back to our room so I could curl up under these big thick quilts and just think.

C.L. Hull

What I believe was so revolutionary, right, above and beyond the film sophistication that Carlo was able to inject into the spirit of the whole endeavor, was the sense of gritty independence that really permeated the set during the whole of the shoot. 'Cause that film really grew, you know. I heard one of the technicians at one point calling it a very organic piece of work, and I like that, I really do, I think that puts it very well. It's probably the most organic film I've ever worked on. Very free-form, and you know, that's what comes from trust. Trust is such an essential element to any kind of performance, and I wouldn't have expected Carlo to have that sort of understanding because that's not really the background he was coming from, but Boone was fucking brilliant at taking the shackles off, you know, setting out the principle elements of a scene and then just letting you fly. Because you've got to be able to improvise. You have to be able to react to what's happening around you, and I really did come to admire the extent to which Boone would go with that.

Because he knew, right, he knew that the work must come first, and that means really taking all the rules, and I don't just mean the rules of soundstage etiquette or parental guidance suggested crapola, I mean sometimes the rules of common decent behavior, and just throwing them the fuck out the window. Abominable stories, I could tell. Christ, I come in one day for some scene in Beethoven's bed chamber. There's gnats all over the place and up my nose, and the bed smells like piss. But I do the scene, right. I don't say a word. I bowl ahead, I'm in the moment. My friend Richard Harris says to me years later, in Cannes actually, he says, "Jesus, Hull, that was a brilliant expression on your face in that scene." And I say, "Bloody hell, Dick, that was no expression, I was sitting in Boone's piss!"

I mean, that's how dedicated you have to be. You have to work with that kind of insanity. You know, Boone, for a whole fucking week at the end of every shot where Chloe's anywhere near— Chloe Webster is the woman who played that little shit nephew's mother, an absolute cunt. Chloe did a wonderful job with it too, really brilliant actress, because she is not a cunt—but anytime Chloe's anywhere near, Boone has to take her off and do this fucking court dance he's learned from some hippie-yippie from the local anachronism society. The sound men are moving their mikes and the makeup people are rushing in for my rash—absolute torture, I don't mind saying—and our fucking director is over in the corner with a puff wig on his head doing some macaroni jig with Chloe, clapping their hands above their heads. You know, it'll drive you fucking bonkers, except actually, you know, he sets a tone, and that's quite right. He has to be free. Just like the rest of us. He's got to be able to do his jig, or put gin in Timmy's thermos, you know, or set out fucking mousetraps if that's what it takes.

Because you know what it is? I really think that to an extent he has to be *un*reliable. You know, he has to be a little bit of what you call a fuck up, even if it's for show, because then everyone says to himself, "Well, all right, this picture is mine too, you know. If loco over there is going to be doing this Germanic mambo all over the place, I'll have to pull my own, won't I?" And I've seen it work, I have—brilliantly—where you've created this sort of air around the set where honestly—and I mean this in a good way because I really do admire it when someone's willing to set his balls aside as a sacrifice to what film can really be—but you've created an air around the set where honestly no one really knows what the fuck is going on. Brilliant.

Carlo Esteban

Boone liked for us all to see films together. Wiseman's *Law and Order* we were able to get copies of, and *Don't Look Back,* of course. *Medium Cool* was very important to him. But he had found out from Timmy Weld that they would be showing *Nanook of the North,* the classic by Flaherty, at his public school in Chislehurst. Boone dragged the technicians there. McMurtry and Randolph I remember at Waterloo station, grumbling and wiping the sleep from their eyes, but Boone had said he thought it was important for us all to keep thinking about the same things. It would be good for us to see another way a movie could look, the different kinds of crudity that were possible. We took the train from Waterloo East and walked all the way to the school, ten or so of us. We found the dining hall, hundreds of little children in flannel pants and black shoes, all thronging around Timmy Weld. We all sat on dining room tables. We were welcomed by the headmaster. The children applauded. They chanted, "Tim-my, Tim-my." When they were finished, the school people started the film.

The projector broke after ten minutes. The film melted. The children all started chanting and applauding, stomping their feet. The film has melted—hurrah! The crew people, they have been dragged to this place on their day off, Randolph and McMurtry go up to Boone and ask if that was what he wanted, a film that melts in the projector. "That should not be such a problem, Mr.

Boone." "Yes, we think we can handle that." Boone smiles. He asks one of them if they will go help with the projector. The children are getting restless. They are down on the floor punching and tickling each other. A woman goes up on stage, the school nurse. She sits down at the piano and begins playing a song, and the children all begin to whistle along. They are all whistling, a medley of these school songs.

We have nothing to do. McMurtry is reading the football scores. I am looking at the lunch menu—London broil and potatoes. Boone gets up from the table and starts walking up to the stage himself, over all these whistling children, and they are all looking up at him, elbowing each other. By the time he reaches the stage, the room is quiet. He walks up to the piano, introduces himself to the school nurse, and then comes up to the front of the stage. He says that we who have come to visit their school don't know their songs very well, and some of us can't whistle—he is pointing at me, three hundred children now know that I cannot whistle—so why don't we sing some songs that we all know while we wait for the film, and he begins to sing "Little Jack Horner." Boone is up there with his feet together and his hands behind his back in front of all these children, and he sings, "Little Jack Horner sat in the corner, eating his Christmas pie . . ." While Randolph is getting the film ready, Boone and the whole school are singing this plum song as a round, the lower forms, then the upper forms, the faculty. When they are finished, Randolph calls up to the stage and says that they are ready with the film now, but all the children say, "Noooo, we want to sing with the man. We want to sing with Timmy's boss." So the headmaster asks Boone, and for the next half hour we all sing. We sing "Little Jack Horner." We sing "I'm Being Swallowed by a Boa Constrictor." We sing, "McCarthy Is Dead and His Brother Don't Know It." We may even sing, "John Jacob Jingleheimer Schmidt," I do not remember. But the last song, when they tell Boone that we are out of time and the children must go back to class, he decides we should all sing, "Nine Bottles of Beer on the Wall"—he wants to sing only nine. Randolph and McMurtry are standing on the table in back, their arms clasped, shouting like this is Liverpool versus Southampton.

Erin Hirt

After I got back, I would come home from some shoot. I'd look up and see the lights off in our flat, and I'd know he wasn't home yet. He was still at the set and I'd never know how long it would be. I hated going in alone. Sometimes I'd just go across the street to this pub and have a glass of water with lime and chew this English gum. Really I don't like gum at all now. I don't know if I liked it then, but I don't like it now. If someone asks me if I want a stick of gum now, I say no.

John Kinsey

Every summer my wife and I had leased a cottage in the Cotswolds, but I stopped in 1965, the year she died, and did not begin again until that summer of 1971. It was close enough to city proper that I could make good use of it without forgoing the pleasures of urban living entirely. For the most part I used it on weekends, and somewhere roundabout the final week of June, I'd summoned up the courage to invite Erin and Eton. Erin had returned from her trip to the North, and I'd thought it might be nice for them both to come out. I didn't think there was much chance they'd accept—even getting in touch with Eton had become something of a task—but weighing the pain of their probable refusal against the unspeakable buoy of their possible acceptance, I felt there wasn't much of a choice.

And they did accept. Eton said they'd come. Or not completely. One never knows what will come up, but he'd given me reason, at least, to shore up the rations. Erin had said that she would be out a day early, that she would come out the Thursday evening, and Eton would follow on the late train Friday. And so

I prepared for their arrival, floating on air, nervous, but positively electric with excitement.

Unfortunately, Erin's spirits were low the night she arrived. We shared a roast with a beekeeper who lived up the road and we all retired early. I showed her to the room I'd prepared, the master bedroom of the house actually, which I had found too large for me. And she'd seemed so quiet and sweet as I set down her bag by the fire and pulled back a corner of the bedcover, and at supper too, she'd seemed dolorous. It was something I was quite unprepared for, and I'm afraid that I reacted rather numbly. I showed her the Casterman edition of Grimm's Tales, wished her a quick good evening, and waited for tomorrow.

She seemed happier the next morning, and we had quite a nice and thorough day. We drove in to the village well before noon to pick up the particulars for the menu we'd planned for Eton's arrival, visited an antique shop or two, stopped in on the vicar, and then returned home to share a lovely lunch in the gazebo. After a short rest, we took a little nature walk along what my wife and I used to call "The Butterfly Trail." It really was a lovely day—largely because we'd spent it together and knew that soon we'd have Eton with us.

In any case, by the time we returned from our hike, we were so warm that we were both quite ready for a dip in the small indoor pool that the owners had unfortunately installed in the time since my wife and I had stayed there last. It was actually quite an eyesore, but it did provide some relief on a hot day, and so Erin and I decided we'd have a dip in the pool, begin preparations for dinner, and then drive in to the station to meet Eton's train.

I'd barely got my trunks wet when the phone rang. I had to grab a robe and rush out to the main house. It was Eton, of course, and he sounded exhausted, too exhausted—he was almost unconvincing. He said that he was terribly sorry, he really was, but that he would not be able to make it. Apparently, they'd had the use of a particular lot for less time than expected, one of his technicians had made this or that mistake, they'd lost a day to Hull's pot valiance—I don't recall exactly, but in any case, he was compelled to spend the weekend in Surrey.

Oh, but I was so disappointed, and perhaps more so because I was hardly surprised. Almost the instant I'd heard the phone ring, with Erin paddling like a frog beneath the surface, I'd known that it would be he, that he would not be coming. It was all too obvious. We can't often get our hopes up without having them dashed.

And, of course, Erin. My heart went out to dear Erin. She was waiting for me when I returned, propping herself up on the side of the pool at the deep end. She asked me if that was Eton, and how I wished I could have said no. But I told her he wasn't going to be able to make it, and that I was sorry, I was sorry for both of us. She paused a moment at the lip of the pool and then slid back into the water. One of the most rueful sights I've ever encountered. She began to make her way to the other end, the shallow end. I walked along beside her as she sliced through the water languidly, and I watched her hair, billowing crimson behind her.

She was so beautiful, so guileless. What reason could there be for treating her with such callous indifference? I remember she touched the side and without lifting her eyes pushed herself back toward the deep end as I waded in myself. The sound of her strokes I can remember, mechanical, eerie. She completed her lap and turned back round, but she didn't finish. Halfway toward the shallow end, where I stood waist deep, she touched bottom and stood up. Lovely but ever so fragile. She walked toward me, putting her hands up to her eyes to clear the hair away, but she kept them there as she waded toward me, toward my shoulder. And I held her, weeping gently, absolutely stricken by him.

Carlo Esteban

There is a photograph hanging in our hallway at home, of Boone on the set, and this is the picture that sums up for me what happened. It is of Boone pretending to feed the camera biscuits with Sinead, the P.A. with black stockings, behind him. They are both smiling, and this is our film—Boone with the camera, entertaining the crew, treating his camera like a pet. He would talk to it, stroke it, pour it cups of tea. It was like a monkey, or the pirate's cockatoo, but always there, so that at any moment he could begin shooting.

Ninety percent of what you see in the film today was shot by Boone. He was like the child in the pool who says, "Five more minutes." He would roam around the set peering through the eyepiece, scouting for shots. I would discover things in the daily rushes that I had never seen before, Chloe and the whore's bath. The opening shot, actually, had come this way, by accident. Hull had been sitting on the set, exhausted and bleary as usual, his shirt undone, one leg thrown over the side of an eighteenth-century armchair. Boone liked the pose. We had been eating samosas. He saw Hull and he told us all to be quiet. He crept up on Hull from behind. It is an appropriate opening. Beethoven asleep, his mouth agape, then waking with a start and staring at the camera in blank, abject horror.

But that became the rule. We did not make a movie. Boone found a movie, and the most interesting character was the camera. The party scene, I remember, it is one long take, a weekend party at Heiligenstadt. I will never forget the image, people milling about this eighteenth-century salon, and Boone among them, weaving his way in his blue jeans through men in frock coats, games of whist, and ladies in petticoats. He would invite people in the door and then follow them over their shoulders, giving coats to a valet, ducking in on all the conversations—about art, politics, breasts, Bursy analyzing a dream of Schindler's. He says, "Dreams, my friend Anton, are all a matter of blood flow." And in another instant, Boone is with Henrikson the chemist and Mme. Bernier. They are dancing a three-way minuet, and Boone is waving them on and on, faster and faster—it is a dizzying scene, but Boone moves on, he staggers away. The camera keeps searching. It is everywhere, on scalps, in drinks, on shoes, the series of buckles, and then zipping up to Hull as he sneaks a swig of scotch by the window. "I am fucking parched," Hull had said into the camera. "Not since I was with Lean in the desert, Boone." In the finished scene, Boone has over-dubbed. He says, "Nonsense is a lean dessert boy."

Erin Hirt

I'd asked him what was going to happen when the movie ended, because it just seemed like a weird idea that we would go back to the way we'd been before, living together. It seemed like it had been so long since he'd even been around or we'd been together, and I didn't know if it was something he'd been thinking about. I'd had a friend, who was actually a friend of both of ours, who was shooting a movie in Paris, and he'd offered me a part. It wasn't any big thing, but I'd never been to France, and I told Boone that I was probably going to say yes, and he said I should too, because he thought he was going to be working on the film for a while more. But I asked him what if *Heiligenstadt* was over by the time I got back, did he really want to have to be waiting in London for me, because I could tell he didn't. I knew that he'd wanted to go back as soon as it was all over, and I thought that maybe I'd want to stay in France too if I liked it. He said that was probably right. He said, "Don't hate me, though," and he meant for being so gone all the time. He said the dumb part was he should have started missing me already, but he knew he wouldn't get to it until everything was done with and he was back in the United States. He said the first thing he'd probably do was just sit down and miss me. I asked him what he thought he was going to do after that. He said, "Laundry."

John Kinsey

Erin had called to tell me that she was leaving. I'd been prepared for news of this type, but still I was very, very saddened by it, and I had her over. It was in the early evening. We had some wine and talked mostly about what she would do after she left, but near the end I'd asked her a question that had been waiting in me, unkindly, for some time. I asked her if she'd ever seen a photograph of Hugh Gardiner. She said no, which of course I knew—if Eton hadn't ever seen him, it didn't seem likely that she had—and I asked her if she'd like to see one. She said yes, why not? I went upstairs and brought down a photograph of myself and Hugh from ten years previous, standing outside a theatre at the Edinburgh festival with Robert Bolt. Hugh looked small and was smiling. It's actually a very happy picture of him, but as I showed it to Erin, I wanted to tell her what she was looking at. I wanted to say, "This is the man that Eton's been writing, Erin, this one in the middle. This is the man who's funded his movie. This is the man he was writing before he knew us, and who Eton will continue writing after we've gone. He knows things about Eton that we never will, ever, so if you've felt a distance from Eton, or that something's been kept from you, this man has it. This man keeps it." I wanted to say all this to her, and more, but I held my tongue, and she only looked at the picture. She touched it. She put her finger on Hugh's smiling face. "He looks like a very sweet man," she said.

She left my home for the last time not long after. She had a gift for me, a pair of tartan socks she'd bought up in Scotland. I asked her if she knew where Eton was that night. She told me that he was taking the final story conferences at a pub in Battersea, and after she left, I made myself a small dinner. I had another bottle of wine to myself and smoldered, and when I was through I went to find him.

They were all in a back room, half a dozen or so of them. I have no memory of what they discussed, except for Hull. He was completely smashed, rambling on about the tragedy of the whole thing and trying his best to keep his seat. I'd sat next to Eton—he'd pulled out the chair beside him when he'd seen me—but it was well past midnight by the time the meeting ended. I remember Eton held me by the coat sleeve as all the members filed up one by one to have a final word with him. He cocked his ear for them and rubbed his chin, but I don't think he heard a word they said. When they were gone, he ordered us two pints of bitter, and said he was glad I'd come. He asked if I had plans to see Erin before she left, and when I told him that she'd come to see me that night, he seemed very relieved. He said that he knew she'd like that. He said that she'd liked me a great deal.

We sat for a while and drank. We may have finished our pints without saying another word, but I asked him finally, and to him it must have seemed to come from nowhere, the question I'd come with—I asked him if he ever had questions about Hugh. He looked very disturbed by the idea, but perhaps not so surprised. He said, "Sometimes, yes." I said, "And you understand, Eton, that I could answer any of them." He nodded, but he wouldn't look at me. He had his arms stretched out over the table, and we waited. He said, "This isn't very kind, John," and I told him it was neither kind nor unkind. That remained to be seen, but if he wanted to know anything, that's what I was there for. He thought some more. He had his chin down on the table, and then at last he said, "Very well." I was rather stunned. As intently as I'd come to him, I hadn't really thought it possible that the conversation I'd been devising in my head might actually happen. Eton would ask his questions about Hugh, and I would answer. In this extended moment of jealousy and drunkenness, I would tell Eton everything about Hugh, all the things to round him out, about his voice, his looks, his habits, the vests he wears, the things in his cupboards, the way that he carves his meat or cleans himself, anything, any question Eton asked, no matter how trivial, I would satisfy, just to make Hugh real to him and shatter their whole game.

But he said, "I have only one question." He looked at me. I waited. I was ready. "Is he alone?" he asked.

Is he alone? Is that all he wanted to know? I'd been so prepared for anything. But this, his question was so brief and enormous, I was very disappointed actually, because there didn't seem to be quite the edge to his question that I'd anticipated. There wasn't any of the mischief or betrayal. But I thought of my answer. I'd promised him one. And at first I considered all of Hugh's students and how much they adore him, how they come to him and throng the way they do, and I thought to myself, "Well, Hugh isn't very alone then, is he, in the literal sense. He certainly doesn't lack for company." But then I thought again. I thought of how lonely Hugh has always been at heart, back at Princeton when he'd first arrived and in that old house with only Emily and the nursemaids. He is very alone, of course. Or had been, I thought, because I tried to think of Hugh at that very moment now, back in Fishkill, and ever since he'd first written me that the boy from the Wilde play was in New York, and finally my answer seemed very clear. "He has you," I said. "How could he be alone?"

I think we were both a bit stricken by my answer—I was, that I'd actually spoken something so miserable, and Eton too. I could see that he was overcome. It seemed to soften all the bones in his body, and we didn't look at each other for some time. I was helpless to stop the feelings of rage and self-loathing from closing in on me, they filled me up like bilge water, but finally Eton broke the spell of pity and contempt, or gave it voice. He said, "Hugh, whoever he is, accepts that I'm not very good, John, that I'm not good."

I was surprised and confused. I said, "But Erin. You don't think that she would?"

He said, "I wouldn't want Erin to know."

We waited a bit longer and rocked our steins, but finally I had to ask him. I said, "And what about me? I wouldn't accept it?"

He looked at me. "If you did, John," he said, "then you wouldn't be here."

I didn't stay much longer in the room after that. He asked if I would leave first, and I did. I left him there very still, with his arms folded on the table, and his head resting in their cradle.

Carlo Esteban

Editing began in the fall of 1971. Boone was there until December and then he left. All along I had looked forward to my moment to shine, my moment to have influence. This was it finally, in the cutting room at LFI, with my transistor radio and bottles of milk. Boone did not abandon me. He was there for three of the six months it took. He learned how to splice film, dub, loop. His attitude was still positive, with his feet up on the table of the Steenbeck as we watched the footage, but in truth, Boone had very little interest in the finished product of this film. The editing room for him was a place to rest, to watch it all again, for himself.

He would say to me that he had made an 83,000-foot movie, but he did not mean that this was some great thing that I could not touch. He meant that he was tired and that his job was done. He had created a world filled with anxious codirectors and wretched actors in silly costumes and powdered wigs and beauty spots, a world with coffee and donuts and technicians and wooden ear horns, and he had decided that the best thing would be to wander around inside it with his camera. That is what he had done, that is the film he had made, and it was a fine thing to do. But cutting this and selling it, thinking of the audience and the critics, he was not against these things, he did not resent the idea of someone editing his work, he just did not care about it.

From FILM INTERNATIONAL, November 1972

DON'T LOOK BACK AT BEETHOVEN
by Andrew Fortenbaugh

Well, he's back, but his act hasn't changed quite as much as he'd like us all to think. He's put an interesting twist on it, though. Eton Boone always worked in guises and disguises. A psychoanalytic journeyman of the first order, he'd put on people's clothes just to skin them in a stand-up act that New York has sorely missed since he left three years ago. He's in film now, and just as much a journeyman, just as fun with fangs still as sharp. The problem with *Heiligenstadt*, due for limited release this winter, is that he hasn't quite made up his mind where to sink his teeth.

The obvious choice here was the meaty flank of Ludwig van Beethoven, and the film's premise is as ripe and innovative as we've all come to expect from Boone. He wanted to turn the eyes of direct cinema on history and follow the great composer around for a week or so. He wrote himself a free-form screenplay, lassoed a crew of cinema verité hired guns to give him the texture he wanted and then let the cameras roll. It didn't look like Beethoven had a chance, and in certain moments of *Heiligenstadt*, he doesn't. Despite the breathy gust of bitching and moaning that this film wafted in on, it still works remarkably well at times. Absolutely, its likes have not been seen before, with scenes as simple as this: Beethoven counts his coffee beans, Beethoven changes his mind while he's going downstairs, Beethoven spits at a stranger, Beethoven takes a piss. Not for the music lovers, but very nice cinema when Boone hits it square.

As it turns out, though, there's just too much in Boone's way to really get at Beethoven. Hilarious and chilling some scenes may be, but a lot of others are excruciating to watch. C.L. Hull, a veteran of the British stage, plays his Beethoven a little camp for a handheld camera, and the film falls to pieces whenever Beethoven's nephew Karl (Timmy Weld) makes an appearance. Hull and company stand in between Boone and Beethoven like the Vatican gates, as if what's inside might be too sacred to risk their director's swaggering iconoclasm.

But while all these elaborate measures of ineptitude were taken to preserve the mystery of history's first rock 'n' roller, no one thought to protect cinema verité, and Boone feasts. That's where he finally does his damage. This film shakes like Leacock, it flirts like Pennebaker, right down a nineteenth-century cleavage. If Boone can't wear the frock of the musical genius, he wears the baggy pants of the filmmaker, and fills them with the same tragic self-contempt he ever stuffed inside any shoes and trousers back when.

Like everything Boone used to touch on stage, cinema verité ends up seeing its own drawbacks and failings. Its presence on the scene is at once too conspicuous and too demure to tell the story it wants to. Hull plays for the camera just as much as Dylan did in *Don't Look Back,* and it makes him just as nervous as it did Jagger in *Gimme Shelter.* And when an actual story threatens to peak through this film's level surface, it finds its hands tied, prohibited by clever device from the omniscience that might have scrounged up a plot for us.

As a result, *Heiligenstadt* is trapped in the hinterland of the cinematic landscape. It pleads either not to exist at all or to be a movie movie, straight from Hollywood, handsome, fake, and quite contentedly absurd. Caught in between, embarrassed, enraged, the film panics and its trajectory is one we've seen somewhere before, same as ever for Boone, spilling towards self-destruction, but always fascinating. One wonders how aware Boone is of his tragicomic fetish. Must the film have lost its interest in the music man? Must Boone have cast these less-than-competents and directed them all so poorly that he had no choice but to direct his cameras so well, sending up the pretensions and flaws of our latest fad? One wonders. One yearns for what was almost there. One smiles, shivers and yawns at what is. And one wishes that Boone might tame his subversive penchant next time, just to see what else might happen.

John Kinsey

One always holds out a small hope, and I confess there was just a glimmer of optimism in me that saw the completion of the film and Eton's leaving England as two completely unrelated events, but I fear they weren't. He found me at Ozymandias to tell me, and I don't believe it was easy for him. It wasn't easy for either of us. It's one of the cruel things about parting that normally one stays and one goes. I don't think it would be half so difficult if we could all leave each other at forks in the road, but it's the waving good-bye and then turning home.

He found me asleep at my desk, and I don't know how long he'd waited there for me to wake, but when I did, he had some tea ready for me. He'd been reading a book of Rilke's letters, and he looked up and said that he was leaving. I was slow to understand, and so reluctant, but I think it was just a matter of acceptance. I asked him if he was here to say good-bye, and he said that yes, he was. Like foul medicine, he'd thought that waking me for one nasty tablespoon would be most merciful, and perhaps he was right. Perhaps he wasn't swift enough, though, because as he sat before me, very much like a ghost I think, I was surprised by a voice within me. I said to him, I did, "Please don't go." I did plead with him. If he left now, I said, we couldn't be together. Wasn't that clear? Now that the film was done, there would be time for us to spend together.

But as this innocent voice kept on, desperately and pathetically, he stood up and he began looking at a shelf of my books, and I could see from something about his manner, something stern but gentle, that he already had left. I asked him if he was going home to California, and he said no. And I thought, damn, I thought to myself, "Is it Hugh? Are you going back to see Hugh?" And standing there, with his hands behind his back and his head bent up at the top rows of my shelf, it seemed to be so clearly the case. Of course he was going back to see him, and I felt as though I'd driven him there. I asked him if that was it, was Hugh the reason he had to leave, now that the film was done? He turned round and he said, "John, don't torture yourself. I may see Hugh," but he spread his arms and he said, "But this is not where I live."

I was speechless. He turned back to the bookshelf and after something of a pause he said very softly, "Which would you like?" almost as though he were speaking to the very childish voice I'd been unable to control. I said, "The Lewis book at the top," *A Grief Observed,* one of the few books that's ever given me any real consolation. He pulled it down, sat across from me in the corner chair and read to me the whole of it. Sitting in my study at Ozymandias the day before he left, he read it to me, perfectly, and it was a moment, as long as it may have lasted, of watching Eton and listening to him, a moment I was lifted well above myself, and despite each word's bringing us closer to good-bye, was happy.

V

Standish, Maine

Winter 1971—Summer 1972

Hilary Richman

It was going to be a big Christmas Eve adventure. You know, I honestly didn't know what had gone on between E.B. and this man. I had only a vague outline of who he was, this shadowy figure who wrote E.B. letters. But E.B. had called me at Harvard. I was going to spend my break there, and E.B. was in Boston, at the Holiday Inn. He'd flown in from London the night before and he said he was going to go down and meet this man. He asked me if I wanted to come along, and I did. I mean, he obviously wanted me to go along. He'd flown to Boston. He could've flown into New York.

So he picked me up at school early on Christmas Eve day. It was always really bleak there on vacations, especially Christmas. It was absurd. The only other people who stayed were these

Nigerian twins who couldn't fly home. But E.B. came up in this rented car, and I remember he was wearing two sweaters. The outside one was this beautiful dark green one, Lincoln green with charcoal diamonds. He'd bought it in England and he always looked freezing in it, but it was a beautiful sweater with his eyes, and he had on blue jeans too, and his sleeves pushed up, and the steam coming out of his mouth. He just said, "Well, let's go meet him." It was right around lunch, it was like twelve o'clock, and we got in and drove away.

We had the address, these return addresses that all said Fishkill, New York, which is near Poughkeepsie. We got these apples and a jar of peanut butter and drove all the way down to Fishkill. We had to get directions to find his house, which was this big dark thing with trees and bushes all around it. It was about five o'clock, it was very dark and spooky outside. E.B. parked down the street, but he wanted me to go first and make sure everything was okay. I was like, fine, whatever you say, and I trudged through the snow and rang the bell.

This timid little voice came through the peephole—"Yes?" It was ridiculous. I felt like I needed a password. I said, "Mr. Gardiner?" and he goes "yes" again, and I just wanted to say, oh, grow up, this is the twentieth century. Stop acting like you're Roddy McDowall owning a haunted house or something. But finally I said, "It's Hilary Richman"—I mean, what was I supposed to say?—I said, "I'm a friend of Boone's. He's here to see you." Then there was this awful sort of rheumatoid fumbling with the locks, and finally he opened the door.

Have you seen him yet? He's very strange, his foot's turned in or something—he has a little deformity. He's very odd. Basically he's hideous. He has these cheeks that are all pocked and scarred, and these little wet fish eyes that are too close together. He's really very ugly, but he had on this brown sweater, and he looked, I don't know, like a professor, but very scared at first, like a little bird. I went into his house. He was very polite, and he closed the door and we stood there in his entrance hall, with this coat rack there with exactly one hat, one coat, an umbrella, and this man's galoshes like Mister Rogers or something. And he just stood there with his hand on the doorknob. I introduced myself, and I think he just sort of feigned ignorance a little bit, but he knew who I was.

And he had this tiny, tiny Christmas tree, with real candles on

it, clipped on, which looked perfectly dangerous. And these decorations, paper angels or whatever. And then his dog—he had this
little yellow dog that looked like it was between seizures. And
finally he invited me in to his living room, and he offered me a
glass of sherry, and there was this music playing, I didn't know
where it was coming from. It was like it was being piped in, some
choir from Daneland or something, and he said something pitiful
like, "Say hello to Mr. Richman, Carnegie." And this little dog
sort of bleated at me without moving.

Anyway, I sat down on this ancient couch and explained who
I was and why I had come. And I said, "E.B. is in the car and
would like to meet you," and he didn't get upset. He just said,
"I know." I mean, he tried to pass it off like something he was
expecting, but he was obviously scared shitless. He just sat there
and thought for a minute, and finally he said, in just this little
voice that barely gets out of his throat, he said, "Will you excuse
me?" And he left the room.

Honestly, I didn't know what the hell was going on. I was just
thinking, what the fuck am I doing here? I'm in this living room
of this strange little man, and he's offered me sherry and he's got
this pathetic little dog and this Charlie Brown Christmas tree and
now he's left the room to get, I don't know, another scarf or put
on some thermal underwear or something. And I remember sitting on this couch thinking I was in one of E.B.'s pictures, you
know, something from E.B.'s imagination. And I didn't know
what to do. I felt like running out to the front lawn and waving
my arms to E.B., you know, he's left the room, c'mon in, E.B., take
a look, he's grotesque. Or whether I should just leave him out
there in the car, because it was such a bleak picture and E.B. had
enough bleak pictures.

But then Hugh Gardiner came back carrying this typewriter. It
was this enormous clunky typewriter in this big black case. It was
practically a tuba case, it must have weighed five hundred
pounds. And he walked right up to me and he said, "I'm afraid
you're going to have to tell him that he can't see me." Surprise,
surprise. I mean, I think I knew from the second I got in there that
Hugh Gardiner wasn't going to agree to see E.B., he was so pathetic. He said, "As long as you're here, I have this typewriter for
him. And there's a note inside." And he sort of clunked it down
on the floor. I thought he was going to have a hernia. And he said,
"Will you take it to him? It's rather heavy."

It was absurd. I was ready to say, "Come on, Jesus, we've driven all this way. Why don't you just go fucking meet him? I mean, cut the bullshit." But then he took the case and he dragged it over to my feet, and he stepped back and looked at me. He'd put on his eyeglasses, these little ancient bifocals, so I couldn't even see his eyes, and he said the weirdest thing. He said, you know, "You really are lovely, aren't you?"

I don't know, so we said good-bye. I went back to the car carrying this incredibly heavy typewriter that Hugh Gardiner had written some story on thirty years ago or whatever and it's cleaving into my shins, and I got in, and I said to E.B., you know, he doesn't want to see you, he thinks it's wrong. And E.B. didn't say anything. He just sat there for a second, and he started the car. We just drove away.

We drove to the city. We didn't stop. We were going to go stay at this apartment over on Central Park South that belonged to some friends of his. But we were driving on the Cross Bronx Expressway and it was snowing out, and E.B. sort of looked over at me and said, "Why don't we go to a hotel?" And I said, "Sure." And we went to a little hotel which was right across the street from the U.N. He actually shelled out a lot of money for it. It wasn't that bad. It had a beautiful view, looking out over the East River. And that's where we began our "fling."

Hugh Gardiner

I think it's because he was so disappointed at the end of *Heiligenstadt,* and not simply because he knew the film could have been better, but because there's always a period of withdrawal after one has devoted so much time to a single project. It's very difficult to know what to do next, and in this state of limbo, it's no wonder that he should have thought to come to me, but it was a diversion. It was not what he needed to be doing. He needed to be gathering his energies again, and I was quite sure that once he was settled on a new project, this fancy of coming to meet me would be revealed to him for what it was—caprice.

Of course, it was by no means easy for me to admit that. The temptation was great, I can tell you, to open my door. This beautiful young man standing before me, offering me the introduction that I had imagined so many times, it was an impossible position, but I simply felt that we still had so much to do, and that our meeting then would only jeopardize that future. What could I do? I said no.

Hilary Richman

Afterwards, it was one of those weird things which after that initial time became common. We made love and then I would fall asleep and he would leave the bed and sit in the chair in his sweatpants and look at me. This first time, I was just dozing but I saw him staring at me. It was sort of scary. I mean, I've had people look at me, but they weren't E.B. It was just different. I must have fallen back asleep five times, but every time I looked up he was still sitting there looking at me, just dark in this hotel chair underneath this lamp chained to the ceiling.

After like the fifth time, I finally sat up. I pretended I was waking up and he just said, "Okay, what did he look like?" He meant Hugh Gardiner, so I got out of bed and I sat down on the floor in front of his chair and described it, this pathetic—oh, I don't want to use that word—this sad little character with his Christmas tree and his yellow dog. And he smiled. I don't know, it was a little confusing, but he smiled. It was E.B.'s smile, and then we just watched TV all night.

And in the morning, we woke up and it was Christmas day. It was like two o'clock, and we didn't have any presents except for this clunky old typewriter from Hugh Gardiner. It was locked. It was one of those old typewriter cases that's like an armored truck. It was made of lead or something, and E.B. wanted to get inside to read what Hugh Gardiner had said, so we took it into the bathroom. We put it in the bathtub, and E.B. went at it with this bottle opener that was attached to the sink by a string. It took him fifteen minutes before he could get the stupid thing open. He completely demolished the case, and then we found this little metal key scotchtaped to the inside lid.

And also this note from Hugh Gardiner. It was handwritten in red ink and it explained that Hugh Gardiner had this friend who E.B. should call in Maine. This friend was an English professor at one of the colleges up there, Bates or Bowdoin or one of those places where all you do is drink and vomit, and he had this house in Standish, Maine, and he was going on sabbatical and he needed someone to housesit. Hugh Gardiner said he thought it would be a good idea for E.B. to go up to this place. I think E.B. already had it in his head that he wanted to write this play about his mother, so it really was this ideal gift, just this totally secluded place where he could go and think and write. Plus it was only two hours away from Harvard.

Camille Walker

There's a restaurant in Boston called Madame Bovary's where they have foot-long straws. Hilary and I used to like to go there, and sometimes, just because it was Hilary, we'd feed our drinks to each other through the straws. I took him there after that Christmas vacation. He looked good. Hilary always looked good, but now he looked happy. He was being his most delightful self, and somewhere near the middle of the meal, he mentioned that he'd gone to see *Picnic* at a revival house and the air conditioning had been on, and he and "E.B." had nearly frozen to death. And I said, "Hold on"—because I like to be kept up to date—"Who's this Edie?" And he said, "Not Edie, silly, E.B." I said, "All right, who's this E.B.?" And he huffed and took a big long draw from his drink, and he said, "E.B. is the eldest son of the man my mother married after Damon." I said, "Eton Boone." I knew who Eton Boone was, and I knew he was Hilary's stepbrother—far be it for Hilary to let anything like that go to waste. I said, "Oh, they call him 'E.B.?'" And Hilary sucked some planter's punch up his straw and held it with his finger. "No," he said, "*I* call him E.B.," and he pea-shot his drink right into the back of my throat.

Hilary Richman

It was understood. It just was. It's not like we had to speak about it. I guess what happened is that he moved in up there, and then surprised me one Friday afternoon. I'd just finished my last exam or something, and I was walking out of the big hall, the one with the beautiful roof tiles where they make you take exams like you're in jail, and E.B. was just sitting out there reading a copy of the *Globe.* They had this special inauguration supplement, and I just stood there looking over his shoulder at this floor plan of the Capitol steps or whatever. He made this joke about us being assassins, and then he just must have said something like, "So, do you want to come up?" And I was like, let's go, I'm already packed. That's how it was.

He was all alone up there. I don't even think he'd started writing yet. But that's how it would work. Either I would some-how get a car or take a bus and scoot up there, or he would come down and pick me up for the weekends. He'd bought a used Volkswagen, a convertible bug that always smelled of old Ritz crackers that I could never find, but E.B. didn't mind. And we'd whiz away up there.

We never really talked in the car. E.B. used to keep the top down, so you couldn't really hear anything. And usually I'd make him stop to buy groceries for the weekend, because he didn't exactly keep a well-stocked icebox. We always got in really late, and the lights would be off, so the place looked gigantic. It was actually an unbelievable house. I had no idea professors lived like this. It was this huge converted barn, and it had this loft that ran the length of the building, with beams. And the third floor had a balcony where we would end up sleeping in the summer some-times. The stars were amazing. It was just beautiful.

But we'd get up there and I'd have to go racing around trying to find all these antique light switches, you know, these pull chains on levers, and E.B. would just go straight upstairs. It was this little ceremony we had to go through. We'd have been together for four hours and said maybe six words to each other, and I'm sure E.B. hadn't even spoken to a human in a week, but he'd just go straight upstairs and I'd hear him throw his shoes in the bathroom. Then he would put on something, Dvorak or someone like that—the professor had this giant classical record collection—so I'd still be in the kitchen with these two whole grocery bags to put away, and this music would just be blaring. We still hadn't even spoken. We wouldn't really speak until afterwards. I mean, all he'd have said was, "gin."

Camille Walker

Plums changed. No fun. No more Peter Pan in your shower, or that Zephyr quality—Hilary rooting through your medicine cabinet, trying on your robes, sorting through your sock drawer—delightful but gone. And say good-bye to the lawyers on Brattle Street and the million different lovers. He shoos them all away, and the trinkets—he's giving them to me now, he says, "Keep them," because that was the old Hilary. That was over. Hilary had "E.B." now, Misstra Know-it-all. Family no less, but that wasn't even the best part. Uh-unh. The best part was "E.B.'s" brain. Catch of the century. "E.B., E.B., E.B., E.B.," his Lord and Master, the All Knowing One. "E.B. E.B." gives us the heebie-jeebies. "E.B." knows. "E.B." understands. He's the only one. It all just became crystal clear—Hilary says Hilary's been a plaything up until now, "Where do we put in the batteries?" But now "E.B." has ridden up on his white steed and he's said, "Hold on a minute here, people. This guy's not a toy, this guy's not the hurdy-gurdy chimp. Can't you see? This guy's incredibly sad." E.B. thinks Hilary's a heartbreaker, and I swear to you the little woozums felt substantiated by it. Who wouldn't? At long last someone spies his substance. "E.B., E.B., E.B., E.B." Thank God for "E.B."

Hilary Richman

He lived like a complete monk. He didn't even like having lights on, ever. He liked candles, and there was only one mirror in this entire house, but E.B. wouldn't get another one—I mean, I'm a very vain person, and I can remember the first time I was up visiting him, seeing that there was only one mirror, in the bathroom, and that was it. I practically had heart failure. And then I would come up after two weeks or something, and the cabinet would be open exactly the way I had left it. It was incredible. Nothing moved. He had this cold all spring long and there was this brass pot next to the bed that he would just roll over and spit into at night. It was completely disgusting, it was completely grotesque. I don't even think he washed it all spring. I made him put a piece of cardboard on top of it.

And I was always telling him, "Please go get a haircut, please." I always thought he looked better with short hair. I cut it a couple of times, and he came out looking like a Martian, but he didn't care. He would just say, "Well, if you want to cut my hair, cut my hair." And I said, fine, and I would set down all these newspapers in the kitchen and make E.B. take off his shirt and wash his hair in the kitchen sink, and I even brought up these good scissors from Cambridge. But he didn't seem to care. He didn't care about his clothes, he didn't care about his food, he didn't care about having aspirin, he didn't care about changing lightbulbs. Sometimes it was almost as if the man had no thought.

But I mean, I think that was just part of it, you know? He wasn't going to roll out some red carpet for me. Standish wasn't just some place I was visiting. It was this place that I was—it was much more my home than Harvard, that's for sure. He just didn't make some big deal out of it. I mean, what else do you need? Here's this man living in this cave and working on this play as if nothing else matters in the world, but he calls and says he wants you up there. And he's still going to sit on the living room floor reading all the record covers. He's still going to be writing every day, but that's just the way E.B. was, you know, just saying, "If you're smart enough to realize that this is your place too—I mean, you're not a guest—then it can be easy."

I mean, I remember, in the mornings I would go downstairs to the kitchen and usually the first I would see him was walking back from getting the *Globe.* It was this road that went like a mile both ways and it would take him at least ten minutes to get to me. He never used the bikes, which there were about ten of, but all the chains were constantly fucked up. He would just walk along the road, and he knew I was there watching him, but he wouldn't do anything different. Maybe he would be reading the paper, and I would be having my cocoa, and it just seemed like, if he could watch me sleep and I could watch him walk all this way up the road, then no matter how fucked up it had been or intense the night before, no matter what had happened, it was all fine. By the time he got back to the house, I don't even know how, but all that shit was just gone.

Hugh Gardiner

The play was a new beginning for him, a project he could take his time with, and work alone on, and I was really quite grateful to be able to provide him with the setting and means to undertake it. No large budget, no crews to assemble, no disputes to mediate, just a place where he could live comfortably and without the distraction of others. I could only hope that any visitors he may have had during this time understood—for their sake as well as his—the paramount importance of his remaining disciplined and keeping his focus on his work. And I think that he did manage to achieve a solitude there in Maine that was much more thorough than he'd yet experienced. He established an almost workmanlike relationship to his craft that I hadn't seen before.

And so, in fact, it was no great surprise to me that the correspondence changed as it did. There was not the quantity that there had been in England, it's true, but the intensity was still there, as strong as ever. It was only more focused on the play—its themes, its structure, its characters—and I think it was very helpful for him to be able to describe his ideas to an innocent ear. It enabled him to see the work in perspective, and I think that was very exciting for both of us. Yes, I can assure you, my involvement with *Studies,* even as limited and as distant as it may seem from this vantage point, was the greatest thanks he could ever have paid me for my patronage. For us to move on from the film so quickly, and from the incident that winter, it was ample recompense, to say the very least.

Camille Walker

It's the classic sleeping-with-a-writer story. This one's for after dessert when everyone's retired to the fire.

I found Hilary coming from the library one afternoon with a big manilla envelope tucked under his arm. I asked him what it was, and he said, "It's Act One of E.B.'s play." He said he'd had to get someone at the library to type it over for him because he'd sullied "E.B.'s" copy during a fight they'd had, "this monster fight," he called it.

According to Hilary, it started because he just wanted to talk more. Poor Hilary wanted to know what "E.B." was thinking. I picture them in bed. Maybe Hilary is sweeping out the strawberry stems. They're through for the night, and Boone has probably grabbed his manuscript or he's doing some kind of rollover routine. Hilary feels slam-bam-thank-you-ma'ammed, and he has nothing to do with himself. He gets out of bed. He gets back into bed. He sighs. He harumphs. He pulls the sheets. He just wants to hear a little something. Just a little, "coo, coo."

But no. For the first time in his life, Hilary doesn't know how good he's been, and the silence is killing him. But finally Hilary gets up. He gets out of bed when he'd had enough of "E.B.'s scribbling" and goes and sits in "E.B.'s" throne, the rattan chair from which his lord and master used to watch his subject sleep. Hilary doesn't have a stitch on, but just to make his point, he's sauntered over, flopping through the moonbeams streaming in the window, he saunters right up to the throne and says, "Dammit, E.B., we can't all have your brilliant thoughts. We can't all sit in your chair and just screw everyone"—not one of the great power moves of the century. Hilary said "E.B." was acting like there was a whore in the room, or like there was something dripping in the bathroom. Whatever it is, Boone doesn't stir. He ignores the gorgeous hyperactive nymph climbing all over the wicker chair.

So then, of course, tears. Hilary goes downstairs, and he said that would have been okay if he'd been able to find an old Bette Davis movie, but "Professor Cuntcaid's TV only gets one channel." Hilary has to watch Portland news. And he said he was still so pissed that he just went into the kitchen and got a bottle of cooking sherry and sat down to watch this "Eye on Portland." He couldn't find any wine glasses, and there were "corklets" in the wine bottle, so he drank it out of a small pot that "E.B." had. He said he had about four potfuls of wine, getting tight as a drum watching some silly little report about Satanic cults in northern New England, and it doesn't take Hilary long to get drunk— sometimes he even blacks out. But not now. Now it doesn't even calm him down, and pretty soon the show ends, and poor Hilary is left staring at a test pattern.

He didn't really remember this part as well. He was still just livid, so he stomped back into the kitchen, still completely nude, completely smashed, to try to entertain himself. And before he knows it, he's waltzing around the living room with two pots, belting out "I Feel Pretty" at the top of his lungs, clanging the two pots together, or hitting a pot with a spoon, just making noise and noise and noise until he finally hears "E.B." from upstairs. "Would you please shut the hell up?" So le petit Hilaire stops his banging and marches back upstairs, pot in hand, walks right up to "E.B.," snatches the papers from his hands and throws them down in the pot, and then relieves himself, lets fly all over the papers.

When he told me this, I said, "You peed all over 'E.B.'s' play?" He said, "Well, Camille, you know how wine goes through me."

Amalie Hindemuth

I went up into Maine to visit Eton actually, when he returned.
He'd written me a postcard saying where he was, and I'd had to
go up to Boston for a weekend to see something at the Hunting-
ton. Actually, I'd thought Boston and Maine were much closer
than it turns out they are, but I'd called Eton and told him that
I would be in the neighborhood and could I come up and see him.
It was a very nice phone call. I mean, I hadn't known how things
had been for him in England, and I didn't know if he wanted to
be left alone. I suppose that's sort of the message I'd gotten from
him before he left, but he sounded genuinely happy to hear from
me. We had just a wonderful conversation, and I asked him, you
know, have you made any friends? Do you ever have any visitors
come by to keep you company? And he said no, not really. But
then he said that Hilary of all people came up and visited on
weekends sometimes, and I thought, well, that's very strange,
isn't it? I mean, that's sort of sweet somehow, that he and Hilary
had remained close and were sort of keeping each other company
up in this house. And I was even thinking, you know, well, I
wouldn't mind seeing Hilary. I mean, I'd rather not, in a way, but
I wouldn't mind.

Anyway, we decided that I would come up on a Friday afternoon. I told him that I would be bringing this friend that I'd
made, Tikki Moore, a young girl from Toronto, who was looking
for theatre companies, just a lovely girl, and she was very excited
to meet him. I think I just thought, you know, well, why not try?
I mean, I'm not this type, I'm not always on the lookout for
people who should get together, but with Eton all alone all day,
just writing off in the woods like some sort of Thoreau person,
it seemed like it would have been very nice for him to have Tikki
there, if she ended up finding work nearby. So Tikki and I drove
up to his house.

He looked wonderful. I don't know why, but with Eton I was
always never expecting him to look particularly good, but he
always did. It was always this sort of constant surprise how

well he looked, and we had a very fun day. We drove to an old movie house in Portland and saw this movie with Robert Montgomery, and then we went to dinner at some lobster and thick steak sort of place where we all had to wear bibs, and Eton was being just very entertaining. I mean, it sounds strange to say that, as if Eton was on his best behavior or something like that, but you know, I didn't know how it would be. He'd been so unhappy before he left for England, and especially towards the end I hadn't really felt very welcome. But this evening in Portland, I actually think that sometimes when there's someone new, you know, someone you don't know at all like Tikki, sometimes things can sort of keep moving in a way they might not if it was just old friends, you know, and it did. It was a very funny evening. I remember Eton had lobster juice all over his chin and pretending not to notice and things like that. Doing these fake magic tricks with the butter patties, and after dinner, he and Tikki rolling up the car window together. He was very funny that night.

But afterwards we had to drive back to Eton's to pick up our car, and when we drove up, we saw this other car in the driveway and the lights were on, and Eton sort of went, "Oh, that must be Hilary." And I thought, you know, how odd. I mean, he hadn't mentioned anything about Hilary coming, but we went in and there was Hilary wearing just a bathrobe and sandals and he had a glass of red wine in his hand, and he said, "Hello, Amalie. Hello, Amalie's friend." He offered us something to drink and I don't think I alone would have accepted, but Tikki did. We had coffee. We all sat in the living room of this lovely old house and tried to have a conversation. I remember Hilary going on about some story about the Harvard policemen. He was actually being very pleasant and sort of hosty. I just remember the way he was sort of crossing his legs, if that makes any sense. But Eton, it was as if the moment Eton sat down, he just turned off. I remember Hilary finished this story and no one said anything. We'd all just sat there in stone silence, and Hilary said to Eton, "I'm sorry. I'm sorry you had to hear that one again."

Because Eton had just turned off. He'd turned back. He sort of metamorphosed back, and I don't think either Hilary or Tikki certainly would have noticed, but I know I felt we all could have been in his apartment on Perry Street when he was doing the impersonations, or up in Chelsea when we were sharing the apartment. He just absolutely became that person again, that person with that look, and I don't really know quite how to describe it because it wasn't even so much of a look. It was more a feeling in the room, you know, like something you'll smell and know, you could be blindfolded but you'd know in a second that you're back in your old school, or back at Williamstown or something like that. It was just very obvious, and I suppose I took it personally. I mean, he'd seemed perfectly happy, we'd had this lovely day and there hadn't seemed to be anything wrong at all, but then it was as if he'd just had his fill, you know. I'd outworn my welcome again, and I even thought, you know, well, thank goodness for Tikki, because apparently I'm making him very unhappy. I really just felt that I was this thing reminding him, you know, of what it had been like before he left. I mean, I'd known this feeling so well.

I don't think we stayed very long. I think we left fairly quickly once this gloom had sort of settled in, and I remember just driving back with Tikki that whole ride and thinking, you know, damn. I'd just completely forgotten, you know.

Hilary Richman

There were these sprinklers E.B. had discovered. They were in this playing field of some high school or something that you could walk to from his house, through these woods, and every morning they would turn on at exactly ten o'clock or maybe it was eleven. I don't know. E.B. knew the time. So we were going to go find these sprinklers because it was a boiling day, and the lake nearby was sort of goopy. E.B. had wanted to go to these sprinklers.

We'd gone into the garage to look for bigger towels, and we'd found this professor's hunting rifle, this shotgun. E.B. took it out and he was examining it. He didn't know the first thing about what the hell you do with a gun. He asked me if I knew anything about guns, and I told him I did. I mean, if you've spent as much time as I did in those horrible military schools, you get to know a little something about firearms. Lucky me. He asked me to do what he called "the shoulder to shoulder crap." So I did that, I "presented arms" with this shotgun, and I showed him how to hold it correctly, how to use the sight, how to plant your feet so you don't fall on your ass, and he asked me if I could shoot well, which I could actually. It's one of the few things I happened to do well at Hoyt was shoot. I showed him all the stuff you have to know, but finally we just got sick of it and went off and found these sprinklers, which were amazing. It was incredibly cold water, and you could stick the back of your head right up against it and just feel this wicked jet smacking your head—it was incredible—and the water coming down through your shirt. And there were these rainbows. Jesus Christ, there were like a dozen rainbows you could see. I've never seen so many rainbows in one place. You could just walk right through them. You could stand in the middle of them.

But when we came back, I just went and lay out in this lawn chair in the sun to dry off. It was glorious. I don't know if it was the lawn chair or the sun or what, but for some reason just frying out there in the back yard of this professor's house was glorious. E.B. got dressed and said he was going to get us some lunch in town, and I think I just dozed off in this heaven. When I woke up, E.B. was in the other chair with a bag of groceries. E.B. had a craving for Rice Krispies. He would get these little boxes, you know, like a six-pack of little Rice Krispies boxes, which were perfect for E.B., because you could pour the milk right in. They made these little bowls and then you could throw them away, so all E.B. needed to eat breakfast was a plastic spoon.

But this day, he'd had to buy like six of those jumbo mixed packs or whatever because he hadn't been able to find an all-Rice Krispies kind, and with the mixed pack you also unfortunately had to deal with Froot Loops and Sugar Smacks and all that sugary crap that E.B. didn't like. He said he'd gotten so pissed in the grocery store that he'd decided to find the shells for the gun. He'd hunted around and found this box of shells in some tool chest in the garage, and he threw me over this box and asked me if they would "fit." They did, so I loaded this shotgun, and he took his chair and he moved it over to a spot next to the open field. And he poured himself a box of Rice Krispies and milk, and he had the carton down on the grass. Then he took the one with the little frog, the Sugar Smacks, and he looked at me. I was at the other end of the lawn, and I knew precisely what he wanted. I was just waiting for him. He threw it into the air and yelled "Fire," and I blew that fucking toad right out of the air. It was intense. I just remember E.B. sitting there in this folding beach chair with these Rice Krispies in his lap, throwing these cereal boxes into the air and getting rained on by all these flecks of sugar crap.

Amalie Hindemuth

He called me. He called me a week or so after I'd visited, and I'd thought he might have wanted Tikki's number or something like that. I didn't really know—you know, someone completely new. But he was actually calling to apologize. He said he'd been aware of his mood and he hoped I hadn't thought it was me. Of course I told him no, but he said he'd realized I might have thought it was. He said it was Hilary, and of course I still had no idea what had been going on with the two of them, but he said he hadn't been expecting Hilary that night and that he didn't normally see Hilary with other people, but that that's what it had been. He said that Hilary only came on weekends.

And I sort of made a joke of it. I said, you know, "I hope it doesn't always have that effect on you." And he said no, it was all right, because Hilary was his only calendar. He said he didn't really know the difference between Monday, Tuesday, and Wednesday because the play just took him. And he never even knew if it was breakfast, lunch or dinner because the shades were always drawn. But he said he always knew it was Thursday, because Thursday Hilary would sneak in. He said, "Thursday Hilary sneaks in and sits on the typewriter keys so I can't get anything done. And then I know it's Friday because he arrives in person." And that's actually how I found out about them, is that, when he called to apologize for that mood that seemed to make him so sick.

Camille Walker

By the middle of the summer I'd have to pick Hilary up at the bus station, he'd come back from E.B.'s so wrecked. We'd go back to my place for tea, and I'd watch the poor little woozums tremble on my kitchen stool, very dramatic, telling me about how E.B.'s shadow was slinking inside him. It was just crazy. He'd have been back for twenty minutes, finally he'd calmed down, and then all of a sudden he'd reverse direction, start begging me, crying, "Drive me to the station, Camille. Please, I have to see him." And of course I'd have to stop him, "Baby, don't. Just look at yourself." He looked awful, his hands—he could hardly hold a mug of cider. I'd tell him, "Find someone new, Plum, because this is clearly not doing you any good." But he'd just scoff at me—ha! He'd say there was no point to anyone else anymore, couldn't I see? *E.B.* was the only person who mattered. *E.B.* was the only person who really understood him. E.B. saw inside, so that made things quite clear, didn't it? E.B. has to love you. "He just has to, Camilleon. He has to." He practically made it sound like a vow.

Hilary Richman

We both knew he'd be leaving at the end of the summer. You know, as soon as the play was done, he was going to be going to New York to put it on. Hugh Gardiner had seen to that. E.B. was going to come down from his little hermitage—you know, because as far as they knew, he'd just been up there all alone, just clacking away in the woods—he would come down and deposit this work of genius in everyone's lap. We both knew it was going to be done by the end of the summer.

I don't know how we knew. It's not like we ever spoke about

it. It's not like he ever said, "Look, I'm going to be finished soon. What do you want to do?" I mean, I don't know what I expected, but I think he just wanted to let it all happen naturally, like if you just leave it alone and pretend it isn't there, you know, it'll take care of itself.

The only problem was, that was a complete crock of shit and E.B. knew it. I mean, you can act that way and hope it turns into real life, but the idea of E.B. doing that, it just makes me want to laugh. God, he tried, though. You know, he's just folding his laundry pretending he didn't know what was going on, what I was going through, shit, just being this pathetic little plaything—that's what it started to feel like—who had nothing better to do but go up there and be with him so he can remember there's someone else in the fucking world.

Because let me tell you something. E.B. knew damn well what he was doing every time he did something. All this sort of stretching and rubbing his eyes and looking at you like, "What? What?" That was bullshit. He was the least casual person who ever lived, and I wish he'd just admitted it or at least admitted I knew it. I mean, he knew damn well what he was doing.

Like this one time near the end of the summer. He actually did something for me, you know, something nice. It must have been the dead of August because there were all these fans all over the place and all these paperweights and rocks. I'd just found him up in his room looking at this linen napkin thing, and the way he was holding it, I was afraid he was going to shove it in a drawer and tell me just to vanish or something. But he said, no, come here, and he let me see it. Levi had sent him this thing. I guess he'd written to Levi and told him what he was doing, you know, what the play was about, and Levi sent him this little napkin from some restaurant in Monterey where Levi had gone with E.B.'s mother. And apparently she'd taken this napkin home and painted on it, just this little picture of Levi in New York City, surrounded by all these buildings, looking completely lost. It was actually pretty cute. It said, "The Adventures of Levi in New York" on it. It was dated and it had her name on it, you know, Love, Blue.

Anyway, E.B. actually showed me this beautiful little thing, which was just bizarre. He never showed me things like that, or let me see what he was writing, but he let me look at this napkin as much as I wanted. I held it in my hands, and I was like, "Why don't you do this? Why don't you let me do this more? It's so easy." But I didn't say it. I just drove all the way to Portland that afternoon and bought him this frame for it, which of course he never used. Of course. It was like, "Sorry, Charlie. Time's up."

VI

New York

Fall 1972 — Winter 1973

From STUDIES, by Eton Arthur Boone*

Curtain rises on an art class. Six easels stand symmetrically placed
in a quarter-circle across stage right, so to create a space in the
middle of the stage where sits a nude man, very well built, chiseled
as from the center of limestone. A seventh easel stands stage left,
alone and larger than the others. The flatboard surface of each
easel should be adjustable, so that their planes can assume any

---

*Eton Boone's *Studies* was first performed at the Brandimore Theatre in
New York City on March 18, 1973, under the direction of Elizabeth
Rubin. It featured Katherine Odeon as Mrs. Singer and Daniel Schrag as
Felix Popper. These opening stage directions appear as they did in the
play's final draft.

slope. The flatboards should be made of a light material, perhaps linen, transparent enough to admit the shadow of the students' movement from behind. The students themselves are seated on stools as well. The two easels at the opposite ends of the stage are unoccupied as yet.

The class instructor is Mrs. Singer, mid- to late-thirties, her hair gathered viciously in a bun. She walks from her easel into the shadows behind the others, surveying the scratchwork of the students without a word. Perhaps only her footsteps attract our attention, that and the command of her index finger, which every so often darts out into the light just long enough to direct the model to a new position. The model has assumed perhaps five positions, one for each surveyed easel, before both Mrs. Singer and Felix, who enters stage right, converge on the last easel, the seventh.

Felix is a student, early twenties. He is tallish and slim, and the colors of his ill-fitting clothes are muted by dust. He carries a wooden case in one hand, a leather bag over the opposite shoulder, and an air of mild frenzy, mild manners, and mild contentment. He is new.

Levi Mottl

A portrait artist I once knew used to say everyone has a set distance that they look best from, and it was his job to find it for them—if he did, then they got their money's worth. He said that some people looked best from ten yards, some from ten feet, others from just a foot away. But no one, he said, wants to be looked at from too close—at some point your pores start to show. And I suppose that might have been my worry, that Eton had pulled out a giant magnifying glass and was turning it in my direction, except that I never thought Eton really worked that way. Proximity for Eton, or intimacy, was more a matter of trying to paint your painting—I'd let him do it already—so I can't say the play ever really worried me. He'd told me not to sweat it. He sent me bulletins whenever Felix developed habits of his own. He'd tell me when his characters had grown their own ideas, bought their own shoes. It was only some of the feelings he was borrowing from me and Blue, but he said he promised to give them back when he was finished.

Hugh Gardiner

By autumn of 1972, *Studies* was worthy of production, and I was able to see that it had a chance. It was a very simple play, two characters for the most part—a love dance of sorts between partners who are quite out of step—the young art student and his teacher, Mrs. Singer, who is at first a character of consummate detachment and cool. That was a very satisfying role, because of course it undergoes change, but not for the purpose of any high moral design. Mrs. Singer's change only further develops her character, it deepens our understanding of her, and of how myriad and profound the human mind really is.

For you must understand that Boone's art, in whatever form, always strove above all to reveal human character. His interests in drama or in suspense, in spectacle or detail, were nothing compared to his concern with character and characterization—that hadn't really changed so much since he'd been in New York. But it's quite clear, I should think, that in the years since he'd left his performances behind, he'd been trying to find new ways of satisfying this desire. With film, he'd seen the possibility of demonstrating character simply by observing behavior, meticulously, and sometimes, one would have to admit, tediously. But in theatre now—and this was something he'd come to understand in writing the play—Boone had to be more stylized. He couldn't aspire to realism as he had with Esteban. There wasn't the room in theatre for that particular kind of irreverence, for microscoping the bald spots and droolings of one's characters, nor was there room for the poetic savagery of the exposures. He had to pull back now and try to convey character through dramatic action.

What was very interesting, though, was the word Boone used to describe this more restrained, narrative approach—he called it "awe-ful," and by that he meant filled with awe. And I think that the decision to base his play on the relationship of his mother and Mr. Mottl was actually a very keen strategy on his part, for finding a subject that he could still marvel at. His feelings about their relationship, he'd written me long before, were indeed filled with awe, and always had been, for what he perceived as being its grace and restraint. Their relationship wasn't something he either wanted to, or felt he could have, invaded with the impiety he was so used to, and I think as new as the experience was for him, of exchanging insight for wonder, he was also thoroughly invigorated by it. One could feel it in his letters, and in the play itself—its slow, rich development—he'd never done something so uplifting. I think he discovered that to have relaxed his obsession with the thoughts and motives of everyone around him, to have released his fingers from their brains, was a far less dangerous, and far more joyful, way of being.

Harry Hampton

He contacted me. I couldn't have been back in the city more than a couple months myself. He saw my name in *The News* and hunted me down. It was nice. You know, it's not something you'd have expected from him, but he called, and I was glad he did. I needed a pick-me-up. You know, newsprint gumshoe, I don't care where you are, it gets a little tired after a while, and I figured Boone would be a real shot in the arm—at least there'll be some laughs.

But I don't know, people change. That's not something I really believe a lot. Basically, I think if you were an asshole in kindergarten, chances are you'll be the same asshole at Morgan Stanley—but things change. You get older, you start to figure out who you are and what you do, and I don't care what anyone says, you set limits by it. It's really the worst part of growing up, I think, having to set your limits, and actually I'll tell you a place where it starts to take its toll is humor. Just as a for instance.

I mean, think about it. You're a kid, you're seventeen, the

world's fair game. You can laugh about anything you want because you're not committed to anything yet. But you grow up, you become a journalist, and all of a sudden you can't make the same kind of fun of journalists anymore because you are one. I mean, you do, you ha ha ha aren't I terrific for telling you what a small dick I have, but it's not the same, it's not the same as being seventeen.

For some reason it's making me think of this guy my dad knew. He'd known him from college, and my dad was always telling me, you know, "Bernie's the funniest guy I ever knew. I never laughed so hard as when I was with Bernie." So you get this buildup and I always just accepted it when I was young, because Bernie would visit every now and then, and I'd think, you know, Dad says he's funny, Bernie's funny. But you grow up, you take a look at him, and one day you realize, Dad, Bernie isn't funny. Bernie doesn't know what the fuck is going on. He's just hanging on like everyone else.

But see, now I'm afraid you're just thinking I'm trying to find a polite way of saying Boone had lost his sense of humor, but I am not. I am not. What I'm trying to get at is, he was older. It was like he'd decided there were certain things out there where he just had to pass. You know, shit keeps piling up and piling up, your dad beats your mom, your dog dies, and the only way to deal with it is maybe just not to. You've got to sort of keep your hands off, and if you think about it, it's true. What's an old man, what's being an adult, if not pulling your hands back a little because they keep getting burned? Doesn't mean you can't be funny, doesn't mean you can't be smart, just means you can't really be a kid anymore.

Liz Rubin

Some parts, when you're casting, you read the play and you know. You see the character, and you know who you want for it—you think, this is Wally, or God, I hope we can get Geoffrey Holder for this. And Mrs. Singer, I knew what we wanted. Someone reserved, smart, a little scary maybe—a woman who's off somewhere else, above the fray. Her mind was on her art, not her relationships—and that's a great woman's role, one of the best of the time—but all I could think when I read it was, where's Katherine Odeon?

Katherine Odeon. Years. A decade since I'd seen her. I met her the summer I was trapped down at Norfolk. Katherine was one of the few interesting women there. Quiet, incredibly quiet young woman, but not timid—tough young actress and she'd done a terrific, spacy Iphigenia that people just fell in love with, fabulous. And also she'd turned _Troilus and Cressida_ around. Made us love Cressida, a terrific presence, wonderfully sympathetic actress. So calm for such a young woman, I had a real crush on her. But last I'd heard, she'd dropped out of sight. No one knew where she was, so I tried to put it out of my mind.

We cast at the Adele, the old studios on Forty-second and Ninth, up in one of the dance studios, an open call—Eton wanted it. He didn't want an actress. He just wanted Mrs. Singer to walk right through the door. No résumé, no photo, just her easels, her brushes, and a peanut-butter sandwich for him. He kept saying, we'll know, we'll know.

It was just the three of us there, me and Eton and Max. Max, this strange little producer Hugh found for us, such a strange man. My God. No idea what he was doing in theatre. Little man, baby face, like a baby in a three-piece suit, with a lisp. Like what's his name, Elmo Fudd, but on speed, that's Max. Anyway, the three of us had been there, auditioning every actress in New York between the ages of twenty and fifty. It was the second or third day, probably eighty people we've seen already. Lawrence, our P.A., has just shown someone out. It's late, we're tired, we're weary. Eton slides over to me. He says, "I haven't seen her yet, have you?" And I just say, "Goddammit, Eton, dammit, yes. Yes, I have. I haven't seen her in ten years, but I've seen Mrs. Singer, and her name is Katherine Odeon." Boone shrugs his shoulders. He says he's never heard of her, but Max is jumping on his chair—"Yes, yes! Let's call her." I keep telling them I don't know where she is, but Max is whirling around with his finger in the air—"A search, a search, a wild goose chase!"—incredibly odd little man, but we did it finally. We committed.

We went out into the office—about fifteen actresses are out

there, lined up—heads turning. Oh, sure, everybody wanted to
work with him. The movie was just out. So we troop down the
hall past these women, and we get to a phone and I start making
calls, anywhere I can think of, just this incredible search—two
hours on the phone, Max the whole time is saying we're FBI. I
call Williamstown, Nikos tells me she got married, older man,
world-class chef, refugee from World War II, he thinks Hungary,
all very sketchy. I call Austin in L.A. and he tells me that Bob
Dishy told him last he heard, Eric Zelman went into a restaurant
near the U.N. three years ago, and Katherine was the hostess.
Half hour later, eight or nine calls we've made to restaurants near
the U.N., I get this man named Boris on the phone, head waiter
at *Esterhazy*—bingo, he knows everything. Boris tells me, "Oh, no,
Mr. and Mrs. Koestler, they're divorced now. Mrs. Koestler left
three years ago." He's whispering. He tells me Mr. Koestler
nearly went crazy. He had to sell the restaurant and then buy it
back two years later, incredible mess, but if I want Mrs. Koestler,
maybe I try Fifth Avenue Hotel. He says she lived there right
after the divorce, family connection. "If you find her," he says,
"give her my regards."

So, finally, two hours later—it's already dark outside—I call
the Fifth Avenue hotel, complete shot in the dark. She's there.
Unbelievable. They connect me. It rings about eighteen times.
Eton keeps saying, "She's in the shower, give it another ring, the
maid's vacuuming, she's just coming in, she hears it from the
elevator." The eighty-ninth ring, she picks up. She doesn't say
hello, she just says, "Yes?" She's just walked in from buying a
rubber tree plant—go Katherine—and she's meeting her aunt in
about an hour, but she'd be happy to come by and read. We talk.
She says she started acting again a year ago. Commercials. One
stint up in New Haven doing Lula in *Dutchman*. We're in the
middle of talking when Eton grabs the phone. He says, "Hi, I'm
Eton Boone," and he starts telling her about the role—he's telling
her that maybe she should come in tomorrow if that's easier. But
he just stops when she starts talking. He puts his finger up to
block the noise—there isn't any noise, he just wants to listen to
her voice—he's got his finger in his ear, and he's listening, but he
looks up at us and starts nodding. Max, Max the whole time has
been flapping his hands, he starts pirouetting around the room—
"Hooray, hurrah, she's here! We've found her!" He tells me, "Liz,
let's go tell the rest of the ladies to go home!"

From THE DOWNTOWNER, *March 29, 1973*

STUDIES IN RESTRAINT
by Elaine Swayze-Gilpatrick

Seductions are as old as the stage, and Eton Boone may have discovered, or rediscovered, that the stage and its various seductions provide a much more comfortable arena for his talents than film. Eton Boone, who is still only twenty-five, is the performer/director who dropped in on the New York comedy scene in the late '60s and graced the stages of an abbreviated club circuit with his riveting penetrations of the celebrity mind.

However, Mr. Boone's short circuit blew soon enough. In June, 1969, he left New York after a celebrated club melee. He moved to London, where he wrote for television, and then produced, directed, and wrote last year's *Heiligenstadt,* a small-budget cinematic experiment which was visionary, but not altogether successful.

Enough time has passed apparently for Mr. Boone's return, marked by the modest triumph of his latest work *Studies,* a play with remarkably few excesses considering the leaky pen that wrote it. Mr. Boone's surprising sensitivity to the power of spectacle has aided him immeasurably in creating a play that is as visual as it is literal, as much the product of subtle choreography as subtle language.

Studies is about the unfinished relationship of an art instructor, Mrs. Singer (Katherine Odeon), and her teaching assistant, Felix Popper (Daniel Schrag). In essence, it is about emotions that pass like ships in the night; it is about characters who exchange, but never share, their feelings towards each other.

Structurally, the play is tight as a bow string. Boone uses three nude scenes, only two of which take place in the figure-sketching class that Mrs. Singer instructs, to mark distinct points in the evolution of Felix and Mrs. Singer's feelings. As Felix and Mrs. Singer trade the roles of model and instructor, the playwright tastefully and powerfully dramatizes the decisions that they are forced to make with respect to their divided attractions.

These scenes are most worthy of note, however, because of the abundant skill with which they are played. The performances of Miss Odeon and Mr. Schrag, as well as the direction of Elizabeth Rubin, whose work at the Women's Theatre Collective has also shown a weakness for excess in the past, are admirable. Miss Odeon's work in particular verges on being memorable, since it is the subtle development of her character that gives the play its emotional force. Odeon's Mrs. Singer makes the transition from the detachment of the instructor to the longing of the seductress believably and almost imperceptibly, so much so that by the play's final scene, her actions are as natural as they are new.

However, as is often the case, especially early in a career, those features that distinguish a piece are the very same ones that hinder it. If *Studies* is remarkable for its structural integrity, it is also bound by a sense of determinism that falls just short of being predictable. By its end, the play's symmetry becomes almost overt and therefore harmful. As Mrs. Singer takes on sexual energy, Felix loses it, and because it is sexual energy that provides dimension to these characters, we may lose our sympathy for Felix. Perhaps the transformation that Schrag presents us over the course of the play simply isn't as smooth or convincing as Ms. Odeon's. Perhaps it is Mr. Boone's fault that they should seem to compete.

But these are minor objections, and certainly debatable ones, in light of the overall achievement of the production. During a period when so much contemporary theatre seems bogged down in wretched excess, it's refreshing to see such a reassuring example of elegance and simplicity, and quite a pleasant surprise to see such a provocative name supplying it.

Max Kleinman

Katherine. She was a pistol, wasn't she, right from the start. I didn't get to meet her until the read-through. It was at my apartment. I don't think I'd have been invited otherwise. We moneybags usually get left out in the cold once we've signed our checks away—but my living room was the only open space in Manhattan that didn't charge rent. Yes, the ever so swank Kleinman penthouse.

They all troop in, in their boots. Rainy day. Raingear, galoshes, shaking umbrellas, brrr. I'll light a fire. But shoes off, everyone, or Consuela will chase me around the apartment with a frying pan! Even once their shoes are off, lined up at the door, they all sit on the floor with their drinks on the carpet, and Mr. Boone is handing everyone sticks of charcoal. Yikes!

But no stopping them. Our playwright passes out sheets of paper next—even to me, with my twelve thumbs—and says, "Let's all draw nudes!" "Nudes?" I say. "Let me at 'em! Where are they?" Ah, says Mr. Boone, they're in our imagination. "But it's better that way," he says. "We'll make them up out of our heads like little boys in church." He said that every time he'd gone to church as a little boy—Christmas and Easter—he used to sit in the pews drawing naked women for his brother, while all the old ladies around him watched. Ha! Imagine.

He wanted us to draw two nudes. One—how shall I say?—one sexy, and one not sexy. Well, well. Intriguing. I remember Mr. Schrag, Daniel, clearing his throat, "Excuse me, Mr. Playwright, but what makes something sexy? Who is to say?" Fine question, Daniel—I snapped my fingers, hear, hear. But Boone looked at him, right dead smack in the eye, and said, "When you look at it and you want to have sex with it, Danny, that's sexy." Ha! "When you look . . ." Yes, precisely. What else?

So we drew. Scribble, scribble, pass the towels please. It was an icebreaker, you might say. Chip, chip, chip away at our icy exteriors. We melt. We were puddles, puddles of tears, tears of laughter, laughter at our drawings. Mockery, I tell you. Boone held our drawings up for everyone to see and laughed at them. Even mine—producer Kleinman—chutzpah, sir, chutzpah to treat your producer this way. Lucky for you he takes his jokes so well. But I was not the only victim. Everyone had their moment in the stocks. Boone pointing at Liz's—tight, clenched figures they were, but females. Brave, brave, Liz. More courageous than our leading man, Daniel. When Daniel saw Liz's, he raised his hand and asked if he could change his.

But enough, enough. The reading. Delightful play, but Katherine—her voice stole the show. The very first line, heavens, it was the calmest, most serene voice you can imagine—she'd have made Mabel Mercer sound shrill. Oh, to be home from school and have Katherine Odeon sit by your bed and read to you, that would have been worth any fever.

When we finished, an hour has passed, two acts, conflict, resolution, end. All was still. Silent. Can we breathe? Can I applaud? Are we finished? Katherine was the first to move. She put the script down and went to get a glass of water, but our playwright was in the way. He had been standing in the kitchen doorway the whole time, leaning up against a pillar with dark smudges on his cheek from the charcoal. They staggered in front of each other for a moment, this way, that way, a two-step at my kitchen door. She took his arm finally, she grabbed his wrist—an untouchable man, she touches—she reaches up and wipes a smudge off his cheek. He could do nothing but look at her—shock, I tell you! But she just thumbed it on her jeans and went by him into the kitchen. He blushed, Mr. Boone blushed so very crimson red. Ho, delightful. He looked down at his sneakers and Katherine came back in and sat down on one of the pillows with her glass of ice water. "This," I wanted to announce, this smudge of charcoal here on Miss Odeon's jeans for us all to see, *"this* is sexy!"

Harry Hampton

We ate like kings. All he could make was pasta, but variations galore. Marinara, clam sauce, marinara, clam sauce, you name it, clam sauce, marinara. If he was feeling tricky, he'd cut up a mushroom. I'd bring a six-pack of Heineken, we'd throw some newspapers over this wood crate he had in his living room, stuffed with books and manuscripts, set dinner up, flip on the game. Knick game, Ranger game, it didn't matter. They were both terrific, very romantic teams back then—a pleasure to watch, and really, that's about all you want from an evening. No need to push it any further than that, an "l" or a "w," makes things simple. His apartment too. It had that same no-shit feel, which means bare walls, a rug, the crate, the TV, a typewriter, and exactly one painting, by his mother, a painting of a coastline, yellow and blue. That's it.

Thing is, I could really go on about that apartment, about those evenings. I could flip open to any page of my notebooks from back then and find you something, and the great thing is, there'd be no contesting it. You couldn't roll your eyes, because it's all just details for me to remember—Harry and Boone, winter of '72–73. I could tell you how many A&P matchboxes propped up his rickety kitchen table, what kind of slippers he wore. I could tell you everything in his icebox door—lots of pickled stuff, Ann Page marmalade, cream cheese, a couple bottles of Thousand Island dressing, I think there was a bottle of aspirin, and a couple of beers we'd frozen by mistake once, just sitting there in case of an emergency—double overtime.

Honestly they're the only notes I took on Boone that ever worked. They just take it in, no questions asked. They just sit there, in their own little pocket, this peaceful season when we'd found something that didn't need any help from me. I'd get home, and if I had anything to write, it wasn't, "The night went down like Beaujolais." It was just a detail I wanted to remember, like the pipe. Out in back of his place was a big factory, a printing-press type of place with a giant pipe running down the side, and every hour or so, at least at night, this pipe would hiss and blow steam. If Boone didn't have the window down, you'd feel like someone just shoved a gallon of india ink down your throat. We called it Old Faithful. I called it Old Faithful.

Camille Walker

Hilary started seeing some of his older flames again, and turning his old tricks on the fourth floor of Lamont Library, but it wasn't the same. It wasn't, "I have a present for you—moi." It was, "Help me out." And believe me, no single person could handle him—I know I couldn't. He needed worship, physical and vocal and emotional and sexual. He needed everything. And to a point, that's kinky, having Hilary roll around on your king-sized zebra pelt saying, "Tell me I have silky skin." Oh, mais oui. Thou art the fairest, lady queen. Great fun while it lasts, but it doesn't. It didn't have the staying power of the old Hilary. The old Hilary didn't have to think. But the new one, post-E.B., do you know what you get? Petit Hilaire gets more petit, rolls off, gets a drink or a towel and says, "Well, I guess E.B.'s made his decision." Oh, how very interesting, lovey, would you excuse me while I go get the Water Pik?

I mean, I tried to be kind, but this is a bed. This was Hilaire, and oh, how the mighty had fallen. Shall I tell you? He became gimmicky. Gimmicky and cheap, not to mention a little bit scary. He'd call up and say, "I'll be right over." Well, no, Plums, I've got a dinner date. I've got papers to get to. I've got the TV set or Gideon's if worse comes to worst. Sometimes I just was not in the mood, thank you, but that did not sit well with the fallen prince. "Not in the mood?" he'd say. "Well, what about this?" and he'd grab my crotch. What about it, love? It just didn't work anymore. I can't tell you why. I couldn't tell Hilary why, but I didn't want to be on the panel of experts anymore. No. 'Twas a millstone round my neck. I come home and find him in the apartment, in my father's robe. I ask for the key, please. He calls while I'm with another man and asks if I'd like to come over and see something. Not now. He practically assaults me behind the bookshelves in Child's Library, displays himself to me and asks if I ever remember seeing it bigger. Hilary! Stop! I'm sorry, but lunches from now on, okay? Lunches and dinners and phone calls when you're feeling blue, but no more of this.

Liz Rubin

Eton was a very solid presence at rehearsals. He didn't say a lot, he stayed in back. We asked him questions if we had any. He'd make a comment if something wasn't coming across. Blunt. Danny would be up doing something, easel scene, when out of nowhere—Aaaaanh!—a buzzer sound from the back row. There wasn't a lot of discussion. He'd have been a director like Mandy Ehrlich, who started out as a musician. He used to tell us things like, "Eagle perched, not eagle fly." Boone was the same, even in the stage directions—for Felix, "Think Gary Cooper in Oz."

"Gary Cooper in Oz?" Danny had trouble with it—odd role too, Felix. Always too much gaga. Eton would tell him, "He's a cigarette burning in an ashtray." But Danny kept losing it, it didn't click with him. "Cigarette?"—Danny's lost by that.

She, though. Didn't need help. Katherine stepped right in. She had it from day one, what we wanted. Autopilot the whole way, key to Mrs. Singer. Key to Katherine, and Eton deferred. Absolutely. I'm talking to Eton about a scene that isn't working. Something's not right and he says, "If Katherine looks out of place, then the play's wrong." Because Mrs. Singer belongs to Katherine. This hello-are-you-there quality. She's someplace else. And you know, that's nothing new, a lot of people are someplace else—that's life—but you can tell where it is—"I'm saying this, but I'm thinking you're a dyke." "I'm saying this, but I'm thinking about my book." Katherine, no, somewhere else, but I never knew where.

I remember from early, early on, an example. We'd finished early, and Eton had been on his way out, but Katherine said, "Wait. We're on the same subway line." She had to go downstairs to get something, and Eton and I waited at the water fountain. She came back, we all walk to the station together. We go down into the subway hole. We pay our tokens, wait for the train, talk about Watergate, Haldeman, Dean, I don't remember, but then, yes, I realize, I'm not going the same way as them. I have to go to the other side of the platform, so I say good-bye. I go underneath. I come out the other side and they don't see me. But I watch them across the tracks, I'm looking at them. They're sitting on a bench, and behind them—this is tangential but great, very memorable—there's this poster behind them, this cigarette ad with the black eye. This man's giant face is smiling down at them like he's going to eat them, like they're on a platter for him to eat. Fabulous image. Like in *Life*.

But okay, this is it. She gets up from the bench and goes and looks down the tracks. She looks both ways, and she walks back to him. She puts her hands behind her back, like a magic trick. "Which hand?" She's standing in front of him with her hands behind her back, and he says, "The train is coming?" She pulls one hand out and opens it. There's nothing in it. Nothing. And he says, "The train isn't coming?" He doesn't know, and she pulls out the other hand, and there's nothing there either.

Nothing. They're just hands. She holds them both out in front of him, these flat palms of her hands, and he's looking at these hands. He doesn't know what they mean, there's no trick. He doesn't know if the train is coming or it isn't, and his face, he's amazed. He's just saying, "Yes, I have no idea. I have no idea. What a beautiful thing." And the train comes, and they get on, and the train goes, and they're gone. Who, who the fuck knows where?

Harry Hampton

Men can be real spastic with each other. This one night I remember we tried to talk about her, what he called this new woman who was the lead in his play. We were out to dinner, celebrating an assignment I'd gotten from *Cue Magazine.* We met at an Italian restaurant on about Sixtieth and Lex—I forget its name, but they've got a boccie court right there in the middle of it—a boccie alley. Whatever. So we had dinner and spoke about my article, which was going to be on the state of contemporary theatre in New York and whether what they called a "New School" was forming, which I concluded there wasn't, stop the presses.

So it was a case of two guys meeting and shooting the bull, you know, tackling another issue, which is what two men do together. But we had a lot to drink. We'd opened with kirs and then split a bottle of valpolicella so we were feeling pretty loose. We let it hang out a little. We've solved the problems of the theatre world, now we can turn to matters more personal.

But if that's what we're going to do, we're going to need something to occupy our bodies while we talk—you know, Don Vito has this figured out, what men need—so we've taken our coffee down to the boccie alley and it's great. He says, first serve, "There's this woman in the play." Leaves it there. We bowl a few balls, take a few sips, let it hang, then I say, "Oh, yeah?" He says, "Yeah." Another couple tosses, go get the balls, bring 'em back. "So?" "So?" "The woman." "Oh, the woman, yeah—" The woman, yeah. I wanted to say, "Yeah, the woman. What? What about the woman? There's a woman in the play and you like her." And he says, "Okay, yeah, there's a woman in the play and I like her." And I say, "She pretty?" He says, "Yeah, she's pretty." "She funny?" ". . . Yeah, she's funny." We gave it another rest. I didn't want to push it. We play another round maybe, discuss spin strategies, finish another game. Finally I say, "So, is there some kind of problem?" And he says, "Problem? No problem."

Basically he was being very irritating. You know, if you don't want to talk about it, Boone, we don't have to talk about it, but if we are going to talk about it, then you're gonna have to stop acting like it's a crime to be attracted to someone. He was acting like he'd never been attracted to anything before in his life. It was like being with a twelve-year-old. You know, I felt like I should be saying, "Yeah, Bucky, that's a hard-on. That's what happens when you rub it." Christ.

But obviously he doesn't want it to turn into locker talk, not that it would have, but he stopped us finally. He was cradling the ball like a shot-put, contemplative pose, and he just says to me, "Harry, she told me about the canals in Holland. They freeze over in the winter, and everyone puts on their skates and they go down the canal." He just says this. "They don't go in circles," he says, "these people. They just keep going straight along these canals. The scenery just goes by. You don't even stop." He looks at me and he says, "Hunh, Harry? What do you think of that? They just let it go by." I didn't say anything. I thought he might be trying to give me shit, I didn't know. He said he'd watched her head off down the block after rehearsals. He said she walks away and all of a sudden, boom, she's there. "It's like she's constantly slipping through into her own world," he said. "She's always passing over the threshold, you know, and it keeps surprising her. She keeps saying, 'Wow, color!' "

I said to him, "You believe that?" He said he thought he did. I said, "If you believe it, I believe it."

Hilary Richman

He wrote me a letter. I got this letter from E.B. He wrote me at Harvard, sort of detailing what he'd been doing. Just what I wanted. It had all these new names and information and funny descriptions. This whole new bunch of people and problems. It was a good letter. I mean, he was great at writing letters, wasn't he? What complete bullshit. I was just sitting out there in the gross little courtyard eating lunch with this moron who was one of my roommates that year. I wasn't going to open it until he left, but he just wouldn't leave. He just kept sucking Jell-O through a straw. He was such an asshole, Gordon. Finally I read it with him there. I just read it twice and put it on my tray and threw the whole thing away.

I mean, I don't know, it was ridiculous, he was acting ridiculous. We didn't even see each other that whole fall. The first we saw each other, it was right after Christmas. I went in this one time to visit him, during my exams. He was just racing around the whole weekend with his play, which didn't bother him at all. It bothered me. It pissed me off. You know, it wasn't easy seeing him. I thought he was going to have trouble dealing with people after Maine, so here I am coming down just trying to help, but I get there and it's like, "I don't need your help." All of a sudden he's acting like Mr. Fucking Adult. It was like, la de da, this isn't so hard. I'd like you to meet Mrs. Whoozeewhatsit. She's playing Mrs. Nerdlinger. Or here's my friend Harry. I'd like you to meet my friend Harrybutt. Maybe Harry'll come to Lüchow's with us tonight. Fuck that.

Max Kleinman

There's a marvelous Turkish coffee shop that's around the corner from the Brandimore, and sometimes in the late afternoons when I needed a pick-me-up, I'd connect my booster cables, yes, I'd drop by the theatre to check on my investment, see how the play was coming along. So I'd bought my cup of coffee this one afternoon. I brought it into the theatre, but no one was there. The stage was set up for dress rehearsal, and there was a floor lamp on stage right, a very bright bulb on top of a brass pole, but no one was there. They'd all taken an early dinner— scoundrels! Their heads! I say. Let them roll! But there was no one there to hear me, so I found myself a seat in the back of the house and decided to wait there and drink my coffee until they got back.

Turkish coffee, yes, but the lights dim, not a soul about, not a creature stirring, and those plush seats. I, for one, sleep. Can you blame me? But I was awakened by voices, entering from backstage. Katherine and Mr. Boone, together, chattering. Just the two of them, and both very alive. Mr. Boone in particular, a bounce in his step. Katherine seated herself on a stool upstage, and Mr. Boone began wandering around looking at the easels, standing behind them like one of the artists, sketching. He went to the floor lamp. He gripped it by the neck and put his feet on the base and began rocking it back and forth, back and forth, gently swinging all the shadows around.

I might have made my presence known, but I'd heard so much from Hugh about the boy's ability to play and improvise on stage, I buttoned my lip. I snuggled down. Katherine got up from the stool and started walking towards him. She circled round some of the easels and came towards him, but he told her to stop right there, because the shadow she was casting against the scrim was enormous, and it was. Enormous.

But Katherine wasn't interested in playing. She went and sat by the edge of our little proscenium and watched—the shadow waltz. He dragged the brass lamp to center stage, and he started whirling it around. All the shadows danced. There were six or seven easels on the stage, and the white scrim behind them as a backdrop. He swung the bulb around like a flag and the shadows all swirled one-two-three, one-two-three. But no sound. Hush.

She lay down on the stage with her hands on her stomach, and he told her to look at the ceiling. He moved the shadows across the wall and told her to imagine it was the ceiling of her bedroom on Lake Shore Drive in Chicago, with cars passing outside, or the roof of her father's Buick, with her lying in the back seat dreaming as the street lights passed by. He kept doing the same pattern over and over, eleven, twelve times—mesmerizing—but finally she stopped him. She reached her arm out for him, and he came over, dragging the lamp behind him. She tugged on his pant leg—enough play for now—and he left the lamp and knelt over her. He lowered himself and they began to kiss. A kiss! Katherine and Mr. Boone! It's a wonder I didn't shout with joy and interrupt it.

When I told Hugh this story, I remember he asked me if Katherine and Boone had been casting giant blue shadows against that back scrim, and at first I thought to myself, yes, wouldn't that have been magnificent? But on second thought, would that have been more magnificent than just the two of them there together on the stage with that brass lamp? I don't think so. I don't think so at all.

Hugh Gardiner

There are bound, I think, to be periods of calm and periods of fury in any relationship, and I don't think it would be fair to venture simple guesses about why they come and go when they do. Even with literature, one finds oneself inclining towards a certain author and away from another, simply because our needs change over time. But it's also important, I think, not to treat our sources of well-being—authors, friends, poems, prayers, whatever they may be—as static presences, for just as we change, so do they.

And yet it was one of the less fortunate conditions of Boone's and my relationship that as simple as it was to understand each other during our periods of greatest interest—because we had our letters to read and refer to—just as basic was the difficulty of understanding our slower periods. His silence, when it lasted longer than normal, was impossible for me to read, and I was often at a loss how to respond, if I should at all. In general, I tried to write him as regularly as possible, because as much as I ap-

preciated his occasional weariness, I did believe that if my re-
minders were constant, they need never sound urgent. The question, I suppose, is whether we prefer having a gentle bird of
warning on our shoulder, chirping away throughout the day, or
an occasional siren, and I chose the former. I wanted him to know
that I was there, and that the particular concerns that he'd been
sharing with me over the past six years should probably not be
forgotten or ignored. They were not the sort, I think, that a mood,
a phase, or an affair, could ever hope to put away, and if his
silence sometimes suggested such a possibility, I hoped that my
consistent biddings would help register my calm, but concerned,
objection.

Harry Hampton

I saw them together once down in the Village. They were shopping, just looking in the windows outside Pierre Deux, and I was
going to say hi. I was going to go up behind them and tell them
I knew Pierre personally if they wanted a deal on the chiffonier
in the window. But I stopped. In the middle of goddamn Bleecker
Street I stopped. I don't even think they were holding hands, or
maybe they were—you don't notice when people are doing it
right—but I just let them be. If they're shopping, and they're
happy, why screw it up?

Hilary Richman

I'd had to go to New York for some reason. There was some
interview I had, so I'd caught a ride down with this bunch of guys
from the house I was living in. Like a dozen of us were all
crammed into this van. It was disgusting. But I hadn't even called
E.B. to tell him. We'd had some pretty bad phone calls. Not fight

phone calls, just phone calls like, I gotta go, Hilary, can I call you back? Well, E.B. does not call back. I knew that, so I guess I figured I'd clear out of the way. Which I did.

But this trip. I'd made the mistake of telling one of these morons I was with about E.B.'s play. It hadn't opened yet, but this guy—I don't even remember his name anymore, some nickname like Moose or Scooby—he was in some college acting troupe and he was begging me to introduce him to E.B., so I guess I just used it as an excuse. I called E.B. from this pay phone in Grand Central—we'd had to drop off like ten of these people for some party in Rye—but I told E.B. that I had these "friends" with me who were dying to meet him. He said okay. He said he'd take us out to dinner.

You know, so we went up there, me and Scooby. It was absurd. We drove up to the theatre, and E.B. was waiting out in front with Katherine. I didn't even have any idea who she was—I'd heard her name—but she was wearing a yellow bandana and they were sitting on some smelly old thrown-away Murphy bed on the street. So we all introduced ourselves and went to this bistro around the block, and I didn't know what the hell was going on. I mean, of course the second I saw this woman I thought to myself, "Oh, great, look who E.B.'s fucking." I mean, it just seemed obvious, but I guess I didn't think it was that important because she clearly had no idea who I was. I mean, not a clue, and it even sort of pissed me off a little—you know, because here we were at this restaurant looking at our menus, and all of a sudden I just felt like E.B.'s stepbrother, you know, who's come down from Harvard for a visit. The whole thing seemed like such bullshit.

But this guy, Scooby, had dragged E.B. into this conversation about how brilliant *Heiligenstadt* was, and I know E.B. was just thinking to himself, "Jesus Christ, it was a piece of shit." But I couldn't even get his attention, I couldn't even catch his eye, so Katherine and I were sort of left there in front of each other with nothing to say. I guess I was ready for her to start asking me some absurd questions about what I was majoring in or where I was living, but she just sat there. She was just sort of observing this restaurant, looking all around at these beer clocks on the wall, and then she took a box of cigarettes out of her purse, which was a knit bag, and started smoking. She just smoked. She didn't say anything, she just smoked this cigarette and I had one too. We sat across the table from each other smoking these two cigarettes with this guy next to me going on and on about Truffaut and jump cuts and shit like that.

But it was weird, because I just remember it getting very quiet inside. It was like this peaceful feeling you get when something horrific is about to happen, like this cab is going eighty miles an hour through traffic and all you can do is sit back and say, "Fuck it," you know. That's basically what it felt like smoking this cigarette with Katherine in this restaurant, because I was looking at her—she was just sitting there with her legs crossed and her arm up on the back of her chair, and she was turned towards E.B.—and we would look at each other every now and then, and we would smile, but there was something about her eyes. She was different. I think her eyes were different colors. She just scared me, and I thought she was incredibly beautiful, I thought she was incredibly powerful, and so basically I was sitting there smoking this cigarette with this woman realizing that she and E.B. are probably not just fucking around. And I mean, I literally started getting light-headed, I started getting dizzy, and she could even see it, I must have been turning green, because she stubs out her cigarette and she goes, "Are you feeling all right?" And I just looked at her, and I couldn't even help myself. It's like it just came out. I said, "So how long have you and E.B. been lovers?"

E.B. almost fucking choked. It's the first time he even looked at me the whole evening. He looked like, what the fuck? But Katherine sits back, and she's smiling, and she says, "Well, let's see." And she put her hand on E.B.'s neck and they look at each other and I practically died, I practically hyperventilated right there in my chair, because it's like they fucking fell in love right in front of me and Scooby. She looks at him, and he looks at her, and I've never even seen E.B. like that, it's like he was just disarmed. His eyes were like fucking diamonds, and Katherine looks back at me and goes, "Since just now, I guess."

It was incredibly fucked up. This guy Scooby, I don't know what the hell he thought was going on, but E.B. gets up and says he's going to go get us all some drinks. He just gets up and leaves, and I felt like I was going to be sick. Katherine, I couldn't even look at her anymore. She starts talking to dorkbrain on my right.

He's saying he recognizes her from something and she's just, you know, taking or leaving him. She doesn't give a shit. E.B. comes back and I can't even tell if he's been laughing his head off or losing it in the bathroom. I basically have no idea what's going on inside his head, so I figure fuck it, I can't deal with this, and I placed my napkin over my plate very neatly and I didn't excuse myself, I just left. I left.

And I went out of the restaurant and I waited out there, and I don't know what I would have done if he hadn't come out finally. But he did, he came out and we started walking up, I don't know where the hell we were, Lexington or Third, the uglier one, and I was just out of my mind. I didn't know what I wanted, but E.B. tried to make some joke. I'm sure he was a little fucked-up too. I mean, he wasn't ready for this. He goes, "Well, that was a fun drink." And I think I just started crying right there. I mean, I was so scared. I just said, "Who is this woman?" I mean, the idea of him having someone else, you know, it just seemed so inconceivable to me. I hadn't even thought about it, and I started yelling at him. I said, "Does she even know about you, E.B.? Does she know what you do, that you're just going to crawl inside her where all the ugly things are and wait for her to come? Because," I said, "it's mean, E.B., it's the worst thing you can do, because she's not going to be able to leave, she's not going to be able to walk away like you— when it all gets too horrible and grotesque to look at, you're just going to disappear, aren't you? You'll fucking vanish, asshole. Does she know that, E.B.?"

I don't know, I'd just been yelling and yelling, but he kept trying to deny it. He kept acting like he didn't know what I was talking about. He was saying, "I'm not doing anything, Hilary. I don't do anything." He's looking at *me* when he says this, and I was just like, "Oh, fuck you, E.B. You do too. Fuck you. Fuck you for fucking me up." I was so pissed, I wanted to tear his eyes out. I just wanted to hurt him, but he wasn't even listening, it's like he was smiling, and I wanted to hurt him. I said, "Oh, look at me. I'm Eton Arthur Boone. I'm Boone, and I'm so above it all, and my stepbrother who I've totally fucked up and I won't even admit it is yelling at me, and I'm so above it all, I don't care, and I've written this play about my mother and now I get to fuck her. I'm fucking my mother."

Okay, well, that was probably a bad thing to say. It was. He grabbed me by the elbow and turned me around, and he wasn't loud. E.B. was never loud. I don't even know if you'd call it angry, but it was intense as hell. He just said, "Look, you can come here and you can do this." He said I could try to get him going again with my little scene on the sidewalk, and he said, "You can stand there and say I can't help it, and that it'll always come back and get me, but it won't. And it won't because of her." Okay? He said, it won't come back because of her. Okay? Have you got it?

Well, I don't know, I'm sure I was already bawling by this point. I just told him I didn't believe that, and he said, "Well, Hilary, I don't give a shit what you believe," and he turned around and started walking back towards the restaurant. We must have been in the nineties by now, like on Ninety-seventh Street. I was just bawling on this corner. I remember just thinking, I can't lose him, I can't lose E.B., just blubbering it like this pathetic fool. I don't even know how long I was there. Finally I headed back. I cleaned myself off and walked all the way back to the restaurant just bleary-eyed, but I wasn't going to go in. I looked inside and E.B. was just sitting there. He was tilting back in his chair smoking this cigarette, and he didn't have any food. Katherine and Scooby had these burgers or something, and she was drinking from this tall glass. And I just looked at her, you know. I looked at her and I just thought, oh, fuck, what if he's right?

Amalie Hindemuth

Katherine and Eton came out to Quogue once, for a weekend. My father died that year, and I used some of the money he left me to buy a house out there on Long Island, and I actually think Eton and Katherine were my first guests ever. The play was changing theatres so they came out for a weekend, and one of the days I spent alone with Katherine. Eton had wanted to sleep late and he said he'd meet us at the beach in the afternoon, so she and I just went antiquing and looking for things I would need for the house, you know, bottle openers and placemats and things like that, the things you find you need when you're just moving in.

But we'd been shopping around and one of the things we'd found was just the loveliest bellows for the fireplace, a beautiful antique black one with a a sort of moon face on it. It didn't seem like a very necessary thing to get, you know, but we bought it anyway, and we'd taken it into a sort of sandwich shop to have lunch. We sat it up in the chair next to us, and we both had these giant iced teas they served, and I think because of the blower, Katherine told me this story from when she was younger.

It wasn't a story actually, but she said that when she was just twelve or thirteen or so, she used to have to make a fire in her mother's bedroom fireplace every night. She said her mother had been bedridden for years with the most awful depression, and that as children they'd just been told that their mother was very sad. Apparently she'd just gone into her room one evening after dinner and didn't come out again for four years. She just stayed in bed. But Katherine said that she would go in and visit her mother first thing every day when she came home from school, and that every evening Katherine's two younger brothers, who were twins, would come in as well. Katherine would sort of usher them into their mother's bedroom and these little boys would tell what had happened at school that day, but most of the time they didn't have much to say. They were sort of frightened of their mother, which you can't really blame them for, and they would stand in front of her with nothing to say quite often, with just their chins down on their chest. So Katherine said that every night her mother used to ask her to build a fire before the boys came in to see her, because the room would be too quiet otherwise.

She said this to me. And I think just the story itself I found very moving, the picture of these poor children standing before their mother and the only sound in the room being this fire crackling away which the daughter had been asked to make, but on top of being sort of overcome by this very sad little scene, I also just couldn't help looking at Katherine as she told it. I was thinking of something Eton used to say when we were back in New York, about watching people. He said, "When you're really seeing things, Amalie, sometimes it will just strike you." He'd say, "Watch the way a man will bend over and pick up a stick, because there's everything you'll ever need to know in that, or the way a woman will touch her hair, she's been doing it for years and years."

But with Katherine, you know, here she was telling me this story from her childhood, and it was very lovely, but I couldn't really find it anywhere in her face, any trace at all of the story she was telling me. It's something that was true of her on stage as well. It's even in the play. Mrs. Singer says something to the young man about a flower. She says you can understand its life very easily if you like. You can think of it as something that's come from a seed, something which has grown and changed and bloomed, and that's lovely, that's very simple—it's what we do. But she asks the young man, can you see it there in front of you and not think of the seed? Don't think of it as a flower, or of the petals as petals, as these things which come from somewhere. Think of them just being there in front of you. Can you still see the life? She says you'll never be the same if you can really do it, and I just know that that's why Eton loved Katherine so much. She just made it so easy in a way, you know, just to see her right there before you, even if she was talking to you about how silent her mother's bedroom was.

Afterwards we went to the beach to meet Eton. We walked along the dunes and sat at the foot of them, and she pointed out at the ocean. She said, "There he is," and he was just this black figure out in the waves. You could only tell it was him from the way he held himself, and there were two or three other people out with him, and I said that he was actually quite good, wasn't he? He was actually a very good body surfer, coming from San Diego, I suppose. He was bobbing up and down in the waves, and he saw us and waved his arms. I don't know who the other people were, but he got them all to wave too. We were all waving at each other from the dunes and the ocean, and Katherine had a straw hat on her head that she had to hold onto.

And just sitting right there up against the dunes, we were both lying back on our elbows looking out at the ocean. I think it may have been the first time I'd really seen those Long Island colors, you know. The sky was becoming that sort of thick blue, and the ocean was sparkling with these little black heads bobbing up and down in the surf and diving under waves like sea lions. Eton's feet would stick out of the water and we would watch him, after he caught a wave, working his way back out to where they were all breaking. And I just remember watching her watch him. She was holding her hat down, and her hair was blowing. She had to wipe the strands of hair out of her mouth, and you could see her eyes sort of glinting out from beneath her lashes, they were blue. She looked so lovely I wished Eton could have come and seen. I wished he could have seen how lovely, and I know he would have told me, "I know. I know she is, Amalie." But he was too busy out in the waves playing for her, catching all the waves for her. She could just look out, you know, and be the one he would do his swimming for. I was moved. I said to her, "Katherine, do you think you would mind if I put my head down on your lap and looked out at the ocean from there?" It's just what I wanted to do, and she said that certainly I could, and I did. I put my head in her lap and sort of listened to it gurgle while the ocean was doing all its smashing on the beach and Eton kept swimming in the ocean like some sort of hero.

Harold Odeon

Katherine hadn't been very forward about the men she'd been seeing after her divorce. When I first met Eton, in fact, I was thinking of him much more as a writer, just a friend of hers. He was so much younger than she was. The only thing I knew of him aside from his having written the play was that he was interested in the chess letters of my wife Margaret's grandparents. Katherine had told us when we came in to see the play that Eton had wanted to talk to us, and to Margaret in particular, about the story of Margaret's grandparents. She said that he was considering using it as a basis for his next project, a book he was intending to write.

Margaret's grandparents, the Uyterhoevens, had lived in Dayton. They'd come over from Holland, and they'd run a little game shop on the main street in Dayton, which Margaret has photographs of. It was a place that people could go to play backgammon or dominoes, pachisi, chess or checkers. There was a garden in back with chairs and tables, and pies were served by Mrs. Uyterhoeven, along with drinks, all different kinds of coffee and lemonades, anything the customers wanted but liquor, I think.

But Margaret's grandfather had gone back to Europe during the Boer War to help his brother run supplies, or he may have been an intelligence man of some sort—it's never been very clear to me—but he was away from Mrs. Uyterhoeven and their children, five of them, three girls, two boys, for nearly three years, during which time he traveled extensively through Europe and Africa. And on his travels he'd hunt around for beautiful games for their shop, unusual backgammon sets or African games he could ship back to Mrs. Uyterhoeven. In Khartoum, he found the most beautifully detailed chess set he'd ever laid eyes on, with individually carved pieces, and a rosewood base, and the legend is that Mr. Uyterhoeven sent the pieces back to Mrs. Uyterhoeven one by one, each accompanied by a letter which told a story of that piece, a fable or an adventure that he'd written and illustrated for her and the children. Mrs. Uyterhoeven kept all of these tales in a backgammon case at the shop, and read them to the children and grandchildren years later. Margaret herself swears to having heard some of them. But unfortunately while the chess set has survived, the stories that Mr. Uyterhoeven had written, as well as the shop itself, were lost in the Dayton flood of 1913.

Mr. Boone had met with us to learn more about the story, to talk with Margaret about them, and in particular to ask if she would mind his undertaking a novel based on the idea of Mr. Uyterhoeven's letters. He had it in mind to write a book, the major body of which would be the husband's letters back to the wife, the fables about each piece that he sent, with very spare explanations of how the letters had come to be, what became of them, and what became of the pieces. Mr. Boone was wondering if we could send him photographs of the pieces so that he could have something to work from. He was extremely polite in our meeting—I should say that—but it was clear that he was a good deal more than a friend of Katherine's, and that this book, if we approved of his writing it, wouldn't be a book really, so much as a gift to our daughter.

Harry Hampton

Oh, the way I found out, it was a real beaut. Story begins at the cast party, though, if I'm going to tell it right, back in March or whenever it was. Tons of people are there. Elaine May is there. Patricia Neal is there. Edward Albert's in the corner with a blonde. Everyone's happy. The play went off without a hitch and it was good. Everyone gets to pat themselves on the back.

So, late, two-thirty or three in the morning, I'm looking for Boone and Katherine. And you know, they'd just looked great. They looked like they were on cloud nine, but I hadn't seen them for a couple of hours. I didn't know if they'd left. I ask that guy, the little guy who played Levi, "Where are they?" He points toward the coat room and rolls his eyes, and I think to myself, "All right. That makes sense. Everyone's having a good time, opening night's a hit, you're a little drunk, you're in love—'Hey, let's go have humpties in the coat room.'"

So ten minutes, fifteen minutes, I don't know, half hour later, out he comes, Valentino emerging from his lair, and he looks like hell. Just out of his mind. His shirt's undone, his knees are shaking, his hair's all over the place, and I'm thinking to myself, you know, "There's a Cadillac. There's an American success story." He saw me through his haze, he came over and we had a little talk, just punching around, a few yucks, but I didn't want to hold him up. It seemed like he wanted to get back to Katherine and I don't blame him. I tell him I hear the bell for round two, buddy, go knock 'em dead. You know, I'm his cornerman.

And I'll admit, a lot of that had to do with the play. I mean, there she was, she'd been out on stage looking great, and every guy, every person in the audience, I don't care how much you liked the play, you look—she was just glowing. And now, a few hours later, 3:00 A.M. the next morning, here's the writer triumphant. Our crush is in love, she's in love with this guy, so you can either ice pick the son of a bitch or give him a slap on the back. And I know it's a little slimy, like Katherine's some slice of cheesecake, but I'm just telling you, I was really feeling like there is a top of the world, because that guy's on it, and it's great to be near it. It's great to be near them, and someday, who knows, maybe there'll be a party for me. I'll get to stagger in and out like Stud Stevens, and I'll look like shit too because, hey, I can afford to.

Well, it's as simple as every dog has his day, and you can even check with seventeen editors up and down BosWash if you want, and not only will they tell you it's true, every dog has his day, but they'll tell you when Hampton had his. Hampton had his months later, and I'm sure you're not interested in the particulars, but if you want to know the difference between Harry Hampton and Eton Boone, well, here it is. Under an assumed name for the only time in my career, I write a series for the *News* about the life of the stripper. Intrepid reporter that I am, I do a goodly amount of research, and the series runs. It sells okay, at least well enough so that when it's all done, there's a little party—every scam has its party. A bunch of my new friends come. They put on a little show, and to make a long story short, the main attraction, the *pièce de résistance*, the headliner, our featured performer for the evening, ends up in my lap, and we end up in the coat room.

Now, Boone was not at this party. Somehow he'd managed to stay away, so he didn't get to see my moment in the sun. But I'd told him about it, of course. We'd gone out to Gallagher's, late summer now, and I was trying to drag him into the conversation, talking about what it feels like to walk down a hall with a drink in your hand knowing that behind the third door on your left, there she is awaiting. You know, isn't that great, I'm saying, isn't that something, and what a country this is where a couple of guys can sit around in a bar and shoot this kind of shit without lying to each other. Not that I'm comparing Katherine to the pasty queen—I don't mean that at all—I just wanted him to know that I'd been watching opening night, and I thought it was terrific. I envied him, I was all for him—all for them—and that he'd even inspired me to action in my own crass way, to get the chick everyone's been looking at all night long.

And I don't know what the hell I was expecting from him, a secret handshake, but as I was telling him this, I started to get the impression that I wasn't really connecting. It was like doing radio, and Boone was realizing it too. He could tell we weren't on the same wavelength and he just couldn't listen to it anymore. Finally he said, "Hey, Harry, I have to tell you. That's not what was going on back there at the cast party. That was a bad night."

I didn't know what he was talking about. What did he mean, bad night? I'm thinking to myself, "Hey, Boone, I was there. Don't tell me you weren't enjoying yourself. You were a friggin' dog that night." He looks at me, he takes a sip of his beer with his eyes on me and he just shakes his head. Such a goddamn sober move that I start to think that maybe he's telling the truth here. You know, I'd seen him bobbing and weaving his way out of the coat room at 3:00 A.M. or whatever it was, I just assumed he was spent, he needed a breather, but he told me he'd just been looking for some coffee. So I'm thinking, yeah, that's right actually, he looked pale as a ghost. Splotches on his cheek, bags under his eyes. If he wasn't post-coital, he was post-something, and he's telling me now it wasn't good. He said he didn't even know where the hell he was.

And so here I am, now I feel like the schmuck of the century. Bull in a china shop, I've gone and smacked my big fat ass into some private moment of theirs that's none of my business. But apparently there had been some things the rest of us weren't seeing, a little more trouble in paradise than we all would have thought—and it surprised me a little. I guess you've just got to expect that, but it surprised me—but here I've been bragging about Candy Fucking Fondue for the last half hour, telling him, hey, aren't we both riding the queen's quim? Jesus Christ, I wanted to crawl into a hole.

But it's right there, understand, while I'm feeling so crummy—I want to tell him just to forget about the whole thing—Boone says to me, "Harry, I've got something you might like to see." He's reaching into his pocket and I'm thinking he's going to pull out some newspaper clipping, some letter to the editor I might get a kick out of, and I don't want to see it. But I look out across the table, and there it is. There's this ring sitting there in a velvet box. Beautiful ring too. Band of rubies, band of diamonds, just nice and simple. My chin's probably down in my plate now. I look up at him, he says, "Harry, will you marry me?"

Camille Walker

Always when you least expect it. At two in the morning, and this is September, because I have writer's cramp from correcting summer-school exams—or finishing off my application to Fishkill, if you like. Yes, let's go with that. There's someone gently rapping, rapping at my chamber door, and I find not a black raven but a miserable little mulatto boy saying, "Lettuce in, lettuce in." Oh, he looked so pathetic. I open the door and in he storms, hands over his face. He rushes into the bathroom and crouches over the toilet, dry spitting and heaving. What is it, mon amour, body or soul? "It's because I'm ugly. It's because I'm ugly and grotesque, horribly, horribly, wretchedly ugly." And I said, "No, no, Hilary, you're a beautiful little man." And he said, "Well, not as beautiful as before." His pouty little face with tears all over it, I started wiping his cheeks dry, "Hey, love, none of us are as beautiful as we were before."

But Hilary wouldn't listen. He was crying and his nose was running—I'd really never seen him look so weepy and horrid. He was saying, "People won't play with me, Camilleon. Why won't people play with me anymore?" Oh, love, oh poor, poor baby, wipe your nose first. And he did, he started to pull himself together. He started to roll the toilet paper around his hand. He rolled so much that he had it going up his arm, and I said, "Hilary, sweet, that stuff doesn't grow on trees," and he said, "It does in Bethesda," and he started to laugh. Oh, my little pet, my little brown baby. And he told me, "I've been crying all day long." He asked me, "What have you been doing?" I told him correcting papers, and he said, "Well, would you like to take a break and come play with me?"

I did. I did. Sometimes I would, sometimes I wouldn't. We never really made a decision one way or the other. Just more of the same, trying to be friends. We tried to be friends, we really did, but with Plums and me it just didn't seem to work. We ended up coughing along like one of those old jalopies, all through the fall, off and on. It might have been worse, and we might have been a little tougher on ourselves if we hadn't both known I'd be gone in the winter. I think I got the acceptance call, from Hugh himself, in early November.

Hugh Gardiner

It had been my opinion that his projects were inclining towards literature as a kind of progression, from the improvisations, to the screenwriting and direction, to playwriting, and so I'd thought of suggesting the possibility to him of attempting a novel. But he'd anticipated my thinking, because when I wrote him that fall, he wrote back that he'd already begun one. He'd said he'd had a book in mind, and I could sense from his letter that whatever this was—and I think he was reluctant to explain it before he had a draft to show me—it was clearly the right thing, perhaps just to be writing.

And I can't express to you how overjoyed I was by the news. I had feared that in this first blush of love, Boone might forget his work. It might seem a bit too grave or dour to include in his life at the moment. But Boone had continued, you see, without prompt. I found that very encouraging, very gratifying. And I must tell you, the prospect itself, of Boone's ambitions finally reaching literature's threshold, it was the thing, I suppose without my knowing, that I had been waiting for—something we could keep and absorb without the worry that it will come and go.

Ellen Bok

The Capper, Lou Cappellino, was still running Hardcastle back then. I was in his office when my editorial assistant, Nancy Manoff, comes in, beet red, says she just got off the phone with Eton

Boone. She says Eton Boone wants to write a book. Capper says, "Who?" I tell him—the movie, the impersonations—he says, "Oh, that guy. I hate that guy." Right off the bat, he's saying, "No, I don't want to work with him. He's the one who stabs people on stage." I said, "Capper, are you kidding? Think about it"—I just assumed this was some kind of celebrity book. You know, these people come to you with ideas, it's their bout with drinking, or what Daddy used to do to them at night. That's what you end up working with. I know. In 1971, I wrote four autobiographies. So when Nancy comes in saying Boone is talking book, already I'm pitching it to The Capper—*Stand-up and Take It: My Years on the Comedy Stage.* Something like that. But then Nancy says, "Hold on." She says, "No, get this," sits down and tells us the chess-set idea.

Well, you've got to work with these things. Nice idea—don't get me wrong, I liked it—but not what you're expecting from Eton Boone, am I right? Capper keeps shaking his head, "I don't want to work with him. Guy's a son of a bitch, I don't want lawsuits." And I'm asking, "Is this a kid's book, or what?" Nancy says, "Yeah, Boone wants kids to like it, but it's a novel too"— you can see, she's just been swept off her feet. She's saying, "It's a love story, Ellen, it's about a relationship." I said, fine, Juliet, give me his number, let's see what we can do.

Joe Boone

We hadn't seen him in seven years, since Anne and I had been together, but he came back that Thanksgiving. He tried to downplay the whole thing, we all did. The other kids weren't even there, so it was just the three of us, which was probably better. We all went and saw some movies together, had dinner in Old Town. Went up to SC and took in the football game. I even think he and Anne had a good time together too. He went over to the museum for lunch with her one afternoon, and he'd given one of the guards a hard time. Anne said he was great.

And you know—I knew—he was only there a week, we

weren't going to be able to wipe everything away. We both understood that. All we can really do in a week is spend some time together, and the crazy thing is, I knew the only reason for that was Katherine. He didn't really talk to me about her, but he'd let Anne in a little, told her he'd found someone, but you could see it too. Seven years he's been away, he's been an actor, he's been making movies, writing plays, but the first thing he wants to show us in seven years is that he's in love, and he didn't even have to bring her with him.

Hilary Richman

I was with Camille. We weren't together, but we'd gone into the city to see her cousin or something who was a cellist in the Cleveland Symphony Orchestra, the CSO. I think she was honor-bound to go into the city and see this person, like she'd gotten a call from her mother saying she was going to be dis-owned if she didn't.

So we'd gone in. It was two days before Christmas or some-thing and I mean, I don't know what started it. There'd been things like this, but we were in Alice Tully Hall, Camille and I were in our seats, and I just started feeling him. These people were playing their violins and pounding their drums, and all I could think about was that E.B. was in the concert hall too. And I was just saying, God, don't let this be happening, I'm so tired of this. You know, because up at Harvard it would happen. I'd just be sitting someplace, I'd be reading at the Signet and all of a sudden I'd know he was thinking about me. I could feel him, and I'm not saying it was true, I'm not saying that, but it's like all I had to hold onto, I guess—you know, this idea—and at this concert it was practically nauseating it was so real.

They even started playing this Beethoven piece. I have no idea which one, the one with all the violins, but I'd heard E.B. playing it when we were in Maine. It's like that just clinched it, this whole insane delusion. It's like it all became obvious to me—Katherine had bought E.B. these tickets to go hear Beethoven for Christmas.

It was comical. On the exact day that Camille drags me into this place, E.B.'s getting his Christmas present from Katherine, and they're sitting up in their own little box. I was just convinced. I was even trying to picture what he was wearing, I mean, to Alice Tully Hall, I couldn't even imagine. I'd never seen him even wearing a fucking tie, much less trying to look nice, but I know he must be in some jacket and she's in pearls. They're so beautiful together, it's like I'd seen it in dreams, E.B. just sitting there next to her listening to these violins, and I knew that's all he wanted to do—he used to tell me about listening to it, about what it must be like for blind people—but I'm in Alice Tully Hall, and I know he can't even listen to a goddamn note, it's all completely fucked up now because he's seen me. I could feel it. He was looking down at the back of my head from his seat, and I could feel his eyes. Just all of a sudden I felt like I could see what E.B. was seeing and it's like, what the fuck am I doing here in this place? I mean, what am I doing? I had no idea.

So like this idiot, I actually got up from my seat. I stood up in the middle of this concert and walked up the aisle, and I went outside and I was sitting by this fountain with all these Christmas lights, like now that I'm out of his sight, it'll be better. God. I practically started laughing at myself. I was like, "E.B. wasn't in there. Jesus Christ. What, am I going insane or something? He wasn't in there." But then I'm like, "Well, fuck, I don't know if he's in there or not, but what difference does it make?" I mean, Jesus Christ, I'd been feeling it up in Cambridge. E.B. didn't have to see me. Shit, I mean, I realize finally, I have my little epiphany at the Lincoln Center fountain, that it doesn't matter where E.B. is or who he's with. As long as I'm going to be fucked up like this, as long as I realize there's something just impossibly absurd about what the fuck I'm doing here, E.B.'s going to know it and he's going to be there.

And I mean, I'd been trying to convince myself, I really had, that maybe what E.B. said was right. Maybe it was all over, maybe he didn't do anything, but I just knew that was bullshit. E.B. did think about me, goddamn it, and why should I have to feel like an asshole for saying I could feel it? That's like the only thing that *isn't* bullshit, you know, that someone actually might stop and think for a second, might use his brain—and fuck anyone who says that isn't real, fuck them. They don't even know.

But, God, I'm lying there. I've got my head down on this freezing cold stone, and I think of Katherine. I think of Katherine and the way she is, and I can just see what she means to him. I mean, I just knew, and so for the first time I can't even fucking tell if it matters anymore what's going on with E.B. and me. I mean, yeah, okay, it's real, it's pounding in my fucking head, but all of a sudden I'm saying to myself, "So what? So fucking what?" And it's the worst, most terrifying thing you can ever think, "so what."

I don't really know how it ended. Camille came out before everyone else. She came out early and just took me out of there and we went back up to her parents' place in Connecticut, and I mean, I just couldn't stay with her. It was a joke. She was making spaghetti or something, and I thought, fuck it, this is ridiculous, I'm looking at her ass against the stove and I'm not even attracted to her. I mean, that's cruel, but I just couldn't deal anymore. I had to get out. I had no place else to go but Cambridge, which was the last place on earth I wanted to go. It was so gray and bleak and disgusting. So I just said, fuck it, do you want to have a fight or not. And she didn't. So she just took me to the station, and I had to take this horrible Greyhound bus to basically nowhere. And I was just shivering in this little bathroom they had.

And I had been seeing this man during the time I was with Camille. He was older than I was. He'd just taken some time off from Harvard. He was a bartender at Casablanca, but when I got back, he was away. His wife said he'd gone and she wouldn't tell me where. It was almost Christmas, and I didn't want to go to San Diego, which I knew would upset my mother. And my room-mates had gone home for Christmas, which was probably just better. So I went out to the river, and there were these morons walking on the ice with these big sticks trying to get the ice to crack, and they were kicking around their hats, playing hockey with these sticks and hats. And I went back to my room and I took pills.

I was in my dorm room and I took pills. I took pills, and I went outside and I just sat outside the dining room, which was closed, and I waited to die, because I didn't want to die in a dingy little dorm room. I really wanted to die outside, and there was this guy putting trash bags in the garbage cans. But they found me. I was hospitalized for a while. And I even called this man, who was back, but I didn't say anything. I hung up. And I couldn't call Toddy, you know. I couldn't bring down Toddy. The only voice I really wanted to hear was E.B.'s, and I didn't even feel like I was allowed.

VII

"The Story of the Lovely Pawn"*

by Eton Arthur Boone

Copenhagen September 8, 1900

Dear Sonja,

Yesterday evening I had the chance to meet "the lovely pawn," and I was unable to write we spoke so late into the evening. You will remember I've mentioned this piece before. The bishop had referred me to him when I'd interrupted his rifle practice last month. I'd been trying to discuss the alecky rook's behavior at the

---

*"The Story of the Lovely Pawn" is reprinted by permission of the Estate of Eton Arthur Boone. This draft provided courtesy of Ellen Bok and Hardcastle, Inc.; Ms. Bok remembers that she received it the week before Christmas, 1973.

aviary, pushing over a domino—what a mess. But the bishop had told me that if I truly wanted to meet someone who represented a threat to the community, I should look further than the alecky rook, who is nothing more than mischief, after all. If I wanted a problem, he said, I should search out "the lovely pawn."

I had been utterly unaware of his existence before my meeting with the bishop, but once this most handsome piece was called to my attention, I can hardly count on my fingers and toes the number of times I have heard his name. The pieces speak of two things about him: his handsome looks, of course, of which I knew nothing until just yesterday, and the number of places he's been. He never seems to stop anywhere very long, though. "If only he would," the young ladies sigh and fan themselves with their peacock tails. But he remains a well-traveled piece, an extraordinarily well-traveled pawn—some say he's utterly unawares taken queens' hearts and left them broken—and would for all his wandering be a very difficult piece to find, except that one can so easily follow the trail of whispers that lead his way.

So by asking questions here and there, especially of the younger ladies of the land, I was able in only a few days to discover his whereabouts. He was in the harbor town of Untilleflu, which is right by the Mirjam Sea, and small enough that I hadn't been there an hour before I found him. He was up in a candletree, but there wasn't very much doubt it was he, all the women about were in such a buzz and pointing. The lovely pawn sat gracefully in his limb, unperturbed, staring landward.

The bishop had advised that if I desired to hear the pawn's tale, I had only to say to him the words, "I have seen her too." He explained nothing more, and so when I first approached the lovely pawn up in his limb, I didn't know quite what to expect. I called up to him, "I have seen her too," and his attention was quick. He looked down, our eyes met, and he climbed down his tree hurriedly.

Oh, but how good-looking he was. Everyone was quite correct about that. In my days here, I've seen several pieces carved with equal care, and some with more detail—his modest khaki coat and plain twill trousers are very simple compared to the Queen of Binghampton's dress—all those smelly oyster shells!—but never have I seen in a chess piece a face of such lovely expression. It wasn't only the flow of his luxuriant hennan locks, the fine straight and well-tanned nose atop his bushy mustache, or the square proud fit of his jaw. It was also a pleasantness about him, a combination of sympathy and purpose in his lovely blue eyes which gave them a twinkle that I haven't seen anywhere else but in our children's. (I wonder if the bishop would be so frightened of *them.*)

The lovely pawn looked me straight in the eye, but with more energy than fierceness. "You've seen her?" he said. "Where?" Such an engaging figure he was, I found I could hardly control my tongue to answer, but I believe he took my confusion for incredulity and sought to reassure me. He placed his hand on my shoulder. "You want to hear my tale then?" he said. I nodded my head. "Then come with me."

Taking me by the arm, he led me to an outdoor cafe across the way that served fried crickets, cicadas, and spiders for just a penny a bug, and this most handsome pawn, without a word to me, ordered us a whole bowlful of them, along with two dishes of chutney and a pitcher of anjelswet filled with mint and cubes of frozen beeswax. I poured us both a glass, we toasted "to her," and he began. This was his tale:

My first memory of this world is she, her lips just parted from my cheek. She was the first thing I saw, and the most beautiful to this day. So beautiful she was and so vivid is the image I keep of her that I cannot suggest fruit to you, marble, milk or cherries to describe the colors of her being. It is that these things have taken their colors from her. Cream is the color of the dress she wore, and golden is the color of her hair. The peach has stolen its blush from her lips, and its blanch from her soft cheeks which brushed mine as I awoke. And all the stars in the sky shine only because she has gazed upon them and shown in her eyes where light dwells, deep within. There is nothing I have seen which hasn't somewhere in its being reflected a moment of her image, but as constantly as it lives in my mind, I saw it only an instant, as she turned from me in surprise when I opened my eyes, and fled from my foundling sight.

In that instant that she turned, though, I saw the rest of the vista which life was giving me—a whole green field, scattered with still lifeless pieces, other pawns, but rooks as well, knights, and bishops. Beyond them was a woods' edge which kept the sounds of birds singing, brooks rolling, and the breeze sifting through its leaves, and beyond them still were mountains softening my horizon, quilted by patches of wildflower, baby's breath, bluebonnets and violet. A drink of life and living so awesome to my new eyes, that when I looked again for the woman who'd lifted me so perfectly from sleep, she was gone.

Other creatures beckoned my attention, though. Some of the pieces began rubbing their eyes and stepping down from their bases, and as each discovered the wondrous use of its novel life, to move about and be free and see the world from shifting perspectives, we all made our way stiffly but so curiously to the woods.

How long I was in those woods in this state of discovery, I cannot tell you, for I had so little worldly understanding at my disposal. I didn't make much company with the pieces I would see, walking in twos and threes through the forest, because I found that though there were always some about, peeking at me through bushes, from underneath mushrooms, and whispering to each other behind tree stumps, they weren't inclined to come very close. And so making my way alone, I learned very few of the lessons which make life traceable. I knew little of time, little of place, little of purpose. I knew only faintly the things I liked most, for all things to me seemed wondrous. I may have stood beside honeysuckle for days in a row, just to smell it on the breeze. And it may have been weeks that I stood beneath the waterfalls of Sistina, to feel the cool mountain wet splash over my head. There were times whose lengths I couldn't hope to measure when I did nothing but stand among the elephants near the Karjiri and listen to them trumpet each other from across their mudslop. Other moments from this period in my life will come to me occasionally—they come as though they were recollections of a life not yet my own, but I'm afraid that as for recalling them with any intention and sharing them with you, though I've no doubt there would be stories there to tell, I cannot. I was too busily happy.

It is the day that I was foraging in the hanging licorice gardens of Tambusco for a wind that might carry some cinnamon on it that my memory begins. I had seen a small vermillion bird which I thought might lead me to my spice and followed it up a trail of ebonystone to the edge of a perfectly sheer, jade cliff. A cousinbird came to join her, but its wings were so long and slow as it flew by that I thought she was waving to me and inviting me to the air.

I'd have followed them on their flight, but no sooner had I taken my first flap from the cliff than I felt a tremendous, angry tug. I looked out and saw a bushy green creature racing towards me at such a furious speed that I was unable to soothe him before he swallowed me whole.

"Good heavens," I interjected. "Were you hurt?"
The lovely pawn smiled at me wisely. "What did I know of pain?" he asked.
"But falling from such a height—"
"What did I know of height or falling?" he asked. "No, sir, I knew very little of what had happened, but that I'd been swallowed from the air by this great green leafy beast. In another world I was, one apparently intent on keeping me from my birds, but no less interesting or wondrous—yet—than the one I'd leapt from."
He popped a cube of beeswax in his mouth, chewed it thoroughly, removed it with his pinky and his thumb, and then continued:

The green creature's wooden bones were brittle, and I snapped my way through them until I found a hole in its spine and climbed through. Once inside its throat, another quick swallow this monster took, and further down its body I fell, until I caught myself by the roots which hung from the dark mud ceiling of an underground cavern, larger than my vision could take in one view. There were torches lining the walls, and I saw little figures, pawns all, marching about below, hundreds of them, all oblivious that I had been so newly swallowed.

There was a low murmur which filled their dark space, and I hung there a long while before I understood what the sound was. But lowering myself further along the root to listen, I could hear numbers, all sorts of numbers, every number it seemed, all muttered in low tones by these little wandering pawns. I began to swing on my root back and forth so that I might be carried over a vaster portion of them, and as I sped over their heads, which were forever bent towards the hardmud floor, I could hear them individually—"One, two, three, four," or "two, four, six, eight." They were each counting sequences, some by fives, some by tens, one with a very consternated expression attempting thirteens! And all the while they walked in circles. After a few passes over their heads, I was able to determine that those who counted by ones were walking in very small circles, those by two were tracing slightly larger circles, and there were others whose arcs were so wide, I can only think they were counting by hundreds or thousands!

I don't know how long I might have swung over their small polished heads listening, but my root snapped and I fell tumbling down at the foot of a pawn who was counting up by threes. I thumped directly in his way, but his surprise was very mild. He merely stepped over me and continued counting.

"Hello," I said, scrambling after him.

"Thirty-three, thirty-six, thirty-nine," he answered.

"Where am I?" I asked.

"Shhhhh," he said. "Forty-two, forty-five, forty-eight."

"Where?" I whispered.

"Here," he whispered back. "Fifty-one, fifty-four."

"Where is here?" I demanded.

"Here, fifty-seven, sixty, is here, sixty-three, sixty-six."

Seeing that I was interfering with his work, I moved on and had other similar exchanges with a piece counting up by fours, another by twos, another by elevens, and finally one pawn with a yellow derby on his head who counted by nines and was in no better a mood to tell me where we were than his comrades. Like them, he merely said, "You are here," and gave me a good shove out of the way, I know not why, since I had done him no harm.

The lovely pawn paused a moment. He took a fried cicada from our bowl, held it to his lips, and expertly sucked its meat from out beneath its shell. He followed the cicada with three large gulps of anjelswet, patted the sides of his mouth with the edge of the tablecloth, as is the custom here, gave a great loud belch, which is also customary, and continued.

I would like to tell you, my friend, that I haven't a very clear idea of how much time I spent with these pawns, for I cannot say it was an experience which compared to the one I'd been having in my upsides world, but I know quite precisely that I was with them for three months, one week, three days, eleven hours, thirty-two minutes, and sixteen seconds. And the reason I know this is that these pieces did nothing with their days but count the moments as they passed. They did so as a duty, and they did it without question. They did so with pride.

Every morning when they awoke, they would check their schedules first thing to see the sequence they'd been assigned for the day. They would announce to their spouses, "sixes today, dear" or "fives. I'll have an easy one," then they would go off to The Main Flat and count until they were done. The differences between the pawns were only very slight. They wore different costumes from time to time as their duties required—the gaolers, for no reason I could see, had to wear giant sombreros on their heads, and the cooks wore monocles and fezzes with blue grass tassles—but for these props, they all looked precisely the same. They sounded the same. They behaved the same, and so I never knew quite whom I was with. Their homes were all set out along the labyrinth of pathways which bordered The Main Flat, but because they were merely round huts which varied not at all inside or out, and because their inhabitants were so wholly inter-changeable, I do not really know how many different homes I stayed at during my time there. It may have been only two or three, it may well have been thirty. Very few ever seemed much bothered by my presence, though, and for the most part, they were only vaguely aware of it, as it was considered a virtue among these pawns to be as unobservant as possible. In fact, those pawns who did commit observation, beyond the relative merits of certain counting sequences, were sent to private caves where they had to walk backward and count down rather than up, in denominated sequences that quite exasperatingly never quite reached zero.

To ensure that there would be as few observant pawns as possi-ble, the schools were quite regimented. The students were made to wear bathing caps and sit in rows of thirty, counting off down the line for their day's lesson, one by one, until the hourglass had been turned over twelve times! There was no sun, of course, but the days were measured by two new workers every day, who wore pith helmets and alternated twenty-four sets of 3,600 by ones. The meals were served promptly, and consisted every day of fifty-six beans, fifty-six kernels of corn, and eighty-four grains of rice. When they were through, having washed it down with two quarts of root beer, they climbed into their separate but similar wood beds, pulled themselves under black straps, and fell asleep to the ticking drip, drip, dripping sounds of the water which fell steadily from the ceiling roots.

Their entertainments were rare. Every so often they all liked to go see a piece who called himself Count Numero, who wore a long black cape, and performed in a giant amphitheatre underneath The Main Flat. Every ten days Count Numero would perform to packed houses, pacing before the footlights, twirling his wax moustache, and reciting in a rich tenor voice what were considered some of the more classic passages of the pawns' favorite number sequences. He never failed to please, but it was generally regarded that his interpretation of a ones sequence through the three-hundred-thirties was a highlight, and if I'm not mistaken, his hushed recitations of the seven-hundred were also something of a favorite.

Now, beyond Count Numero, who was a district legend, the only pleasure I ever saw any of them take, they derived from their peculiar ventures up a particular ladder-root, which hung all the way down from the ceiling of The Main Flat, down onto a wooden gallows platform. There was always a steady line of pawns waiting to climb its whole extent, which was long enough from top to bottom that twenty-four pawns, set at a distance of twenty rungs from each other, could fit on the root at once. At the top of the root, right to the side of the final rung in the ladder, was a hole in the ceiling that the pawns would stick their heads through, and though I couldn't see from the ground what was through this pinhole, I did observe that almost from the instant any of these pawns peeked through it, he became so excited that his legs would fly out from beneath him, he would begin shaking uncontrollably, and then fall, only to be replaced in another ten rungs by the next pawn on the ladder. The fallen pawn would land on a pile of mattresses stacked seven high, tumble off, and his smile would last another twelve paces exactly before his very same face resumed its very same expression.

At this point, the lovely pawn took a break. The process of describing the world of these little counting pawns seemed to have drained him. His complexion had grown pale, and his eyes looked tired. He grabbed a passing waiter by the sleeve and asked him if we could have more beeswax for the anjelswet. We waited in silence until the waiter returned, and when he set down six more frozen cubes, the lovely pawn popped them in his drink, took a gulp, and resumed:

Though its effect appeared ephemeral, I had by the end of my first month there stared at this ladder-root so long and with such curiosity that I resolved one morning to attempt the climb myself. But as I took my place in line, the pawn directly before me turned and asked me suspiciously if I had done my counting for the day. When I told him that I had not, he said he'd thought so, shooed me away with a lion's hair broom, and instructed me to go see the leader at once.

The leader's platform was located up where everyone could see the incumbent at all times, on a rather smallish shelf on the wall of The Main Flat, counting faithfully. As with all other functions in the community, leadership changed hands daily, almost without notice or ceremony. And so it was that the day I was sent to the leader, I found a pawn like any other, counting a brisk set of twos and circling with his hands behind his back. He wore glasses with no lenses, and he would not speak to me until I stood in the middle of the circle he was pacing.

"Why have you, fifty-six, been sent to me, fifty-eight?" he asked.

"I think it's because I haven't done my counting for the day," I said.

"Sixty-two, why not? Sixty-four, did you lose your schedule, sixty-six?"

"No," and I was afraid of alarming him, but remembered he was the leader and supposed he should be understanding as a result. "It's that I don't very much enjoy counting," I told him.

The leader looked so puzzled by this, I felt as though I had set him with a paradox. "But counting, seventy-six, is all that matters, seventy-eight. You must count, eighty."

"But I don't want to sometimes."

The leader paced about for some time considering my predicament. He paced so long, in fact, that he finished his sequence to one-hundred and had started over again before I interrupted him, fearing that he might have forgotten me. "Is there anyone here," I begged him, "who doesn't count?"

"Oh, two, cheer up, sir, four, we all count, six."

I found this a very frustrating response and was considering leaving the platform when he raised his hand. "Wait, sir, please, eight, and listen to your leader, ten," he said. "Although I don't, twelve, count myself a very, fourteen, perceptive pawn, sixteen, I can see, eighteen, that you might do, twenty, with a trip up the ladder-root, twenty-two." He seemed very pleased with the idea he'd suggested. "That is where I, twenty-four, go when I am, twenty-six, feeling as you do."

"But that is why I'm here," I explained as patiently as I could. "I wasn't allowed to go up the ladder-root."

The leader pawn looked stumped by this and a trifle embarrassed, so much so that I felt obliged to end his confusion with a question to which I was more certain he knew the answer. "By the way, sir leader, what is up the ladder-root?"

"Up the ladder-root, thirty-eight," he said, quite pleased, "is our ruler, forty, of course." He beamed.

"You have a ruler?"

"Why, yes, forty-four."

"And does he count?"

The pawn smiled at the innocence of my question. "No, forty-eight," he said. "The ruler simply measures, fifty, what his subjects count, fifty-two."

To me this sounded like nonsense and was much more than I could fathom, I was still so young. The leader looked at me, sensing my annoyance, and without quite admitting an observant expression, pointed his finger at me loosely and began nodding his head as he walked. "Perhaps, fifty-eight, you should go see the sick ones, sixty," he said. "They have forgotten, sixty-two, the virtues of counting, sixty-four, just as you seem to have, sixty-six, sixty-eight, seventy. Perhaps if you visit them, seventy-two, you will see the folly, seventy-four, of your ways." The pawn looked quite pleased with himself for this and resumed his count with the vigor of one whose wisdom has just shone in all its glory. But I left no wiser and no more satisfied than I had been when I came to him.

So by my fifth week among these pawns, I had begun to sense a change in myself that I was unable to give a name, but recognized as wholly different from any of the feelings I'd known on the brighter side. There were still mornings I would wake up, as I had above ground, to the feeling of a kiss upon my cheek, and they were the only moments of hope I think I knew there, but I did not allow to myself that she had been anything but my imagination, her figure seemed so distant from the life I now knew. I found myself feeling exceptionally lonely most of the time.

I had taken the leader's advice, though, and visited the sick pawns, who were kept in cells far along the labyrinth which surrounded The Main Flat, purposely hidden to keep the sick from infecting the general community with their dementia. I had searched them out at some pains, and came to do so quite often, for rather than feeling repelled by the sick pawns, and replenished of my sense of good fortune and priority, I actually found them quite appealing. They weren't in any way physically deficient compared to their likenesses outside the cells. They did not cough or stumble, they had no boils and didn't pus or leak in any way. They were only considered sick because they'd grown incapable of, or unwilling to, recite perfect sequences anymore, a condition which didn't bother me in the least, I assure you. In fact, I found the unpredictability of the sequences they barked out quite soothing, and also discovered these sick pawns to be a bit more personally interesting, as they tended to be more liberal with their insight.

There was one in particular, a much older pawn who wore earmuffs over a bent bottle cap on his head, had fingerless gloves, and always carried a lump of coal with him so that his nails were perpetually black. He was one of the few pawns who would have me as a sitting partner. We would sit side by side in the rubber room of the sick cells as he called out his numbers, "Fifty-seven, three, one-hundred sixty-one," and all the gaolers would gather round and laugh at how ugly and absurd his sequence sounded, but this older pawn always insisted they were wrong. "It certainly is, seven, a sequence, four-thousand six-hundred and eight," he would tell me, "and it isn't, nineteen, ugly in the least, eighteen. It's the most beautiful, one, they've ever heard, nine-hundred ninety-two, only they don't understood it yet, nine-hundred ninety-four."

Tribute to his lenience with observation is that it was he, my old demented friend, who first impressed me with the fact that my appearance was different from those around me. He always told me that I shouldn't be there, that this was no place for a pawn like me. When I asked if there were a way I could see this appearance of mine he found so exceptional, he said no, that there were no mirrors anywhere in the community for me to look at, as the rest of the pawns only needed to look at one another to understand their appearance, and that the brooks which ran through their houses were too fast and muddy to show me back to myself.

But he continued to insist that I belonged elsewhere. Whenever we said good-bye, he would tell me that he didn't want to see me anymore, that I should soon be gone, he was sick of me. I always returned, though, until one afternoon, my ninety-ninth, he called me over to his side as I was leaving the cell for the evening. We knelt down beside each other and he said to me, "I, forty-three, have been thinking about you, twelve. I've decided, seven-hundred eighty-eight, that it's time that you left, nine-hundred sixty-three, for good, twenty-four, I'm so tired of you, nine." He lowered his voice. "I want you to go, nine-million three-hundred-thousand and two, up the ladder-root, thirty-three, and when you get up there, seven, hold tight to the hole, six, don't fall, five, climb through the hole, four, and leave, forty-one."

The idea, I must admit, hadn't even occurred to me. I asked him, "Wouldn't the ruler mind?"

"The ruler," he said, throwing the lump of coal down at his feet, "won't care." It seemed like a very nice plan, and I would gladly have undertaken it for my friend, but I had to explain to him that I wasn't allowed up the ladder-root because I never did my counting. The sick pawn looked about us to see if anyone was listening, put his arm around my shoulder, his crusty mouth up to my ear, and said one word. "Lie!"

As I left the cell, my sick pawn friend was waving me away, shouting that he never wanted to see me again, "Go, sixteen, go, three-hundred-one!"

I stayed one more night among these pawns, and early the next morning arrived at the ladder-root, which was already filled. I found the back of the line, where again the last pawn asked me if I had done my counting for the day, but taking the advice of my one friend, I told him that I had—sixteen sets of 320 by four. He was very impressed and let me stay, so I took my place on the ladder. One by one I watched the pawns reach the top and peek through the ceiling hole, and one by one I watched them fall by me, with the expressions of tickled babies on their faces, pawn after pawn, twenty-four up and twenty-four down, until I finally reached the top myself.

I looked through the hole, which was only barely large enough for my head, but shaded from the outside by a tuft of milkblades.

Sitting there in a clay jar quite glumly at the foot of a spoon tree was a ruler, a long, tall wooden one, thirty-feet high at least, with measurements along its sides quite clearly marked at increments as small as your knuckle, from top to bottom. I couldn't see what was so very pleasant about this ruler, why he was a figure so worthy of the little pawns' worship and delight, although he seemed neither stern nor frightening. I called out to him, "May I have a word with you?"

He was surprised and stiffly turned my way to see me. "Certainly," he said, "come." I crawled out of the hole and climbed up to the base of his clay jar, but his face was still so far from me, up at his own twenty-seventh foot, I climbed up the tree to meet him, and sitting in its limbs, in the bowl of a tarnished silver spoon, we had a conversation.

I pointed down towards the tuft of milkblades, from beneath which were two delighted pawn's eyes gazing. "You are their ruler?" I asked. The ruler looked towards the pawn and it fell from sight, giggling. "Yes. No. I am *a* ruler," he said casually. His big black eyes looked tired. He yawned and stretched a full six more feet before he came back down to my level. "Well," I told him, "you don't seem very excited about it. Is there anything you tell them?" He looked at me woefully. "No," he said. "I don't say anything to them." He looked back at the tuft of milkblades, and two more pawn eyes peered through at him gleefully. "Boo!" he said, and the pawn fell down, screaming with joy. We kept our eyes on the hole until we heard the little pat of pawn against the landing mattresses.

The ruler looked at me curiously. "What on earth were you doing with them?" he asked me.

"Why? What's wrong with them?" I asked. "I have been with them for a very long time."

"Well, nothing's wrong with them, I suppose," he said and blew a leaf which had fallen down onto his nose. "It's just that they are lost."

"Lost?" I said. I had never heard such a word.

"Lost, yes," yawned the ruler. "They haven't any idea where they are. Lost and they'll never be found. There are buttons and thimbles that can do their work just as well up here sunnyside, so no one bothers to look for them." He looked at me then, and it was an expression of greater interest than he'd yet shown. "I'm surprised you were with them as long as you were. It doesn't seem that a pawn like you could be lost for very long." I, of course, still didn't know what he meant, having no understanding yet of the word lost, and no notion of my own image. "You're the kind," said the ruler, "that she lingers over."

"Who?" I asked.

"The wakening woman," he said.

In an instant, although she'd passed my mind all this time, I knew precisely whom he was referring to. "Why, yes," I told him. "She is the first thing I saw of this world, and the most beautiful to this day."

"Yes," said the ruler. "She *is* lovely."

"You know of her?" I was overjoyed. "I haven't yet met anyone who's seen her. I had begun to think she had come from my imagination."

"Well, you've been living with *them.*" The ruler glanced at the milkblade tuft, and another pawn fell tittering. "But it is true. Not many have seen her. I have only seen her because I am tall. I see her sometimes waking pieces."

"Yes," I said, "that is what I saw."

"Well," said the ruler, "but normally, you see, she is gone by the time the pieces fully awaken. Every lost pawn down there has been kissed, but I'm sure she was gone by the time they each awakened."

"Oh, not for me, sir. I saw her very clearly."

"Yes, well," the ruler pondered. He seemed doubtful at first. "I have seen her linger sometimes over the more beautiful pieces, waiting for their eyes to open, but I have never seen her wait so long that the piece could see her back. The bishop tells me she's been known to, but I have never seen it." Then he looked at me more deeply. "But I have also never seen such a lovely pawn as you, sir." I still had no notion of what he was saying, and it may have shown in my face. He asked me, "Are the lost pawns the first pieces that you have been with?" I nodded. "Ah, then you have never seen yourself."

"No," I said, "never."

The ruler chuckled. "I am gold on my back," he said. "Turn me over and you will see."

I turned the ruler over, and for the first time saw my own face. It was true, I had never seen such a thing before. A face, and these eyes, the very same color as I had first seen in hers, the color of the sky. But deep within them was an aspect completely new to me. All this time, I hadn't known what I'd been feeling, but as it was reflected in the mirror before me, the whole of my sorrow fell upon me at once and I shed my first tear. "I am very sad," I said.

"Maybe that is it," said the ruler, whose back was still to me.

I continued looking at my reflection, bewildered. "What has made me this way?"

"I am no wise man," said the ruler, "I am only tall. You might ask the bishop if you dare interrupt him, but for myself I have only known things to be sad because of their difference from other things." He looked at me over his shoulder. "Why do you think you are so different from the others?"

I looked at my reflection. "Is it this face?" I asked.

The ruler spun around to look at me. "Yes," he said, "but you had not known that until now. And yet these tears have been waiting for some time."

"Yes, I think so."

"Then?" he said.

I looked at the image closely and my eyes were wet, but in those pools I saw reflected that first image I had ever known, her gaze upon me, with her lips parted in wonder. "Then it is only that I have seen her as she kissed me?"

"Perhaps," said the ruler, and he was strangely impatient, "but it is *your* sadness. I do not know."

"Yes," I said, but my attention was no longer with my tall friend in the jar. I realized, only moments from first seeing my sorrow, what I must do to be rid of it, that I must look for this woman and not cease until I found her. There could be nothing else, I was certain, and even as I sat on the limb, considering the first direction I would strike, I heard the ruler cry, "Your face!"

"What?" I said.

"Look!" He spun around again so that I could see, and in the reflection, as clear to me as my sorrow had been at first, I could see that my features now had taken an expression of . . .

The lovely pawn searched a while for the words, but he could not find them. He said at last, "The expression I saw in the reflection of the ruler's back, it is the expression that sits here before you. Can you see it?" I looked at him. Oh, indeed, there were flecks of sorrow deep in his eye, but surrounding those and filling the rest of his features was an assurance which glowed. "Do you see it?" he asked. I nodded my head. "And ever since that moment that I was in the spoon tree beside the ruler," he said, "I have been looking for her. I have traveled this whole land in search of her and traded stories with pieces of all kinds, many who claim they've seen her but haven't, some who didn't remember until I reminded them, but none who could ever send me her way."

He leaned across the table to me with his arms folded. "But I will tell you something, my friend, because I can see that you might understand. If I am sometimes discouraged that I haven't yet found her, I am consoled by two ideas," he said. "Would you like to know them?"

"Very much," I said.

He took a sip from his glass of anjelswet, which was warm by this time, with clouds of beeswax hovering near the top, and he looked out towards the bay. "I am consoled that I know she is there, as I see life in all the things around me." We both looked around us as the twilight fell and it was true. A family of red checkers rolling into the berry market next door, a constellation of dice tussling in a pile by the gingermill. The balloons drifting home from their day at the needle factory, even a deck of cards gathered round and teasing a poor little whistle too frightened to scream. There was life everywhere and in everything, and even as we watched it, all the candles in the candletree across the way lit one by one and shone very golden underneath the periwinkle sky. The lovely pawn looked back at me, and his face was glowing now. "And I am consoled," he said, "that when I find her, sir, the love I'll feel will be as much as this world can hold. I will love her as the sky loves the sea and the land, and as they all love our senses at every moment."

If it were possible that his expression of peace and purpose could deepen, it did at that moment. Then he remembered me at the table. "And you have seen her, sir?" he asked me.

I was barely able to speak, as it dawned on me that moment what my answer had to be. I realized that I had lied to him from the moment we had met, and how horrible my lie had been. I was overcome with shame for having deceived him so, but I knew I could only make amends now by telling him the truth. "No, sir," I said. "I haven't seen your woman."

He looked down at the bowl of uneaten insects, squirming out from beneath their deep-fried shells. "I didn't think so," he said. "But it is all right. I thank you for listening."

I saw more sadness creep across his lovely features, and partly for fear that it would reach mine as well and stay less beautifully on my face than his, I tapped my finger on the rim of the chutney dish for his attention. "But I have seen mine, sir," I told him, "if that should console you as well. I have seen mine, I love her as you say, and am always consoled by the same."

He looked up at me. "And you know where she is?" he asked.

"Yes," I said. "I know."

He stood up from the table and he looked even more invigorated now than when he had leapt down from the candletree so many hours ago. "Then that is where I shall go next. Mine may be there as well. Do you think?"

"Perhaps," I said.

"Do you mind?"

"Not at all," I said.

"Tell me where," he said.

And he has found you.

Kiss the children goodnight for me.

Your faithful Gus

VIII

New York

Winter 1973 — Spring 1974

Harry Hampton

That morning when he woke up, Katherine was already gone. She'd gotten a spot on an orange juice commercial, a thirty-second spot, part of which they'd filmed down in New Jersey, but that day, it was December 31, and they had some final shot to take in a studio in New York over on Columbus in around the seventies. Not the ABC place.

Boone didn't get out of bed until around ten, I don't think. He gave me a call at my office around eleven o'clock. He wanted to talk about *The Exorcist*, which he'd seen the night before and loved. He was in a very energetic mood. He said as soon as his Pop-Tarts and his coffee were ready, he was going to go take a look at an old three-story brownstone over near the studio where Katherine was working, between Central Park and Columbus.

My notes say Seventy-eighth, but that can't be right. It was further down. But I asked him where the hell he was going to get that kind of money, and he said, "Hey, Harry, need I remind you, Katherine happens to be shooting a very lucrative OJ commercial at this very moment," and that actually his second errand of the day, right after he made a down payment on a Shetland sheepdog that just happened to live in the very same brownstone, was to go knock off "that Bryant bitch," who, he had on good sources, was lunching at Tavern on the Green.

So it was somewhere in there, running errands, that he found out. He walked right into it. He must have left his apartment at around 11:15. It was a very bright day, one of those crunchy winter days when you want ski goggles it's so bright. He walked up Fifth and then through the park to this brownstone on I think Seventy-fourth to see this dog that belonged to an old man named Avvy who'd worked with Hank Piedmont. And even then, as he was talking to this old man and buying one of his new puppies, he heard sirens outside. You live in New York, you never even notice sirens until something happens. But you can remember them, and he ended up buying the dog, and then he took it over to meet her.

Harold Odeon

Eton called us at about 1:30 in the afternoon and said that Katherine had been in an accident. I remember both Margaret and I were home because I'd taken the whole week off, and the boys had just left. We'd all had Christmas together, except for Katherine, but the boys had to get back to their homes before New Year's for parties or what have you.

Margaret could tell something was wrong the moment I picked up the receiver and said hello to Eton. She rushed to the extension, which is in the upstairs hallway, so Eton had to begin twice. His voice was icy. He said he was at Roosevelt Hospital, that there had been a fire at a television studio and that Katherine was in a coma, that she was burned, and that she had nearly suffocated. The official cause of death was suffocation by smoke inhalation. Margaret began crying immediately. I think women have a greater capacity for understanding tragedy as soon as it strikes. I could hear her put the receiver down, not in the cradle, but on the table, and I asked what the chances were, how good a chance did she have, and I remember very much wanting to hear him say, "Oh, they expect it will be all right, sir." But his voice was brutal over the line. Brutal and straightforward—I think he was in shock. He said, "No chance. She'll die before the New Year." I told him we'd leave immediately.

Harry Hampton

I was supposed to meet him and Katherine late in the afternoon at O'Neal's, but he called me at two and said there had been a fire at the studio, and that Katherine was in the hospital in a coma. He sounded very calm. I asked if I should come down, and he said no, don't, don't come down.

Harold Odeon

It was a very brief phone call. It seems there should have been so many other questions, but of course there weren't. We caught a plane out of O'Hare that evening. Margaret had neared a collapse by the time I was off the phone. I called the boys, but neither of them were home, all day, so we caught a ten o'clock flight. A nine o'clock flight. The winds took us over Manhattan, and you could almost see, even from that height, that it was New Year's, that it was New York on New Year's, and we were dipping in for the worst moments. Margaret had taken some Valium and had become deathly quiet, and Manhattan looked so brilliant from the sky, glassy, and there was also smoke rising from some of the rooftops, horrible smoke.

Fortunately we didn't have to go through midtown to get to the hospital, but the cabdriver, I remember, was a talkative man, and I remember saying to him, "Please, please just drive." That ride is a blur. Margaret had tucked herself deep into the coat she was wearing, a camel-hair coat.

Eton was the first thing I saw as we entered the hospital, Roosevelt, a brick hospital. He was down standing by the elevator bank, and there was a small dog next to him, at his feet. He walked up to us and hugged Margaret and said, "She's gone," and he shook my hand. His face had taken on an entirely different look.

Toddy Boone

Dad and I were home watching the Rose Bowl. I was back on vacation, and we were in the living room. It was USC, I think against Ohio State, and it was late in the game. USC had this guy Sam Cunningham who Dad was crazy about. I guess everyone was. SC'd get down to the goal line and then they'd give the ball to Sam "The Bam" Cunningham, and he'd just take off around the three-yard line, just jump over everyone, and fly into the end zone. I remember Dad telling me, "You can't stop Sam the Bam, you can't stop Sam the Bam. Who's going to get in the way of a two-hundred-forty-pound torpedo?" So we were in the living room and USC had just scored a touchdown, and Dad had gone back into the kitchen to get a sandwich or something, and I could hear him going "Sam the Bam! Sam the Bam!" like that. And the phone rang, and I remember Dad saying, "That's going to be Mendikoff," who always used to call during the games. He picked up and said, "Sam the Bam!" and he was stretching the phone around the corner into the living room so he could watch the game. There was this weird pause, and he said, "What?" And he turned to me and sort of motioned for me to turn the volume down. And he said, "No, he's not here." Then he said, "No, he didn't come back from school for vacation. Can I take a message?"

I think that was it. He hung up and he came back. He was sort of shaking his head, and he sat down and said, "That was your brother. He didn't say, but that was Eton, and he was asking for Hilary." And I said, you know, why didn't you say something, Dad? If that was Eton on the phone, why didn't you say something? But Dad just shook his head and turned the volume back up. I remember telling him that it probably wasn't Eton, it didn't sound like Eton to call up like that, but Dad just gave me a look.

Ten minutes later—the game was almost over by now—the phone rings again. And this time Dad isn't marching around the place. The phone rings, and Dad shuts off the set and answers it. It was Amalie Hindemuth, and that's when I knew something was up. Dad had his eyes shut, and he just starts saying, "Oh, jeez, oh, Jesus, Jesus Christ." And, you know, I was sitting there for a moment, and then I stood up. I just stood by Dad, and Anne came in from the kitchen. It's weird how people know. Anne came in and stood right in the doorway, and Dad held her arm while he talked to Amalie. All I remember is Dad asking Amalie, "Is he there?" And I kept waiting for him to say, "son," or "Eton," something like that, but he just said, "Is he there?" And nothing. He was silent for a while, and then he just hung up. I guess he thanked her.

And he just told us about Katherine. Anne started crying, and she was leaning on his shoulder, and he was telling me the details, and shaking his head. That's all I remember, is him shaking his head. He looked really confused.

Hugh Gardiner

Oh, it's the kind of tragedy that leads one to believe in some sort of divine being, that one man should be so targeted for pain. I believe that Boone really loved only twice in his life—twice in his life he'd known a love that could lift him—and disease had taken his first. What a tremendous relief of that loss Katherine had provided him only he could know, but now to have her taken as well, by different means, but equally cruel—it made one want to shake one's fists at the heavens.

I dispatched a letter to him as soon as I heard. I wrote in lieu of my possible appearance at her funeral, which I did very seriously consider attending. John advised that I should, and I actually did give it some thought, but I decided against it in the end. I would have been no help to him, expressing in person the condolences that I'm sure he was hearing from all those who knew him and were living in his circle. It was not my place.

Instead, I realized the value of his continuing his work. I felt that he should continue it, to channel his grief. Art is a vent, and that's what I chose to tell him in my letter. To press harder with his work, to concentrate on his art. We can really only turn to ourselves for consolation—that is not an outrageous statement in the least—and I think he ultimately did see the truth in it. I told him that there was little I could offer him, little anyone could offer him of substance during times such as these, save distractions, but that if he needed to express himself and heave this tremendous burden that fate had shouldered him with, I would be an attendant ear, as always.

Harry Hampton

Boone called me and asked if I would come to the funeral, which was on the fourth, see if I could help the Odeons out, lend a car, because they were having it up at her grandmother's house in Martha's Vineyard. And of course I could, it wasn't even an issue, but, you know, there was a part of me that felt out of place. I really felt I didn't have the right. It's a feeling you get. When someone invites you to a funeral, you've got to think to yourself, do I deserve to be here? And I guess I was feeling that I just didn't. I'd only just come back into the guy's life and then this thing happens, and I don't mean the accident. I mean them. They happened. Then came the accident. That's how it worked. And just because I happened to be around, does that give me the right to be someone at her funeral? That's just timing. It's all timing. It just felt like one big coincidence that I was there.

And I know, for God's sake, a friend is supposed to be supportive, and that's what friends are for, and you lend a shoulder and you lend a car. But you looked at him, and you thought, well, what does he need now, and what he needed now was her, and I'm not her. That's not a brilliant piece of analysis, but at least it's the truth. I mean, what else? What else do you want to know? The weather? My notes say it was "cold and crisp." But I can remember that funeral. I don't need my notes for that. I remember Boone standing there in Harold Odeon's coat, which was much too big for him, with his "head bowed," it says—great. He wasn't showing much. You know, here's "a million miles." "A million miles"—it seemed to me then that the human body can only register so much pain. You get to a point after which it's no use, and Boone was about a million miles past it. Which covers that.

"The dog," though. The dog was at his feet, looking for birds. There were a few other people, and I didn't really know who they were, and I'm sure they didn't really know who I was, and we're all just standing around in big coats. But, you know, this dog. Me, I'm some kind of friend—Katherine's body is lying in this coffin, and I'm thinking about how this dog spent its first few days living with some old Jewish comedian, and then it gets shuttled through some crazy street scene, with smoke and fire and sirens and ambulances, and how it spends the night in a hospital with some guy who's probably not giving it the time of day. And then it goes home with him for a couple days, and then gets put in a box and driven up to Martha's Vineyard, and it doesn't know what the hell is going on. I mean, Martha's Vineyard's the best place this dog's ever been, and he's watching people stand around a pit and cry. I don't know, is that mourning, trying to figure out if anyone's given the dog a name yet?

After the service, which was "too short and too long," the Odeon boys and two kids in white altar-boy robes lowered the casket into the ground with ropes—okay, here's some meat—one of the ropes gave way, I don't know who it was, but someone let his rope go for a second, and the goddamn casket slid down and kind of thumped, and that's when Mrs. Odeon started to cry. That's the story of how Margaret Odeon started to cry. After that we went back to the Odeons and Boone let me have the dog, which I ended up turning over to Max Kleinman. I don't know what he did with it, sorry.

Amalie Hindemuth

Those were horrible days, right afterwards. He couldn't eat anything. The only things he could eat were apples and nothing else. He would slice them up with a paring knife and eat the slices. I would sleep in the living room. We'd sit on the couch with the television on, and he would just begin crying. He'd curl up and put his head in my lap. He would actually put a dishtowel on my lap and rest his head down on it and cry while I touched his head, and his whole body would shake. It would come in waves, and then after long enough he would say he had to go to bed. He'd get up and go into the bathroom. I'd lie there listening to him brushing his teeth, washing his face, and then getting in his own bed. I'd pray that he could go to sleep.

Hilary Richman

Toddy called to chastise me that I had not done everything I could, like put in some appearance at Katherine's funeral. I myself had just one day earlier checked out of a facility north of Boston and had moved back to my dorm, and I hadn't told anyone. But that's when I find out, in some telegram from Amalie that's three days old, that Katherine has been killed.

It was just too much. And of course I felt awful for him, of course I did. I mean, it would just break E.B., I knew. Don't tell me I didn't know. What do you think I was doing in the hospital? I knew what she meant better than anyone else. And of course I wanted to speak to him, but I was just too fragile. I mean, I didn't know what Toddy's point was. None of *them* flew East, but then Toddy's telling me that E.B. had called for me, so I bore some responsibility or something like that. I mean, he didn't know what he was saying, but he was confused and he was just being incredibly nasty, and so I blurted it out. I just told him that he would never understand, that he would never know why I couldn't just rush down and say "Here I am, E.B., at your disposal." He would never know what E.B. and I had, and maybe Toddy already knew what had gone on between us, but he's such a good soul, I don't think he ever wanted it to get in the way of his love for E.B., but when I said it, when it was finally out in the open, it just freaked him out. He didn't know what to say. He just kind of hung up.

But I did have to tell him. I'd had it with having this secret. I'd had it with being this secret, and maybe it wasn't the best time, but, you know, it made me feel a lot closer to E.B., and I wasn't just being full of shit, because he did call. I mean, it's just not right having these secrets. I know E.B. lived with buckets of them, and I don't know how he did it. I have no fucking idea, but I wasn't going to be one any more. I mean, it had practically killed me.

John Kinsey

Eton wrote me a very disturbing letter in March of that year. It was about Hugh. He'd become very, very disenchanted with him, and most of that had come from Hugh's reaction to Miss Odeon's death, which I'm afraid had offended Eton a great deal. He hadn't liked being told to go back to work, and though I think I understood what Hugh had intended with his advice, Eton was so put off by it, and still so despondent, I'm sure, that he'd even suggested that Hugh was relieved by what had happened. It was a very disturbing letter. He said that he was intending to cut Hugh off, and he wanted neither advice nor encouragement, just to let me know that I might have to pick up the little pieces of Hugh that he would leave behind.

He was right. Hugh called me two or three days after he'd received Boone's final word, and he was devastated. His emotions were playing havoc with him. There was no way he could have expressed them all to me, in so many words, or would have, I suspect. Hugh has never been one for revealing himself, and it's partly that which emboldens me to speak on his behalf here, because I suspect that he'll probably keep some things to himself that he shouldn't, for fear that it might reflect poorly on Boone. But he was in pain. It wasn't so much that Boone had called for a break—I'm not sure that Hugh ever completely admitted that— what struck him most deeply was that Eton had accused him of being unfeeling. I can still hear Hugh's voice quivering over the line. "John," he said, "it's dreadfully unfair, and it shouldn't have been written, because"—and Hugh knows this as well as any- one—"we all have our ideas of suffering." We all have our ideas of suffering. If I'd been able to put Eton on another extension to listen in, he'd have seen it. Hugh was reeling. Everything he'd done for Boone he'd done out of love, and that included his advice to continue writing. That was Hugh's most honest and tender condolence, and I don't imagine that he would rescind it even today.

But he was still groping, trying to understand what had hap- pened. "Perhaps I didn't make myself clear to him," he said. "Do you think that could be the case? Should I write him, John? Do you think I should?" Oh, to appease him in the short run I suppose I could have said yes, go ahead, apologize, kiss his feet. But no, if Hugh had somewhere lost sight of his dignity, I had not, and I also knew that Eton's feelings, however unfortunate and misdirected, were quite fierce. If Hugh had tried to explain himself, he very likely would have felt an even sterner slap. The most I could advise him in good conscience was to be patient, and to continue to keep his eyes and ears open, wait for a sign.

Eton Arthur Boone to Ellen Bok, March 25, 1974

Dear Ms. Bok,

I assume you know about Katherine. I have tried to continue with the chess pieces. There are a couple more you haven't seen yet, but I don't think that I'll be able to finish the project. I am sorry, but it is not easy.

I will try to continue writing. Something. I will send it to you. I don't imagine there'll be much publishable, but I don't really care at this point. Just keep your mailbox open, clear it once a day, and

do what you will with the stack. I am sorry about the chess book.
I will let you know if it seems like a possibility again.

Have a pleasant spring.

Sincerely,
E. A. Boone

Ellen Bok

We'd been excited about the chess pieces, we really had, once
we'd started seeing the stuff. He'd just been pouring it out, rough
drafts, and it worked. People in the office were making xeroxes,
sneaking it off for their kids. And I'll admit, I couldn't wait to read
the bishop piece, but he never got to it.

We were still keeping our fingers crossed, though. We didn't
know what to make of this new writing he was talking about, but
we didn't want to lose him. I wrote him back. I said we were sorry
as hell, we understood, and whatever he wanted to send us, okay.

Levi Mottl

Toddy had wanted to tell Joe about Eton and Hilary. He'd written
me a letter about it. I wrote him back and told him not to tell Joe.
That seemed like a bad idea to me. I said I'd do it. At the time
I was staying on Ibiza with my friends Lance and Sylvia, and
Toddy had said that Joe and Anne were planning a sort of second
honeymoon to Europe that spring. I told Toddy that I'd catch
them and tell them myself if he would just hold on.

I met them in Venice. I didn't really get to Joe until my last
night there. We'd been out to dinner just off San Marcos, and
Anne had excused herself. Joe and I went out onto a sort of
veranda overlooking one of the canals. We'd already spoken
about Eton and Katherine—Joe and Anne and I had—but I said

to Joe that I thought we had something else to discuss. It was very difficult, because I could almost see it there, how much he wanted to stop me. He was sort of draped over the railing, and when I told him it was about Hilary and Eton, it looked like he'd been pierced. His eyes shut. I remember a gondolier slipping into view from around the corner perfectly black, and Joe looking out at it, nodding his head as he watched it. He watched it until it disappeared again, and when he turned back around to me, his expression sort of darkened. I was going to ask him what he knew, but before I could open my mouth, he just said, "No." He was leaning over the railing dropping splinters into the water. He said, "And not a word when Anne gets back." That was all.

I left the next morning. When we said good bye, Joe asked me to do what I could for Eton. He said, "Please help him," and I'd never seen Joe look like that, so helpless. I think he was just terrified by the whole thing. But I'd have called Eton either way. I didn't like the idea of our all stranding him. I hadn't even spoken to him.

Hilary Richman

My roommates and I were getting stoned. The doctors of course, these moron doctors at the place I'd gone to, had given me these prescriptions that didn't really work for me. So I was smoking in my room instead, and the phone rang. I picked up. I always picked up, because I was one of the few people in our room who could deal. I must have sounded different, because he said, "Hello, is Hilary Richman there?" And I said, "Oh, E.B., I was just thinking of you." Which was true. I mean, no matter when the phone rang, it was always true. But I really couldn't believe it was him, I couldn't believe I'd just heard him say my name. I felt like I hadn't spoken to him in years, and you know, the last I'd heard was that E.B. had tried to call me but he obviously hadn't wanted to find me that much. I mean, if you want to talk to someone, you can.

I asked him how he was and he just said, "If she offers to make me omelettes one more time, I'm going to go buy a machete." And

I knew exactly what he was talking about. Amalie was driving him crazy. And we talked. You know, he'd called up in one of his good moods, one of his fun moods. Of course he was sad still, but he was in a good mood, and he'd called me. But, I mean, we couldn't talk that long before I had to ask him, you know, why have you called me, E.B.? And there was this long pause. I don't know, it probably wasn't that long, but it was very good dope so it seemed like forty-five minutes, and finally I just said it, you know, "I'm lonely." I wanted to say, Jesus, E.B., I miss you and I've had it with being alone, but I thought that would be pushing it. That's not what he wanted to hear, so I waited. I just waited. And I remember I thought, Oh, fuck, he's hung up, he heard my voice and realized he hates me. And I was about to say, hello? But then he said, "Well, actually, I was thinking of coming up to Boston for the weekend," which was obviously what I wanted to hear. It was exactly the only thing I wanted to hear, but I just said, "Oh." You know, but my mind was racing. I mean, what did he mean? Where was he going to stay? Were we just going to have dinner? I mean, what's going on? But he just said he'd call me when he got into town, and I tried to be really cool, you know, great, E.B., whatever, and we hung up.

But, God, did that really happen? I mean, was he really coming? I remember later I'd gone upstairs to this party in some room, and they were all sitting around listening to Pink Floyd—like I gave a shit—you know, it was this room of people who did nothing but burn incense all day long and listen to *Dark Side of the Moon,* but they always had drugs and they left you alone. And it just hit me. You know, you have to keep reminding yourself. And I got so happy I nearly cried. I probably did, in this cheap beanbag chair that was ripped and had all the Styrofoam pellets all over my sweater, I was probably crying. I mean, for the first time I wasn't even worried about what we'd do, or what we'd say to each other. I was just so blown away that he was coming and that he wanted to see me. All the rest of that shit—I mean, part of me was clearly like, who the hell does he think he is? He thinks he can just call up and snap his fingers—but I practically had to laugh at myself, like, finally he's called, so I'm going to say, fuck off, I'm busy? Come on, it was E.B., and what else would I possibly have wanted to be happening? Nothing.

He called me on Friday afternoon. I'd basically been sitting on top of the phone. He said he was at the Brattle Street Theatre. He wanted to see a movie, and it started in approximately seven minutes. It was this old Frank Capra thing, Mr. Something goes to Someplace, I don't even remember which one. So I raced over there, and he was just standing out there with the tickets.

He looked different. His features looked really defined, but it was weird. It was like someone had taken his face apart and put it back together or something. He actually looked a lot like Joe Boone, that same sort of beaten expression, sort of weary eyes, all bleary and sad. You know, I knew E.B. had that look, because I'd seen it before, and it would come and it would go with moods, but I don't know, it looked like it was just there now. It looked like it had just invaded his face.

But we just said hi and went racing in to the theatre and the movie had already started, and it was obviously impossible to pay any attention. It was ridiculous. I still wanted to know what was going on. And after the movie I didn't know what we were going to do. I mean, he'd come up for a reason, but it was like he wanted me to take charge or something. So I did, I said, "Do you want to go down to the river?" And he said, sure, so we went down there and walked down towards M.I.T., and he told me about these people in Madison Square Park, these old ladies and old men who would go to this wretched little park in the afternoons and just wait with their rotten bread. He said he couldn't stand them, but he went every day anyway to look at them. And he said he could just feel himself with all these old thoughts. He'd look at these old people or at Amalie, like every time she would come in, he would just start thinking about what the hell she thought she was doing there, what good was she doing. I mean, he knew Amalie so well, he really did. He just couldn't help himself from looking at her sometimes and, you know, just skinning her, or these old people in Madison Square Park. And he knew he shouldn't be doing it, he knew it wasn't any good, but he just couldn't stop himself, and he didn't feel like he had anywhere to go. I mean, he didn't want to be with the people from the play, or his friend Harry. And he said he'd had it with Hugh Gardiner, all that was too ridiculous. And he wasn't about to go to his father—Joe Boone was the one who fucked him up in the first place—and Toddy was probably still reeling in shock, thanks to me.

So, I mean, I was all he had. I was all he had left. Which wasn't a bad thing in the least. It was obviously special, but it was very scary, to both of us. And I just looked at him, and we were down near M.I.T. by now, and I really just wanted to make him know that it was still okay. It was more than okay. And I asked him, "E.B., can I kiss you?" He just looked at me, so I did, and he let me. Then we went back. He went back to New York that night.

Levi Mottl

I wrote Eton and invited him to Ibiza for the summer. Lance and Sylvia had said it was fine, and it seemed like that was all I had to offer him. He wrote back and said he'd come. He said he'd fly out late spring, but I couldn't really get a sense of what was happening with him. It was sort of like trying to find something in a barrel of mud.

A week or two later, he wrote me asking if Hilary could come along. I didn't know how to respond. It certainly wasn't what I'd had in mind, and I suppose if I'd been following my intuitions, I'd have said no. But I guess I didn't feel like I was in any position to decide what was best for Eton right then. I left that to him. I said, fine.

Harry Hampton

I was seeing a woman that spring, an up-and-coming television journalist who I probably shouldn't name. I don't want to be cute, but I'm going to give her an alias. Let's say Doris. I was walking down Broadway with Doris. We'd just come from a party thrown by a Columbia science professor up in Morningside Heights. It was late. It must have been 2:30 or so, and I was walking her back to her place in the nineties, on West End. At around 108th Street, I mean really in the middle of nowhere, we ran into him. He was walking in the other direction, but it didn't look like he was going anywhere. He was just walking, and we stopped.

We said hello. I was embarrassed. I even screwed up her name, Doris's last name, pretty much on purpose, to let him know, you know, I'm just making time here. I don't even think he looked at her. We shook hands hello, we shook hands good-bye. That was about it, and he just kept heading in that same direction, for no reason, just whichever way the wind blows, and she said to me, Doris did, "That was Eton Boone? Eton Boone?" And I said, yeah, that's him. I turned back around to take a look, same gait, same pace. You know, there was a time I'd have been pleased as punch to say, "Yeah, sure, that's Eton Boone, my buddy." But now, I just wasn't sure if I could get away with it. He'd hardly even broken stride. I swear to God, if someone had come up to him five minutes later and said, "Hey, have you seen Harry Hampton around?" he'd have said, "Who?" And just like that, you're right back where you started.

IX

Ibiza

Summer 1974

Levi Mottl

I spent the early part of that summer on eggshells. The three of us were living out in the guest compound. I'd lived with Lance and Sylvia in the main house before Eton and Hilary arrived, but I moved out to the compound when they got there. I put them in separate rooms up on the second floor, overlooking the beach, and I took the bedroom downstairs. I'd thought that would be the best arrangement, but it didn't make for a very comfortable stay. I would lead myself around the house clearing my throat and whistling, and I can remember climbing into bed at night wondering what I'd hear. What would I make of two doors closing?

They spoke to each other almost never. They stayed pretty clear of each other physically. They wouldn't even share a couch.

Evenings, Eton would thumb through Spanish soccer magazines, and Hilary would sit by the hearth arranging dominoes. That was as close as I saw them. But I didn't tend to be around the house all that much. I spent the better part of most days outside painting. I'd thought Eton might join me on excursions to the churches there or the coves, but he seemed more concerned with his writing. He commandeered a room in the downstairs to work in—he set up a typewriter on an old sewing table.

Hilary, I had no idea how he would spend his days. He didn't paint. He didn't read. There were some old World War II bicycles he could use. There was a pool. He swam in the pool. I'd wake up and see him standing on the diving board looking up at the first plane of the day as it buzzed us all good morning.

Hilary Richman

It had this beautiful little pool with black tiles. I adore black-tiled pools. I had a friend in Montecito who had a black-tiled pool, but the one in Ibiza that belonged to Lance Link was the most beautiful one I'd ever seen, up on this little hill above the house, looking towards the mainland. The whole place was gorgeous, but the day before we got there Saliva had slipped by the pool or something and broken her elbow, so she was in this sling. Which she'd made. She was one of those people who makes everything, including these big wooden salad forks. I'd help her in the kitchen with the cooking. It was someone else to talk to, you know, especially in this place with these three artistes off doodling with their pencils all day long.

So I would cook with Saliva, and I would go out and get some rocks or shells to put on the table for dinner because she had to have rocks and shells on the dining room table. I think it was her idea of homemaking. But I'd just watch her cook and listen to her complain about how immature Lance was, and I'd think to myself, you know, "Complain complain, Saliva, at least you know what the hell is going on. At least you know what you're dealing with." I mean, I had no idea. I was there because he wanted me there, but sometimes I didn't even know why. Sometimes it was like I didn't exist, but I wasn't going to say anything. I mean, he was still incredibly depressed. He just wanted me around, which was fine.

So I don't know. I guess I complained a little too. I definitely complained. Saliva and I would sit there and cook and bitch, and I remember one of the first days E.B. and Lance had gone some-place—I don't know where Levi was, probably conversing with a goatherd or something—and we had cooked this rabbit, which was grotesque. But when E.B. and Lance were coming back, we were out on the front porch peeling these horrid little carrots which had come directly from the ground, and Lance and E.B. were just laughing hysterically and falling out of the jeep. They had these crab nets stuck in their pants, and they were just limping around like two eleven-year-old boys. But I hadn't seen E.B. laughing in so long, and it was nice, you know. Saliva looked at me, and we looked at these two complete assholes staggering around this dirt driveway, and I don't know, she goes out to kiss Lance Link hello, and I keep peeling the carrots.

Levi Mottl

You tended not to see him for largish portions of the day. But you could get the sense of his presence. He left a sort of conspicuous trail once you were aware of his routines. Lance had a book of Diane Arbus photographs that Eton would flip through. He'd stare at them like a child. I've always envied the lengths of time that children can stare at illustrations. I had a friend from Germany who died not so long ago, and she gave me a book of Norwegian fairy tales she'd had when she was a little girl, and when you hold the book in your hands, it opens right to the most beautiful plates. When you lay it down you can almost feel her leaning over them as a little girl, lying on her bed at night staring at those pictures so long she's broken the book's spine in a dozen different places, a dozen different places that say she was there and what she liked to look at. Eton left Lance's photography books the same way, with inclinations that sort of remember him. The chairs and couches too. Because there were habits, patterns and postures, the same poses over and over. He'd fold paper napkins into tiny tight squares and then unfold them again. You'd find them on the end tables, soft as cottonballs. You'd find the same glass of milk sitting in the sink every morning, next to the same dish, the knife set the same way. Shredded popsicle sticks in the living room ashtrays. The labels of beer bottles rolled into little cigarettes. All Eton's grooves, just indications of someone's presence, who you weren't allowed to see. He'd either be in his room typing, or where I'd find him in the mornings, sitting out on a deck chair that faced the ocean, with his legs crossed and the Arbus book sitting in his lap, and his left hand up against his forehead, rubbing.

Ellen Bok

We started getting packages almost as soon as he got to the island. Whether anything was going to come of them, we didn't know, because most of the stuff was just formless, late-night remorse, deep pain. But so steady and so much of it, wow. You didn't want to discourage him. You didn't want to commit one way or the other, but the man had an athletic mind. You did get the feeling that sooner or later he was going to let her rip.

Eton Arthur Boone to Ellen Bok, June 6, 1974

It is raining very hard, almost violently, and there's a canvas canopy above my window that's snapping in the wind and catching the rain louder than a copper pot. They sound like little bullets outside my window. The night frightens me lately. Darkness takes control of my mind with the same tight grip as guilt, but with a greater sense of conspiracy, so powerfully and so reliably that I've had to devise ways to fend it off. I have found ways that see me through until sleep or until morning, and tonight I will need them.

If I did not have methods and ways, I sometimes think that morning wouldn't come at all, and if morning never came, I would go mad. I have to settle on images that I know, plots that I command and that comfort me.

I think of a woman I first saw standing in a window, selling herself. A violent rain was spanking Amsterdam that night as well, so hard that a low sparkling mist covered the ankles of the men on the sidewalks. I was with Levi, who is downstairs now, fending off night with handmade cigarettes, a little tip of light searching for morning indesperately, almost casually.

The rain was so hard and thick that June. I was drunk, and Amsterdam was standing on edge for us. We could only roll along the sides of buildings, like drunken boys on golf courses at midnight—only the drunken boys look up at a clear summer sky, and we look up at whores in red frames.

We're plastered to the brownstones and theatres of the red-light district and attracted to the particular window of a woman whose name I never got. She is older than me, thirty or so, and the center of my drunken gravity. She is not quite a silhouette. Her white slip is cast pink by the single red light of her window display. Behind her I can see a small bed up against the back wall, and a lamp on her bed table. She is standing with one foot up on the seat of a simple wooden chair, and her hand caresses her hip and thigh. Her body is flawless, balanced and smooth, without a single imperfect line. You can see her nipples through her slip, large, and she is unashamed.

She looks out her window right in the eyes of the shoppers, sailors and middle-aged men under umbrellas and felt brims. I don't know how many times we pass her by, but one final time we return, and the rain curtain splits long enough to give us away. She sees me across the street and her eyes dig in like painted nails. With the trace of a manicured hand up her belly, she lures me out into the rain, and with a gentle cup of her left breast I am yanked back out of the rain to her door. That pull is so breathless and welcome. A resignation, an acquiescence, a deliberate mischievous limpness. Like that same drunken teenager, on a rollercoaster, I give in to her.

Very few words pass between us. They may concern her rates. Probably I explain that I am not alone, but when I turn back around, Levi is gone.

Levi Mottl

Eton and Hilary had been there maybe a month. As I say, they hadn't seemed very familiar with each other when the rest of us were around, but I'd started noticing how often they were away from the compound at the same time. They never left together, but most of the time if I found that one of them was out, more than likely so was the other. I assumed that they were seeing each other. I don't think I was being suspicious, though, because they'd actually established a sort of conspicuous pattern. It was maybe over the course of two or three weeks that it really came to my attention, that they were leaving in staggered starts. I'd watched it from my room, Hilary going off down the path on his bike and then maybe an hour later Eton following. Then they'd return the same way, in what I guess I thought were equally obvious intervals—Hilary first, normally, and then some time after, Eton. It could happen any time of day.

Eton Arthur Boone to Ellen Bok, June 6, 1974

She takes me in. I have no expectations. Everything, the light, the rain, and her movement in particular, seems to follow naturally. She leads me by the hand over to her bed and seats me there without a word, then returns to her window and draws the curtain. It occurs to me that she will have trouble distinguishing me from the others, but I cannot keep that worry long. She turns back to me and as her shoulder strap slips, the silk slides across her body like a linen kerchief in the breeze, but the way it settles is more comfortable on her flesh, more pleasing and temporary.

She's looking at me, seeing me for the first time, sizing me up, figuring the portions of business and pleasure that my look and manner promise. I think I impress her. I think I am younger than most of her customers, and I am determined to affect her as much as she does me. Her slip falls to the floor quietly and I can't suppress a faint moan. I can see her whole figure as she turns back to the window. Perfect, catching light the way only skin can, smooth, spread by a palette knife on the finest canvas, on stretched satin. She reaches up, enough to rouse her breasts a moment, and pulls the chain of her red lightbulb. She leaves a light more blue, seeping from the street through her shade. She is pure silhouette, a challenge.

I rise from the mattress and meet her in the middle of the room, with my hand first around her neck. I have never wanted anything like this ever. It's heartening that the passion is so true. It feeds itself—my passion devours my passion—and it feeds on her, on her mouth and neck, down over her breasts to her stomach. I'm down on my knees with my hands around her waist and her solid hips, encouraged by the little waves that tremble through her body. Has anyone ever loved her as much as I want to? Has anybody cared about her so much? I am beginning to lose myself, beginning to forget where I am, who I am, that I am anything but my body. Drunkenness and this woman, and the consistent, muting rain outside would have me forget everything but sensation. I am using my teeth, running them along the tight skin of her stomach and her hips. My mouth is dry and I am gnawing on her. My grip begins to tighten and my fingers are strong, molding her flesh, imprinting it, and biting it. She turns around me so that I have to follow her with my mouth; like a cripple I'm straining for her as she stands before the bed and then lies back on it. I kneel next to her, up against the bed and continue working my way up her body until our mouths meet, like an explosion, swirling and deep. I want to be down her throat, absolutely inside of her.

But my mind can never push that far. Not with her. I shy from the moment of pushing inside her. I cannot imagine it, and the rain distracts me, the Ibizan rain, ticking on the canopy now. The wind has died down, so it seems to be leaving me alone as well. And I know I've been away long enough that maybe Levi has stubbed out his cigarette and pulled the covers over him, but not long enough, nowhere near long enough, for me to begin looking for morning. Only once has that woman allowed me to stay until dawn, and every other time she's left me feeling more frightened and hollow than when she let me in.

Levi Mottl

It all came out in early August. Hilary had excused himself after a dinner we'd all had together and said he was going down to the beach to watch the moon. After ten minutes or so, Eton followed him. It was one of their less subtle exits, and I kept an ear open for them that night. I read very late. I didn't get to sleep until around four o'clock in the morning, and I hadn't heard anyone return.

The first I heard when I woke up was sobbing from outside, coming from the terrace that connects the main house to the guest wing. It was a sort of jolt. I stumbled out to the kitchen and met Eton at the screen door, coming in. His expression was a blank. He didn't look at me. When I got out to the terrace, I found Hilary with his face in his hands. Lance was standing over him in his painter's cap and Hilary was shivering—it takes a while for the sun to burn through in the mornings, it was still chilly, it was still foggy.

When I reached them both, Lance drew me aside. He actually took me into the main kitchen. I remember him holding me by the elbow, and he said, "I'm afraid we've had a bit of a nasty scene here." He said he'd gone out walking on the beach early and found a maroon silk scarf of Hilary's in one of the dunes, and then he'd continued on a ways and found them. He said at first he thought they were in a wrestling match, but the closer he got, the more clear it was, that it was Eton on top of Hilary, forcing himself, and Hilary was crying. Lance said it looked like two crabs fighting. He'd given a shout and they'd separated. Hilary had scrambled away.

Lance sort of left it at that, and I still wasn't exactly clear, but sometimes I guess your body has more instinct than your mind, because I began to feel very nauseous. I don't think I said anything to Lance. The first thing I did was go into the bathroom, a small one down below the main stairs there. It was very cramped and I was sweating. I was kneeling by the sink, running the water

and trying to sort through his story. I had an intuition that there
was more to this than what Lance had seen, and I think I just had
to brace myself for a moment, or collect myself, before I actually
went outside and went up to Eton's room, because I felt like that's
what I should do. I can't really say why I was feeling so determined about it—and motherly, it strikes me now. I suppose I just
must have felt that there was a great deal to be resolved, and that
going up and confronting Eton, which is something I'd been
reluctant to do all summer, was the only way.

I got myself out of the bathroom. Hilary was still on the patio
where I'd left him. He looked like he was recovering. Sylvia had
gotten him a cup of coffee. I went back into the guest house and
actually I put some dishes away before going up to Eton's room.

I remember rolling myself a cigarette. The door had been open.
Eton was lying on his bed with his hands behind his head and
his feet crossed. I pulled up a chair from an old school desk that
Lance used to have in there, and I sat down straddling it backwards. I rolled myself the cigarette and then I just asked him if
this was any of my business.

He was looking out the window. He asked if I had another
cigarette. I gave him the one I'd rolled, lit. He said, "I assume you
know already," and I told him I didn't. I asked him if he'd been
going out and meeting with Hilary all summer long, outside the
compound, and he smiled. He said no, he hadn't been meeting
with him. He lifted the sash and stuck his arm out on the sill. He
held it out there sort of testing the air with the cigarette, and then
he said he'd been "finding" Hilary. I told him I didn't know what
that meant. He said, "Do you really want to know?" I said yes,
and he told me.

It's actually a little difficult to begin. I've had some trouble
deciding if I should say what Eton told me that morning, because
it seems like a fairly grave invasion of his privacy—I've thought
to myself that there wasn't much point in revealing details like
this, that people are so liable to misunderstand—but Eton was
very confused that summer. He was in an unhealthy frame of
mind, and I guess I think that maybe the only real way of measur-
ing his despair is to know the truth or know what he told me was
the truth that morning in Ibiza.

He explained that he'd been hunting Hilary down, all summer long. He said it had just sort of evolved. Hilary would go

out first and usually leave some indication of where he was going to be. They'd even used me once or twice—apparently Hilary had told me where he was going and then Eton had come down and asked me—but more often Hilary would keep it simple, write it on a piece of paper or in the dirt in the driveway, somewhere Eton could find it. Then Eton would go out after him. Hilary always had the head start, but Eton said it didn't usually take too long to track him down. It's a small enough island. So he'd find Hilary and trail him a while. Sometimes he'd follow for hours and not do a thing—sometimes all he wanted to do was let Hilary know he was there. But more often, at some point, he'd ambush him, attack him. Hilary would struggle, but Eton said he was the stronger of the two and the faster, and that he could take Hilary whenever he wanted. He listed some of the places they'd used—Isla Vedra, the Caves of Cala Portinax, Figueretas, behind the English pubs, the jetty. He said there were too many, but that there probably wouldn't be any more now, now that they'd been busted. He'd said he'd followed Hilary by moonlight for hours the night before, on the beach and in the woods, but that he'd let the hunt drag on too long—he'd waited till daybreak before taking him, in the dunes, and that's where Lance had found them.

He'd been watching his hand through the window pane the whole time he told me, and flicking his cigarette ashes in the breeze. When he was finished we both just sat there. He let the cigarette burn down to its end, and then he placed it on the sill. He didn't look at me, but he said, "Hilary. Don't mention it to Hilary that we talked. That you know." Then he withdrew his arm. He left the butt on the outside sill and closed the sash. I was starting to feel ill again. I stood up to leave, but Eton just kept looking out the window. He said, "Does this surprise you, Levi?" I said yes, this was not what I'd expected. He put his cheek up against the pane, smushed, and he said, "Well, I'm sorry."

I left the room. I went downstairs and got a chocolate, a sketchbook, and a bottle of mineral water, and I went to the gypsy camps on the other side of the island. Some of the gypsies in Ibiza try to breed wild dogs, *Podenco Ibizenco,* a caramel-and-white breed with ears that stand up on their head like dingos or Egyptian dogs. I tried sketching them, but I didn't feel very well. I tried to sleep it off. I found a little tuft of grass on a hill.

After Blue died, I had dreams. I used to dream that she was still there. I would go into her studio to clean up her things, and she would be there. She would have her brushes in her hands, and pads, and she would want me to come out and paint with her, and we would go out but we could never find the place. I had that dream for years. But lying there on the hill in Ibiza, I had dreams about Eton, that I would go back to the house and Eton would come out of his room with brushes and he would say, "Why don't you and I head out and do some painting?" "Why don't you and I hit the beach or go up to Majorca or into Spain and just paint?" But drifting in and out of sleep, I had dreams that that could never happen because Eton had died too. He was dead. Hilary had killed him. Lance had found their bodies on the beach, and he would come find me to tell me, but I'd be dead too, lying on the hill with my hands folded over my chest, waiting for the Egyptian dogs.

Hilary Richman

I don't know. It's not really that easy to remember, to tell you the truth. Things just changed. E.B. changed. He would just write and clack away at his typewriter all day long, and what the hell was I even doing there? I would do all these things, I would go shopping, I would make us these little picnics to take to the bullfights or whatever, but he'd just say I was trying to steal him away from his writing. And I mean, his writing was obviously important to him, I knew that, but it didn't seem that good for him. It wasn't making him happy, so what was I supposed to do, leave him alone with these gloomy thoughts?

But, I don't know, how do you trace these things? One night I'd just been walking on the beach and I was incredibly upset. I'd just had it. We weren't talking, we weren't even dealing with each other at all, so I'd gone down to the beach and I was just laying there looking at the moon, which was full. And E.B. came. I guess he'd come down to the beach to find me. So we just lay there looking at the moon and we fell asleep. We didn't say a word.

And when I woke up, E.B. was getting up to go. It was like six in the morning, and the sun was coming up and it was practically red, just this red I've never even seen anywhere else, and I said, "No, E.B., stay with me. Just stay for once." But he said he was going to write, and I don't know, I just didn't want him to. I mean, I was just sick of his writing, but he kept walking away like I wasn't even there, and I told him to stop. I had to fucking scream it, and I told him, I said, "You know the only reason you go write all the time is so you don't have to think about the fact that all you've got right now, E.B., is me." I said this to him and he turned around. He just stood there looking at me. He was in this sweatshirt and his pants were rolled up, and he had his hand on his hip, and I mean, I didn't want to have to beg him anymore, so I just told him to go the fuck ahead. I said, "Oh, go then. Go write whatever the hell you have to write, and then you can go send it all off to your fucking little Hugh Gardiner friend or this editor woman whoever she is," but I told him it was pathetic. It was pathetic that the only people he could ever talk to in his life were these little moles he didn't even know. I mean, it was so obvious. You know, I said, "What the hell are you so scared of, E.B.? What are you trying to hide?"

And he's standing there. He like laughed. He goes, "I'm not scared of anything, Hilary. I'm not hiding anything." And I just said, "Jesus Christ, E.B. Bull shit." I mean, he knew that wasn't true. I said, "What about me? Haven't you been hiding me?" You know, we had to act like these strangers when Levi was around, we had to go through all this bullshit, and E.B.'s telling me he didn't have things to hide? Jesus Christ, of course he did." And I just, I mean, I'd never mentioned what Joe had done to him. I don't even remember when he'd told me exactly—it was when we were in New York. We were probably stoned someplace. But E.B. was standing there looking at me, and I knew we were both thinking it—it's like he was daring me—so I said it, I said, "What about your mom, E.B? What about cheating on your fucking goddess mother, being Joe's little postboy?" I mean, Jesus Christ, sometimes I felt like that was the only reason E.B.'d ever wanted me at all, just so he could have his little revenge on Joe Boone. I said, "What about that, little postboy?"

He just went after me. He hit me. He hit me with two hands. He went crazy, and I've never been so scared in my life. The next thing I remember is just this pain, and I was crying, and then Lance came, I guess thank God. It just stopped, and we all walked back to the house. I was probably hyperventilating, and all this sand was in my mouth. I don't know, it was really sad in a way, because E.B. hadn't wanted to hurt me, he was just so angry. But I mean, that's what the book was. That's where *Ruth* started, right there on that beach.

Eton Arthur Boone to Ellen Bok, July 3, 1974

I went to find a tree today that I had seen my first morning here, which was not yet a month ago. I didn't know that I was headed for the tree until just before I found it. As it came into view and I realized it as my destination, I was surprised that my familiarity with the island had grown so intimate so quickly that it could guide me without my even knowing.

As far back as I can remember, when I was only just walking, my mother took me to a garden that sits on the western end of the park where I first played. I did not know the hedges or trees or flowers of the garden by name. I did not know how to find the garden, but once I was there, set down from my stroller, I am told that I could work my way through its maze at least to find the places I liked to be, a concrete bench by a shallow coin pool, and a tree that I think must have been a willow, whose boughs fell down in twisted green braids. Even now as the images drift back to me, I can imagine that I knew where each turn led, where what was around this enormous hedge would not surprise me, it would satisfy me. The garden drew its designs in my mind even as I was only just beginning to understand space. Perhaps that is why even today I can remember certain of its pathways. I still have dreams I suspect are plotted by the schemes of that garden.

I know the same is true of feelings. Those that settle on us when we are first beginning to understand—what a feeling is, that it is independent of the mind, but knowable, like a garden—these first-known feelings leave a print that remains long after them. And when they return later on, when they are recalled by dreams or by moments, it is like the violent recovery of a first self. The power of it is breathtaking and vengeful, as if having pretended to pass beyond them was a kind of mistaken impression that should never have been allowed.

It was that way with Katherine. Twice. But even as it happened the first time, there was a sense of recurrence. I'd been there before and felt the fear, of hovering over a body and feeling the loss and punishment, that there was a force somewhere that could take her away, that could make her change like that, where one moment she is the woman you love, and the next she is someone else. Katherine had been acting differently that night, louder—I had to leave the rooms where she entered. She scared me. And so I watched her from around corners and across rooms, one drink after the other. Mixing—from beer and then to wine—seemed innocent. I asked her, "Have you been drinking wine all night?" and she said, "No, I'm switching"—innocent, or just a hint of danger—"Just switching, not changing." Or so I heard, and left the room. I was silent and hesitant as I watched her change. I did not completely believe it, or perhaps it was a kind of faith that had me denying. Either way, I was dumb, just dumb with fear.

And I remember a soothing feeling of vindication when she came to me at 1:30. We bumped into each other in the hall accidentally and she said, "There you are. Come with me." She took my hand and led me to the single bedroom past the coatroom where we'd gone to kiss before. There was something then, something in her eye that said "remind me, find me," and the relief in it was painful and exquisite, like blood rushing back into a sleeping limb, my hand, as she held it and said she wanted to be alone with me.

But when we got there—a bright room, too bright with the light on, and much too dark with it off—she sat on the bed and then sunk down, her body curled inward, and she took my left hand in both hers and began to cry. She said she felt horrible, and it didn't seem she was speaking to me. She said she wanted to be left alone there for the night, and as she spoke, her face sickened so violently that all my relief vanished, its blood turned cold and I wanted to be able to touch her for warmth, feel her temples and lie down beside her. But her sickness frightened me, parried and sliced me with all its possibilities, the lashing, terrifying glances of someone drunk, someone not herself, someone nearly alien, or someone dying.

I knelt down beside the bed and removed my hand from hers. I touched her gently on the shoulder and bent over her face as her crying subsided, and her eyes rolled beneath her lids, searching desperately for sleep. I watched as all the life seemed to leave her. All the blood drifted from her face and the breath from her nostrils was faint, almost undetectable. There was no swell in her breast. Her sleep was poisoned and the deeper it fell, the more pale her face became, and the skin of her forehead would tighten and tremble. No confusion, though. No voices or dreams. Nothing. Just sleep, neither fast nor restless. Sick. Bacterial.

Loneliness crept in the room from under the door, or was a vapor that rose from her body as she slept, the smell of loneliness and abandonment. It was familiar to me, like a song or a poem or a garden, waiting for my return. I could feel the terror and bewilderment just as I had before, of losing someone before we became inseparable, of watching her disentangle herself from me, pushed from my net by an inescapable current, and acquiescing. The power of it must seem so friendly to them, softening and liberating and inescapable, like deep space, but terrifying to me, and purposeful—Take this love from him, he isn't capable of it. His mind is savage, it is not innocent. I felt it as I knelt beside Katherine's bed, awkward and desolate as before, nothing learned but the feeling of helplessness, as if nothing I could do then could keep her, the force was so mysterious—remote and soft and momentous, the current—disease. Where is its power, and how has it known so well to punish me?

That was the first feeling I ever knew, the one I grew into. That was the garden I could never hope to leave behind or forget. Not as I watched Katherine sleep. That was my skin and it was ashen. And she was blue, just like before, blue and gone, just like before and just like after, blue and burnt.

I saw her death. I saw her die before the fact. I knelt beside it and imagined it, and I knew the feeling of it long before it happened. I imagined our separation and after such a long period of calm I felt the powerlessness to stop it. It made the years in between seem like just a respite, when I'd had the fortune or good sense neither to want inseparability nor grieve the fact that it could never ever be permanent. Impermanence returned that night and ran its fingers up my spine and cupped the back of my head. It had stinking breath, and I grew weaker and more frail in its presence, almost as if all I could do was sit beside her, lie down beside her bed and slowly bruise.

Hilary Richman

E.B. was very cold for a while. I don't know, I didn't know what to think. I just left him alone to his writing. I mean, it was the book now, and that's what he wanted. I guess I just gave him some distance.

Of course this was around the time that those bastards were doing their little planning, making their little schemes. It was ridiculous. I mean, no one needed to. I didn't even know what was going to happen with me and E.B. No one needed to be so fucking scared. You know, we stayed an extra month, and then I was going to go to New York and live with a friend and look for a job, but I got a letter from my mom right before we were going to leave. It was this letter inviting me to Japan and two plane tickets. I guess my brain had clicked off. You know, she'd always wanted to go to Japan with me, and now finally it had come through, but it was just so ridiculous. They'd just gone to Europe and sent me to Ibiza, and now I was going to Japan. You know, we're not the Rockefellers. I don't know. I had this ticket from Madrid to San Diego. I can't believe how blind I was.

Levi Mottl

Towards the end of the summer, Joe started calling. I began getting messages from Joe, and I don't know why it dawned on him to get in touch with us, but I welcomed it. The idea of actually talking to him I dreaded, and I didn't get back to him immediately, but the sense of Joe being there, sort of ready to field anything that came his way, made me feel a little less lonely. I finally called him. We had a conversation. I didn't tell him what the specifics had been. I just said that things hadn't been working out with the summer, and I remember Joe asking, "Is it Hilary?"

I told him it was both of them. And I remember Joe's voice, "Do I want to know about it?" I told him no, I didn't think so, but I said something should probably be done, and he said, "Yep, yep." He said, "Okay." He'd slipped into a kind of Emergency Father Mode, like he was finally going to put a stop to it, Goddamn it. He told me to keep them there until the end of September, which was a month longer than we'd originally planned. He said that if I could keep things under control until then, he'd set something up for their return, something, to be honest with you, that would keep the two of them apart.

X

Ruth

Winter 1974 — Spring 1975

Camille Walker

Hate to say, but Hugh was just a kiss-and-tell, that's all, quite a little tramp, at least while I was at Fishkill. It was the spring right after Boone's fiancée had died, and apparently Boone had just given Hugh the old heave-ho. Hugh didn't let on. He kept a stiff upper lip, but that was the talk around the colony, that Hugh had been hit hard by Boone's Dear John, and you could see the man was in pain. I could. Remember, this is not the first person I'd seen devastated by Mr. Boone—I knew that lovelorn look. But Hugh's response I thought was much more entertaining than Plums's— he started showing off those whoop-de-do letters of his. He'd read them aloud at teas, and it was always a real tearjerker. He'd pass them around like pressed leaves, and some people, the really "in" crowd, they'd even managed to get some copies of their own—kiss-asses. So that's how the whole thing got started.

Now, the first person I ever saw with the *Hilary* letter was Sarah Palmeroy Moore, then Sarah Palmeroy, a Cliffie like me and still unpublished, as yet undiscovered by Mr. Moore. She had it posted right there on her office corkboard, a nice big gold star from the professor himself. I read it. I'd heard so much from Hilary about these things that I felt almost obliged to. I had it on her bed, wading my way through, and Sarah tells me, "Oh, sure, Hugh says that one is about Boone's obsession with his stepbrother." "His stepbrother?" I said. My little heart must have skipped a beat. I probably quiffed. "Mmm-hmm. Hugh said so." Well, I said, "Ms. Palmeroy, do you have any idea who Eton Boone's stepbrother is? Eton Boone's stepbrother is our darling Hilary." She wouldn't believe me. We read the letter again together, and it was incredible—"the major's head bobbing up and down on Marabou's humongous swannee"—I loved it. Besides, who wouldn't just want it to be true? It was the most scrumptious thing I'd ever heard of. We have in our possession not only a private letter of Eton Boone's—eh—we have a letter that's about his obsession with his beautiful, mulatto, stepbrother-slash-lover, who is only the loveliest little bitch on the eastern seaboard, our little lambkins Hilary. Dee-lish.

News spread. Let's face it, these writing colonies are a little hard-up for action and all ears for gossip. I'll take some of the credit, but Ms. Palmeroy was a bit more popular than she lets on. People got their own copies. They got the scoop on Hilary and the affair, third-hand, fourth-hand, but it's a pretty incestuous world. That letter became a cult classic on the circuit—Boone should have been quite proud. I was up at the MacDowell Colony that summer, in New Hampshire, and people there already had it. They knew I had it, and those without really made me feel like some college drug dealer, seriously. They'd knock on the door and ask if they could see.

And at Harvard, where people actually knew Hilary, in many many many senses of the word—please. By the time I got there, half the damn school knew about it. All of Hilary's little conquests. Standing on line for books at the Coop, it was like one giant game of telephone. A copy gets posted on the bulletin board at the Signet Society, I remember—Andrew Holden, then editor of the esteemed *Advocate,* had Magic-Markered above it, "Savoir Faire is everywhere!" And before you know it, word is they're going to stick it in the winter issue, just print it without asking—a regular literati scoop, Eton Boone's angst. Fun for that alone, a cheap thrill, but an absolute sophomoric blast for anyone who'd had a taste of Plums, especially Andrew, who'd been tupped somewhere along the line, I'm sure. You should have seen his face when I asked him about it at a Signet tea—how on earth did he think he was going to get away with printing that letter? He had his hands behind his head, smiling—"Hey, what's the problem, peaches? The University's got lawyers." Such arrogance. I said, "But what about Hilary?" Andrew just looked at me. "It's free publicity, babe, and if your little caramel friend isn't going to eat that up like a big ol' slice of watermelon, then I'm Jack Reed." He said, "I'll be expecting a thank-you note."

Harry Hampton

Joe Boone had called me that August at work and scared the shit out of me, basically. I'd never met the man, Boone's mentioned him maybe twice, but all of a sudden out of nowhere he calls up and asks if I could help find a place for his son, a professional place. I thought it was some kind of prank or something, but he said he didn't know anyone in New York well enough, so he was calling me. He sounded like hell. He said Boone was in trouble, and he thought he might need an institution. I kept asking him what had happened, had Boone tried to hurt himself or something, but he wouldn't tell me. He just kept saying that Boone wasn't bouncing back too well. He said I should call Levi if I wanted to know more.

I called Levi and he sketched out what had been going on, all the stuff with Hilary, and I don't have to tell you—it was a little hard to take. I didn't talk to Levi that long. I got off the phone, and it took me maybe two hours to find the place, Hanover House. It was a private clinic out on Long Island, in Sagaponack. I got the tip from Boone's editor. She said it was just the thing, run by a guy who had some experience working with artists. Sounded right, but I didn't really know. The whole thing threw me. I called Joe Boone back the same day, gave him the address, and he took it from there.

Levi Mottl

There were a few days on Mallorca before Eton left. We'd gone to Mallorca to see Hilary onto his plane in Palma, and right after, I'd told Eton that we'd found a place for him to rest when he got back to the States. All he'd asked was whether he'd be able to write. I'd said yes, and that seemed to be all he needed to know.

We were there for about four days, staying with some friends of Lance's who lived in a colony of British expatriots whose families had come down during the Spanish Civil War. We slept in an office, head to head in beds that were up against a bookshelf filled with rocks, and Eton would make notes late into the night. He'd turn the lamp in against the shelf to keep the light low.

We'd taken walks during the days. We'd stay out as long as there was light, hiking out around the landscape with sticks. Eton said it was like wandering through a fairy-tale kingdom, the mountains there are so enormous. They rise from the sea at an almost cliffish pace, and the sheep graze on inclines.

I think it was our second to last day, it had been very beautiful. A thunder shower had cleared thick fog, and late in the afternoon we split some bread and cheese at an old stone well. We were eating across from each other, and he asked me if it had been Joe's idea to find a place for him. I didn't lie. I said yes, but that I hadn't been against it. I'd thought it might be a good idea. Eton sort of chewed and nodded his head. He said, "Have I ever done my imitation of Dad for you?" I said no. He pulled the wineskin out of his sack and poured himself a mouthful. Then he came over. He was bent over and peering at me. He put his face near mine and then pushed out a long, slow, warm breath. And it's funny, if you'd asked me before then if I was familiar with the smell of

Joe Boone's breath, I'd have probably said no, but what Eton had just blown in my face, tannin and sweet and stale, was it almost exactly. Eton smiled and he said, "Pretty cool, hunh?" I think that's probably as close as he came to explaining to me what his book was about.

Harry Hampton

It had been my job to pick Boone up at the airport. Levi and Joe and I had turned into a real SWAT team, setting everything up, making sure everything went smoothly, but Boone was on to it. I could see the second he came through the gate. He didn't even say hello. He just said, "Harry," and went off to the luggage belt to wait for his bags. I followed. We didn't talk. He was just watching the bags spin around. He looked tired, tan, a little sinister, he didn't look happy. Finally, it was taking so long, he went off to the restroom. He said he had to go wash his face, and he told me what his luggage looked like. It was just one of those Navy sacks, drab green sausage things that always weigh a ton. It came around while he was gone, so I dragged it over to the restroom to wait for him there.

And even that, you know, standing outside the men's room, I was thinking, "Look at me. Drop of a hat, I'm helping out. Gotten him a place to stay. Dealt with his landlord. I'm here to pick him up at the airport, no fee, and now I've got his goddamn ton of a Navy sack on my back. You know, I'm not happy that my friend is a little screwy right now, but he needs my help—that's what they tell me—and here I am giving it, no questions asked. I'm okay." It's in the way I've got his duffel bag balanced on my hip. I'm a trooper.

Boone comes out of the restroom finally, fresh, clean, but he's still looking a little sour. He's not giving me anything, and I'm wondering—I mean, it's a little thing—but I'm wondering about his bag. Is he going to take it and carry it out to the car, or is he going to let me do it? Well, long and short, he didn't even make a move for it. He just started outside, went right through the doors—if they hadn't been automatic, I don't think he'd have held them. So I heave the duffel bag up on my shoulder, and we make our way out to the car. It was raining, and it was a long walk. I'd parked about half a mile away, and the point is, Boone didn't even think about offering to take his bag, didn't even mention it until finally I say, "Hey, Boone, do you want to take this for a second?" I mean, do you want to take your own god-damn two-ton luggage? I'm having a hernia. And he just says, "Oh, sorry, Harry, I didn't want to ruin your moment."

Ellen Bok

Ruth didn't really happen until he got to Hanover. The idea he'd had for a while—the painting trip with his mom—he'd sketched it out for me before he left Ibiza, but I think he wanted a change of scenery before he started in. I could tell he was on track, though. He sent us the diary entries right up until he left, and you could feel it, he was just revving his engine. Some of these things were classics—one about the speckles on his mother's smock that'd tear your heart out.

So by the time he got to Hanover he was raring to go. Perfect place, too, especially in the fall. I haven't been out there for years, but I used to go when friends were in. It's just a house, but enormous Georgian, red brick and the spanking-white trim, a perfect lawn out front with red maples and beech trees. They've got a duck pond out behind the main building, with a weeping willow, and it's right across from a horse stable, the ocean's around the corner, corn fields, potato fields, tractors. The whole Long Island bit. Hanover is not a very gruesome place, believe me. It's a room of one's own, and that's all he was looking for. Listens if you want to talk, leaves you alone if you don't, and most important of all, gives you a fresh ribbon if you ask for it. That's all most of these people need.

Hilary Richman

I was flown back separately from the others, back to San Diego. It wasn't even convenient. They'd gotten me one of these twenty-hour flights with a stopover in Atlanta. My mom was on cloud nine. She'd gotten all these guidebooks about Japan or whatever, and we were going to leave in a week or eight days, I don't know. I was completely exhausted. But you know, they'd set everything up. They put me in Toddy's room with Toddy. And, I mean, Toddy'd already moved out, he was living downtown, but they'd brought him back so we could bunk together. I guess they thought he'd be a good influence or something, and they certainly didn't want me in E.B.'s old room anymore.

I don't know why in the world I'm saying "they." It was just Joe, doing all his plotting and scheming. I practically think he'd hired Toddy just to tell me. Toddy and I were in his room, and I was packing and writing down his new address downtown, and he said something like, "I guess you'll need E.B.'s address too." And I had E.B.'s address. I said, "I have E.B.'s address." And Toddy just told me, and it was ridiculous. I mean, who were they? A clinic. What the fuck. Toddy said that E.B. had gone along with it, but I knew that wasn't true. I mean, only Joe Boone. I'm sure E.B. didn't go along with their shipping me all the way to the other side of the fucking world. It was ridiculous. Asshole. Joe Boone deserved everything he got.

But when Toddy told me, I didn't want to make a big stink with Mom in the house—I was such a simp—and Joe wasn't home. He was at work down at the radio station, so I just took Toddy's car and went down there. I was going like ninety miles per hour. Joe was in some programming meeting when I got there. I just said to the lady, "Tell him his stepson's out here." I guess he wrapped up his meeting pretty quickly because he was out in about two seconds. He came out into the reception area and we went into this old studio, into this control room they had with these leather stools, and he just goes, "So. Hilary. What's the problem?"

Really. I wasn't in the mood for any of his bullshit. You know, on the ride down I'd been thinking about what I wanted to say. I had this whole speech, but I just blurted out exactly what I thought, which was something like that he was this pathetic man who couldn't handle things, who had no idea about his son, so he had to send him away because he'd hurt him so much. And he just said something, some lie like he was only doing it because E.B. was sick, which was total bullshit. E.B. wasn't sick. E.B. was sad maybe, or alone or angry or something, but he wasn't sick, and this was just going to make it worse, sending him off to some hospital or whatever. I mean, what did he know? What the fuck did he know about it? They could've just let nature run its course—I mean, I was so pissed, but I get twice as pissed just thinking about it. And Joe, Joe Boone, like this fucking politician, says something like, "It's not a hospital. It's a house to relax in. I checked it out." He checked it out. Oh, fuck you, Joe. Just fuck you. He didn't check out shit. This man didn't know the first fucking thing about what he'd done. But he looks at me and he goes, "Maybe some peace and quiet will help him get his writing done." I nearly laughed in his face. I said, "Oh, that's very interesting. Do you know what he's writing, Joe? Do you have any idea what he's writing about?" And he's just looking at me and he put his hand up like, you know, let's keep our voices down Hilary. God. I just said, "He's writing about how you fucked around on E.B.'s mom when she had cancer, you prick. And you fucking made E.B. help. That's what fucked him up, Joe, and you know it, so don't look at me like it's me. It's you. He's writing about how you fucked him up. You know it, and I know it, and he knows it, and now everybody's going to know it." Jesus. Asshole.

Well, I don't know. Joe was basically blanched by this point. He was just standing there looking blanched, and I just walked on out of there and went to Japan with my mom like a good little boy, and I haven't had a conversation with Joe Boone since.

Hugh Gardiner

It was Ms. Rubin who'd informed me, actually. It was very kind of her. She'd dropped by my office at Vassar on her way to a theatre collective upstate. We had tea, and she told me that Boone had placed himself in the care of the people at the Hanover clinic out on Long Island. I was obviously very concerned. I'd had no idea, and I couldn't bear feeling so ignorant. I realized that I'd completely lost touch with what he'd been going through, and I even began to question myself, that perhaps it had been wrong of me to withdraw as I had, so quickly, because my absence hadn't seemed to do him much good. It was a very difficult piece of news to accept.

I decided to write him. I had to, but this time in a somewhat different vein than I had previously. I wrote him about myself, really for the first time. I'd given it a great deal of thought, but I believed that it was the only real alternative. I wrote him of my past, of my family, of my professional work as a teacher. I wrote him of the things I keep most private, and it was not easy for me to do, I assure you. I am not comfortable discoursing in any way about my personal life, and I struggled with that letter through several evenings, but all the time encouraged by the idea that my efforts might help him, in a strange way, to make a new friend.

When I was through, I found before me a document of some forty-two pages. It was a bit surprising, I admit, that I'd been able to turn out such volume, and I was reluctant to send it—it seemed in many ways just burdensome and selfish of me. I even resolved several times to destroy it. I came very close, but I didn't. I sent it finally. Not all at once—I thought that might be too much, and I only wanted to help. I sent my letter to him in installments, three to be precise, all packed tightly and stamped twice, and mailed over the course of two weeks in October, 1974. I took them down to the post office myself.

Claire Sullivan

My cousin Alice and I went to see him. I think that we were the only ones. It was after Thanksgiving and we were bringing him some turkey from the get-together that we'd had at Alice's place in Wallingford. We muscled our way in. It was a lovely place, with a perfectly charming clientele that seemed to roam about so freely, lounging in studies and so forth—and to think of the people who must have lived there first. There was a gallery of them all, portraits of shipping magnates and robber barons and the like. We were given a tour when we finally got in, and they showed us the china and crystal and silver. It was quite a show. And the loveliest mantel pieces in every room.

We had surprised Eton coming. We found him in a lovely room up on the top floor with the fire ablaze and him hunkered over his papers. It wasn't a sight that I found particularly enjoyable. Seeing Eton so much younger than all the others, and holed up in that room there with nothing but himself and his papers, it made me very sad. He was still such a young man, but him coming to the door with his back curled over from hours and hours of such quiet, lonely labor, it's not how a strong young man should be spending his days. And having nothing but a turkey sandwich to celebrate Thanksgiving. There's very little thanks for that.

We took a blanket from his bed and brought it outside to the lawn there, with a bottle of wine, and we had our own little party in the late autumn sun. He was so preoccupied with his work, but we had a very nice time. We talked about Alice's family actually, because all the boys were getting married, and Eton was very nice. He gave us both some little drawings he'd done and we all looked through a little sketchpad of his, of all the interns in their baggy white pants running all about. I think he'd been so surprised we were there.

When we left, all I have is the sight of him, bundled up and shivering, kissing us both good-bye on that enormous lawn and then turning to go back in. We couldn't help watching him as he went. He had his hands deep in his pockets and was walking back briskly. Half way there, he broke into a trot, with stiff legs and such a burdened little head tucked between those shoulders. I doubt that he thought about us again that day. He just trotted back indoors, back up to his fireplace and went back to his papers like Bartleby the Scrivener or that Cratchit man.

Toddy Boone

When Anne got back from Japan, I think that's when things hit rock bottom. Hilary hadn't come back with her. He'd gone straight to San Francisco for a while to visit friends, but Dad was still in a daze. Anne said he wouldn't talk, and he wasn't eating. All he did was sleep. I started going over to dinner because she'd ask me, and the place was like a graveyard, all these flowers everywhere and no one talking. Anne would clear the plates after dinner and just leave the two of us there, and I wanted to talk to him, tell him just to let her in a little and explain about Hilary, but we hadn't even discussed it. I couldn't say anything. We'd just sit there in front of the TV until I said I had to go. Anne would call me at my place later before she went to bed and thank me for coming. She'd say Dad was out walking.

And he knew how hard it was on her. He didn't mean to leave her out, but I just don't think he knew what else to do. He kept getting her flowers. We'd gone to Del Mar this one time to pick up a bedframe for my apartment, and we'd had an all-right time. It wasn't great, but on the way back Dad drove through town. It was in the evening and he was sort of sliding around everywhere, looking out the window for something. I asked him what he was looking for, and he said a flower shop. He wanted to get flowers for Anne. It's like that's all he could do, but there weren't any flower shops open. We ended up going to the place where I was working, an architecture firm in Mission Beach. I'd just got my first key, so we snuck in together to steal some flowers for Anne, and while we were in there he told me about meeting Mom, and their first kiss. He said he'd picked her up for a dinner party in Philadelphia with wild roses. She'd gotten in the car and he'd given her the flowers and told her how beautiful she looked, and she'd said, "I like your tie." Dad said that was her big mistake, complimenting his tie.

We found some flowers. There was a nice arrangement out in one of the reception areas. We drove back, and I'm sure Dad didn't say anything to Anne about it. The flowers were probably just waiting there on the kitchen table in the morning, and they were probably in a vase on the dining room table when Dad got home that night.

Ellen Bok

He sent us a complete draft just before Christmas, right before all that baloney with *Harper's*. Interesting story. The manuscript was ready, in my opinion. I hadn't wanted to change a word. I was very happy. Last fall the man had come to us with some idea for a kids' book, and now a year and a half later we've got *Ruth* in our hands. Much better, much more personal. It's about Boone, people are going to know it, people are going to want it—that's what I'm banking on, at least—so I just want to keep the ball rolling before anyone changes their mind. I've got a good feeling about this.

But Capper was still dragging his heels. Every time the book came up, he'd start grumbling, saying he still doesn't like the guy, doesn't want the trouble. He was going to bury the book. He'd been talking to the sales people about maybe five thousand copies, first printing. I was trying to tell him he was crazy. Five thousand? This is Eton Boone, give me fifty. The man was a name—that's what I kept trying to tell him. So we sent the manuscript out to certain readers, just to get some reaction, see how people take it. We do not send one over to Larry Wolfe, though, at *Harper's*, because frankly Larry Wolfe cares too much. Always has. He always wants to talk to the writer. Turn your head for two seconds and he's on the phone with your author, messing with his head, asking him questions about narrative parabolas, and it's six more months of revisions. We don't want that. We just want to get going.

I start getting messages from Larry, though, and I'm thinking, dammit, who the hell? Love the guy, but the last thing in the world we need now is Larry Wolfe sticking his ever-conscientious nose in Eton Boone's business. So I don't call him back. He gets through finally, though, persistence pays off, and he says to me, "Ellen, where is Eton Boone? We've been trying to find him for the last two months now. What have you done with him?" I didn't know what he was driving at, so I told him a half-lie—I don't know where Boone is, the book's done, maybe he's off drinking champagne somewhere. Larry says, "No, no. It's not about the book." He said he didn't even know Boone was writing a book. He said, "We want to reprint *The Advocate* letter." I said, "*Advocate* letter? What *Advocate* letter?" He says, "Oh, you haven't heard?" All of a sudden he gets very uncomfortable. I said, "What? Tell me." He tells me.

He says that a month or so ago, out of nowhere some letter of Boone's shows up in *The Harvard Advocate*. No one really knows where the hell it came from. The kids at Harvard are saying they got permission, which Larry doesn't buy, I can tell, but "the fact of the matter is, Ellen"—this is what he tells me—he says, "I can't imagine it'll be a problem. They've been dropping bundles of these things from the sky all summer long." He said he saw the same letter three months ago in P-town and loved it. Fine, great, I didn't want to hear any more. I told him, "Larry, I don't know what's going on here, this sounds like April Fool's to me, but I'm saying good-bye now." I hung up.

Next day, Larry sends me a copy of *The Advocate*, hand-delivered to my desk, and there it is, just like he said, knock your socks off. I take it in to Capper's office, I said, "Would you get a load of this, Cap? Take a look. You stick this man in Hanover House, you hide him underground for six months and still there's smoke. Could we get a little enthusiasm here?" Capper took a look. "Okay, okay," he says, "I'll talk to sales." He was smiling.

Excerpted from the Editor's Note, THE HARVARD ADVOCATE, *Winter 1974*

. . . And last but oh baby not least . . .

Try as we might, we poor souls of tardy didn't quite catch the sixties head-on. Ours is a generation just a half-step behind the good stuff. We all but missed Hendrix. We all but missed Joplin, and Morrison too. Only the most precocious among us caught the full meaning of Camelot, and even fewer Sputnik. We missed Flower Power and the Motherfuckers, and any of us who saw Daley's butchers in Chicago were probably only watching it on TV. We missed the maharishi, John and Yoko, not to mention Bobby and Dr. King.

Scan down that list three or four more inches and you'll find another sixties treat that came and went before us was the stage work of Eton Arthur Boone, mimic extraordinaire. Yes, indeed. In 1968 *The Downtowner* wrote of Boone's performances that "it's difficult to know which is more entertaining, watching Boone climb inside a celebrity's skin or watching him eat his way back out." Seems that Eton Boone was the classic "you had to be there," and once again we weren't.

Ah, but not so fast. We can't go back in time, it's true, but the Gods have shined down just this once and offered us, the beleagured and punchless class of '75, a stunning glimpse of Boone's most notorious insight. A letter from the man himself has landed softly in our laps here at 21 South Street. Written while he was filming *Heiligenstadt* in England, and addressed to his long-time patron, Vassar English professor Hugh D. Gardiner (*The War with Rupert Brooke*, Chicago University Press, 1972), Boone's letter offers us much more than the suggestion of his legendary cannibalism. It's an actual feast unto itself, and the main course—that we may better sample Boone's epicurean flair—happens to be quite a well-known campus dish. Enjoy.*

---

*The text of the letter appeared in *The Harvard Advocate* exactly as it did in *Harper's Magazine* (see pages 211–15), with the exception that the names James and Nina were supplied as John and Erin by *The Harvard Advocate*.

Hilary Richman

When I got back to San Diego, I'd been expecting to find maybe some letters from E.B. I'd written him a few times when we were away, postcards mostly, but there weren't any. I'd brought back this pair of ivory chopsticks from Kyoto and I'd sent them to him for Christmas. I didn't really expect anything back, but you know, even E.B. acknowledges Christmas presents. All he sent were these little cards of him and his doctor waving at the camera really sarcastically—it went something like, "Eton and The Doctor send Season's Greetings!" exclamation point. They were absurd. I don't know, it depressed me. I was supposed to be looking for a job, but I wasn't. I hated being in San Diego, and I didn't know what was going on with E.B. I got ill, literally physically ill. I was in bed for like a month, and that's when I found out. I was just lying there in my room wallowing when my mom brought up this package from Harvard, from Camille, and it was this fucking *Advocate.*

And at first, you know, I had no idea what it was. Camille had put this note in congratulating me and I didn't know what she meant. But then I saw they had it written on the cover. It said—"A letter from E. A. Boone," and I couldn't believe it. I thought I was going crazy. I looked inside to see if it was some joke or something, but it obviously wasn't—I mean, the way they were treating it and everything, I could tell it was real—and I actually had to get out of bed and lock the door before I could even start reading it.

But I mean, it's ridiculous. It's impossible for me to tell you what that letter was like for me. There was so much to deal with, and it all just seemed surreal, but I guess the biggest part was—I mean, the part that wouldn't go away—was just, I felt so betrayed. I don't know. I don't know if that's the right word, but it's just that I'd trusted E.B. so much, you know? I mean, that sounds weird, but it's true. I mean, with E.B., it's like every time he even looked at you, you were trusting him with your life. Like when we were up in Maine and it was the middle of the night and he'd just be sitting there smoking his cigarette looking at me, I would always want to ask him, you know, "What are you thinking, E.B.? What do you see?" But all he'd ever do was shake his head and smile like it was nothing. You know, so I'd just have to turn over. I'd just think, "Fine, you know, I guess I have to believe him." What else could I do if he was going to act that way? Over and over I would just have to keep telling myself that E.B. wasn't a liar, you know, and that if he really had something to say, he would. I mean, he wouldn't just let me twist, because it was E.B. and he wanted me there.

But I don't know, when I read this letter, I mean it's really like all that trust just fucking blew up in my face. Like everything that I'd been trying so hard to believe just turned out to be some ridiculous delusion that E.B. would give a shit about making me feel better, and I mean, I just hated him, I hated him when I read it, and it wasn't just these things he'd written. I hated him because I felt like I'd been lied to. You know, every time he'd ever tried to calm me down, telling me it's all right and I shouldn't worry, it turns out he'd just been lying through his teeth, because now, you know, I could hold this letter in my hand. I could actually wave it in his fucking face and say, "Look, goddammit, don't tell me it's in my fucking head." I mean, E.B. was writing this shit in England, for Christ's sake, and so I know, every goddamn second we were together, whether it was in Maine or New York or Ibiza, I know he must have had this shit in his head—you know, that I'm some freak, I'm just this perversity— and I couldn't stand it. I mean, I hated him. I just did. I hated him for making Hugh Gardiner the only person he ever talked to. I hated him for not protecting me from this fucking magazine. You know, and I hated him for the way he'd been acting since Katherine died, so scary—I mean, I'd been trying to understand it, and just accepting the way he'd been treating me, but after reading this letter, I didn't give a shit anymore. I mean, fuck him. Fuck him for all of this, for making my whole life feel like just this giant grotesque lie all of a sudden, and making me have to hate, just fucking hate his guts, and he's the only person I ever really loved.

John Kinsey

Hugh's sister died in early January of 1975. Hugh had asked that I come over for the funeral, and it was only in view of his insistence and an uncharacteristic tug in his voice that I felt compelled to do so. Emily had been sick for quite some time, and it certainly hadn't come as a surprise. In many ways, it may have been a blessing, for her—she suffered horribly, despite all that Hugh had done. She'd been completely helpless for over a decade. I flew over at Hugh's request.

He'd withered. Visibly. For the most part, of course, I'd thought it was due to his sister's passing—one less life in the home. But there was something more that plagued him, it was very clear, something nibbling away. Apparently he'd been trying to win Boone over again. He'd been writing him furiously at the clinic, from what I could gather, but he'd received no response and was quite despondent.

The way he chose to demonstrate it. I'd been unpacking my valise my first night there when he came into the guest chamber and said that he had something to show me. He took me by the arm and led me down to his office. He'd set out the sea chest of Boone's letters by his desk, in arm's reach. Without a word, he opened it for me and indicated with trembling hands the most recent postmark, which I must say made me quite uncomfortable. It was dated some time the previous winter, and I knew very well what it was—Eton's letter of renunciation, or denunciation—but here Hugh was presenting it to me as though its finality were some impossible mystery. I looked at Hugh and nodded—"Yes, that's a long time, Hugh"—and he placed it carefully back on top of the heap.

I was very uncomfortable. None of this seemed like any of my affair. Hugh went back to his desk and poured himself another glass of sherry. He looked ghostly. Finally he turned to me and said, "John, you must go see him. Please go see Boone. I must know, why does he not respond?" Ah, I thought to myself, so this is why I've come—to be your legate. Apparently Emily's funeral was only a pretense. I said, "Hugh, man, go see him yourself. I won't be your scout. Enough is enough." And Hugh returned to his chair, and he sunk his body into it and said, "John, I can't. Not like this. I'm too weak. John, please go."

Oh, the decisions we are forced to make as friends. I looked at him there in his dressing gown with his decanter on the table next to him and his lonely sherry glass. I looked at him as honestly as I could, and finally seeing him so alone, alone completely now that Emily was gone, I did see that perhaps his fear wasn't wholly selfish. It seemed like a far more profound dread than that. Every day that Boone did not respond, every day Hugh returned from his mailbox empty-handed, it only confirmed his worry that Boone was in trouble, that he might truly be sick, or insane, or dying, or that drugs were taking his precious mind. Even as it occurred to me, I was convinced that that was Hugh's fear, and that is the reason I decided to go. As a friend, I didn't like the idea of Hugh having to make his only sojourn just to find Boone not Boone.

Amalie Hindemuth

We'd planned on Eton's staying with me in Quogue for a few weeks after he got out, just to use my house as a sort of stepping-stone back into the city. I hadn't seen him at all. I'd been in California, so I didn't really know what to expect, but he actually looked very well. He seemed very calm when I'd picked him up at the clinic, and that whole first few days actually, I feel as though we were living by candlelight out there. The first night I remember we'd made dinner together. He'd just been cutting the vegetables and trying to get better reception on my radio. It was very lovely. I even remember thinking to myself that I hadn't seen him so calm since England really, because he wasn't even being jovial the way he usually was after we hadn't seen each other, being sort of clever and entertaining and things like that. He seemed much more serene.

But the third night, which I'd never forget because it was really so soon after he'd come out, we'd been in the living room reading. Eton had a biography of one of the musicians—it may have been the Schumanns—and I was reading Jane Austen, I think, but we'd just been sitting there gently turning our pages and sipping our tea when we heard a car in the driveway, and we both looked at each other, as if, you know, "Who could that be?" And the car door closed, and these footsteps came up the path and Eton knew immediately, I think. He said, "That's Hilary." And then we heard Hilary knocking and calling, "Hello, hello." I was overcome. I mean, I just knew the last thing in the world Eton needed now was Hilary. It just seemed like a horrible dream. But Hilary sort of burst into the living room unannounced, and I was looking at Eton. I don't think I'd ever seen him so humorless. His face sort of tightened, and he actually excused himself, he went upstairs, so it was just Hilary and me in the living room.

And, you know, this isn't the sort of thing I'm very good at, I'm not a very aggressive person, but I just had to ask Hilary what on earth he thought he was doing there, and he was very pompous with me actually. He said he had something to show Eton, and that he was staying that night. He said he had nowhere else, so I told him that he could, on the couch, but I said that he had to go first thing in the morning, because he hadn't been invited.

But then Eton came back down. He'd put a sweater on, and he seemed very under control. He was very pleasant. He said to Hilary that he and I had been planning to go skating that night, which was true, with an older couple we'd met at the market, and he said that Hilary should come along if he liked. So we all went skating—I mean, I don't think Hilary had much choice, but it was a great bother finding skates for him. I think we must have stopped at at least six different houses in the area asking if anyone had any skates we could borrow, and Eton had ended up leaving his own shoes on this Italian man's porch as collateral or whatever.

But once we got to the pond, it was much better being outside. We could all sort of keep whatever distance we wanted. There was a stick hockey game going on, and this older couple was there. They were wonderful. They'd taught ballroom dancing for years and years, and they showed us their fancy sort of swooping moves on the ice, and then the woman tried to teach them to

Eton. It was very sweet. But Hilary had sort of stayed on the side. He ended up going back to the car early because he said his ankles were breaking, and I know it sounds horrible, but I remember being so relieved. I remember thinking, "Oh, just go, then."

John Kinsey

There was an enormous reception desk in the mansion foyer, and I asked the rather sinister battle-ax who manned it if I might have a word with Eton Boone. She thumbed through an absurdly oversized binder and informed me that Mr. Boone was on what she termed a "provisional leave." I remember I was quite hungry—Hugh had whisked me out of the house in such a hurry that I'd scarcely had time for toast and marmalade—so I suppose I was a bit testy. I demanded to speak with Boone's doctors. She, and I use the term loosely, escorted me to the office of the clinic's director, a wiry jackal of a man whose name I'm overjoyed I can't remember. He explained to me the meaning of this provisional leave. He said that Boone had completed his "project" and that he'd been granted furlough with the possibility of return if he felt he needed more time. Or some sort of revision, I suppose. I asked him if any of this meant he knew where Boone was, and if the answer was yes, would he please tell me.

I don't blame him for asking me at this point who I was, and what right I had to come in there demanding the specifics of his patient's condition. I told him that I was there for a friend of mine, a dear sweet withering man in Fishkill, who, I assured him, cared just as much for his patient's well-being as he or God or anyone. I told him I was there for Hugh Dunleavy Gardiner—I was quite lofty about it—but how well I remember the expression on this mooncalf's face as he recognized the name. Smug. Fascistic. He said, "Mr. Gardiner's been declared off-limits."

Well, that'll teach him, won't it? Hugh, quarantined. I can't imagine a man who deserved such a thing less. Poor old dog, kept himself off-limits. I asked the doctor what on earth any of this could mean, and he explained to me, with noxious arrogance, that it meant that all correspondence between the patient and the civilian—by my life, this was his term—had been provisionally suspended. "Egads, you don't mean to tell me that you've been intercepting his mail!" Oh, Hugh, look what they've done. They've taken your mail. You've been aborted. I was astounded. I asked the doctor if they kept the censored material. Did they practice that much courtesy or was it given to the orderlies for packing? He said there was a file.

To make a long and harrowing argument short, I was on the road by 1:00 P.M. with detailed directions to a place called Quogue, and a bulky manilla envelope, filled with Hugh's letters, riding shotgun. I admit, I felt utterly triumphant. I imagined trumpets and fanfare accompanying me as I sped on my way in Hugh's Falcon, and of course some soothing music too, strings to reassure us all that Boone was well and that his silence had had nothing to do with cruelty or sickness. I'd even considered calling Hugh from the clinic to let him know, but decided it might be best if I saw the letters into Boone's hands, completed my mission, before telling him the news. I suppose it was a good thing I did.

Hilary Richman

Look, I didn't know what I wanted. All I knew was I had to do something. I mean, I'd been basically dying at home. I hadn't been able to eat or sleep or do anything. All I'd been doing was reading this letter over and over and having it torture me, so I'd just gone. And I didn't even know if I wanted to see him—I couldn't make up my mind—but I knew he had to see this magazine, and I wanted to be there, I guess. I don't know. It wasn't some big plan. I mean, I certainly had no intention of staying at Amalie's—you know, when I got there she just kept telling me how much E.B. needed to rest. I basically told her she could go fuck herself—all I wanted to do was give him this thing and get the hell out of there.

Because, you know, I'm not going to lie about it. The idea of E.B.—I mean actually being with him—it scared the shit out of me. I just didn't know what I was going to feel like when I saw him, if I was going to want to tear his eyes out or just start crying, I didn't know. The night I was there at Amalie's we'd gone out to this freezing pond—I had no idea what the hell we were doing—and he'd just been skating around like he was trying to be Hans Brinker or someone—he was a shitty skater—but I was looking at him from the car and I mean, I was just thinking, "God, who the hell is that?" I mean, I was looking at the shape of his head and his shoulders and the way he moved, and I knew it was him, it was E.B., but he'd just come out of this place, and then I would think of this letter—it's like I couldn't put any of it together anymore. He basically scared me to death.

So when we got back that night, right before we all went to bed, I just went up to his room with the magazine, and he was standing there in these long johns trying to balance his shoes on this heater. I just said, "Here," and I put the magazine on the bed. He asked me what it was, but I couldn't even tell him. I just said he should read it and I started to leave, but he stopped me. He said, "You know, I finished the book." And he was just like this little boy, he was like this little kid in his pajamas, and I didn't know what to say. I said, "Oh. Great," and I started to leave again, but he said, "Don't you even want to know what it's called?" So I said, "What?" He said, *"Ruth."* We just looked at each other. I didn't know what I was supposed to say, I felt so separated from him. I said, "That was your mom's name," and he sort of bounced his head around. He said her name was Blue. It was scary. I couldn't stand it. It was like talking to a stranger, so I left.

And I couldn't get to sleep that night. I was just on this couch downstairs, thinking about E.B. upstairs reading this letter. And I was having this fantasy of him coming down, and he would look at me, and I would know it was all right finally, like somehow he'd do something and this whole thing would go away, this feeling I had—I just felt so lonely—but he didn't. I even went up to the top of the stairs and saw that the light under his door was off, so I basically spent all night just crying on this couch into this rotten pillow, and I ate toast and milk at Amalie's kitchen table. I left at like five-thirty in the morning. I drove back to New York.

John Kinsey

By the time I arrived at Miss Hindemuth's house in Quogue, my energy had been somewhat dampened by the circles I had taken to find it. I discovered Eton and Miss Hindemuth in the living room. They were playing backgammon. I actually crept in upon them, and when Eton saw me, I had expected it might give him quite a jolt, or that I might seem like some sort of specter, the ghost of drudgeries past, but in fact from the expression on his face, it looked as though he'd been expecting something like me. I tried to explain my presence as quickly as I could. I told him it was wonderful to see him, wonderful to see him looking so well, but that I'd come with a purpose. And there was a twinge of sadness in that for me, I admit. Coming upon him there, seeing him again, I'd have liked nothing more than to be near him, to be in his presence, without purpose. To visit. To share a *New York Times* with.

But Hugh's letters were heavy on my arm and quite conspicuous. I presented him with the prodigious envelope, and when I explained the delay, that these had been arrested by doctors, I don't think it was a complete surprise to him, either that the doctors had been protecting him, or that Hugh had been writing. As peremptory as Eton may have been in breaking off with Hugh, as clean as he may have wanted the cut, he must have known that Hugh couldn't simply bow his head, "Yes, your majesty," and leave for good. No, there were sure to be struggles, pleas, supplications, and here they were, bulging in a manilla envelope, here to show Eton once and for all that you cannot completely command a man's attention, no.

Miss Hindemuth had excused herself. Eton took the letters back to where he'd been sitting. He opened the envelope and spilled them out onto the backgammon felt. He hardly needed to cut them open to see the romance they contained. Some were thick and others slim, obviously panicked, scribbled off at a late hour when Hugh's imagination had gotten the better of him. Eton showed nothing outwardly, though. Before he actually took any of them up to read, he pointed over to a magazine on a coffee table, and he told me what it was. He explained it very calmly. He said that someone had gotten hold of one of his letters to Hugh, from England. They'd printed it already in a student journal at Harvard and were apparently intent on printing it again in _Harper's Magazine._ I was a bit confused. I said, "With your permission?" He glanced down at the postmarks of Hugh's letters. He said, "Nope," and lifted his eyebrows at me.

I was having great difficulty reading Eton's attitude. I looked at him searchingly for some sign of how this had affected him, but there was no hint of venom or pain anywhere in his expression. He looked down at the letters before him, as though the answer might lie there, and he said, "Do you know if Hugh knows anything about this?" And I'd love to have been able to tell him for certain that he didn't, but with all those letters clumped there on the table, and the urgency with which I'd been summoned from London, I wasn't altogether sure. Maybe Hugh did know something. I told Eton that perhaps he should read what I'd brought, and he agreed, but before he began, he turned to me and nodded at the magazine in my hands. He said, "You may read it if you like," and his intention was completely obscure to me. Eton started reading Hugh's letters, and perhaps from some desire to maintain a kind of balance in the room, that we should either both be reading or neither of us, I opened the magazine and found the published letter.

But as I began to read, it was something like the mental analogue to sniffing sour milk. My mind gagged at the words. A letter from Boone to Hugh, I simply couldn't read it. I know there was some mention of Paul Cézanne in the first line, and I remembered taking Eton to an exhibit at the National Gallery, but I simply couldn't press my eyes through it. I had to put the magazine down, but even as I'd survived my own shamefully extreme reaction, I began to feel absolutely sick for Hugh. It dawned on me slowly what this letter, published here for all the world to see, actually meant. The letters were all Hugh had. How had he let them out of his sight?

I looked up at Eton, wondering if he was aware, or sharing the queer intensity of my moment, and I was amazed, I can say, by what I saw. It was an impression, but absolutely striking. He was sitting in the chair there, upright, struggling to keep the bundle of Hugh's letters on his lap, and the frown on his face was so peculiar. It was a strange bewilderment. He held the letters almost as though they had nothing to do with him, as though he'd been laden with the correspondence of someone else, like a student of history, or a grandson who finds the love letters of a long-dead relative—he was interested, fascinated, I can even say, but also distant and slightly awed by them. It was simply unmistakable, as I watched him there, that Eton had changed. The difference was in his eyes, and not by any means for the worse, because they weren't dumb or slow. They just didn't seem to have quite the same focus.

He looked up at me. He startled me actually, and I felt I should have a question for him. I asked if there were any explanation yet in what he'd read, and he said no, no direct explanation, but he gestured at them all, and there were so many, so many pages and words, he said, "This may be explanation enough." I was suddenly overcome with the desire to leave, to let him go through the whole bundle without my peering over his shoulder. I stood up from my seat and told him that I was going. I said that I thought I should get the letter to Hugh as quickly as possible, just in case he didn't know. Eton said yes, but he looked a bit startled. I think he was surprised at the power that all this still seemed to wield over two old men. I didn't choose to explain myself. I gathered my hat and coat, and took the journal from the table. He smiled. He said, "You've come an awfully long way just to save me postage, John. Will I see you again?" I said that he would, of course he would.

Hilary Richman

I was staying at this apartment on the Upper East Side that belonged to a friend of my mother's who was in Europe. I basically sat there in this woman's house all day long just waiting for E.B. to call. You know, I'd left him the number and my address, and I certainly wasn't going to call him. I mean, I didn't feel like

I should have to. But it was something like five days and I still hadn't heard a thing, I was going crazy, but then finally he called. He'd left a message with this woman's answering service when I was out getting food or something, so I had to call him back.

It was horrendous. He said he'd read the letter, but he didn't go into it at all. He told me the reason he hadn't called before was that he'd wanted to find out exactly what had happened and what the whole legal situation was. He just had all these facts. He told me about *Harper's,* and he started explaining to me how if we wanted to stop them from reprinting it, he was going to have to deal with the people at Harvard because they're the ones who'd claimed rights—you know, some legal ramification bull-shit—and I was just confused as hell. I had no idea why he was acting this way, but I asked him what he thought he was going to do—I mean, about the whole *Harper's* thing—and he just gave me this really considered response. He said he'd been talking to people, these lawyers or something, and they'd all decided it would just attract more attention if we tried to stop the letter. So E.B. said he thought maybe the best thing was just to let it go, but then he says, "I'm really sorry about you and Hugh." He said, "I'm sorry the two of you had to get dragged into this."

It, like, stunned me. I didn't know what to say. I just felt like, is he out of his mind? That letter didn't have one fucking thing to do with Hugh Gardiner. How could he say that? I mean, Hugh Gardiner, he just *reads* that letter, he just gets it in his fucking mailbox, what difference does it make to him if it's published? I wanted to say, "Jesus Christ, E.B., Hugh Gardiner's not getting dragged into anything. No one's getting dragged into anything. You wrote a letter, and I just want to know what the hell it means." I mean, shit, was that asking so much?

But I couldn't say it. I couldn't even talk to him at all, I just wanted to get off the phone, I was so pissed. I said, "Look, E.B., if all you care about is someone reading this shit, I mean, if you just want to protect me and your little gimp friend, then you can stop worrying your little head—I mean, about me, because I don't give a shit." I said, "If you want it in *Harper's,* put it in *Harper's.* Be my guest." And I think I just slammed the phone down in his ear. I mean, I was completely obliterated.

John Kinsey

I'd called Hugh from a roadside inn and told him I was coming
back. I'd told him Boone was well and so when I reached his
home, everything seemed brighter. There was a skip in Hugh's
step, and even Carnegie was lapping at my feet like a pup as I
walked in. Hugh'd kept dinner for me. He served lamb chops—
Hugh has always been under the impression that I like lamb
chops. But it wasn't until we'd sat down and poured the wine that
he said to me, "I understand that he's in good health and spirits,
John, but what kept the boy from responding? Was it the doctors?"

He was so animated, he was so alive that I didn't know quite
how to treat him—he seemed to have completely forgotten the
fact that Boone had cut him off, which puzzled me. But I told him
that yes, indeed, it had been the doctors that had retained his
letters. I told Hugh that he was considered a rather dangerous
commodity at Hanover, and that he probably couldn't have gotten word to Boone with a carrier pigeon. Which delighted him.
He was carving and chewing his food with embarrassing energy.
"How odd," he said. "How odd, John. Do you think I should
write his doctors about their reasons?" Oh, Hugh. I told him no,
he needn't worry with their kind, and he agreed, nodding, grunting, pouring himself another glass—Boone was free now, that's
all that mattered, so what purpose would it serve?

It was very difficult to look at, Hugh so cuddly, and as I
watched his mind churn with the new ideas he could send off to
Boone, what lovely blossoms the new flowering of their relationship might bring, I resigned myself to the fact that I would have
to tell him about the magazine. Clearly he didn't know. I took out
my copy and slid it across the table to him, face down. I said,
"You should turn that over."

He was impatient. He said, "John, don't ask me to read and eat
at the same time." He asked me not to play games with him, and
how I wished I could have obliged. But I urged him to look at it.
Finally he did. His curiosity was too keen. He pushed his chair

out from the table and picked up the magazine. He saw Boone's name on the cover. He flipped to the page, and it was heartbreaking having to watch the slow transformation in his eyes, from confusion to absolute horror. They lit with fear the moment he fully understood. He put his hands to his lips and looked up at me, and perhaps it was the expression on his face, but I felt compelled to speak. I said that before he fell full-fledged into his reaction, he should know two things—first, that I had chosen, for reasons of my own, not to read the letter, and second, that *Harper's Magazine* was apparently intent on printing it again in an upcoming issue.

Oh, to look at him. You cannot imagine, after such a peak, how sheer the precipice. He was bewildered, he was saddened, he was frightened to death. "Do you know if he plans to do anything?" he asked. I told him I didn't know. I wanted desperately to ask him how this had happened, but I could see that he was in no condition to answer me. He'd taken it all in rather quickly. His elbows were up on the table. He'd removed his glasses and was rubbing his temples, his hands were trembling. "Oh, John, what have I done?" He looked up at me and there were tears in his eyes. "Is he angry?" he asked. I didn't know what to say. I had an impulse to assuage him with what I'd seen out on Long Island, that Eton hadn't seemed angry at all, but as I looked at Hugh, shaking, absolutely electric with fret, I wondered if that's what he really wanted to hear. I decided no. For the moment at least let him think that Boone was outraged. Let him think Boone was writhing.

We sat there another minute or so until he stood up. He said, "You'll have to forgive me, John, but I really must excuse myself." He got up from the table slowly. He left his plate and wandered off to the den. I was paralyzed with sympathy and indecision. I left Miss Hindemuth's address on top of the journal.

Hugh Gardiner

I make no excuses for myself. I can only tell you that it is very difficult sometimes to resist the temptation to share what we cherish with others. I had shown certain letters to students, I admit. I had read portions to them, passages relevant to the things we would discuss. I believe it was very helpful for them to hear the words of someone whose career they were familiar with, and to see the terms in which a contemporary artist actually thinks. It was never my practice, though, to give the letters out, to show them off, or to reveal what I considered to be the more personal passages. It's simply that over the course of such a lengthy correspondence, one is bound at moments to lose sight of which passages are appropriate to share, and which passages deserve privacy. If I ever confused the two, and I know that I did, then I was wrong, it was an abuse. I was wrong.

I only wished at the time that I had been able to tell Boone these things, but I thought I'd said too much already. I felt that I'd exposed myself in the letters I'd written him over the winter, and it didn't seem there was much more I could say on my behalf. I preferred relying on his sensitivity. I sent him a very short note telling him that I had learned what had happened and that I was very, very sorry. Then I waited.

Harry Hampton

He'd come back into the city from Amalie's in around mid-February. He was living in the Chelsea Hotel, and I don't think anybody really saw him at all. No one knew what his plans were or what he was doing. Late March I started getting messages at work. It was like he timed my departures. I'd get back from lunch and find these pink slips saying, Ho Chi Minh called. Tony Perkins is in town. Nanette Fabray wants to have lunch with you. I'd been slow getting back to him, though. I don't know how long it was, until one morning he just showed up without calling. He had a Herman's shopping bag with him full of old clothes and a fungo bat sticking up. He was taking them to the Salvation Army, and he said his publisher had been pestering him about the jacket photo, but he didn't want to use some glossy. I told him there was this Korean kid in the Sports Department, Gi Min, just out of college, who used to sit up there all day waiting for people to tell him what to do. We went up there looking for him and he was playing chess with himself. Boone came up behind him, stood right over him and yelled, "Min! What the hell do we pay you for?" The kid nearly wet his pants.

Anyway, he said he'd be happy to do it, so we all went up to Central Park together. We actually took a baseball with us from Gallo's desk, his Babe Dahlgren autographed, and on the way down in the elevator, Boone pulled these two old mitts out of his shopping bag. They looked like they'd fallen behind a refrigerator someplace. Boone said he'd got them at a yard sale for fifty cents. He said he couldn't pass it up.

So we went up to the park. It was probably the first decent day of the year, and I remember flipping the ball back and forth up Sixth Avenue. We got hot dogs at the Plaza fountain and then went up to the zoo, then out by the bandshell. Boone and I played catch while Gi set the light level, and that's why Boone looks like he just ran a marathon in the photo. I have about thirty other pictures from that afternoon. We got pictures of his swing, and there's one with him getting good wood on it. My hand is coming in the side, holding the ball up against the bat. There's one where we're both just standing there and he's got his arm around my shoulder, I look like I'm with some great aunt I never met before, and I always thought it was a funny picture because I think we got on film the only time the two of us ever made physical contact.

Joe Boone

Anne picked up. It was early on a Saturday morning and we keep the phone on Anne's side of the bed. She didn't recognize him. She just told me it was some man who wanted to speak to Joe Boone. I was still groggy, I think I just said, "Joe Boone," and his voice comes over, three thousand miles away, and I feel like I haven't heard it in a hundred years, but it's the most familiar thing I've ever heard in my life. He says, "Joe Boone? Eton Boone." Nearly gave me a heart attack. I had to sit up. Anne had gone into the bathroom. I moved to the edge of the bed, and Eton started asking me how I was and what was going on. We were talking back and forth, but finally I had to say, because I didn't know what else he'd be calling about, I said, "Does this mean you're finished? Are you done with the book?" And he kind of laughed. He said, "I've been done with the book for a while now." And then he said, "I've been thinking about maybe coming out there. I want to see you."

I think I just held the phone. There are some things you hear, you've dreamed them long enough, you figure they're never going to happen, this thing is just going to torture me for the rest of my life. But he's on the phone with me now. He's said the book's done and he wants to come out and see me—he says, "Is that okay?"—and I realize, you know, it's just hearing his voice. It's not even what he's saying. He could have called up and said, "The cow jumped over the moon, Dad," and I'd have listened, because every word, I realize the thing that's been scaring me isn't this book. What's been scaring me is the idea that I'm never going to hear his voice again. Maybe we'll just be acting like strangers the rest of our lives. That's what's scary. But now he's on the phone with me. He's called me up and he says he wants to come home.

Anne had come out of the bathroom. She was in her robe, and Eton and I were wrapping it up. It wasn't a long call. I was telling him we'd fix up the room. I must have been ear to ear. Anne said, "Is he coming back?" and I nodded. I nodded like crazy. She was squeezing my arm, and Eton said, "Is that Anne there? Can I talk to her?" I looked at her and said, "He wants to talk to you." She took the phone—you should've seen the expression on her face. She said, "Hello, Eton." She was so happy. I was holding her, we were huddled around the phone, and I couldn't really hear what he was saying. I couldn't make out all the words, but it was something about cats—we don't have cats—but he was telling her to please feed the cats, something crazy like that, and she was laughing and saying she would. She was crying. He even made her write it down. She had the pencil and the paper, and she was writing down, "Cod liver oil for Claude and Fred," and she was wiping her eyes. And I'm telling you, we got off that phone, we said good-bye, I was out of my mind happy. We opened up all the windows in the house, we just aired the whole place out. We went downstairs, had the radio going, music, and Anne put on some coffee. I made us some blueberry waffles and bacon, and we stayed in our bathrobes all day, just talking. We had a lot to talk about.

Hugh Gardiner

I was in my dining room, settled down before a grapefruit with the Sunday *Times*. I'd only recently let my housekeeper go, so I was still adjusting to preparing my own meals. I was eating my grapefruit when the doorbell rang. I'm certain I took longer than I might have, and I was wondering who could be in such a hurry on a Sunday morning in early April, but I recall I did not look through the peephole as perhaps I should have. I simply opened the door to find him.

I must have had a rather alarmed expression on my face, because even he looked a bit startled. Bashful, though, and I remember he was careful to keep my eye. He was wearing a gray sweatshirt with a collar underneath, and blue jeans. He was dressed very comfortably, and there was an envelope under his arm. My first thought as he extended his hand to me was that he'd come unaccompanied. He means to be here. I invited him in, and it was a bit awkward at first. I could offer him little but half a grapefruit, which he refused. He'd eaten. I gave him a brief tour of the downstairs, the living room, the dining room, the parlor. He walked about them all gazing, and I could see that he was comparing everything he saw, including myself, to the things he'd been imagining all these years. He conveyed the aspect almost of a newlywed husband. It was a strange charm, and as I looked at him standing in front of the photographs in my hall, I must tell you that I was at a loss.

I showed him into my study. He asked where I kept his letters and we took the sea chest down from its shelf. I told him it was locked, in view of what had happened, but I offered to open it for him. He only looked at the lid. He knocked on it and said, "No, they're yours," and I wanted to tell him how grateful I was that he would say so, but that it wasn't really true. I said, "No, no, they are yours, despite what anyone else may say. These letters are yours, and they are gifts to me." And I told him that when I passed on, he should reclaim them.

He smiled. He looked embarrassed that my gesture had had to seem so grand. He had his foot propped up on the arm of my chair, and I could see his reflection in the glass of the painting that hangs above my cabinets. I was so slow to fathom his presence. He took the manilla envelope out from underneath his arm and placed it on top of the chest, and for a moment, I thought that they might be the letters I'd sent him at Hanover, that he was returning them. But he looked at me and smiled. He said, "No, I still have those. I'll keep those." He patted the package with the tips of his fingers, then he stood up. He said that the *Harper's* people had asked if they should change my name in the letter, but that he'd told them not to. He said he didn't see that there was anything either of us had to be ashamed of. John and Erin's names would be left out, but mine would remain. He asked if that was all right, and I said it was.

Then he said he was going. I offered him tea, but I think we both understood that perhaps it was better he should leave quickly, this once. We shook hands at the door, and then said good-bye, and he went off down my path swiping at the forsythia as he passed.

I was still in quite a state as I went to the kitchen and poured myself a fresh cup of tea. I returned directly to my study, to the envelope which he had left there, and opened it. Inside was a manuscript, some two-hundred pages, but not, I could tell, the one he'd been writing at Hanover. This was not *Ruth*, and it's not a work of his that anyone else has yet known about, I don't believe. The manuscript was untitled—it merely said, "For H. G." on the cover page, and the dates, March 11 through 21. It was the book of letters he'd embarked on before Katherine died, the chess piece tales he'd left off but had apparently taken up again, for eleven days late that winter, and finished at once. That afternoon just after he'd left I read it the whole way through and I could never express my emotion as I read, I never could, but that simple book was an assurance, I can tell you, every bit as clear as the one he'd offered by coming to deliver it in person, that there was still so much generosity in him, and so very much creativity. It is his imagination cut free finally, with nothing there to ground it or disturb it anymore. It was only the beginning.

I've never shown the book to anyone else, though. It's something he gave to me quietly, and something I've tried to keep just as quietly, not, I think, from selfishness or pride that it's mine—I hope that's not so—but there are some things we simply cherish too much, some things we occasionally need to keep and know are ours and ours alone.

Hilary Richman

I hadn't even known he'd been in the city. Apparently he'd just holed himself up in the Chelsea Hotel and disconnected his phone, but it was like two weeks before this *Harper's* thing was going to come out. It was a Tuesday, and I was sleeping. I'd been busing tables at night at this restaurant on Irving Place, but E.B. actually came by in person, and he said he was going to try to go to this baseball game. He said it was Opening Day and did I want to come along. I was completely freaked out. He was still acting like nothing was going on, but obviously he was thinking something. I said fine, I'd never been to one, so we went out on the subway. It took like ten hours, and I still couldn't tell what he was thinking. He'd brought the *Post* along and he was reading all these articles about ballplayers to me. I just thought, you know, maybe he just wants to have this day, you know? Maybe he just wants to try or something, so I tried to relax, but I couldn't. I mean, I would see him look at someone on the subway, these transvestites came on and E.B. was watching them and I mean, just the way he looked, it was still E.B., goddammit, whether he was trying to read these stupid articles or not.

So we got out there finally after ten hours, and we were about to buy tickets from some scalper. E.B. was haggling with him, and I just said, "Stop," you know, "Stop." I mean, I couldn't go in. I didn't know what was going on, and he knew—we couldn't possibly just go to some baseball game together, I'm not just this hunky-dory pal. So I said I was going back to the city, and he said, "Look, we can talk if you want." That was like the first real thing he said the whole day, and I don't know, I didn't want to fuck up his idea or anything, but we just had to. We had to talk.

But we couldn't even find a place at first. This stadium is in this land of parking lots, and there were still a million people trying to get in, so we just wandered around until we found these police barricades, and we were leaning up against them. He wouldn't even look at me. He was just sitting there in this floppy tennis hat waiting for me to say something. I just said, "Please, E.B., I just want to know what the hell is going on with us." I mean, I told him, I said, "This letter is coming out and I still don't know what it means. You know, I read it every day, and it makes me sick, and it makes me sad and it makes me mad, but I don't know what to think because you won't tell me. Is that letter the truth? Does it still mean anything?"

We were just standing there and you could hear all these people in the stadium like these waves, and E.B. just had his arms crossed. I didn't think he was going to answer. We just stood there, but then he was looking up at these trains waiting up on this track, and he said, "Hilary, do you love me?"

God. I was so confused. I just looked at him. I said, "Of course I do, E.B. I mean, you know I do, more than anything in the whole world. Why do you think I keep coming back?" He was just standing there. He had his hand on his face, and I was like, "What? Tell me. Tell me for once." He was looking at his feet. He said, "I think you come back here to see if I love you." And he said, "I don't blame you. When I read that letter, I want to know too," and he looked at me and he said, "but I've got to tell you, I don't know the answer." He said, "I don't really know." And I looked at him, I was dying inside, and he said, "But do you love me?"

It was just so hard. It was so weird to hear because it had always been the other way around, you know? I'd never even thought about do I love him, just because it seemed so obvious. But he was looking at me now, and his eyes—I mean, there was this look on his face, and I just didn't know—why did he have to take on everything like that? Why couldn't he ever see anything nice? I mean, I could be happy, but he was just looking at me and I wanted to cover his eyes. You know, stop. "Jesus, if it's going to do *that* to you"—I told him—"then don't look."

But God, I think that's the hardest thing I ever had to do, you know, having to tell E.B. to stop. It was the hardest thing in the world, because I'd just always felt like I was the only person who ever said it was okay, you know? I was the one person who told

E.B., "It's all right. Be in me. You don't have to have your rules with me." I mean, it's like the only thing I ever really wanted. But now just because I'm the one person who ever had the guts and loved him that much, now I can see, he can't even stand looking at me anymore. His eyes. I mean, it was in his eyes, all this shit that he's always had to deal with, the stuff he sees in people that's just been fucking him up and cleaving these hunks out of him for his whole life, it was all just me now, I'd just become this monster to him. So when he asks me this question, "Do you love me?" I want to say, "God. Yes!" I want to say, "More than anything," but he's looking at me, and what does that mean? What does that mean, yes I love you. Does it mean I'm supposed to stay around and just be this thing that I know is torturing him? I mean, shit, I couldn't do that. I didn't want that. I just said, Okay, I'll go. Of course I'll go, I do love you. Why didn't you tell me to leave? Tell me to get the fuck out of your face if I'm making you so miserable.

I'm sorry. I told him I would leave. I told him that I would go somewhere, and when I figured out where, I wouldn't even tell him if he didn't want to know. I said I could just leave him there. I said, "Why don't you go see your game?" and he said okay. I don't know what he was feeling, but I left him, I walked away. I had to go up these stairs for the subway, and when I got to the platform I looked down once to see him. I wasn't going to do it, but he was talking to this man in a windbreaker about buying himself a ticket. And I didn't even want him to look up or do anything. I didn't need some look from him or some picture of him. My fucking thoughts go through my fucking head, these little ideas I have, and there isn't a single one going through my head that E.B. doesn't hear.

XI

Home

Toddy Boone

He actually wasn't home for that long. Two weeks and two days. But Dad wanted to get him a present for coming back. He really wanted to do something nice, and I'd seen an ad in the paper for a used motorcycle. Dad said, "Great, a big, giant dangerous toy." We went over to this woman's house on Balboa Road. She was selling it for her boyfriend, and we bought it right away, and a helmet with leopard spots. I don't think we'd have done it if it hadn't happened so fast. I rode it home about ten miles an hour and we put it in the garage, under a bedsheet.

The first thing we did when Eton got back was take him out there to look at it. He was pretty excited. It surprised him. He said he was going to be the next Steven Kiley. We had a family dinner that night, and it was actually a lot of fun. We stayed up pretty late in the living room, all four of us.

But it seemed like he left again so quickly. He'd been riding the bike everywhere, and he'd wear the leopard helmet indoors watching TV. He loved the helmet. We played golf, the three of us, and he even wore it on the course. Dad said he thought we'd hit the spot. But Eton said he wanted to give the bike a real run. He called it his hog. He said he and his hog were itching to hit the road. He never even got an operator's license. He just went. He left on a Friday. He packed some watercolors and a painting block in an old knapsack. He said he wanted to go back down to New Mexico to see some of the places he'd gone with Mom. He said it was real good country for a man and his hog, and he'd be back in a week or so, which I think he meant, because I know he wanted to get back for my birthday. He said he was going down there to get me a present.

Anne Richman Boone

I was in the kitchen, making sourdough bread. I had just come back from the library. I had taken out a copy of a book by Leon Uris that I have never read to this day. The phone rang. It was the police from New Mexico. The first thing they asked me was whether I was related to him, to Eton. Was I his mother? And I said yes. I have always been glad of that.

Toddy Boone

He was outside a place called Red Hill, just across the border from Arizona. He'd actually spent the night in Arizona someplace. The motel owner there said he'd got up early in the morning and paid and left. I guess it was about six o'clock when it happened. It was a very cold morning and Eton was still getting used to the feel of the bike. He skidded for some reason. The truck driver said there may have been an animal, but there were marks. He might have just been going too fast, but the bike shot across the yellow line. He nearly made it all the way off the road, but the truck was coming from the opposite direction—it swerved away from the yellow line too, so they hit flush on.

Anne Richman Boone

I didn't want to call Joe. I didn't even think of calling Joe. I called for a taxi. I didn't want to drive. The taxi took about twenty minutes, and I'm not sure what I did. I think I may have turned on the television set. I know it was on when we got home later. I took the taxi down. It was a very hot day. And when I got there, Joe was in the station lobby for some reason. He was out there and he had a bottle of apple juice in his hand, and he was talking to a young man with a clipboard. I don't know the man's name. But Joe left him fairly quickly when he saw me. I remember I felt that I should have had something for him, like a sandwich or a sweater. But all I had was my purse.

I don't know how I said it exactly, but I told him Eton was dead. I know I said dead first. I didn't want to say Eton had been in an accident and was dead because I didn't want Joe to hope for a moment. And I hadn't wanted to do it in front of everyone, I wanted Joe alone. But I had to tell him. He went straightaway out the doors. There was a bench out to the left of the doors, on some grass, next to a trash can. Joe just took his bottle and he threw it down on the grass and he tried to stomp it, he began trying to stomp it with his shoe. And then he just collapsed on the bench. You know, I don't even know where certain sounds come from.

Harry Hampton

It was incredibly humid. A very hazy heat, thick. The tent they'd put up didn't do a damn thing. Not that many people were there—twenty, twenty-five, all fanning. I stood next to Max Kleinman in the back. He had an umbrella with him. Levi and Joe and Anne and Toddy were together, standing near the head of the grave. Harold Odeon came. Peter Finney was there, and Amalie spent the whole service on his shoulder. Liz Rubin was there. And Kinsey, from England, and Hugh Gardiner, of course—I was surprised at how solid he looked. There were aunts and uncles I didn't know who were sprinkled around the outside. Hilary did not come. Amalie had spoken to him and urged him to, but he'd said he wanted to mourn alone, which was a relief for us all, I'm sure.

It was a strange funeral. It was so delicate. You know, everyone has their own idea, their own reasons for coming and standing there and watching Boone get lowered into the ground, but I don't think anyone wanted to leave a real stamp or mark. The priest was very brief and gave his service in Latin, and there'd been no eulogy. I've just never felt such a strange connection to people. It was like being connected by cobwebs. No one wanted to move. No one wanted to say anything. The most you could have said—I would have told them, "Just keep your heads down, folks. Look at anyone else here, it'll kill you."

Levi Mottl

Joe told me the day of the funeral, we were being driven back in a limousine, just Joe and I and Harry, and he said to both of us that the instant he was told, it just sort of flashed before him, the picture of Eton careening toward the truck on his motorcycle. It was how Eton had gone into it. I don't think Joe thought Eton had deliberately driven his motorcycle into a truck. What got him was that last moment, where Eton must have known that he would hit, and Joe said he was almost certain that Eton must have let himself go, really thrown himself into the truck head on, just to make sure that the impact was as hard and complete as it could have been. It was that moment of seeing what's going to kill you and lunging at it, that was the moment in Eton's life, his last, that haunted Joe. He said it was the first thing he thought of after he'd been told, and it was what he woke up to every day.

Hugh Gardiner

He'd left no will, of course, but I had mentioned to Harry Hampton the meeting that Boone and I had had in Fishkill, and he saw to it that soon after I returned home, I received a package of my letters. It was very kind of him. I keep them with Boone's, and with the manuscript he gave me. I don't take any of them out any more, though. The chest is locked—it has been since his death—and sealed tight.

But knowing that the letters and his book are there, that a great part of my past rests there on my closet shelf, was great solace, and is. Having to open the chest and look through them—it's not so much to read the words, the words which I remember well, as to see them, and consider the hand that laid them down—I had always known that that would cause me to grieve too much.

Harry Hampton

I remember the day I first saw a copy in a store window, Brentano's. It was fall. I was walking uptown in the late afternoon, and the cover just caught my eye. Simple, a cutout horizon and the word *Ruth*. I didn't want to see it. I didn't want to see it on Fifth Avenue. They had the jacket photo on posterboard, and they'd put a black border around it with stenciled lettering, his name and the years, 1947–1975. You know, part of me wanted to storm in there and take down the posterboard, rip it up, buy out all their copies, just keep it from Amalie's eyes, keep it from Joe Boone's eyes, keep it from mine. Just get the ghost the hell out of that window.

But there was another part of me, the part that eventually prevailed I guess, that saw all of us, anyone who'd been at the funeral, anyone who'd known him, all wandering around Manhattan or the West Coast, just creeping all over the world with our own lonely ideas about a friend we'd lost. And from the grave, he'd sent a note, just something for us to think about, so however separate and lonely we may have felt, we could all carry his book around in our hand and wave it at each other when we wanted company.

From RUTH, by Eton Arthur Boone

By the time we reached our neighborhood, I'd broken my last promise to myself. My mother and I hadn't spoken for hours. The shadows passed over our faces quietly in imperfect patterns and they made me queasy. When we pulled in, my throat was thick and I had a bad taste. We'd been somewhere so far away, the house seemed stodgy and dumb. It was violet. The lights from inside were a garish yellow, and as the station wagon tugged to a halt, I could even see my father in the living room, sitting in front of the television's pale blue glow. My mother glanced over at me and put her hand on the nape of my neck as she tapped the horn lightly twice.

I took the keys from the ignition and got out. By the time I'd opened the back door of the car, my father was walking stiffly up the pathway and my mother was going to him. He hugged her and looked at me without worry and without dividing his attention. They walked over to me, to where I'd set down the lightest bags. My father picked one up with his arm set on my mother's waist. I told him that it was okay, I would take the rest. They walked up the path to the front door together, and I took the bags in through the garage. I returned the paint boxes to the studio and brought our suitcases upstairs. I left my mother's outside her door and went to my room.

It smelled stale. The air was empty and lonely, and I sat on my bed without moving. I wondered whether I should go downstairs and join them. I could hear they'd gone into the kitchen to get themselves something to drink and that they were back in the living room now, on the couch. I heard my father say, "Let me turn off the TV." His left arm was around her, and his chest pulled up high and jutting out like a fat man's stomach. They'd sit and say nothing, and he would know it was fine.

I looked around my room at the mayonnaise jar of marbles on my bookshelf and the crate of wood blocks by the window. They seemed childish, and I imagined them staring back at me confused, as if they'd finally given up, figured me for lost, and had begun waiting for other little boys. I went over and put the jar in my closet. I left the crate, but tomorrow I would take them into my brother's room.

My father knocked just as I'd begun to unzip my suitcase. I hadn't heard him. "Son," he said. "Are you coming down?" He stayed behind the door and waited.

"You can come in." He pushed it halfway open and took one step inside.

"Are you going to come down? Your mother and I were just going to have a drink in the living room before going to bed." He looked so genuine. He looked at me with neither caution nor urging, and as I looked back at him, I realized I must have been doing the same. He said, "You tired from the trip?"

"A little."

"You just want to unpack and go to sleep?" I nodded. "You want me to bring you something to drink?"

"No," I said. "I've got a new way of making a Walter Brennan."

"They make those different down there?"

"I figured out a new way."

"Are you sure you couldn't tell me right here, and I'll go get you one? We have vanilla."

His questions weren't nagging me the way they usually did. After so long away they even seemed welcome, and I considered letting him go down to fix me the drink, but I heard my mother coming upstairs. I heard her open the bathroom door. She would be putting her hair up, rubbing cream on her face, massaging it into her cheeks and forehead and then down onto her shoulders and hands. I didn't want him to have to go downstairs while she got ready for bed.

"No, I'll get it when I need it. I'll show you in the morning."

"All right then." He stepped back into the hallway and began to pull the door with him. "If I don't see you again before you go to sleep, or even if I do, welcome home." He shifted his weight from the knob back onto the frame. "You know, your brother tried to stay up for you. He made it to eleven o'clock." And I knew my father had carried him upstairs, with my brother's neck flung back, pretending. He'd tucked my brother in and sat by the bed an extra moment to say good night, to see if my brother would smile, to watch his eyelids flutter.

"Good night, Dad." He pulled the door with him but left it just open. I took a dirty sock from my suitcase and wrapped it around both knobs to soften the slam as I shoved the door shut in its frame. I turned off the light and went back to my bed. I lay on top of the covers, looking up at the ceiling.

I thought about my father sitting on his own bed, waiting for my mother to finish in the bathroom, and the way all of his worries would melt when he heard the bathroom door open and saw her coming down the hallway in her cotton nightgown. She would sit next to him, fresh and smooth from the cream she'd put on, the fragrance of peace and safekeeping. For the first time in weeks, I would fall asleep without it.

I heard her pass outside. She knocked but I didn't answer. She said, "Thank you, Eton, for coming with me." I didn't say anything. "I love you," she said. I just lay there and waited. I heard her feet padding down to her room, only seven steps, and the door close.

Bed was simpler at home, alone. The questions wouldn't hover as close tonight, I could tell, and they probably never would again. There wouldn't be the endless resolves keeping me from sleep, and my heart beating, thumping in the bed next to hers, as I came so close to telling her what we'd done. Our secret was safe tonight, my father's and mine. She was with him. She was sitting down beside him and setting the clock, and I could feel him waiting. She would pull back the covers, they'd climb underneath and hold each other. All of his miseries would fall on water and sink as she held him. He could touch her and forget. And as I thought of him there, safe again, if only for the briefest time, I wondered if I had been allowed to go back and paint flat landscapes and slabs of color with my mother for the rest of my life, whether I would have gone. Lying there so near the gentle ebb and flow of my father's mind, I knew that I probably couldn't.

Chronology of the life of Eton Arthur Boone

1947	*August 7*	Eton Arthur Boone born to Ruth Sullivan Boone and Joe Boone in San Diego, California
1959	*December*	Ruth Sullivan Boone diagnosed as having cancer
1960	*June*	EAB and Ruth Sullivan Boone's painting trip to Southwest
1961	*December 21*	Ruth Sullivan Boone dies
1966	*May–December*	EAB travels in Europe
1967	*January*	EAB joins Ratliffe Theatre Company in England, headed by Peter Finney
	February	makes stage debut as Dumby in Oscar Wilde's *Lady Windermere's Fan*
	June	moves to New York
	July	makes comedy debut at Jes' For Laffs
	July 25	Joe Boone marries Anne Richman in San Diego
	September	EAB begins the exposures
	December 8	exposure of Richard Burton
1968	*January*	EAB begins correspondence with Hugh Gardiner
	February 4	exposure of Jack Kerouac
	February 22	exposure of J. Edgar Hoover
	March 7	exposure of Janis Joplin
	March 14	exposure of Syd Barrett
	August	begins work on the comedy-variety program, "The Hank Piedmont Show"

	September 19	the Glenn Hupert incident at Jes' For Laffs
1969	*May 9*	Jes' For Laffs' fifth anniversary party
	June	EAB moves to England with Erin Hirt
	August	begins painting for British detective series, "Color by Numbers"
	November	writes first episode for "Color by Numbers"
1970	*Summer*	EAB writes screenplay for *Heiligenstadt* (with Carlo Esteban)
1971	*January 23*	shooting begins on *Heiligenstadt*
	September 11	shooting completed
	December	EAB moves back to America
1972	*January*	EAB moves to Standish, Maine, writes the play, *Studies*
	Fall	EAB moves to New York
1973	*March 18*	*Studies* opens at Brandimore Theatre in New York City with Katherine Odeon as Mrs. Singer
	Fall	EAB begins work on "Chess Pieces"
	December 31	Katherine Odeon dies
1974	*Spring*	EAB abandons "Chess Pieces"
	Summer	goes to Ibiza
	Fall	enters Hanover clinic in Sagaponack, Long Island; writes *Ruth*
	December	*The Harvard Advocate* publishes letter from EAB to Hugh Gardiner from November, 1970
1975	*January*	EAB leaves Hanover
	Spring	*Harper's Magazine* reprints 1970 Boone-Gardiner letter
	April	EAB returns to San Diego
	May 6	Eton Arthur Boone dies in Red Hill, New Mexico
	August	*Ruth* published

Acknowledgments

Boone would not have been possible without the support, assistance, and generosity of many, many people. We only hope that they forgive the modesty of their billing, but space does not permit the kind of attention that their acknowledgment surely deserves. Trust that our gratitude is profound, and that you are remembered not just here but in our hearts, minds, and on every page of this book. All of this has been a true dream come true, and for that we now offer our deepest appreciation.

First, then, to those who spoke with us in person about Eton Boone and offered their insight, memories, and imagination:

Jason Bagdad, Adam Barr, Ellen Bok, Anne Richman Boone, Joe Boone, Toddy Boone, Elizabeth Buckley, Jenn Burton, Kelso Chaplin, Linda Chaplin, Sylvia Clark, Marty "Solly" Cohn, Buddy D'Angelo, Allison Demos, Eleanor Sullivan Downes, Aaron Edison, Carlo Esteban, Peter Finney, Hugh Gardiner, Linus Gelber, Heather Gunn, Rudy Hack, Harry Hampton, Amalie Hindemuth, Erin Hirt, C.L. Hull, Lance Johannsen, Christian Kanuth, John Kinsey, Max Kleinman, Lisa Lindley, Jeff Korn, Ursula Maggone, James McCarthy, Chris Moore, Alice Sullivan Morgan, Levi Mottl, Rich Murphy, David Nacht, Bert Neimann, Chuck Odeon, Harold Odeon, Lew Odeon, Margaret Odeon, Eric Oleson, Stuart Osha, Hank Piedmont, John Plotz, Dr. Sidney Randall, Barbara Regan, Hilary Richman, Kate Robin, Eric Ronis, Liz Rubin, Daniel Schrag, Frank Smythe, Claire Sullivan, Lionel Thubb, Jon Tolins, Hector Uribe, Camille Walker, Michael J. Young, Daniel Luke Zelman.

To our patient and forgiving transcribers: Brian Anastasi and Mary Kinzel.

To the Estate of Eton Arthur Boone and his publisher, Hardcastle, Inc.

To the publications and the people at each who have helped

us: *Baywindow* and Carey Hogan; *The Downtowner* and Elaine Swayze-Gilpatrick; *Film International* and Andrew Fortenbaugh; *Harper's Magazine* and Charis Conn, Michael Pollan, and Larry Wolfe; *The Harvard Advocate* and Andrew Holden; *The Village Idiot.*

To those whose contributions were more personal than professional, for their moral, inspirational, and sometimes financial, support: Isabel Bigelow, Patty Dann, Tim Davis, David Dishy, Lewis Friedman, Zack Gleit, Sam Hansen, Whitney Hansen, Cynthia Lambros, John Lambros, Chang-rae Lee, John Mankiewicz.

To those who read the manuscript in its early stages and offered encouragement, criticism, and Ockham's address: Peter Becker, Peter Davis, Hope Hansen, Peter Hansen, Hugh Nissenson, Virginia Priest.

To those who have helped turn *Boone* from something we had done into something we could share: Amanda Urban, of course, for her enthusiasm and all subsequent enthusiasm it miraculously yields; to Jim Silberman and the entire team at Summit—Virginia Clark, Wendy Nicholson, Jennifer Prost, Fran Tarshish; and most of all to our editors, Ileene Smith and Alane Mason, for the patience and determination with which they waited for us to discover the difference between a good life and a good book.

And finally, for the record, to each other.

About the Authors

Brooks Hansen and Nick Davis were both born in New York City in 1965, and have been friends ever since. In 1987, they graduated from Harvard, where Davis studied history and literature and was a founding member of the improvisational theater group On Thin Ice. Hansen studied philosophy and English and was editor of *Padan Aram: The Harvard Literary Review.* Currently, Davis is acting and writing in New York City, and Hansen is at work on a second novel. They are Mets fans.